SPECIAL MESSAGE TO READERS

THE ULVERSCROFT FOUNDATION
(registered UK charity number 264873)
was established in 1972 to provide funds for
research, diagnosis and treatment of eye diseases.
Examples of major projects funded by
the Ulverscroft Foundation are:-

- The Children's Eye Unit at Moorfields Eye Hospital, London
- The Ulverscroft Children's Eye Unit at Great Ormond Street Hospital for Sick Children
- Funding research into eye diseases and treatment at the Department of Ophthalmology, University of Leicester
- The Ulverscroft Vision Research Group, Institute of Child Health
- Twin operating theatres at the Western Ophthalmic Hospital, London
- The Chair of Ophthalmology at the Royal Australian College of Ophthalmologists

You can help further the work of the Foundation
by making a donation or leaving a legacy.
Every contribution is gratefully received. If you
would like to help support the Foundation or
require further information, please contact:

THE ULVERSCROFT FOUNDATION
The Green, Bradgate Road, Anstey
Leicester LE7 7FU, England
Tel: (0116) 236 4325

website: www.foundation.ulverscroft.com

Tracy Buchanan is a web journalist and producer who lives in Milton Keynes with her husband and daughter and their puppy, Bronte. Tracy travelled extensively while working as a travel magazine editor, sating the wanderlust she developed while listening to her Sri Lankan grandparents' childhood stories — the same wanderlust that now inspires her writing.

You can discover more about the author at www.tracybuchanan.co.uk

HER LAST BREATH

Food writer Estelle Forster has the perfect life. And with her first book on the way, it's about to get even better. When Estelle hears about Poppy O'Farrell's disappearance, she assumes the girl has simply run away. But Estelle's world crumbles when she's sent a photo of Poppy, along with a terrifying note: *I'm watching you. I know everything about you.* Estelle has no idea who's threatening her, or how she's connected to the missing teen, but she thinks the answers lie in the coastal town she once called home, and the past she hoped was behind her. Estelle knows she must do everything to find Poppy. But how far will she go to hide the truth — that her perfect life was the perfect lie?

Books by Tracy Buchanan
Published by Ulverscroft:

NO TURNING BACK

TRACY BUCHANAN

---◆---

HER LAST BREATH

Complete and Unabridged

CHARNWOOD
Leicester

First published in Great Britain in 2017 by
Avon
London

First Charnwood Edition
published 2018
by arrangement with
Avon
A division of HarperCollins*Publishers*
London

*A catalogue record for this book is available
from the British Library.*

ISBN 978–1–4448–3767–4

Published by
F. A. Thorpe (Publishing)
Anstey, Leicestershire

For Dad, who told me to dream big

Prologue

Extract from Section 7 Report on Estelle Forster prepared by social worker Jean Biden

2 May 1994

This report has been prepared for the court and should be treated as confidential. It must not be shown, nor its contents revealed, to anyone other than the party or a legal adviser to such a party.

4.1 Description of the child's daily life and experience at the time harm was identified

Estelle is a seven-year-old white British girl born to parents with long-standing drug addiction issues. Estelle lives with her parents in a two-bedroom local authority flat.

My observation during visits is that the flat is kept in an untidy state. Unclean plates are often left out, carpets are stained and filled with debris, and discarded bottles of alcohol can be seen. Estelle's bedroom is kept in a reasonably tidy state with a small single bed and a wardrobe. On closer inspection, however, her duvet appears to have not been cleaned for several weeks.

Estelle has informed me in private on several occasions that her parents are still asleep when

1

she wakes. She learnt to dress and feed herself in the morning from the age of six. A typical breakfast is toast and butter, or leftover dinner from the evening before. Estelle noted that she would prefer cereal, but the milk she finds is often sour.

Estelle attends school at Greyswood Primary, a ten-minute walk from her home. Her head teacher, Mrs Jenny Pyatt, informs me Estelle is rarely accompanied by her parents on the short walk from her flat, and parents report having seen her walking to the school alone since she began at the age of four, something Estelle's mother denies.

Mrs Pyatt informs me Estelle arrives at school dishevelled and unclean on a regular basis. On first starting school at the age of four, she arrived wearing a nappy. But with the help and care of her teachers, she is now able to go to the bathroom.

Estelle's attendance rate is below average and her parents have only attended one parents' evening. On this occasion, the police had to be called due to Mr Forster's abusive behaviour towards the teachers.

In the evenings, Estelle informs me she eats dinner — often chips bought from the local fish and chip shop by her parents or a microwave meal — while watching TV. As detailed in previous reports, there have been two occasions where she has been reported as being left alone while her parents were at the local pub. Her average bedtime is 11 p.m. This continues into the weekend where Estelle spends the majority of her time indoors watching TV or reading.

Estelle does not benefit from any extended family due to both her parents being solo children and her grandparents having passed away.

Estelle has struggled to form friendships due to her low attendance rate at school and her generally shy and reserved nature. Her teachers inform me she takes comfort in retreating to the school library during breaks and has shown a keenness in improving her reading and writing skills. She takes particular joy in any lessons involving food.

The last time I visited Estelle before the distressing incident that led to her being removed from her parents, she was attempting to teach herself how to bake a chocolate cake. It is clear she is a bright girl who could thrive given the right circumstances. But when I mentioned this to her, she informed me her father laughed at her when she told him she wanted to be a chef, and told her the closest she'd get would be 'working at the local chippie'. I detected a real sense of sadness and pain when she said this.

Combined with the terrible recent incident, I strongly recommend Estelle is permanently removed from her parents before long-lasting emotional damage occurs. It is my professional opinion that we may already be too late.

1

Tuesday, 2 May

Estelle's dinner party was going perfectly. A soft breeze filtered in through the chiffon curtains, lifting the corners of the organic cotton napkins she'd so carefully chosen. There was the distant tinkle of a police siren above the acoustic guitar music drifting out from her speakers, adding to the 'sophisticated get-together in the city' ambience.

On the wall was the painting she'd bought with some of the advance she'd received for her book: a minimalist canvas featuring a simple apple tree against brilliant white. And, of course, laid out on the large misshaped driftwood table were her signature dishes: a vast cauliflower pizza sprinkled with locally sourced lamb cubes; zucchini fritters with Greek yoghurt; carrot quinoa muffins; and chunky chickpea dips with crunchy vegetable crisps.

In the middle of it all, taking pride of place, was the first edition of Estelle's book, fresh off the printers. On the cover was an apple tree, much like the one on the canvas, plain and simple against a blue cloudless sky. Beneath the tree stood Estelle beside a wooden table filled with fresh vegetables, fruit and meat, her short blonde hair swept across her forehead, her slim body casting a shadow on the grassy knoll behind her. She was dressed in her signature white, this time a plain white cotton dress, highlighting her subtle tan. She smiled into the sun, her oval brown eyes looking at the camera. Held up in the palm of her hand was an apple. And above it all, four letters in glossy white: PURE. The name of her first book.

Estelle took a photo of the table with her phone, and uploaded it to Instagram with the caption: *Early copies in of my book! Let the celebrations begin . . . #Pure foodie #nom*

Her editor Silvia leaned over and smoothed her fingertips over the book cover. 'I always love the feel of a first edition,' she said, smiling at Estelle.

'And the smell,' Giles, her husband, another eminent editor, said, leaning down for a quick sniff.

Everyone laughed and Estelle joined in. God, it felt good to be here with her closest friends, celebrating the success she'd worked so bloody hard for.

'Everyone dig in,' Estelle said, standing up. 'I'll just get some more wine; can't believe you've already polished off three bottles!'

She walked away from the table smiling to herself, the bottom of her long white skirt swishing around her ankles as she padded barefoot into her large state-of-the-art kitchen. When she was out of sight, she closed her eyes, leaning her head against the large cool fridge, taking in a deep breath. She'd spent half the day cooking; she was exhausted. But it was worth it. She turned back around, taking in the happy scene in the room next door. Yes, it was worth it.

She'd fought so hard for this. She deserved to celebrate.

Didn't she?

She clenched her hands into fists, silently berating herself. Yes, she *did* deserve this. Look where she'd come from.

She took in each of her friends. Had they had to battle so hard to get where *they* were? She doubted it. Her guests were a mixture of people from her publishing house, a few fellow bloggers, plus her boyfriend Seb, his brother Dean and Dean's pregnant wife Laura. All born to well-off families; privileged with happy innocent child-hoods. Only Christina had come from what Estelle would call a 'normal' family. They'd met at a foodie awards event three years ago, just as both their blogs were gaining traction: Estelle's focusing on healthy 'pure' recipes, Christina's on balancing motherhood with crafting. Out of all the people sitting around the table, it was Christina she felt most herself with, even more so than her own partner Seb.

But even Christina didn't know much about Estelle's background . . . and Estelle wanted to keep it that way.

'You okay, gorgeous?'

She looked up to see her boyfriend frowning at her, his muscular frame filling the doorway of the kitchen, a serving spoon in his right hand.

She forced a smile onto her face. 'I'm fine! Just thinking how lucky I am.' She pulled her phone from her pocket and pointed it at him. 'Hold that pose.'

She took a photo then shared it with her

7

followers on Instagram with the caption: *A new paddle for my Olympic rowing darling*.

Seb rolled his eyes. 'I'm just social media fodder for you.'

She gave him a peck on the cheek. 'You need to stop looking so cute then, don't you?'

She grabbed two bottles of wine from their fridge then walked into the dining room.

'Who's for some more wine?' she asked. Everyone cheered in approval. She went around the table, topping up everyone's glasses. When she got to her own glass, she added a dribble. She didn't much like drinking, just the odd sip here and there.

'Might want to calm down there, darling,' Silvia said to her husband as he took a huge sip.

'Oh please. We have a child-free night; I'm making the most of it,' he replied.

'Not a child-free morning though,' Silvia reminded him.

'Don't remind me. Honestly, the stress of getting that girl up in the morning. You wait until you have a teenager,' Giles said, quirking an eyebrow at Dean. 'Nightmare.'

'Oh come on, don't exaggerate,' Silvia countered. 'She's a dream compared to most teenagers . . . ' Her face darkened. 'Like that TV presenter, Chris O'Farrell's daughter. Did you hear about her running away?' she asked.

Estelle thought of the brief glimpse of news she'd seen, the silver-haired presenter pleading to camera for his daughter to return.

'I did,' Estelle said with a sigh. 'He must be so worried.'

8

'I wish Annabelle would run away,' Giles drawled.

'Giles!' Silvia exclaimed, flicking her serviette at her husband. 'How could you?'

Estelle smiled at the banter between the couple. They were the publishing world's most celebrated couple; it was still blowing her mind they were sat at her dinner table.

'Admit it,' Giles said. 'She's a nightmare at the moment.'

Silvia shook her head. 'She's a teenager. They're supposed to be nightmares.'

'Much like writers,' Giles said with a raised eyebrow. 'Bar present company, of course!'

'I do apologise for my husband, Estelle,' Silvia said. 'He's had particularly bad luck with his writers. He never quite believes it when I say mine are a dream to work with, especially *you*.'

Estelle quirked an eyebrow. 'You weren't thinking that when I made those changes to the proofs at the last minute.'

Silvia pretended to scold Estelle and Estelle laughed.

'I'm intrigued, what bad luck have you had with your writers, Giles?' Seb asked.

Giles leaned back into his chair, resting his glass on his rotund belly, clearly pleased to be the centre of attention. 'You must've heard about Krishna Sandhill?'

'I remember reading something about her,' Seb's brother said. 'Wasn't she some meditation guru?'

Giles nodded. 'The Queen of Calm, we called her. Advocating a new form of meditation that

9

promised calmness and clarity after just five days of following her little regime. Just before we signed off the final copy of her book, we received news she'd spent several months in prison for aggravated bodily harm to an ex. So much for calm.'

'No!' everyone around the table exclaimed.

'The book was cancelled at the last moment,' Giles said with a sigh. 'It was a complete fucking mess. You can't publish a book claiming to calm people down when it's been written by someone so angry they beat up their husband.' He shook his head. 'We lost tens of thousands of pounds thanks to her dark past.'

Estelle felt a tremor of fear inside at his words. *Her dark past.* But she trampled it down.

'Ah,' Kim, Estelle's publicist, said.

'What's wrong?' Estelle asked her.

'I hate to tell you this, but the journalist who exposed Krishna is the one who's interviewing you tomorrow.'

'Which one?' Dean asked. He presented a radio show called *Outing Rogues*, which investigated cowboy builders and dishonest businessmen, so knew lots of journalists.

'Louis Patel?' Kim said.

Dean raised an eyebrow. 'Oh yes, he can be quite tough.'

'Don't, you're making me nervous,' Estelle said. This was her first proper profile with a national newspaper. All her other interviewers had focused more on either her book deal or cooking tips.

Silvia put on a mock-serious face. 'I hope our

Queen of Clean doesn't have any skeletons in her closet?'

Estelle forced a smile.

'Okay, I admit it,' she said, putting her hands up. 'I *might* have taken a bite of a Disney princess cake at my goddaughter's birthday last week,' she said, referring to Christina and Tom's five-year-old.

'Yep,' Christina said with an exaggerated sigh. 'I can confirm she did. But *only* because my daughter insisted.'

Everyone laughed and, to Estelle's relief, they soon moved onto a lighter subject — Seb's new radio documentary about aspiring rowers, which was airing the next day.

But Estelle felt herself retreating, thoughts of the previous conversation stirring around her mind. She'd deliberately glossed over her childhood when she'd written the introduction to her book. What if the journalist she was meeting tomorrow had done some digging?

She played with the stem of her wine glass. Outside, the stars twinkled mischievously, the sound of laughter from the streets below drifting towards her on the breeze. She peered towards her book again and tried to draw comfort from it. *Look how far she'd come!* She refused to let anything ruin that. She had so much to be proud of and *so* much to look forward to.

Christina leaned over, putting her hand on her arm. 'You okay, Estelle?' she asked quietly.

'I'm perfect,' Estelle said, taking a sip of wine and smiling at her friend. 'Everything's perfect.'

As she said that, the doorbell rang out.

'Bit late for more visitors,' Seb said. He stood up and walked down the hallway, unsteady on his feet now, the bottle of wine he'd consumed showing. Once a teetotaller, he'd been drinking a lot since the injury that had taken him out of competitive rowing. Estelle's heart went out to him. It must be tough, not being able to do what he loved.

Christina topped up Estelle's untouched glass. 'Here, more wine for the superstar author. Let's raise a toast,' she said, raising her wine glass.

'An *organic* toast,' Silvia said.

'Of the finest gluten-free variety,' Kim added with a raised eyebrow.

'All wines are gluten-free, silly,' Estelle said.

They all laughed.

'To Estelle!' they all said, holding up their glasses. She looked at each of them. Her friendships with them might not be very old, but they were all she had and she was so grateful.

She thought then of one of her few friends from childhood, and saw an image of a girl with long red hair biting into a rotting apple against a stormy sea.

She forced the image away as Seb appeared in the hallway with a small bouquet of bright red flowers. 'Flowers for the hotshot writer,' he said, bringing them over to Estelle.

'What a strange time for flowers to be delivered,' Silvia declared, peering at the clock.

Estelle followed her gaze. Nearly ten at night.

'It is a weird time,' she said. 'Maybe they got ten at night mixed up with ten in the morning.'

She took the flowers from Seb, breathing in

12

their scent, then picked out the card that came with them.

To Stel. Congratulations on the birth of your book. x

Estelle felt a shiver run through her. She hadn't been called Stel for many years. That was another lifetime, another world, long before she became the person everyone around this table now saw. The memory filled her with anxiety.

'What flowers are these?' Silvia asked, brushing her finger over one of the crimson petals.

'Poppies,' Christina said. 'How unusual.'

Seb took them from Estelle. 'I'll put them in water,' he said.

As he walked to the kitchen, one of the poppies tumbled to the floor, where it was trampled by Seb's foot.

2

Estelle stared out at the Thames in the distance, watching as the bricks from the new development being built there crumbled onto the river's banks.

The doorbell went. Estelle cursed, realising her fingers were gooey from the honey she'd been using for a recipe. How long had she been stood there in her kitchen, staring into space? She peered at the clock. Ten minutes wasted. She wiped her hands on a damp cloth and took a deep, nervous breath. She knew who would be at the door: the national newspaper journalist who'd once exposed the 'Queen of Calm'.

Estelle took a deep breath then jogged to the door, opening it to see a young dark-haired man smiling at her. She smiled back, feeling a little relieved. He *seemed* nice enough.

'Louis?' she asked.

He nodded.

'Come in!' Estelle said, holding the door open wide.

'Gorgeous place,' he said, looking around him at the stark white hallway as he walked inside. It was actually Seb's house, but she'd moved in the year before, renovating it from a run-down mews house near the South Bank to a contemporary home for them.

'Yes, we adore it here,' she said, leading him to the kitchen. 'People always seem surprised; I think they expect me to live in a cottage in Wales or something!'

'No, that's what I love about you,' Louis said. 'Clean city living. It's realistic. Not everyone is able to up sticks and move to the country.'

'Nor indeed *wants* to,' Estelle said, gesturing to a row of stools by an oak-topped kitchen island. 'I love the city.'

'Baking something?' the journalist asked, looking around at the busy kitchen surfaces.

'When am I not? I thought you'd like to take something away with you.'

He slung his bag onto the island's surface, pulling his laptop out. 'I'm in heaven. Looks like flapjack mix?'

Estelle nodded. 'With a twist. But I'll leave it up to you to guess what that twist is.'

Louis peered around the kitchen. 'Hmmm, are those chia seeds?' he asked, pointing to a mason jar of small seeds.

Estelle laughed. 'I've hidden the evidence. Here, have a sniff.'

She handed the bowl of gooey mixture to him and he took in a deep inhalation. 'Dates, banana, honey.' Estelle smiled. He seemed to know his stuff. Louis frowned, then added, 'Is that a spice in there?'

She snatched the bowl away, laughing. 'You'll have to wait. I have another batch on the go that will be ready in five minutes, so you can do a taste test then.'

He smiled to himself, flipping open his laptop.

'Woman of mystery,' he said, raising an eyebrow.

Estelle shot him a nervous smile before slathering the mixture into a ceramic dish and placing it in the oven. She loved the baking and the writing. But the publicity, not so much. She hated talking about herself. It had to be done though; that's what her editor and publicist had told her.

'Would you like a drink?' she asked Louis. 'Water? Green tea? Organic beer?' She leaned forward, lowering her voice. 'Or we do have *normal* drinks that Seb keeps stowed away in a cupboard somewhere.'

He laughed. 'Water would be perfect, thank you.'

She poured them both some water from the jug she kept in her fridge, then sat down across from him, brushing her blonde fringe from her eyes.

Louis peered towards the oven. 'Don't you use a timer?'

'No. I've been baking so long I have an instinct for time.'

He laughed. 'Why doesn't that surprise me? So, just a month until your book launch. How are you feeling?'

Estelle felt a tremor of nerves. She'd been waiting so long for this moment and thought she was ready for it, but the closer she got, the more she felt like a fraud. Did she really deserve this? A friend of hers who'd had a novel published said she'd felt the same. Despite the fact she knew how hard she'd worked, it still felt alien, unearned. She called it 'imposter syndrome' and Estelle had it bad.

'Nervous,' she admitted. 'Excited too though.'

'No need to be nervous. So, let's start at the very beginning. Where do you think your interest in food first came from?'

Estelle hesitated a moment. She could tell the journalist it had all started with how scarce good food was when she was a child, pale meals shoved in a microwave, cheap takeaways bought by her parents. She could tell him how, when she went into care and foster homes, it wasn't always much better so she'd had to learn from an early age how to prepare food, the simple things like making scrambled eggs. She could tell him about how she paid attention in cooking classes at school because of this, unlike her peers, because she had no choice if she wanted to feed herself. She could then go on to tell him about Lillysands and the Garlands. Finally a place where food was something to be treasured and enjoyed, making dishes with her foster mother Autumn, helping to serve up business lunches for her foster father Max.

But she didn't.

'I really don't know,' she said instead. 'It's just always held a fascination for me.'

'And that's why you chose to study food science?'

It was almost tempting to tell him the truth here too — that it was one of her last foster parents who'd suggested this subject to her, a gentle chemistry professor called Justin. He'd noticed her interest in food, and the way she'd take notice when he talked about the chemicals in food. But she didn't even want to tell the journalist about Carol and Justin Hall, the lovely couple she'd gone to live with just before she turned sixteen, because that might lead to more questions, to more delving into her past, and that was something she needed to avoid.

'My teachers at school,' she said instead. 'They helped steer me towards food science as a degree subject.'

'And after your university course,' Louis asked, looking at his notes, 'you decided to do a short accredited nutrition course?'

'That's right. But I was very naïve back then.'

'What do you mean?'

'I'd been so full of hope. I presumed the more I learnt, the more success I'd have. But the truth was, it was a tough time.' She didn't mind talking about this. Each writer needed their rags to riches story and this was hers. And it was less complicated than the *real* story, the one where she was a neglected little girl dragged through the care system. She wanted to keep that to herself.

'Tell me more,' Louis said, leaning forward.

She sighed. 'I moved out of uni digs into a small flat of my own. I'd saved up money for rent while working at a patisserie nearby during uni. I knew my savings wouldn't cover me for more than three months if I didn't get a job, but I was hopeful it wouldn't be long before I'd have a steady stream of income as a nutritionist.'

'And that didn't happen?'

'Nope. I quickly learnt you can't just create a reputation based on qualifications. Weeks then months went by with no income. I ended up having to move out of the flat into a room share in a rough part of town.'

Estelle shuddered as she thought of that time. She'd ended up sharing a filthy room with a skinny strung-out girl who reminded Estelle too much of her birth mother. There were dark times then, very dark times, all too familiar to Estelle.

'I was just about to give up,' Estelle continued, 'when the blog stuff started paying off.'

'You set the blog up eight years ago to help a friend, right?'

Estelle nodded. 'Yes. My friend Genevieve was diagnosed with type two diabetes. It was a shock to her but not anyone else. Her diet was *terrible*. I basically took over her kitchen. The improvement in her health was amazing, so she convinced me to start blogging. With each post, I gained more followers and some advertising too.'

The income generated from those ads had been minimal but enough for Estelle to move from that grotty bedsit. She remembered crying in relief. It wasn't just about the filthy surroundings, the noise and the anxious flatmate. It was about extracting herself from her past, moving herself as far away as possible from the destiny her childhood could have moulded for her.

'And eventually, you set up on other channels such as YouTube and your social media platforms?' Louis said. 'Is that when it all really took off?'

Estelle nodded. 'Yes, that's when the clients really started to come in — so many I couldn't keep up!'

Louis tapped away on his laptop. She watched

him, trying to control her nerves. Was she coming across okay?

He looked up. 'So why the pure-eating ethos?'

'Studying food sciences at university gave me an insight into the chemicals you can find in everyday foods. I guess it became a bit of an obsession.'

'And thus your crusade against toxics in foods, as you describe it in *Pure*, began?'

'Oh, you've read the book?' Estelle's heart started to hammer. Was he leading up to telling her he hated it?

'I got a review copy on Friday and devoured it in a few hours. I *loved* it.'

Estelle smiled, full of relief.

'Have you managed to try out some of the recipes?' she asked.

'Absolutely! I loved the *Rower's Delight* cocoa mousse. I presume your other half Seb inspired you with that one?' he said, peering towards a photo of the couple on the fridge: Seb in his Team GB uniform, arm around Estelle, who was smiling into the camera.

Estelle nodded. 'It's his favourite.'

'You met in 2015 after being brought in to assist a nutritionist advising Team GB in the lead-up to the Rio Olympics, right?'

Estelle nodded. She still remembered the day she got the call from the nutritionist she'd met a few months back during a friend's party. She'd been having a down day, wondering when her career would go up a gear. It felt stagnant. Sure, she was getting clients, her social media channels were doing well. But something inside her — the desire to put her childhood well and truly behind her — yearned for more. That was the problem. When you knew how bad it could be — how vast and black having *nothing* was — you always lived with the fear you'd return to it again. So the scramble for more wasn't about greed, it was about fear, pure and simple.

'Was it love at first sight?' the journalist asked.

Estelle thought back to that time two years ago when she'd arrived at the Olympic rowing team's UK training camp where they were gearing up for Brazil the following year. She'd been over-whelmed. It was the accumulation of all she'd worked hard for, so she'd been so overtaken by emotion, she'd felt tears spring to her eyes.

'You okay there?' she'd heard a voice ask. And there was Seb, water dripping from his wet dark hair, shoulders broad and strong in contrast to his narrow waist. He looked so clean and so pure, the perfect specimen of health. Just being around him made her feel the same way too. So she'd taken a deep breath, forced the tears away and smiled. 'Perfect,' she'd said.

Estelle's doorbell went, shattering the memory.

'Do you mind just waiting a moment while I answer the door?' she said, wondering who it might be.

Louis nodded. 'Of course.'

She skipped down the hallway, adrenaline buzzing from her interview. It made it all feel even more real, having a national newspaper journalist in *her* kitchen, talking about *her* life. Maybe she wasn't such a fraud after all.

She opened the front door, surprised to see

21

the son of her local butcher on the doorstep. Then she remembered she had a delivery due that day. 'Of course! Come in, William,' she said, leading the young red-cheeked teenager to her vast kitchen. He smiled shyly as he carried in the large wooden crate, various meats wrapped in white crinkly paper inside it. 'Just here will be great,' she said, gesturing to the kitchen top closest to the fridge. He placed it down and Estelle pulled out a five-pound note, handing it to him as a tip.

Louis smiled. 'You get your meat delivered?'

'They don't usually do deliveries, but it's impossible to lug around all the meat on the back of my pedal bike,' she said. 'So I sweet-talked the owner of the local butcher to do a weekly delivery. I think it's important to support independent businesses whenever possible, and I'm lucky enough to be able to do so. Plus, it's mega cheap,' she added with a wink.

Louis turned to the butcher's son. 'How does it feel delivering meat to a soon-to-be published chef?'

'Cool,' William replied as he took the money. 'Dad's going to the book launch too, he's really looking forward to it. Even got a new suit and everything.'

Estelle smiled, hiding the slight note of worry she felt. Her publicist Kim had been the one to come up with the idea of inviting her local suppliers to the launch. What better way to highlight just how clean and local Estelle was by having her butcher and greengrocer at her launch party to mingle with journalists? But now she was wondering if it would seem a bit contrived. Would people see through it?

Would they see through *her*?

After William left, Estelle started placing the meat in her large American-style fridge.

'So do you do all the cooking in the household?' Louis asked.

'Yes, of course.' She caught Louis raising an eyebrow. 'This isn't about being an obedient housewife,' she quickly added. 'It's pure selfishness on my part. I love cooking.' And she really did. The whole sensory experience of it, the feel of food on her fingertips, a thousand different textures. The smells and the colours, the sound of sizzling meat and whisking flour. The taste too, of course. It was a form of therapy for her: kneading, mixing, slicing everything away, all thoughts, all memories gone until it was just her at her simplest in that kitchen, focused on making the best dishes she could.

She pulled away the white paper from a large slab of beef ready to put it in the fridge. Then she frowned. There was something on top of the meat, square and white.

She looked over at Louis who was busy tapping away at his laptop at the other end of the large island, then she grabbed a fork and lifted the item off the meat. It was an envelope, a name scrawled on the front.

Stel.

She peered at the windowsill, where the poppies she'd received the evening before had been placed in a vase. The note that had come with them had been addressed to *Stel* too.

23

She quickly opened the envelope and pulled out a Polaroid photo. It was a close-up photo of a teenage girl. Sad brown eyes. Freckled button nose. Dyed red hair . . . red hair that made her think of another girl, another time.

Alice.

But it wasn't Alice. In fact, Estelle had no idea who the girl in the photo was. But as she looked into her eyes, she still felt a flare of recognition.

She looked at the bottom of the photo, where a message had been scrawled, droplets of blood from the beef blossoming around the words.

They say you're as pure as the driven snow.
But I know you're not.
    I'm watching you. I know everything about you.

Estelle dropped the photo with trembling fingers, watching as it floated to the floor, the blood from the beef congealing in her nails.

Who the hell had sent this to her?

3

You've changed. You're barely recognisable
from the girl I first met.

All fake though. An attempt to cover the real
you. The dirty you.

Did the people you were with last night see
it, the charade?

I wanted to storm in, smash all those glasses,
rub all that food in your face.

But I didn't. I kept my anger in check and
watched as everyone's eyes poured all over you:
especially the men.

I know the truth. I know you're spoilt goods
and soon they will know too.

That terrifies you, doesn't it? People seeing
the real you.

I can see the fear in your face as you look at
the photo — at my message.

Good.

Time you were taken down a peg or two.
Time you learnt this new life you've created for
yourself is a sham.

A sham that will soon be smashed to smith-
ereens.

4

'You okay?' Louis asked.

Estelle looked at him. She'd almost forgotten where she was. Should she say something? No. Kim and Silvia would tell her not to. Louis was a journalist. He'd ask too many questions. She'd deal with it when he left.

'I'm fine,' Estelle lied, carefully pushing the photo beneath the fridge with her toe before putting the rest of the meat away.

'So, where were we?' she asked as she sat down again, heart thumping uncontrollably against her chest. Why had that Polaroid been sent to her?

'I want to talk about your childhood now,' Louis said. 'You grew up in the care system, didn't you? I found a photo of you; you look very different now.'

So he *had* done some digging. She tried to compose herself, stifling the anxiety building inside. 'That was a long time ago.'

'But interesting, nonetheless. Can you tell me more about your birth parents?'

Estelle folded her legs, her cheeks flushing. 'I don't think it's really relevant.'

'I'm writing a profile piece, Estelle,' Louis said, voice suddenly hard. 'I think it's very relevant.'

Now she saw the man who'd exposed the 'Queen of Calm.'

'They just couldn't cope with a child, they

26

were very young themselves,' she said, glossing over the truth. 'Then I was in care and lived with some foster families. It wasn't ideal. I don't know what else there is to say really.' She added a smile, just to make it light.

'You lived in Devon for a bit, didn't you?' He looked down at his notes. 'Lillysands?'

She tried to keep her face neutral. She'd worked so hard to leave her time in Lillysands behind, but now here it was again, bringing all those memories to the surface. 'You really have been doing your research,' she said with a nervous laugh as she peered towards the fridge where the photo lay.

'I spoke to an old geography teacher of yours, Mr Tate. He said you left the town abruptly when you were fifteen.'

Estelle swallowed. He'd been talking to her old teacher? Had he talked to anyone else in Lillysands . . . ? What else had he discovered?

'That's the way it is with foster parents,' she said, trying to remain calm. 'I never knew how long I'd be with them.'

'But *you* chose to leave?' Louis said. 'He told me your foster parents were devastated.'

Estelle closed her eyes. She'd left a note for them, a nice note, thanking them. But how could she have stayed in Lillysands? It was impossible.

'It was time to leave,' Estelle said. 'My foster parents understood.'

'Yes, your foster parents. Autumn and Max Garland,' Louis said, looking at his notes. The mention of their names made Estelle tense up. 'They're quite well known in Lillysands, so I'm

27

told,' he continued. 'He's a local property developer, right? She's a food taster. Was *she* the reason you got into nutrition and food?'

Estelle put hers finger to her temples, massaging them as she closed her eyes.

Calm down. Calm down. Calm down.

'Estelle?'

She quickly opened her eyes. 'I — '

A loud noise suddenly pierced the air. *The smoke alarm!* Estelle peered towards the oven to see smoke drifting out of it. In the tension of the moment, she hadn't even noticed the scent of burning in the air.

'Fuck,' she hissed.

Louis raised an eyebrow as she darted to the oven, pulling the flapjacks out.

They were burnt.

She took a deep breath. 'Well,' she said, looking at Louis with a shaky smile. 'Maybe I need a timer after all.'

He looked into her eyes, frown deepening. 'Is everything okay, Estelle?'

'Fine, fine! I'll do a new batch and get them over to you.' She peered towards the front door. She needed him gone. The photo, combined with his questions, were making her lose her grip. She needed to be in control when talking to someone like him, especially when it came to her past. 'So you have everything you need?' she asked, picking his jacket up for him.

Louis peered at his watch. 'I've only been here twenty minutes. I was hoping — '

'Great,' Estelle said. 'Thank you so much for coming.'

28

He slowly gathered his stuff up, frowning as he looked at her. 'If this is about the line of questioning . . .'

'Oh no!' Estelle said in a too-high voice. She could feel herself losing it, the stench of the burning flapjacks clogging her nostrils, the memory of the bloody Polaroid and her past seeming to burn into her too. 'It's all fine. It's just that I have an event to run to,' she lied. 'You'll be at the launch party, right? How about we grab ten minutes then, just you and I, to finish this?'

Estelle walked him to the door, legs shaking.

'Is everything really okay?' he asked as he stepped out onto the doorstep.

'Perfect, just busy busy busy.' Then she closed the door in his face.

She stayed where she was a few moments, sensing his presence outside. When she heard his footsteps, she ran back to the kitchen, getting on her hands and knees and scrabbling under the fridge to find the photo. She pulled it out then leaned against a cupboard, staring at the girl, heartbeat going a million miles a minute.

She frowned, peering closer. The girl looked like the TV presenter's daughter they'd been talking about last night; the girl who had run away.

She grabbed her laptop, and searched for stories about the missing girl, clicking on the first one she found. As she opened the article, the first thing she saw was a photo of the girl with her arms around a dog, her cheek against its whiskers, a huge smile on her face. Estelle looked at the Polaroid she'd received, then back at the girl.

Yes, it was the same person. She was sure of it. But why was this photo being sent to Estelle? She didn't have any connection with the girl. And why that message? It didn't make sense.

Estelle read the article with the photo.

TV presenter makes appeal to missing daughter

TV presenter Chris O'Farrell made a desperate appeal for the return of his fifteen-year-old daughter, Poppy. The presenter of daytime show Here and Now looked distraught as he talked directly to the camera, explaining to viewers that Poppy had run away in the early hours the day before, leaving behind a note.

Poppy.

Estelle peered again at the poppies that had been sent to her. It must be connected.

The thought sent a shiver down her spine.

She quickly clicked on a video accompanying the article about the missing girl. Chris O'Farrell, handsome and silver-haired, looked imploringly into camera. 'Poppy, please come home, darling. We all love and miss you very much. Sandy's at the door waiting and whining for you. There will be no harsh words, no accusations. We just want you home.' His voice broke, his eyes filling with tears. Then the video stopped. Below it was a number to call with any sightings.

Estelle looked at the Polaroid again. She should call the number. She quickly took a photo of the Polaroid as back-up, then dialled.

'Hello, Metropolitan Police,' a woman answered.

'I'm calling about Poppy O'Farrell. Can I be put through to DC Jones?' she asked, looking at the name of the detective in charge of the case.

'Can I just ask a few details about why you're calling first?' the woman on the other end asked in a bored voice. 'We're getting quite a few calls after her father went on air.'

'I received a photo of Poppy this morning,' Estelle said.

'Okay. Do you mean in the post?'

'With my meat delivery.' Estelle peered at the blood still under her nails from the meat. She felt nausea build inside.

'I see.' The officer was clearly intrigued now. 'Are you connected with Poppy?'

'Not as far as I know.'

There was a pause, a rustling of paper in the background. 'Tell me more about the photo.'

'It's a Polaroid photo, a close-up of her.' Estelle looked at the message on the bottom. 'And there's a message on it.'

'What does it say?'

'It says, 'They say you're as pure as the driven snow',' Estelle read out the note in a trembling voice. ''But I know you're not. I'm watching you. I know everything about you.''

There was the sound of scribbling. 'Are you sure it's Poppy in the photo?'

Estelle looked at the image on the news site. Poppy was peering into the camera, a castle behind her, her long dyed red hair lifting in the wind. Then Estelle looked at the Polaroid photo. 'It's definitely her.'

Holding the phone against her ear, Estelle looked up more images from other news sites. In them, Poppy had brown hair. She must have dyed her hair recently.

'Okay, let me put you through to DC Jones. Can I first take your name?'

'Estelle Forster.'

'Do I recognise that name?'

'I'm a food writer,' Estelle said. Estelle got that spark of pride she felt when people recognised her name. The publisher's PR firm had done a great job of getting her in a variety of magazines and newspapers so it was happening more and more.

'Of course! How interesting. So, is there a number we can contact you on just in case we get cut off?'

Estelle reeled off her phone number, and her address too. Then, after a wait, she was put through to DC Jones.

'Hello, DC Jones speaking,' a deep voice answered. 'How can I help, Miss Forster?'

Estelle repeated everything she'd just told the other woman.

'I see,' the detective said. 'And to confirm, you're not connected to Poppy O'Farrell.'

'Not that I know of. It's all so strange.'

The detective sighed. 'It doesn't surprise me, to be honest. Her father's famous. It brings all the nutters out of the woodwork. I hear you're a well-known food writer, so your name must be out there too? Maybe it's just someone trying to get your attention.'

'Maybe,' Estelle murmured. She ought to feel better, calmer, speaking to the two officers. But she only felt more confused.

'We'll have an officer stop by to take a statement.'

'When?'

'We will call you to let you know, probably today, maybe tomorrow. As you can imagine, it's been rather busy since Mr O'Farrell put that plea out.'

'Of course.'

'Call us in the meantime if you receive anything else.'

'I will.'

He hung up. At least she'd made the call, Estelle thought. But as she looked down at the photo, she couldn't help but feel frustrated. Why *had* it been sent to her?

She took a deep breath. She'd done all she could.

* * *

'Interesting cleaning technique there.' Estelle peered up at Seb, who was watching her with a frown as she scrubbed for the hundredth time at wooden floorboards later that afternoon. The blood from the meat was gone but Estelle had to be sure.

She wiped her hand across her forehead and smiled. 'Just want it spic and span.'

'What's going on? You only clean like this

33

when you're anxious. We *do* have a cleaner, you know.'

She paused. She knew she would have to tell Seb about the photo and the note. But she needed more time to figure out how she felt about them.

'Oh, you know, just the launch of my book in a month,' Estelle said.

'You don't need to worry about that; it'll be perfect.'

She blew her blonde fringe from her eyes and stood up. 'You're right. Want a snack?'

'Not if you're going to offer me those,' he said, looking at the dish of burnt flapjacks.

Estelle followed his gaze. She was going to see if she could salvage them in some way; she hated waste. She'd seen enough of it when she'd lived with the Garlands. But Seb was right, they were a lost cause.

'I have some chia energy balls in the fridge,' she said, forcing a smile. 'Let's have some outside with some peppermint tea.'

Seb smiled. 'Sounds great.'

A few minutes later, they were both sitting in the rooftop garden. Estelle looked around, trying to still her busy mind. When she'd moved in, it was just made up of fake grass. Seb hadn't had time to maintain a garden with his busy schedule before his injury: daily intensive training, media interviews and appearances, meetings with his trainer, all meaning his house and garden were neglected. She'd set about changing that, paving it over with beautiful reclaimed stones, and introducing vegetable and fruit boxes. She'd also put up trellises around the edges, interlacing fairy lights with a variety of climbing fruit plants. Whenever anyone came around, they commented on how pretty it was. It played a part in her book too, a whole section on creating your own 'city allotment' at home. It usually calmed her sitting out here, especially when it was early summer: not too hot nor too cold, the tops of the trees heavy with blossom, the sun a warm yellow globe above.

But there was no sense of calm today, the Polaroid photo kept playing on her mind.

'That girl we were talking about last night hasn't returned yet,' Seb said. Estelle froze. 'They've delayed my radio piece because of some special on runaway kids,' he added.

'Oh, Seb,' Estelle said, leaning across and placing her hand over his. 'I'm sorry about that; I know how excited you were about it.'

He shook his head in disgust. 'And all for a teenager. She's probably gone off with some boyfriend or another.'

Estelle closed her eyes. She had to say something. 'Seb, I need to talk to you.'

He frowned, putting his paper down. 'What's wrong?'

'I received this strange photo in my meat delivery this morning.'

She showed him the photo she'd taken of it on her phone — the real photo she'd placed in a drawer in her office.

He examined it then peered up at her. 'I don't understand.'

'Don't you recognise the girl?'

He looked closer, then it dawned on him. 'The presenter's daughter. Why the hell would you receive a photo of her?'

'I have no idea.'

'Have you called the police?'

'Of course. I'm not sure they're taking it too seriously.'

'But the message written on it!'

'You're telling me.' She stood up. 'I need some fresh air. I might go for a bike ride.'

Seb looked up at her in surprise. 'You're not going to even tell me what it means?'

'I have no idea myself! I'm sorry, there's not much more to say. I — I need to get out.' She grabbed her keys and jacket, giving Seb a quick peck on the cheek. 'I'll be back in an hour.'

As she headed out of the door, she heard the clink of glass and the hiss of Seb opening a bottle of beer in the kitchen. Fine, if that was the way he wanted to cope. This was her way. She wasn't prepared to open up about her past. She wanted it to remain there, not here in her present life.

She went around the side of the house and got her bike from the shed, jumping on it and pedalling straight to the Thames. It was busy out (wasn't it always in London?), but there was a jovial feel in the air too, smiles on people's faces as they took in the sun's soft rays.

But Estelle couldn't feel happy. She mulled over the photo and the note scrawled on it. The words rang a vague bell. *I know everything about you.* Maybe they meant her past. Her *parents*. Was it a threat to expose her background? Not great for someone who was advocating pure and healthy living. And then there was what happened in Lillysands.

But what did all this have to do with Poppy?

She pedalled faster, harder, her breath quickening to catch up with the thoughts running through her mind.

'Watch out!' someone shouted.

Estelle looked up to see she'd nearly knocked a man over.

'Sorry!' she shouted over her shoulder. She slowed down, calming her breath. In the distance, she saw Borough Market. She jumped off her bike and pushed it towards the market, immersing herself in the hubbub of the stalls, breathing in the scent of spices, the tangy meat and salty fish. The market calmed her, the familiarity of all the smells and noises; the nod to her normal routine. It felt to her like everything had changed with the arrival of that photo; her whole world had tilted on its axis.

She'd felt that way when she'd been taken from her parents too. Out of control, floating on a turbulent sea, but also the certain knowledge things were to change for good.

She needed an anchor now just as she did then. An anchor in familiarity.

She stopped in front of a fruit and veg stall, taking in the exuberant colours in front of her. She picked up a papaya, cupping her hand around it and weighing it, feeling its yellow skin with her thumb. It yielded slightly. Ripe. Delicious.

'Hello, Estelle!'

She looked up to see her greengrocer, a stocky

man with a pierced ear, smiling at her.

'Hi Tomas.' She handed over the fruit.

He frowned. 'Just this today?'

'Just this,' she replied, distracted, her mind too full to focus on buying anything else.

Why? she kept asking herself. *Why send it to her?*

Estelle paid for the papaya then walked back into the crowds, leaving the market and finding a quiet alleyway as she pulled out her phone. She needed to find out more about Poppy O'Farrell.

There must be some kind of connection.

She explored all the articles she could find about Poppy, eyes glancing over her pretty face in the various photos of her; the familiar media shots of her famous father.

Then a headline came up, a story from that morning. As she took it in, Estelle went completely still.

Poppy O'Farrell Adopted

'Oh Jesus,' she whispered. The walls of the alleyway seemed to press in around her.

Calm down, she told herself. *Plenty of kids are adopted.*

She snuck a look at the photo she'd taken of the Polaroid on her phone, at the girl's brown eyes, the brown roots showing . . .

Estelle closed her eyes, heart thumping. Then she quickly dialled the number DC Jones had given her. He picked up within a few rings.

'It's Estelle Forster, we spoke earlier,' she said in a hurry. 'I just read Poppy O'Farrell's adopted. Is it true?'

A sigh. 'Yes, I heard that had got out. Why are you asking?'

'It's just — ' Estelle paused.

'Just what?' the detective pushed.

Estelle swallowed, mouth feeling unbearably dry. 'I — I gave a baby up for adoption fifteen years ago, a girl.' She thought of the photo of Poppy again . . . brown eyes just like Estelle's.

'I see,' the detective replied slowly. 'Where did you give birth?'

'Lillysands, a town in Devon.'

He paused a moment. 'I think we should come and have a chat with you now, Estelle.'

Estelle leaned against the wall, blinking away tears.

Was Poppy O'Farrell the beautiful baby girl she'd said goodbye to fifteen years earlier?

5

I see you standing there. Can you sense me watching you?

You're usually so good at hiding your feelings. Not now though.

You look so sad. So confused.

I ought to feel guilty. And yes, it oozes at the back of my mind, briefly. But it doesn't take much to shut it down.

You deserve this, after all.

You told me you felt like this when they put you into care. Like you were helpless on a stormy sea. But then Autumn and Max came along, your anchors.

Well, they're not here for you now, are they?

So maybe you'll drown.

And then you'd be really pure, not just covering up the filth inside like you're doing now with grown-up dresses and pretty hair.

But clean inside and out, just like you told me you wanted to be.

And then you'll realise what you've done.

You'll understand why I'm doing what I'm doing.

To save you, in a way. To save all of us.

6

Estelle cycled back home in a frenzy, heart galloping, mouth dry. By the time she got there, there was a police car outside. She placed her bike back in its shed then took a deep breath and walked inside.

Seb was chatting to two police officers in the kitchen, a man and a woman. Estelle quickly looked in the mirror in the hallway, smoothing down her hair. Reflected back at her were her startled brown eyes, skin ashen beneath her tan.

'Hello,' she said, walking into the kitchen.

'These officers wanted to talk to you about the photo, Estelle,' Seb said, an edge in his voice. He was clearly still annoyed at Estelle for rushing out like that.

'I'm Detective Richard Jones,' the man said, putting his hand out to Estelle. He looked younger than she'd expected, late twenties. But Estelle had a feeling he was older. 'And this is PC Alex Thorburn.'

The policewoman, pretty with long dark hair up in a ponytail, smiled at Estelle.

'Mind if we chat alone?' the detective asked Seb.

'Sure,' Seb said. 'That okay, Estelle?' He was looking into her eyes like he wanted her to insist on him staying.

But she didn't. 'It's fine.'

Seb grabbed his hoodie then gave Estelle a

hard look before heading outside. Estelle turned back to the officers; she had more important things to deal with.

'First thing's first,' the detective said. 'Can we see the photo?'

'I just need to get it from my office. Would you like a drink?' Estelle asked, unable to help herself going into host mode despite wanting to scream one big question at the police officers: 'Is Poppy O'Farrell my daughter?'

'Coffee would be great actually,' the detective said with a wry smile as he sat on one of the stools. 'Was on the late shift last night.'

'I'm afraid I don't have any coffee. But I have green tea?' The detective wrinkled his nose slightly. 'There's caffeine in it,' she quickly added.

'You sound like my wife. All right, that'll be great, thanks.'

'Same for you?' she asked the female police officer. PC Thorburn nodded.

Estelle quickly flicked the kettle on then went to her office, using the chance to compose herself out of sight. The fact they were here, and so quickly too, clearly meant there was a clear connection now. She retrieved the Polaroid photo and stared down at Poppy, a storm of emotions running through her.

Could it be . . . ?

She took a deep breath, then walked back towards the kitchen, handing the Polaroid over to the detective. He looked at it for a few moments.

'It *is* Poppy O'Farrell in the photo, isn't it?' she asked.

'Looks like it.'

42

Estelle went to the kettle, pouring boiling water over two teabags, trying to stop her hands from trembling.

'Do you know who her birth parents are?' she asked carefully, taking the mugs over to the two officers as she examined their faces.

'Not yet,' the detective said. 'But we know where she was born.'

Estelle took in a deep breath. 'It was Lillysands, wasn't it?'

The two officers exchanged a look.

'As I said, we can't divulge that information yet,' the detective replied.

Estelle scrutinised the detective's face. 'Okay. You can tell me Poppy's date of birth though, can't you?'

He held her gaze then pulled his notepad out. 'Twenty-eighth of April, 2002,' he said to Estelle.

Estelle's head started to buzz. This was it, proof.

It was the same date she gave birth.

She pulled a chair out, its metal legs scraping against the floor, and slumped down on it, putting her head in her hands as she got a brief flash of memory: soft brown hair, red face, a tiny body . . .

Poppy was her daughter. She had to be. It explained why Estelle may have been targeted with the photo; why the police had arrived quicker than they'd first said.

She looked over at the photo.

Someone knew about her connection to Poppy and they had sent her that photo as a way of — what? — telling her that?

43

She looked up at the officers. 'She's my daughter, isn't she?'

The detective sighed. 'We can't know for sure.'

He didn't say anything but the look in his eyes told her all she needed to know. Estelle felt a debilitating mixture of emotions: elation that she'd got to know the face of the child she gave up. Fear that same girl was missing. And then trepidation that someone knew about that child, someone who wanted to torment her.

'Is this a recent photo?' Estelle asked. 'Do you think it was taken after Poppy ran away?'

'We can't be sure until we show it to her parents,' Detective Jones said.

Parents. That stung Estelle, but she buried the hurt down. They *were* Poppy's parents, of course they were, she was silly to be hurt.

'But she's wearing the same top she wore the day she ran away, look,' the policewoman said. 'Her mum told us it was brand new, only got it the day before. Plus her hair is red too, her dad said she only dyed it a couple of weeks ago.'

'Yes, I noticed,' the detective said.

'So we have to assume whoever took this photo,' Estelle said, 'is with Poppy right now. They know me; they're *threatening* me.'

'I wouldn't call it a threat,' the detective said.

'Not exactly nice though, is it? If they're with Poppy, they — '

'Calm down, Miss Forster,' Detective Jones said, interrupting her. 'We're confident Poppy just ran away, she's done it before.'

Estelle frowned. 'So she's unhappy?'

'I wouldn't say that,' PC Thorburn said gently.

44

'You'd be surprised at the number of well-adjusted happy kids who run away. I guarantee she'll be back in the next couple of days, always the way.'

Estelle fell silent. She thought of the tiny baby she'd given up, the aching she'd felt as she'd handed her over. She'd hoped in the days, months, *years* afterwards she might one day see that child again. But with age came acceptance. She probably wouldn't and that was a good thing. The life she would have given the child would have been a shadow of the life a couple desperate for children could have given her. And looking at the happy family photos she'd seen, maybe she was right.

But if Poppy was so happy, why would she run away? She wasn't sure about PC Thorburn's statement, it felt like she was appeasing her.

'But in the meantime,' Detective Jones said, interrupting her thoughts, 'if Poppy turns up here — '

'Turns up here?' Estelle asked him in alarm. She hadn't even considered that. How would she begin to explain it to Seb?

'If she *is* your biological daughter and she found out who you were, it makes sense she might try to seek you out.'

'But how on earth would she know? Other than the authorities, only two people know I gave a baby up for adoption.'

'So the father and — '

'No, the father doesn't know.' Estelle swallowed.

The police officers exchanged surprised looks.

45

'Just Autumn and Max Garland, my foster parents,' Estelle said. 'I — I never told the father.'

Guilt threaded through her. It felt cruel now, with hindsight. But it had felt like the right thing to do at the time. She could barely admit the pregnancy to herself back then, let alone him. It had come as such a shock — she was only fifteen. She'd thought she'd finally found her place in the world, there in the beautiful tourist town of Lillysands with the Garlands. And then suddenly there was a child growing inside her, a threat to it all . . . and to *his* future as well, on a cusp of exciting things. That's why she'd kept everything from him, including the fact she'd given their baby up for adoption.

'Can you tell us the father's name?' the detective asked her.

'Why do you need to know?' Estelle replied, heart thumping.

'Same reason,' the detective said. 'If the girl is indeed yours, she might have run away with the intention of tracking her parents down.'

Estelle took in a deep breath. 'Aiden. Aiden Garland,' she said reluctantly.

The detective's eyebrow shot up. 'Garland?'

Estelle swallowed, looking down at her hands, cheeks burning with shame. 'He was my foster brother.'

'I see. And the Garlands knew he was the father?'

Estelle shook her head. 'No.'

Autumn and Max had no idea her and Aiden had slept together — that they even had any attraction to one another. As far as they were concerned, the father could have been one of several boys, from what Estelle had allowed them to think. She'd hated that, them thinking she'd slept around. But what choice had she had? Better that than know their son was the father.

'Will you be talking to Aiden?' Estelle asked.

'Maybe.'

Panic took hold of Estelle. 'Can I talk to him first if you do?'

'You're welcome to call him. Right,' the detective said, snapping his notepad shut and standing up. 'I think that's everything. Do keep us posted if you receive any more of these,' he said, gesturing towards the photo, which PC Thorburn was zipping up into a plastic bag.

'So what's next?' Estelle asked. 'Will you do tests on the Polaroid photo, see if there's any DNA on them?'

'Well, I doubt that — ' the detective said.

'But Poppy's missing!'

'She ran away, Miss Forster. Right now, it's a waiting game. The last time Poppy ran away, she was back within twenty-four hours. We're hopeful that she'll be back before long. We'll be in touch if we need any more information.' He looked her in the eye. 'Try not to worry, Miss Forster. Usually runaways return within a few days, a bit hungry and tired, but fine otherwise.'

'But their birth mothers — *if* I am her birth mother — didn't receive Polaroid photos like I did.'

Detective Jones nodded. 'True. But then most birth mothers aren't internet stars. For all we know, other celebrities might be receiving similar Polaroid photos. You'd be surprised at the things people do for kicks.'

'That would be quite a coincidence, I'm not that well known. Will you keep me informed?' Estelle asked as she followed them down the hallway. 'I know you can't divulge much information. But — ' She took in a deep shuddery breath. 'If she really is my daughter, I have a right to know, don't I?'

'I'm afraid you relinquished all your rights when you gave her up for adoption,' the detective said matter-of-factly. Estelle flinched and the detective's face softened. 'Sorry, that sounded harsh. I was just stating the facts. I'll do what I can. Obviously, if we can ask you to keep this to yourself, that would be good.'

'Of course.'

He gave her a pointed look. 'It benefits both of us, not saying anything, especially with your book coming out soon.'

Estelle frowned. How did he know about her book?

'Your boyfriend told us,' the PC added, sensing her confusion.

'All that matters is Poppy returning safe,' Estelle said.

'Of course.'

After they left, Estelle stayed where she was for a few moments, taking in some deep breaths. After all these years, today, that moment, she knew who her child was. Knew what she looked like. Knew what had become of her.

Knew that she had run away from her

seemingly perfect family.

She blinked away tears and strode into the kitchen, getting her laptop out and searching for information on Poppy and her new family. They clearly had money: her father a TV presenter, her mother an interior designer. She learned they lived in a huge house overlooking Richmond Park. My God, they'd been living less than a half-hour train ride from each other! Poppy attended one of the UK's top schools and was a keen hockey player. There were photos of Poppy with her father. A beach shot. Another of them walking through muddy puddles as they laughed. There was the dog again too, a golden Labrador puppy.

Poppy had a good life with a well-off family who could provide her with everything she needed. If anything came out of this, Estelle reassured herself, it was that she'd done the right thing giving her up for adoption. There was no way a fifteen-year-old Estelle could have offered the kind of perfect life the O'Farrells had.

But, then, why had Poppy run away if it was all so perfect?

She was a teenager, Estelle reasoned. Teenagers rebelled. Estelle knew that more than anyone. She'd return safe and sound soon, just like the police officers said.

But why the Polaroid photos, the messages? And there must have been an inkling of concern if the police had decided to talk to her, and maybe speak to Aiden too.

Oh God, Aiden.

He had to hear it from Estelle first. It wouldn't

be fair to find out from a stranger. She thought of the teenager she once knew. He'd be a man now. What would it do to him to know he had a child out there somewhere . . . and that Estelle hadn't given him the chance to know that child? Her stomach dropped. Aiden was a good person, kind, caring. She felt terrible. And she'd feel even worse if he found out from the police.

She googled his name but nothing came up. Then she googled the Garlands, finding a website for their property business. Images of Lillysands flashed on screen: the vast cliffs, the white beaches, its distinctive pastel-coloured houses dotting the coastline. So beautiful, just like she remembered.

She clicked on the contact page, finding a number and grabbing her phone. She hesitated a moment. She never dreamed she'd need to speak to the Garlands again, though there had been many times she wanted to pick up the phone. Like when she'd received a cheque from them for five thousand pounds via her social worker. *A little something to help you in your new home*, the note had read. *Please call us, Stel darling, we so desperately miss you. Autumn, Max and Aiden* x But she hadn't called them, instead she'd stuck to her guns, and left her life in Lillysands far behind her.

But this phone call was different. She owed Aiden this.

So she took a deep breath then dialled the number with shaky fingers.

'Hello?' a familiar husky voice answered.

Estelle found herself mute when she heard her

50

foster mother, a plethora of memories hitting her.

'Autumn?' she eventually said, finding her voice.

'Jesus Christ, is that Stel?'

Estelle couldn't help but smile. After all these years, Autumn remembered her voice. Maybe that was part of the talent with foster carers like Autumn and Max, remembering each and every child they welcomed into their home.

'It is,' she said, trying to keep her voice normal. 'How are you?'

'Shocked and delighted to hear from you, honey — that's how I am!'

Estelle imagined Autumn sat at the large dining room table, a cigarette smouldering in her ancient black-marble ashtray, her expensive gold necklace nestled in her cleavage, the light outside the vast windows behind her catching on her blonde hair.

'It's so good to hear your voice, Stel,' Autumn continued. 'We've missed you; all of us have.'

'I'm sorry it's been so long.' That was a lie. She would never have got in touch with them all again if it weren't for what had happened.

'We're so proud of you, darling, what a life you've made for yourself!'

So they'd been following her progress? That thought made Estelle's heart clench. 'Thank you. Look, Autumn, the reason I'm getting in touch is I need to talk to Aiden.'

'Why?'

'I just — ' She peered at the photo of Poppy again. 'I'm having a launch party for my book. I

51

thought Aiden might want to perform there.'

She heard Autumn sigh. 'Sorry, sweetheart, but Aiden's musician days are way behind him. He's a rock climber now, helps tourists climb the cliffs here.'

Estelle frowned. She was so sure he would have ended up becoming a singer or a song-writer, he was so ambitious back then. 'Okay,' Estelle said, trying to think on her feet. 'That's good enough, he works with cliffs, doesn't he? My next book's on coastal food,' Estelle lied. 'Maybe he can help with that.'

'I see,' Autumn said, not sounding convinced. She always had a knack of seeing right through to the truth. 'Well, here's the number.' Autumn reeled off Aiden's mobile number. 'He might not answer, he doesn't always answer when working.' She paused. 'You okay honey? You sound anxious.'

'I'm fine!' Estelle said in a faux happy voice. 'Just busy.'

'We'd love you to come visit some time. I've missed you, darling.' Autumn's voice was full of emotion. Estelle wouldn't be surprised if her green eyes were full of tears. She had so much love in her, so much intense emotion. Max always said that's why they fostered, Autumn had so much compassion to give out.

'I will visit,' Estelle said, knowing she wouldn't. But as she thought that, a tiny voice whispered, *Why not? Years have passed. Would it really be so bad to be back in the place where you spent some of your best years?*

'Promise?' Autumn asked.

Estelle squeezed her eyes shut. 'Promise. Take

52

care.' Then she put the phone down, staying still and quiet for a few moments as she thought of Autumn, of her kind green eyes, her warm arms.

Estelle snapped herself out of it, looking at Aiden's number. Emotions whirled inside as she remembered the time she broke things off with him. It had been just after the secretive scan Autumn arranged for her to have. She'd had to call in a favour with an old nurse friend. But it had confirmed she was indeed pregnant, too late to do anything but have the child. Estelle had lied, told Aiden she didn't love him, pushed him away. In the weeks that followed, she'd had to watch him angrily go from one girl to the next before being packed off by Autumn and Max to a boarding school to try to focus his mind on his studies. He'd never got on at the local school, getting in the odd fight, missing lessons. But Estelle also suspected part of the reason his parents wanted him away from Lillysands was so he wasn't touched by any scandal that might occur when Estelle had her baby. So there he was, completely in the dark about his child growing within Estelle.

But now, fifteen years later, he was going to find out.

Estelle took a deep breath and dialled his number, keeping her breath held while it rang and rang. Then it abruptly cut off. She tried it again but the same happened. 'Damn it.' She thought about texting him. But it would seem weird, after all these years, and she certainly couldn't tell him about the child she gave up in a text.

Estelle closed her eyes, exhausted from it all. Then she heard the front door click open. She sat up straight, heart thumping.

How would she explain all this to Seb?

Tell him the truth. Something she should have done a long time ago.

He appeared at the door to the kitchen, face hard. 'How did it go?'

'Sit down,' she said, gesturing to the stool next to her. 'I have something to tell you.'

'Something *else*?'

'Yes, something else,' she said with a sigh.

When he walked over, she could smell beer on his breath. He'd clearly popped to the pub. That didn't bode well. Seb could get angry when he was drunk lately. He'd never hurt Estelle, but he liked to shout, to rant. That's what the injury had done to him, made him feel like a caged animal. She remembered the phone call she'd got from his trainer after Seb had been rushed to hospital in agony during a training session three months before. There had been a collision with another boat and he'd seriously damaged his leg as a result. He'd even seen the muscle hanging from the bone. After an operation, it was a waiting game, one that was looking increasingly worrying with each consultation, delaying his return to practice more and more, the bone too weak.

Of course, Estelle understood how demoralising it must be. But other times she found his attitude towards her, the person trying her best to help and support him, hard to tolerate.

'What is it?' he asked roughly.

'I had a baby fifteen years ago.' There. Better

done quick, like a plaster being pulled off.

His eyes widened with shock. 'A baby?'

'I was fifteen. It was a mistake, of course. I gave her up for adoption.'

Seb raked his fingers through his dark hair. 'Jesus, Estelle.'

'I know it's a shock.'

'A shock? That's an understatement. This is *huge*.'

'It's in the past, Seb. I'm not that girl anymore.'

'But people won't see it like that. Your readers. The press. Our *friends*.'

Estelle frowned, surprised by the venom in his voice. 'Friends? If they're true friends, they'd understand. I thought *you'd* understand. You do, don't you?' She looked into his eyes but he avoided her gaze.

Great.

'How's this all connected with the police?' Seb said. 'And the photo you got?' That was when she saw it dawn on him. 'The runaway girl. Is she your . . . ?' Estelle nodded and his face paled. 'This is even worse than I thought.'

'You mustn't tell anyone.' She thought of Detective Jones's plea for her not to tell anyone. But how could she continue withholding information from her own boyfriend? It wasn't fair.

'Too bloody right,' he said. 'This could be disastrous for us.'

'Us? I'm more concerned about Poppy!' Estelle said, biting her fingernails as she looked out of the window over London's rooftops, imagining Poppy out there alone.

'Concerned for the girl? You don't know her!' Seb exclaimed.

Estelle looked back at him in shock. 'She's my daughter; I gave birth to her.'

'Yeah but . . . ' He sighed. 'Look, all I'm saying is if this gets out, especially this close to the launch of your book, it won't look great. We've worked so hard for it.'

'We? I wrote the book, Seb. And this isn't about my image.'

He laughed. 'You think people would watch your YouTube videos if they knew you were once a pregnant teenager? It's *all* about image, Estelle. Why do you think they offered you that six-figure deal in the first place? Image, image, image. *Especially* the fact you're the girlfriend of an Olympic rower.'

Estelle resisted the urge to slap him. 'Oh, so it had nothing to do with my cooking and writing skills, did it?'

He crossed his arms, looking her up and down. 'Be realistic, Estelle, come on.'

Estelle shook her head. That was the problem with Seb, he could be so shallow sometimes. But then he'd go and do something kind and true — like leave pink petals stuck to the wall leading to a gift in their bedroom. Or cook her (admittedly terrible) chicken soup when she was ill — and she'd forget how unfeeling he could sometimes be. But the petals and chicken soup were starting to wane, especially since he'd had to take a break from rowing. He seemed to be more and more reliant on her growing success

— on her money too. She sometimes wondered if he truly loved her for who she was, or for what she was becoming: a published writer able to support him in the lifestyle he'd grown accustomed to.

And this conversation was bringing that right home.

Estelle sighed, standing up. 'I'm going upstairs. Let's talk again when we've both calmed down.'

She went to walk past him but he grabbed her wrist, stopping her. 'Don't you dare let that kid ruin everything, Estelle. I can see it in your eyes. It's got to you.'

She yanked her wrist away. 'That *kid* is my fucking daughter.' Then she stormed out of the kitchen.

'Let me guess,' he called out after her. 'You're going to go up to your secret junk food stash to stuff your face like you always do when you're stressed?'

She paused, turning around to look at him. 'Says the man who's done nothing but drink since he got his injury?'

His face exploded with anger. 'Don't play the holier than thou act with me, not you: the daughter of a junkie who got knocked up as a teenager just like her mother.' Estelle looked at him, shocked. She'd only told him about her parents after he'd forced it out of her a few months ago, moaning she never talked about her past. Now he was using the information she'd been so desperate to keep to herself against her. He stood up, pointing his finger at her. 'Clearly history likes to repeat itself with your family. Be careful, Estelle, or your dreams could come collapsing on top of your head like a pack of cards and you might well find yourself back in that scummy council estate you grew up in.'

Estelle opened her mouth to retort but found she couldn't. As Seb looked her up and down in disgust, she suddenly felt like that pregnant girl again, huddled in the corner of her room, the shame of her situation washing over her in dark ugly waves.

'That was cruel,' she finally said, finding her voice.

A brief flicker of remorse showed in Seb's eyes. But then his face hardened again. 'I'm going to the pub,' he hissed. Then he stormed out.

Estelle took some deep breaths then she forced herself to walk upstairs, making her way to the bedroom and curling up on their bed, going over Seb's cruel words in her head. Was he right? Could she find herself back to square one again because of all this, despite all her hard work?

But that wasn't what mattered now, even though the thought terrified her. All that really mattered was Poppy getting home safely.

After a while, she found herself falling asleep. She dreamt she was standing outside a small room. Inside, Poppy was held captive with her hands bound, masking tape pressed over her lips, the walls around her shaking. Estelle banged desperately on the window but Poppy wouldn't look at her. Then, as she watched, Poppy suddenly grew younger and younger until she was a newborn, her tiny body wrapped in masking tape, desperate eyes turned to look at Estelle, then the walls of the room started to crumble.

Estelle woke to darkness, strangling a scream. She grappled for the light switch, turning it on as she calmed herself. Seb's side of the bed was untouched. She looked at the time. Five in the morning. She'd slept that long? And was Seb still out? She checked her phone, no calls or messages from him. Then she checked for updates on Poppy, but nothing. She found the photo of the Polaroid she had on her phone, staring into her daughter's eyes.

Her daughter.

Poppy was in danger; Estelle could feel it in her bones.

She got up and grabbed an overnight bag, shoving as many items into it as she could fit, and slung it over her shoulder. Then she stepped out into the darkness of the hallway and walked down the stairs. She saw Seb asleep on the living room sofa. So he *was* back. She paused, watching him for a few moments. She realised she felt nothing. When she'd left Lillysands, her heart had ached for Aiden. It seemed to her as though that intensity of feeling had been there from the very first moment she'd seen him, the first afternoon she arrived in Lillysands eighteen years ago. He'd been scrunched up in a cave, tears falling down his face, his long blond hair dirty. He'd looked up at her with green eyes that were vivid against his tanned skin, holding her gaze as he continued to cry, and something had gone 'pow' in the core of her. She'd felt nothing like it since.

As she watched Seb sleeping, she wondered if he was just another man in a succession of men who *weren't* Aiden.

She sighed and scribbled a note for him, sticking it to the fridge.

Going away for a couple of days. Need some space. xx

As she opened the door to step outside, something inside her told her she might be saying goodbye to this place forever. A look in Seb's eyes the night before. The exasperation in her own voice. The writing had been on the wall for a while: arguments, not as much affection as there used to be. She looked around her. Could this really be goodbye?

She'd learnt to leave places behind, to see them as simple, emotionless roofs over her head as a child in care. But as she thought of her kitchen, the pretty rooftop garden, she felt the grief, just as she had when she left Lillysands all those years before. She'd created that kitchen, that garden. They'd played a role in the making of her these past two years. And now she was turning her back of them, and had no idea what she was heading for.

She stepped outside and closed the door, inhaling the early morning air. Then she strode to Waterloo Station. When she got there, she was quiet for a few moments, aware this was another pivotal moment in her life, another ending. There had been so many, one chapter to the next, another door closing. But she kept moving, kept running, because that's all she knew.

No more running. It was time she faced her realities.

It was time she returned to Lillysands.

7

Thursday, 4 May

Estelle stared out of the window as a taxi drove her through Lillysands four hours later. She felt tears flood her eyes, her tummy tingling with nerves. She hated this jumble sale of feelings: trepidation and excitement, sadness and giddiness. She hadn't felt that in such a long time. The past few years had been plain sailing, very clear, no confusing emotions. But now everything seemed to be unravelling . . . including her relationship with Seb. The fact she'd barely thought of him during the long train journey suggested she'd made the right decision. She'd instead tried to focus on looking through a copy of her book to find quotes to read out at her upcoming launch party. But it was impossible, her mind filled with Poppy, Poppy, Poppy.

And Aiden.

She needed to tell him face to face about the child they'd conceived. It felt unimaginably cruel for him to hear it secondhand from the police.

But this trip was more than that. She had a feeling all the answers to Poppy's disappearance lay in Lillysands. The people who knew about Estelle giving birth all lived in Lillysands. Even her social worker hadn't found out, she'd kept it so carefully concealed. But the information must have got out somehow and someone was using it against her. But why? And *who?* She didn't have any enemies in Lillysands, not that she knew of anyway. But Lillysands was a strange place, close-knit and judgemental. She'd learnt that a long time ago.

The air inside the taxi felt close and stale. She powered down the window.

'You all right, love?' the taxi driver asked, a local man with greying dark hair.

'Fine, thanks, just breathing in the seaside air.'

The air seemed to rush in at her a million miles an hour, bringing with it a montage of memories, like the first time she'd been driven to Lillysands by her social worker that freezing December day eighteen years ago. She hadn't been delighted at the prospect of staying by the sea. The first seven years of her life had been spent in a grotty seaside town, sand in her sodden nappies, shoulders red raw from sunburn, the echo of screeching seagulls the backdrop to her stoned mother's snoring. So the seaside just meant neglect and pain for her. But as her social worker's car had rounded the corner and the whole town came into view, Estelle realised Lillysands was nothing like the rotting town of her childhood. Colourful houses dotted the cliff; sailboats gleamed under steel skies; people strolled by with smiles and expensive winter coats, faces pink from the cold sea breeze.

'Lots of money here, Estelle,' her social worker had explained. 'Don't mess things up, this place could be good for you.'

'It's Stel.'

Her social worker rolled her eyes. 'Alright, *Stel*. But listen, this is the best placement we've had for you, even better than the first one. So behave.'

The first one. Her social worker always held that up as the holy grail, better than the care home and the other unsuccessful foster placements. But it hadn't exactly been wonderful. A run-down house with a huge garden. Three dogs and two sneery teenage girls. And then Julie and Pete, friendly enough faces but clearly in desperate need of money. Even at seven, Estelle noticed the mounting bills and scuffed wallpaper; the overheard arguments between the couple about money, making it even more obvious. She'd been placed in a box room that had obviously been home to other kids like her, scrawled messages on the walls not very effectively hidden by carefully placed cushions. She remembered curling up on the bottom bunk bed that first night, yearning to be back home with her parents despite what they'd done to her. At least her filthy childhood flat was familiar. The new place seemed alien to her, scary with the angry teenagers and barking dogs. She was quickly removed from there a month in after the couple split up, and she ended up at a tiny house with an older couple who kept telling her to 'talk for god's sake, child' when all she wanted to do was sleep and wait until she was back with her parents.

After that followed a succession of foster homes, some stints in care homes. She preferred the care homes at times, bumping into familiar faces, a semblance of independence. Just before she went to live with the Garlands, she fell in with a bad crowd at the care home: skipping school, drinking, kissing boys, the sorts of things a twelve-year-old shouldn't be doing. Something inside her stopped her going too far though: placing that bottle down when her head swam too much; pushing the boy away when his fingers reached inside her waistband. It was like standing on the precipice and knowing that even though what greeted her at the bottom could be sweet oblivion, it would also mean no coming back. And there was an urge inside her to come back, instilled ironically by her dad's boasts about what he *could have been* if he hadn't injured himself as a young footballer. Every week in care would begin with Estelle wanting — needing — to do better. Head down at school, reading, writing, baking — she particularly liked baking. But then something would happen. A girl shoving her. A boy telling her she was a skank. A woman passing her on the street who looked like her mum. A missed visit by her parents. And she'd be at square one again. Bunking off school, drinking. In the end, the pool of foster parents willing to put up with her narrowed, especially when she accused one of abusing her — a stupid lie to get her placed elsewhere. So the time she spent in care homes in-between being with foster parents began to increase, and started to look like a permanent prospect.

The Garlands were her last chance. But she'd messed that up too in the end, falling pregnant too, giving her child up.

And what of that child? Had Poppy run away to give herself a chance at something; at finding her birth parents and maybe herself in the process? Estelle felt a pinch of guilt. There had been times over the years she'd considered tracking down the newborn she'd given up. But she knew she wouldn't be allowed to search for her daughter until the girl turned eighteen. She hadn't even known her name, for Christ's sake. Autumn and Max had said giving her daughter a name might make Estelle form an attachment to her. She'd agreed numbly, just as she had to everything that day — too weak, too traumatised from what had happened to argue.

How naïve she'd been, to think something as simple as giving a name to a child was what caused attachment. Those first few months after, no matter how hard she'd tried to forget, it was a knowledge, a bond that curdled inside her. But time had made it fade. And while there were days, weeks, when her mind would be dominated by the baby she'd given away, she felt sure, even now, that she'd done the right thing. What sort of life could she have provided for the girl?

Estelle looked out of the window, shielding her eyes from the morning sun as she peered out at a Lillysands that had barely changed. She resisted the impulse to put her arm out of the window, just as she used to when Max would drive her up this very road in his bright red convertible.

The town was dominated by a huge white cliff face, the pastel-coloured houses lining it painted pretty blues and pinks, yellows and greens,

66

perfect postcard fodder. Along the bottom of the cliff was the town's famous white beach and pretty marina, a plethora of shops and buildings sitting on cobbled stones across from it. And overlooking it all, Lady Lillysands as the locals called it, a huge hourglass shape that curved in from the cliff face, created from years of wind and rain. It looked like the side profile of a woman's body, hence its name, and folklore had built up around it over the centuries, one of the reasons tourists flocked to Lillysands so regularly.

As they drove further into town, Estelle noticed colourful posters stuck to walls and lamp posts, advertising the upcoming festival. It was an annual event held in May to celebrate the legend of Lady Lillysands. Lots of stalls, games, entertainment and fun.

'They still hold the festival here?' Estelle asked the taxi driver.

'Of course,' he replied. 'You're not new to the place then?'

'No, I used to live here a long time ago.'

'In Seaview Terrace?'

'Yes.'

The taxi driver's face darkened. He went quiet and focused on driving further up the cliffs, passing streets of small pastel-coloured houses. The farther up she got, the more people watched the car suspiciously. Tourists rarely ventured up here so it was unusual to see strangers in taxis this far up. The people of Lillysands didn't take to strangers, unless they were tourists ploughing money into the town. And even they weren't supposed to venture beyond the centre. That was why it felt so wonderful to have been accepted as Estelle was back then. As cold as Lillysands could be with strangers, it was irresistibly warm to those it knew and trusted.

As the taxi reached the street where the Garlands lived, two terraced cottages came into view: one pretty blue cottage with a well-kept front garden, the other pink and long abandoned with boarded-up windows. The cottages weren't officially part of Seaview Terrace, that started with the grander houses farther up the street.

Estelle leaned forward as the car approached the cottages, gripping the taxi driver's headrest. 'Can you stop here? I can walk from here.'

The driver came to a stop in front of the cottages and helped Estelle with her large bag as she handed him his money. He peered further up the road towards the Garlands' mansion, a frown puckering his brow. 'You take care, alright?' he said.

Estelle looked into his eyes. He seemed wary of Autumn and Max. But then Estelle remembered there had been jealousy in the town, the rich residents sometimes sneered at by the less well off.

As the taxi drove off, Estelle didn't go straight to the Garlands' house, instead walking towards the pink cottage, memories accosting her of her foster sister Alice sitting cross-legged on the dusty floorboards, red hair dangling to her knees as she read a book; Aiden sitting on the windowsill, strumming his guitar as he looked out over the sea. And Estelle — or *Stel* as she was known then — her long brown hair a tangle around her shoulders, lying on the floor next to Alice, drumming her fingers to the music as she watched Aiden. She quickly peered into a window to double check it still wasn't occupied, finding the same empty rooms and peeling wallpaper. Still empty, just as it had been when she'd been a teenager.

Estelle's fingertips glanced over the cottage's bumpy walls as she walked around its side, heading towards the small garden at the back with its large tree, branches trembling in the early summer breeze. She paused. Was it her imagination or did there seem to be barely any garden left now? The tree she was sure used to sit in the *middle* of the garden was now so close to the cliff edge. Perhaps she'd just remembered it wrong.

She paused as she peered past the tree. At the edge of the cliff was a withering bunch of flowers. Pink roses, edges browning, green stems wilting. A memorial to a life long lost.

'Oh Alice,' she whispered to herself.

'I thought it was you.'

She turned to see a man in his fifties with glasses and greying hair standing behind her. She frowned. 'Do I know you?'

He smiled sadly. 'I've aged that much, have I?'

She looked at him in shock. 'Mr Tate?'

He nodded. He *had* aged. Mr Tate had been the school's most beloved teacher, one of those hip teachers who let you sit on your table and discuss the interesting anthropological learnings from last night's *Eastenders* when you should have been learning about the Treaty of Versailles. And yet he still managed to get top marks for his students.

Estelle had been particularly impressed by him. She'd come to Lillysands being suspicious of teachers, her first experience of them in her old primary school chequered. But soon she grew to adore Mr Tate just as much as everyone else did.

'I'm surprised you recognise me,' she said to him with a smile.

'The famous chef? Of course I do. So, what brings you back to Lillysands? Autumn's sixtieth?'

Estelle closed her eyes. Oh god, she'd forgotten it was Autumn's birthday that weekend. This was the woman who'd been like a mother to her for several years. But, then, Estelle hadn't been in touch with her for even more years.

Thinking that made her feel even worse.

'It's going to be quite the party,' Mr Tate continued. 'I hear they're even getting in caterers.' He raised an eyebrow. 'But then the Garlands have always known how to throw a party.' He'd never been a fan of Autumn and Max. Maybe as a self-proclaimed leftie, he found their excesses a bit much.

'No, it's just a fleeting visit,' Estelle explained.

He flinched. 'Look, there's something I've been meaning to get in touch about.'

'The journalist?' Estelle asked, thinking of what the journalist who'd visited her had told her about speaking to Mr Tate.

He nodded. 'It was Mary. She answered the

phone to him, he got her talking. By the time I realised who it was . . . ' He sighed. 'Sorry. I tried to remedy it by talking to him but I probably just made it worse.'

'It's fine, really. How is she?'

He peered towards the blue cottage where he lived with his wife, another teacher who'd been at the school when Estelle was there. His brown eyes filled with sadness. 'She's ill, I'm afraid. Cancer.'

'Oh, I'm so sorry to hear that.'

'We'll fight it, don't you worry,' he said, clearly forcing himself to be bright. 'I retired early to make sure I'm there for her.'

Her heart went out to him. She'd always liked them both.

He looked towards the dried flowers at the side of the cliff. 'It still pains us to think of what happened to Alice. She was such a bright girl, had so much promise.'

Estelle followed his gaze. 'Yes, she did,' she whispered.

Fifteen years ago, Alice had jumped from this very cliff. They'd discovered Alice's body the day after Estelle gave birth, swept up on the beach at the foot of the Lady Lillysands cliff, a suicide note eventually found in her room.

'She'd have been proud of how far you've come,' Mr Tate said. '*I'm* proud. You did it. You really did. And with a recipe book too.' He put his hand on her shoulder, looking into her eyes. 'You've come a long way, Estelle.'

'Thank you.'

He sighed, peering back over his shoulder. 'I

better get back to Mary. I just saw you here and thought I'd come over to say hello. Hopefully see you around?'

Estelle smiled. 'Hopefully.'

'Take care, Estelle.' Then he walked off towards his cottage.

She watched him go, noticing how he limped slightly. Would Autumn and Max appear aged as well? Somehow, she couldn't imagine it. They'd always seemed invincible and timeless to her. Only one way to find out.

She shrugged her bag over her shoulder, walking up the road towards Seaview Terrace, home to the huge house where the Garlands lived.

When she'd first arrived there as a child, a large sign had welcomed her: 'Seaview Terrace. Luxury 5- and 6-bed clifftop houses for sale, the ideal seaside home or holiday let.' Her foster father Max had developed these houses with an investment from his rich friend Peter. They were so grand and modern, a dozen pastel-coloured houses, the jewel in Lillysands' property crown.

Estelle approached the Garlands' house now, the first of the houses, heart thumping. Its pale lilac walls felt so familiar to her, the pebble-lined lane that ran up to the glass front door like a walkway through her memories. She remembered how it had felt to look at the house all those years before. She'd been used to the houses she was carted off to getting progressively worse (cause enough problems with foster carers and word gets out). But this house had blown her mind.

Autumn was the first one to come to the door when Estelle arrived there as a girl. Estelle had been as awestruck at her as she had been the house. Autumn was so glamorous, with blonde hair tumbling down her shoulders, wearing a long-sleeved blue dress, neckline plunging. She'd met Estelle's eyes, compassion in her own green ones, as Estelle had trudged up to the door.

'Come here, darling,' Autumn had said, opening her arms to her.

Estelle had recoiled.

'Come on,' Autumn had coaxed.

The social worker had shoved Estelle towards Autumn and Estelle had taken a reluctant step, peering suspiciously at a man who'd appeared in the hallway behind the woman. He was tall with short spiky white hair and sparkling blue eyes.

'It's only a hug,' Autumn had said. 'It won't kill you.'

So she'd stepped into Autumn's arms, flinching, and Autumn had held her close.

'You're home,' she'd whispered into Estelle's ear. 'You don't ever have to be scared or alone or hungry again.'

Estelle had seriously thought about bolting then. But she knew if she did, that would be it, her social worker had told her that. No more chances. She'd be thrown into the melting pot, a lost cause. A small part of her feared that. So she'd let Autumn hug her despite hating every minute.

That was the thing back then, she was so unused to affection. Her father had come from a family who'd rather die than show anyone

73

anything close to warmth. Estelle still remembered the occasional visits to her grandparents' house in those very early days before they passed away when she was six: her parents showering and pulling on their best clothes (the ill-fitting navy suit her father always wore to court; a tight black dress and ugly red jacket for her mother). They'd put bows in Estelle's curly brown hair, force her into a pretty but oversized dress and shoes so tight they made her cry. She'd grizzle throughout the entire thing and it would make her parents argue, make her grandparents tut and roll their eyes. 'Can't control her,' they'd mutter under their breaths. 'Look at her filthy face.' No love, no hugs. Nothing.

It seemed to pass down to Estelle's birth parents. Instead, hands reaching out for her would often scare her, signalling a telling off, a gripped wrist, slapped cheeks. Looking back now, Estelle could see why her parents were the way they were. Her mother's parents were alcoholics, neglectful and violent. Estelle's father's parents were lacking in a different way. On the surface, they seemed like upstanding members of the community. But beneath it all, they were harsh with their son, judgmental and critical. It made Estelle's father so angry at the world, always trying to prove himself. He liked to tell her and anyone else who'd listen he'd have been a famous football player if it weren't for a knee injury he'd sustained as a teenager (caused by a fight with another kid — the same fight that had got him slung behind bars for eighteen months, Estelle eventually found out). 'We could be living in a mansion right now, Estelle. A proper mansion with a butler and everything.' To give him his due, Estelle had once found a grotty much-used article of him holding up a medal for being 'player of the match', black hair sweaty, brown eyes sparkling. She remembered staring at that athletic fourteen-year-old, trying to find the skinny, angry, spotty father she knew.

When she'd first walked into the Garlands' house, she'd remembered her father's boasts. *Now, this is a mansion,* she'd thought to herself.

Estelle peered up at the house now, battling a riot of emotions as she smoothed her white cotton dress down, tucking her sweeping fringe across her tanned forehead.

Then the front door suddenly opened — Autumn appearing there as she had all those years before. She was wearing a long white dress and gold sandals, her lips painted red, her eyeliner a bird's wing above each green eye. Autumn's hair was a little shorter, but she looked the same as she had fifteen years before, bar the odd wrinkle or two.

Autumn shielded her eyes from the morning sun with her hands as she looked at Estelle. Then her eyes widened. 'Stel?' she called out.

'Yes, sorry,' Estelle said, walking up the path, memories chasing her with every step: Alice and her skipping down this path, arms interlinked. Aiden and Estelle whispering their goodbyes in the darkness, lips briefly touching before sneaking back into the house. 'I should have called. It was quite impulsive.'

'No, no, not at all, you're always welcome!'

That was the way it was with the Garlands; their door was always open to the people they cared about. But it had been fifteen years. Autumn grabbed Estelle into a hug anyway, as if those fifteen years hadn't passed, her musky perfume overwhelming Estelle with memories. Estelle peered over her shoulder towards the house, looking in at its beautifully wallpapered cream walls. Autumn had it redecorated every couple of years by her interior designer friend Becca so it always looked clean and fresh. Estelle remembered feeling filthy in the house's presence the first time she arrived; her dark hair a tangle down her back, her tartan trousers grubby and her black jumper too tight.

Now she felt clean by comparison, so clean she could almost smell the scorching bleach come off her.

Autumn pulled back, looking into Estelle's eyes. 'I just had a feeling when you called me yesterday, we'd see you before too long. Please, come in,' Autumn said, beckoning her inside.

Estelle paused a moment before stepping over the threshold. The house seemed to reach out to her, pulling her towards it, and she felt a heady mixture of an intense need to get in there and a roaring desire to run away.

'Max!' Autumn shouted, her voice echoing around the large hallway and giving Estelle no choice but to step in as she gently led her inside.

Max appeared at the top of the stairs, looking the same too with his short white hair and sharp blue eyes.

'Look who's come for a visit,' Autumn said.

Max peered closer at Estelle then shook his head in disbelief. 'Is it really you, Stel?' he asked, laughing his charming laugh. The sound of it took her right back in time. It was overwhelming. How had they barely aged? 'Autumn's been dreaming about this for years,' he said, jogging down the luxuriously carpeted stairs. 'You never call, you never visit,' he joked, reaching out to Estelle. She walked towards him, letting him envelope her in his arms.

'I'm sorry I left it so long,' Estelle said, eventually extracting herself from his grip. 'Life caught up with me.'

'Stop with the apologies,' Autumn said, stroking Estelle's short hair. 'You're here now and that's what counts. Look how different your hair is!'

'It suits you,' Max said. 'Must've been a long journey. You're in London now, right?'

Estelle nodded, taking in the vast hallway with dark wooden floors and walls adorned with various family photos — including one of Estelle, face calm as she looked out to sea, her long dark hair in a ponytail. Estelle looked at that girl, tried to find herself in her face. But all she could see was Poppy.

She'd looked *just* like Poppy. How could she not have seen that before? But then she didn't have many photos from her childhood like other kids did; she'd left it all behind.

'Look at this place,' Estelle said, dragging her eyes away from the picture and feeling like that awe-filled teenager all over again. 'It looks just as amazing as it did the first time I was here.'

'Bet it's bringing back some memories,' Max said, his arm back around her shoulder.

Estelle nodded, stepping away from him. She should be used to the over-affectionate ways of the Garlands, but it all felt like too much now. That was the thing with them. Nothing by halves. All the emotion and the love thrown at you until you just found yourself wrapped up in it and rolling down a cliff so fast you forgot the old you was standing at the top, watching.

She supposed that's how she felt all those years ago, standing in the very spot she was standing in now, peering up at the large balcony above and trying to reconcile it with the house she'd lived in as a child with her parents: the tiny cramped hallway with used nappies on the floor, dirty toys flung all over, empty wine bottles and discarded filthy scraps of foil, her mum weaving towards her, ash falling from her cigarette.

'You must be starving,' Autumn said, taking Estelle's hand and leading her through the house. Estelle stopped as she reached the threshold of the kitchen, mouth dropping open. It looked just like her kitchen at Seb's house. White floor-to-ceiling cupboards across the wall to the left with a line of low units dominated by a pale blue Aga cooker. Then, in the middle, a sleek wood-topped island with four chrome stools overlooking the stunning views outside.

Had she unwittingly moulded her kitchen design from memories of this place, without even realising?

She felt her eyes drawn towards the view through the vast windows. An endless sea, the white of the cliffs. How familiar a sight, one that used to greet her each morning.

She walked to the windows, taking it all in. This garden seemed so much smaller now too. Her teenage eyes must have magnified things in her memories.

'The view still has that effect, doesn't it?' Autumn said, squeezing Estelle's hand. 'I still have to stare at it for ten minutes each morning when I wake up, just to convince myself it's real. We are so lucky to live in a town like this.'

Estelle peered out towards the heart of Lillysands and hints of the white glimmer of sails from its marina. She wondered if Aiden were out there somewhere.

Behind her, Autumn went to the fridge. 'So, what will it be? Pancakes and maple syrup? Poached eggs and muffins? Or the full shebang, the famous Garland fry-up?'

Estelle took in the contents of the bulging fridge freezer. Autumn was a food taster for high-street stores and always brought home boot-loads of food.

'People have between two thousand and ten thousand taste buds,' Estelle remembered Autumn telling her on her second day there. 'I'm one of those with tens of thousands. Taste is everything, darling. Taste is the epicentre of what it means to be alive.'

'I ate on the train,' Estelle said now. 'But thank you, I appreciate it.'

'*I'm* hungry,' Max said.

Autumn rolled her eyes. 'Aren't you always? Tea then,' she said to Estelle. 'Or coffee?'

Estelle reached into her bag, handing over some sachets of peppermint tea. 'Tea would be good, thanks. I hope you don't mind using these for mine?'

Autumn and Max exchanged a look. Then Autumn took the teabag, holding it with her fingertips as though it were poison before dropping it into a mug.

'Honestly, it feels like we've gone back eighteen years,' Autumn said, sighing contentedly as she slapped some bacon onto a pan. 'Doesn't it, Max, having our Stel back in this kitchen, sitting at that stool?'

'Poor girl,' Max said, shaking his head. 'Still makes me ill thinking of the state you were in when you got here. We've all had our fair share of difficult childhoods but yours was particularly difficult. We soon changed that though, didn't we? And now look at you,' he said, smiling that magnetic smile of his. 'Author, vlogger, Olympic advisor. I'm so proud of you, and so proud we played a part in that.'

'Yes, we really are,' Autumn said, leaning over and squeezing Estelle's hand. 'It's good to be able to tell you that to your face, darling, how very proud we are.'

'Thanks,' Estelle said, feeling her face flush.

'You'll stay tonight?' Max said.

'Of course she will!' Autumn exclaimed. 'Your old room is ready and waiting for you, I'll even add some chocolate to the pillows,' she added with a wink

'Oh, you really don't have to; I was planning to find a hotel in town.'

The truth was, she wasn't even sure she'd need to stay overnight. She just knew she needed to get to Aiden before the police did *and* try to get a sense of whether anyone else knew about Poppy here. She peered out over Lillysands. Someone out there must know *something*. She could feel it in her gut. But the police had no hope of squeezing any information out of the people here if they decided to ask questions. Only someone who was part of the community could — or someone who used to be part of the community, at least.

'You will not stay in a hotel,' Autumn said, pouting. 'If you're going to stay, I insist it's here.'

Estelle smiled. 'Okay, I'll let you know. I take it you don't have any foster kids staying?' Estelle asked as she sat on the stool Max pulled out for her. 'It's very quiet.'

They both shook their heads sadly. 'Just too busy now,' Max replied.

'With the property business?' Estelle asked.

He nodded.

'I've even gone part-time with the food tasting to help out,' Autumn said.

'That's good news though,' Estelle said. 'Means it's expanding.'

'Very good news,' Max said in a bright voice.

Estelle yawned.

'Keeping you up, are we?' he said with a laugh.

'Sorry! I've just been on the go since five this morning.'

'*Five?*' Autumn and Max exclaimed.

Estelle laughed. They'd never been early risers, she was surprised to see them awake and ready at this time in fact. 'Like I said, it was an impulsive visit.'

'So you just woke at five in the morning,' Autumn said, moving the pan about as the bacon sizzled, 'and thought 'what the hell, I'll go visit Autumn and Max'.'

'Something like that. I wanted to talk to Aiden too.'

'About your next book?' Autumn asked, pausing to look her in the eye. Estelle nodded, trying to avoid her gaze. 'He should be around later,' Autumn said, turning back to the hob. 'I'll give him a call, let him know you're here. You really do look exhausted, Stel. Why don't you go upstairs for a nap? You can't have got much sleep.'

'No, it's fine, really,' Estelle said, rubbing her eyes. But Autumn was right. She'd been up late with the dinner party too, so the combination of two nights with disrupted sleep was taking its toll.

'Come on,' Max said. 'A couple of hours' kip in your old room and you'll be as right as rain. You can barely function, girl!'

Estelle found herself nodding. Autumn switched the hob off. 'I'll get you settled in.'

They walked out of the kitchen and upstairs, Estelle pausing as they passed the room Alice had once occupied. It looked completely different, the once sky blue walls that Alice had chosen had been wallpapered over with shiny grey. She imagined Alice as she used to see her, lying stomach down in the middle of her bed as she flicked through a schoolbook. She was always reading something or another, her curiosity about the world seemingly endless. Her red hair would usually be pinned up, face fresh. 'Shall we watch a film, get some popcorn?' she used to say to Estelle when she caught her watching her. Estelle loved that, lying on Alice's bed and watching films into the night with her. 'We're like sisters, aren't we?' Alice used to say as she peered up at her.

'Darling?' Autumn said, pulling the door shut hard. 'Come see your room, we've kept it just the same.'

Autumn was right, Estelle's room was exactly as it had once looked, down to the same four-poster bed and red and white quilt. The quilt wasn't the original but it was the same pattern. One window stretched across the entire wall looking out over the sea, a window seat in front of it plump with red and white cushions. The room had wowed Estelle the first night she arrived, so large and pristine compared to what she was used to. She used to leave the curtains wide open when she slept there, staring out at the distant waves and pinching herself at how lucky she was.

Estelle caught sight of a small unmanned boat bobbing up and down in the middle of the sea. She felt like that now, afloat, not anchored to anyone or anything. She thought briefly of Seb. She peered at her phone. Still no call or text from him. He'd be fuming, her just walking out on him like that.

'Just have a lie-down, darling,' Autumn said. 'I'll get some lunch ready for when you wake up.'

She looked into Estelle's eyes, her own watering. Then she pulled Estelle into a hug. 'It's so good to have you back.' Suddenly, it was like Estelle was anchored again, still and safe in Autumn's arms.

When Autumn left the room, Estelle swept her hands over the bed. A memory flashed to her then, pain ripping through her body, the sound of her own guttural screams crowding her ears. And then the cry of a baby, delivered on that very bed. At least Poppy hadn't been born in a refuse site, like Estelle had been. Her mother had gone there with a friend to find a cot after hearing one had been dumped there. As Estelle's mother had argued with a burly man over the cot, she went into labour: Estelle's grand entrance into the world surrounded by rubbish and shocked faces peering into a clapped-up old car owned by one of the refuse workers.

Estelle sighed and went to the window seat, curling up on it like she used to, peering out at the views from the vast window. She loved the beginnings of summer in Lillysands. It gave it a different quality, the way the setting sun would turn the sea gold; the rising sun offering a smattering of pink, red and yellow. In fact, it almost looked like there were leaves floating in the water sometimes.

As Estelle looked outside, she caught sight of the wooden decking. The Garlands liked to eat outside as much as possible, even in winter, with the patio heaters they dotted around the decking providing plenty of heat. Estelle thought of her first ever dinner there. She'd walked out onto the freezing decking, Autumn's fur coat around her shoulders, the fire pit crackling nearby. She'd expected it to be just her, Autumn and Max. But there was a boy and girl at the table too: the girl a little younger than Estelle and, she'd realised with shock, the boy she'd seen at the cave a few hours before.

Nobody had told her there'd be other children.

'This is our son, Aiden,' Autumn had said, gesturing to him. He'd shot her a lazy smile and put his hand up in greeting, acting as though she hadn't seen him crying. 'And this is Alice,' Autumn had continued. 'She was our first special girl — came here a year ago and made us realise how much we could help children.'

It turned out Alice was a local girl, but her father was violent, her mother long dead. Autumn and Max had offered to take her in. She was a tiny girl of about eleven, a year younger than Estelle, with a smattering of freckles on her pale skin and long red hair. She was enveloped in one of Autumn's fur coats too, a black one that made her red hair look even more vivid. She'd smiled shyly as Estelle had mumbled a *hi*, sitting in the seat Autumn pulled out for her. Across from Estelle was a huge pot of thick creamy stew, a pile of bread next to it, the first home cooked meal she'd had in days. As Estelle ate and the family chattered away, she felt like she was in an alternate reality and that, any moment, she'd be pulled away from it. She kept quiet, staring out at the dark sea, counting the stars reflected in its surface as she ate the delicious fat-laden stew.

Every now and again, Aiden watched her with unblinking eyes, throwing her his crooked smile whenever she caught his gaze.

Estelle sighed at the memory, and leaned her head back, catching sight of the trendy abstract art piece on the wall. She remembered seeing that the first time she stepped into the room and thinking, *Dad would nick that. He'd nick everything in this house.* Autumn had seemed to sense what Estelle was thinking that day, looking at her sadly.

At least Poppy hadn't had to endure a father like that. The TV presenter looked like a nice man. The articles she'd read suggested he was kind and well-regarded. She thought of the pain Poppy's parents must be feeling at being estranged from her. It was bad enough for Estelle, but she didn't *know* her daughter, didn't have a personality to grasp onto, memories, smiles and tears.

'Where are you Poppy?' she whispered, looking out to sea.

Her eyes started drooping. Just a few minutes' sleep, that's all she needed . . .

8

I can see you up there, forehead pressed
against the window.

You look so innocent, gazing out to the sea,
just like you used to when I first met you.

But that was before I heard what you did.

Even after you'd been handed everything on
a plate! Sure, you had a difficult childhood.
But so did I.

I didn't try to bite the hand that feeds me,
did I?

Watching you, I can't help but imagine the
window opening, you falling through it.

I see you spiralling towards the ground,
imagine the impact.

How would I feel? I used to care for you, so
very much.

The old me, the one who didn't know you
for what you truly are, would mourn your loss.

But now?

I'm not so sure.

9

Estelle woke to the sound of laughter downstairs and the front door being opened. She pulled herself up, raking her fingers through her hair as she fought the fog in her mind. She peered at her watch. Past twelve. She'd been sleeping for nearly three hours! She quickly picked her phone up, noticing she had an email from her publicist checking in after her disastrous interview with the newspaper journalist. Estelle ignored it, instead scrolling to the news to check for any updates on Poppy.

But there was nothing.

She looked around her at the familiar room, so similar it was like stepping back in time, back to where it had all been so right and then gone so wrong. Suddenly, it seemed terribly rushed and irrational to have come back. But she was here now, wasn't she?

She got up and walked out into the landing, peering down. Voices were coming from the dining room.

Was Aiden in there? She swallowed, feeling nervous. She'd need to somehow get him away from his parents to tell him everything. She quickly checked her hair in the mirror then padded downstairs.

'Surprise,' a chorus of voices rang out as she opened the door.

Estelle reeled back, shocked to see twenty or

so faces smiling at her from the large dining room table, which was piled high with food: goat's cheese and vegetable tarts; cold spicy wedges with a plethora of tepid-looking dips still in their plastic containers; shop-bought sandwiches and a slab of honey-glazed gammon. Everything Estelle used to love . . . and everything she now avoided.

'I thought I'd have a few people over,' Autumn said, putting her arm around Estelle's shoulders. 'A little impromptu welcome back lunch.'

'You invited half of Lillysands,' Estelle exclaimed as Max laughed. She noticed Mr Tate among them, looking embarrassed. He smiled at her, raising an eyebrow slightly, and she smiled back.

'Of course!' Autumn said. 'We've missed our girl, I wanted a proper homecoming.'

Estelle looked at them all, not sure what to think.

Max gave Estelle a gentle nudge and she walked in. The faces were all so familiar, it was disorientating. She searched each of them to see if Aiden was amongst them. But she couldn't see him.

'Is Aiden here?' she asked Max.

'Not yet.' Estelle felt a strange mixture of relief and disappointment: relief she wouldn't need to tell him the unbearable truth, but disappointment not to be able to see him right now. 'Left a message for him though,' Max added.

'Stel!' a pretty woman with a brown bob exclaimed as she hugged her.

'Hi Veronica.' Veronica Kemp was Autumn's vivacious best friend, a regular feature at the Garlands' house when Estelle had lived there.

She was the only woman who didn't seem to fade in Autumn's presence. They both gave as good as it got, with their glossy hair and made-up faces. Veronica was a particular *tour de force* in the Lillysands community, organising events, pushing the town's reputation, a confidante to many.

Veronica held Estelle at arm's length and appraised her. 'I prefer the dark hair,' she said as Autumn nodded. 'But still beautiful. Isn't she beautiful, Peter?'

Veronica's husband, Peter, a tall man with greying dark hair and penetrating grey eyes, nodded as he looked Estelle up and down in approval. He was the richest man in Lillysands, owning half the property there. He'd been the one to invest money in the properties Max had had built on the cliff top and they remained in business on various ventures around Lillysands according to what Estelle had seen on Max's website. Estelle always thought Max aspired to be like Peter, but never quite matched his income levels. They had an interesting camaraderie, the two men, competitive but friendly. Estelle wondered if Peter had benefited even more from Max's growing business ventures than Max himself.

'*Very* beautiful,' Peter said, giving Estelle a kiss on both cheeks. 'How are you, Stel? Your book's launching soon, isn't it? It's all Autumn's been able to talk about for months, ever since she saw that article in *The Times*. She still has it hanging in her office.'

Estelle looked over at Autumn who was

fussing over the food. It made her heart clench to think Autumn had kept track of her all this time.

'Estelle, you look fantastic,' a deep voice said. It was Veronica and Peter's son, Darren, tall and dark with grey eyes like his father. A memory came to her of them tangled together in the sand, his hand on her thigh.

She buried it away and tried to smile.

'Darren, how are you?' she asked.

He smiled. 'Great now you're here.' He pulled a face. 'I never got a reply to my email, young lady.'

Estelle smiled awkwardly. She'd received a few emails from him when her name started appearing in the papers, congratulating her on her success and suggesting they meet up for a drink when he was in London. She'd ignored the first one, remembering what a jerk he was. Then he'd sent her chaser emails, so she'd moved them to her junk folder.

'Oh gosh, yes,' she said. 'So sorry. I meant to reply but things got crazy.'

He shrugged. 'I get it.' But his eyes betrayed how disappointed he was.

'Darren is a proper property mogul now,' Veronica said proudly.

'Following in my father's footsteps,' Darren said, patting Peter on the back. 'Looks like you and I have both made successes of ourselves, Estelle.'

'Well, I don't own a property at all yet, so I'm not so sure,' Estelle said.

Darren pulled a business card out and handed

it to her. 'If you have plans to buy, just call. In fact, I'm holding an event tomorrow morning for potential investors. Would be great to see you there. I can show you off, local success story and all that.'

'Great idea,' Peter said, smiling at Estelle. 'There'll be lots of champagne!'

'Or organic wine,' Darren said, winking at her. 'I've done my research.'

Estelle tried to smile back. 'I'm not sure how long I'm staying.'

'If you change your mind, call me,' Darren said. 'I can assure you, you'll have a good time. I put on the best events in the county.'

'I will,' she said, slipping his business card into her pocket and trying not to roll her eyes. Darren had always been a show-off at school, popular and a hit with the girls, but predictably shallow too. Aiden had hated him, said he was the stupidest kid he knew. Estelle wondered what Aiden thought of him now, a leading business-man in the community, and Aiden a rock climber. It was all supposed to be so different.

'Will you stop hogging my guest of honour?' Max joked to Darren, taking Estelle's arm. Estelle saw Darren giving Max a hard look, but Max didn't notice.

'Lots of people want to say hello!' Max said, leading Estelle away.

An hour later, Estelle was sat at the large glass table, delicately nibbling on the edge of a goat's cheese and red onion tart as she looked at the small circle of people surrounding her. It felt tribal, sitting in this enclosed space with all eyes on her as she ate. She'd spent the past hour being grilled about her book and her life in London. There were, of course, also some questions about why she'd left Lillysands so abruptly, but she batted them away by changing the subject. She could tell from the slight frowns on Autumn and Max's faces that they'd overheard.

When people weren't asking her questions, she tried to bring Poppy into the conversation somehow.

'Isn't it awful about that TV presenter's daughter who ran away?' she said, checking to see if anyone responded in an unusual way. But everybody seemed to be acting normally.

Despite feeling like she was back in the arms of Lillysands' community, she knew they had their guard up. Behind the smiles, they were scrutinising her too. She looked so different; she could see them thinking that as they looked her up and down. Could she be trusted? Was she *really* still one of them?

Estelle looked at Veronica. 'All set for the Lady Lillysands Festival?' Estelle asked, trying to show she really was still one of them.

'All set,' Veronica said, smiling as she bit into a cream cake. Estelle watched as the cream oozed over the sides of the pastry, her tummy rumbling in response. 'This year promises to be bigger and better,' Veronica continued. 'We have our last meeting to discuss it on Saturday, how times flies.'

'Maybe I can help?' Estelle asked. 'I know lots of bloggers, journalists too. I could help you drum up some publicity. I'm not sure how long I'll be staying but can still help from home.'

The woman sitting next to Veronica raised an eyebrow. It was Lorraine, the neighbour Autumn had been gossiping about. She lived in the house two doors down. The only thing Estelle could remember about her was that she had a huge white fluffy dog that dragged her down the road whenever she took it for a walk. She looked the same as she had when Estelle was a child, short black hair and layers of make-up. How did the people manage it here, hardly seeming to age?

'I have that in hand, sweetheart,' Lorraine said slightly haughtily. 'But thanks for offering.'

'Lorraine runs her own PR firm, remember?' Veronica explained. 'Now, about that band we said we'd hire . . .'

Estelle looked at the two of them as they turned away from her. Maybe getting back in with the Lillysands community would be a lot harder than she thought?

'I might get some air,' she said to no one in particular.

She let herself out and walked around the side of the house, heading to a veranda that offered clear views of the marina. Max caught her smoking there the first week of her arrival and she remembered thinking to herself: *And so it starts, another set of foster parents throw me out.* She'd braced herself for a telling-off but he'd just asked her to make sure she didn't throw the cigarette butts onto the beach.

As she approached the veranda now, she saw a man leaning over the side, blowing smoke out into the air, a cigarette dangling from his fingers.

Even from the distance, with his back to her, she knew it was him.

Aiden.

10

Aiden still had the same messy blonde hair, same vivid green eyes. But his face was stubbled now, circles under his eyes. She wondered if he'd recognise her.

He turned, sensing her presence.

'Stel,' he said, knowing her instantly.

'I didn't realise you were here,' she said.

'Just arrived.' His voice was deep, still a slight Devon twang to it. He seemed nervous, like she was. It had been so long after all.

They stood staring at each other for a few moments, memories shrinking and expanding between them. Then Aiden tilted his head, looking her up and down. 'You look so different,' he said, smiling slightly. 'You're like one of them now.'

'Them?'

'A Garland.'

She smoothed her short blonde hair down. He was right. The Garlands were all tall and slim with almost-white hair. 'Don't you mean *us*,' she said. 'You're a Garland too, remember?'

He quirked an eyebrow. 'I guess.'

He sighed and looked towards the side of the pink cottage.

Estelle followed his gaze. 'I saw some flowers there. I presume they were for Alice.'

Jesus, Estelle, tell him about the child you had. Tell him!

His green eyes looked sad. 'Yeah, I put them there every year on the anniversary of her death.'

Of course, Estelle realised. Alice died on the 28th of April. The day Poppy was born. Estelle hadn't known it at the time, but Alice hadn't come home that night and her body had washed up ashore the following day.

The anniversary had barely been a week ago and she hadn't even thought of Alice, her mind so focused on the book launch then Poppy.

This was the first time she and Aiden had seen each other — *talked* to each other — since Alice had died. Estelle had wanted to call him at boarding school after Autumn had broken the terrible news. She'd even picked up the phone, ready to dial his mobile phone. But she'd stopped herself. She'd promised herself when she woke the next day, she would leave Lillysands behind, leave the Garlands behind. And that included Aiden.

And now here she was, back in front of him, back feeling that roar of emotions again.

'I'm still shocked she killed herself,' Estelle said, eyes filling with tears, feeling like she was making that phone call now. 'Even fifteen years later, I'm shocked.'

'Me too.' He frowned slightly. 'The whole suicide thing just didn't ring true for me at the time. It just wasn't Alice's style. You knew her.'

He was right, it hadn't rung true for Estelle either. Alice would talk about her mother who hung herself when Alice was just a toddler. She'd get this tough look on her face, jaw set, eyes hard. 'I'd never give up like she did,' Alice had

97

said. 'No matter what happened.' Estelle had believed her, which made the news she'd jumped off the cliff even more dreadful.

What if she hadn't meant to die?

A swift wind ricocheted over the cliff and wrapped itself around Estelle now. She circled her arms around herself, shivering. 'You said her suicide didn't ring true for you. Do you think she didn't mean to die? That she — ' She paused. 'That something else happened?'

Aiden frowned. 'No, of course not. She left a suicide note, remember?' he said, but there was something in his eyes suggesting otherwise.

They were quiet for a few moments as Aiden smoked, taking in the view in front of them: the spires of the church on top of the highest cliff, the quiet marina and, above, seagulls glazing beneath blue skies. Below them, colourful houses curved along the cliffside, the reflection of their windows sparkling in the sea below. A couple walked on the beach, swinging a little girl up and down.

Aiden sighed, turning to Estelle. 'Why are you here? I know it's not just a passing visit like Dad said in his voicemail. It's been fifteen years.' His face looked pained as he said that.

Estelle took a deep breath. 'I came because I have something to tell you.'

He looked at her expectantly. It took her back in time, seeing those green eyes search hers as they had every day all those years ago.

She swallowed, throat dry. She'd thought over and over on the train journey down how she'd tell Aiden. But the words evaded her. In the end, she thought she'd know what to say when she saw him. And yet here she stood, staring at him — at her *past* — and it was even more difficult to know where to start.

Just tell it straight, that was what Mr Tate used to say to her.

So she did.

'I had a baby,' she said softly. 'A girl.'

'Well, congratulations,' he said, jaw tensing. 'How old is she?'

'Fifteen.'

He went quiet. She knew what he was doing, counting down the years. When it dawned on him, his eyes widened. 'So you had her when you were fifteen?'

She nodded.

He curled his hands into fists, his breathing strained. 'And the father?'

She felt sick. 'I only slept with one person then, Aiden. She's yours.'

The air between them seemed to swirl with emotions. 'Mine?' He looked at her, eyes blazing with anger. 'But I didn't even know you were pregnant!'

'I hid it well the first few months. Then you went away, remember?'

He took in some deep breaths, trying to wrap his head around it. 'But why keep it from me?'

'I was scared,' Estelle said, tears springing to her eyes. 'I was confused too. I — I thought it would distract you from all your plans and — and I'd decided not to keep her anyway.'

'Jesus.' He walked away, raking his fingers through his hair. Then he came back, looking at

Estelle with pain-filled eyes. 'Where is she now?'

'I — I gave her up for adoption.'

'When?'

'When she was born.'

Aiden stared towards the sea, looking dazed. 'You gave away our child.'

All the feelings she'd felt as she'd handed Poppy over came back to her then. How everything inside her exhausted body had roared to keep hold of that tiny baby, even though her head was telling her it was the right thing, the *good* thing, to do. And yes, she'd thought of Aiden too, of what he would say if he knew. But she'd convinced herself she was doing the right thing by him too. That didn't stop the pain she felt though, then *and* now.

Estelle's heart thundered. 'I had to give her up.'

He turned back to her, the anger still there. 'No, no you didn't. We could have looked after her.'

Estelle closed her eyes, trying to squeeze away the memories. She'd wondered about that possibility too as she'd looked down at the baby in her arms. *Why not give it a go? Would it be so terrible for the child to have her as a mother?* She'd yearned for Aiden to be by her side, to make her strong, make her see the right thing to do. The same way she'd been desperate for him to be there as she screamed in pain during labour, stifling the urge to call out his name. But he hadn't been there and she'd made her decision.

'Jesus, Aiden, we were kids,' she said, as she

had said to herself then through the doubt. 'We'd have made terrible parents. I had no choice.'

He took a step towards her, fists clenched. 'Not everyone's your parents, Stel. We would've pulled ourselves together.'

'I made the right decision,' Estelle said firmly.

'It wasn't just your decision to make though, was it?' He shoved past her and headed towards the steps leading down to the beach.

She ran after him. 'We have to talk!'

'No we fucking don't.'

'She's missing!'

He froze. Then he slowly turned around. 'What?'

'The girl on the news, Poppy O'Farrell. The TV presenter's daughter who ran away. It's her.'

'How do you know she's our — ' He swallowed, eyes filled with pain. 'Our daughter?'

Estelle dug her phone out, finding the photo she'd taken of the Polaroid before the police came. 'I got this — someone sent it to me. The police couldn't confirm Poppy's the baby I gave away, but it was bloody clear, just look at her. She looks just like me. It can't be a coincidence, she must be our daughter. And whoever took her knows that.'

Aiden stared at the photo, eyes shining. 'I can't believe this.'

Estelle's heart ached for him. It was awful to see him like this. 'I'm sorry, I should have told you.'

He looked up at her. 'Who could have sent this?'

'I don't know.'

101

'Who else knew about her?'

'Your parents.'

'My *parents*?' Estelle nodded. Aiden closed his eyes, pinching the bridge of his nose. 'So they knew I was the father?'

'No,' Estelle quickly said. 'I never told them.'

Aiden looked relieved. 'What about Alice? Did she know?'

Estelle nodded. 'Yes. She knew everything . . . including the fact you were the father.'

'And yet you didn't think to tell *me*, the father.'

'I — I didn't want to distract you, you had all those preparations to make for getting into stage school and fulfilling all your dreams of being a musician. I didn't want to ruin things for you.'

'Yeah, and that worked out really well, didn't it?' he said bitterly. 'You know I'm a rock climber now?'

'Autumn mentioned.'

She saw a flicker of pain cross his face then he collected himself. 'Do Mum and Dad know the baby is this missing girl?'

'Not yet. I'm not sure they need to know. I'd rather they didn't, to be honest.'

'Police have any leads?' he asked, jaw clenched.

'I don't think so. They're not taking it hugely seriously; kids run away all the time.' She put her hand out to him, suddenly desperate to touch him. 'Aiden, I'm *so* sorry.'

He stepped back, shaking his head. 'I need time to digest this. Are you staying in Lillysands for a bit?'

102

'I hadn't thought that far ahead. But I'll stay as long as you need me to.' As she said that, she knew she would, no matter how long that was . . . and no matter what Seb thought.

'Ah, there you are.' They looked up to see Max watching them, nursing a brandy. 'You got my messages then?' he asked his son.

Aiden nodded, eyes faraway as he took in what Estelle had told him.

'Autumn dug out some old photos,' Max said. 'You both coming inside to have a look?' He raised an eyebrow. 'Some major fashion errors to witness!'

'I don't think so,' Aiden said, eyes sliding over to Estelle's. 'I'm going home.'

'You don't still live here?'

'I might not make much money compared to you, Stel, but it's enough to get a place for myself, you know.'

Then he jumped over the side of the veranda, striding to the steps leading down to the beach. Estelle wanted desperately to follow him, she didn't want to leave it like this. Of course, she knew he would be angry. But she'd hoped it would all end with some acceptance, maybe even a coffee somewhere, a sense of closure. Not like this, with him storming away.

But Max was watching her. And how would she explain chasing after his son? So she stayed where she was.

'As you can see,' Max said as he watched his son, 'Aiden's manners haven't improved.' He fixed a smile on his face. 'Come on, let's get you inside.'

Estelle let Max guide her back into the house. Before she stepped in, she looked over her shoulder to see Aiden at the top of the steps, watching her. Then he jogged down them, disappearing down to the beach.

★ ★ ★

After everyone left, Estelle and Autumn sat in the kitchen, nursing hot drinks while Max tidied up. Estelle stared out towards the beach, thinking again of the look on Aiden's face when she told him. The anger. The disappointment too.

'Max told me about Aiden storming off,' Autumn said. 'Everything okay?'

Estelle pursed her lips. She wasn't about to tell Autumn the truth. She'd promised Detective Jones she wouldn't tell anyone and she'd already broken that promise by telling Seb. Plus she just couldn't deal with two confrontations that day. 'I think he's still annoyed I left Lillysands without saying a proper goodbye.'

'That boy, head always stuck in the past,' Autumn said, shaking her head. 'You know, he was a mess when he got back from his first term at his new boarding school. First hearing about Alice, then that you'd left without a word.' Autumn peered towards the side of the pink cottage where Alice had jumped to her death. It must have been hard to stay here, not far from where their foster daughter had jumped. But they'd put so much into this house. 'It hit Aiden hard,' Autumn continued. 'It hit *all* of us hard.

104

Things got even worse between us and Aiden after. Well, you know it was never perfect before then.'

Autumn was right. You'd expect relations between foster parents and their wards would be tough. But it seemed harder between Aiden and his parents. He was always starting arguments with them. Whenever Estelle quizzed Aiden about why he was so tough on his parents, he'd complain that they were shallow, that they cared more for materials than for the natural world around them. But Estelle just couldn't see it. Sure, they were well-off and liked their little luxuries, but they'd always been so loving with her.

'Okay sweetheart?' Autumn asked, breaking into her reminiscences.

'Oh, just lost in memories.'

Autumn leaned forward, grasping Estelle's hand. 'Why are you here really, darling? I can tell something's on your mind.'

Estelle stared down into her tea. 'I broke up with my boyfriend.' Well, it was half the truth, wasn't it? Not the main reason she was here. But a fact. Her and Seb were history, even if they hadn't quite confirmed it with one another.

'Well, that explains it,' Autumn said, putting her arm around Estelle's shoulder and pulling her close. 'Poor girl. He was the Olympic rower, right?'

Estelle nodded.

'I'm not too disappointed,' Autumn said. 'I never liked him in the interviews I saw. Too perfect, too clean, it didn't ring true to me.'

Estelle raised an eyebrow. 'Tell it like it is, Autumn.'

'You know I always do. Were you living together?'

Estelle nodded. 'It was his house, even though I was paying some of the mortgage.'

'What will you do when you go back to London? *If* you go back. There's some gorgeous new apartments overlooking the sea that Darren and Peter have just developed.'

Estelle shook her head. 'I won't leave London.' But in truth, it was more the fact she wouldn't return to Lillysands. There were too many secrets there, too many ghosts.

'Why not?' Autumn wrinkled her nose. 'I can't imagine living there, all noisy and smelly, not like here.'

'It smells of seaweed here,' Estelle said, raising an eyebrow and trying to make the conversation light.

'Good fresh *clean* seaweed, perfect for a pure-eating guru.'

Estelle smiled. 'I see what you're trying to do and it's very sweet. But London's my home now, I'll never leave.'

'Never say never.' Autumn said with a wink. 'I saw you and Darren talking. He's quite a looker now, isn't he? Always was, I suppose, but now he's rich with it too.' She leaned towards Estelle, eyes sparkling. 'He'd make a good match for you.'

Estelle laughed. 'Honestly, Autumn! Are you trying to set us up?'

She shrugged. 'Why not?'

'I think it's a bit soon.'

Autumn didn't answer. Instead she held Estelle's gaze for a few seconds, as if looking into her thoughts. Just as Estelle was beginning to feel uneasy, Autumn looked down at her watch. 'So what's the plan? It's nearly five. If you get a train now, you'll get back very late.'

Estelle looked at her watch. 'You're right.' She wouldn't get back until after nine, which wasn't too bad. But the truth was, she didn't want to face Seb, not in the mood she expected to find him in when she returned. And anyway, she needed to stay in Lillysands a little longer. She couldn't leave things as they were with Aiden.

'So will you stay tonight?' Autumn shot her a cheeky grin. 'You know it's my sixtieth birthday tomorrow and having you here for it would be the most *wonderful* present.'

Estelle thought of the promise she'd made Aiden, that she'd be there if he needed her. 'If that's okay?'

'Okay? It's the best news I've had in years, darling!' Autumn grabbed her face and kissed her firmly on the cheek.

Estelle laughed. 'Autumn!'

'Sorry, I'm just so excited. Thank you, darling. And surely you've got used to my hugs and kisses? It took you a while to get used to them when you first arrived, I remember you used to freeze in my arms.'

Estelle sighed at the memory of how she'd grow brittle in Autumn's arms, embarrassment turning her cheeks hot. Even worse when Autumn hugged and kissed her goodbye at the school gates on her first day, two weeks after she had arrived. A girl in class had even taken the mick out of her. 'Still being kissed at the school gate by Mummy, are we?' After a few days of it, she'd shoved Autumn away. But the wounded look on Autumn's face had played on her mind all day. That afternoon when Autumn picked her up from school, her foster mother had been quiet and that had scared Estelle. While the affection was difficult, she was growing to love her time with the Garlands, the walks on the beach and movie nights with popcorn, snuggled up under blankets in the living room. What if Autumn didn't want her anymore? Her social worker had told her it was her last chance before an indefinite stay in a care home.

That evening, after dinner, Autumn had asked her to stay behind while the others went into the living room. Estelle had braced herself: *Here it comes, she's going to tell me it's not working out.*

'I know I'm too much with the hugging, Stel darlin',' she'd begun. 'Max always tells me off for being overbearing.' Estelle waited to hear the words she'd become so used to. 'I promise from now on I'll stop,' Autumn had continued. 'That's if you want me to?'

Estelle had looked into her eyes, desperate to tell her she didn't mind, if it meant she could stay. But so unused to expressing her feelings, she'd just nodded, pained when she saw the disappointment in Autumn's eyes. She hadn't been able to sleep that night, still seeing that disappointment. So, the next morning, she sought Autumn out in the kitchen and marched over to her, wrapping her arms around her and burying her face in her foster mother's hair. The way that had made Estelle feel had surprised her. It was wonderful.

'Don't stop hugging me,' she'd whispered to Autumn.

Then she'd walked out, catching the smile on Autumn's face in the reflection of the glass.

Max walked into the kitchen now with a bulging bin bag, the memories dissipating. 'I take it Estelle is staying for your birthday party considering that smile on your face, Autumn?'

'Oh, I'm not sure I'll be able to stay for the party,' Estelle said. If she could find Aiden and resolve things with him, and things felt right for her to return to London, then she would. Autumn's face dropped. 'But I'll be here when you wake! I didn't get you a present though.'

'You being here is the best birthday present Autumn could have,' Max said.

'That's what I told her!' Autumn said, the disappointment gone.

They both laughed and Estelle found herself joining in, their exuberance infectious.

Over the next few hours, Estelle helped Autumn cook a hearty stew, somehow finding enough organic, whole foods to make it with. They talked into the night, reminiscing about the good times, glossing over the bad times . . . and the baby too, not one mention of the child they'd helped Estelle give up all those years before. Estelle went along with it and allowed herself to pretend everything was okay, that her daughter

109

wasn't missing, that her relationship hadn't fallen to pieces . . . and that Aiden wasn't angry at her. But she kept watching the door, hoping he'd walk in.

When midnight approached, she made her excuses and went up to her room. After she got changed into her nightwear, she looked again at the bed where she'd given birth. The mattress had no doubt been replaced, but the sturdy mahogany frame was still there. She took a deep breath and got beneath the thick duvet, the familiar smell of the berry washing powder Autumn still used filling her nostrils. She'd held Poppy as a newborn here, very briefly, staring down into her red little face before she'd handed her over. She'd been shocked by the solidness of the baby, the warmth and the smells; the gentle tugging of love that was beginning to swell. When she'd taken a pregnancy test months before, bouts of nausea and a few missed periods driving her to the chemists to buy one, she hadn't seen the red cross as representing something that was *real*. Not at first anyway. Alice had been there and had pleaded with her to tell someone, even just to go to the doctors. But Estelle had blocked it all out. The test was wrong. She wasn't pregnant. It was easy at first. She was so slim, it barely showed. But then one morning, she woke to the baby kicking her. She'd jumped out of bed — that very bed — and stood at the mirror, examining her growing belly. She'd been surprised as something close to affection had risen inside her for the baby she was carrying.

110

Then she'd heard breathing and turned to see Autumn watching her from the hallway through her half-open door. She'd quickly covered herself but it was too late. Autumn knew, she could see it in her eyes. They'd sat on the bed and Estelle had confessed everything except who the father was. Autumn had promised to support her and had even agreed to keep it a secret, telling her she'd get a nurse friend of hers to help with discreet scans and the birth itself so the authorities weren't alerted and Estelle wouldn't be taken away from the Garlands. In that moment, that promise, Estelle had felt a weight lifted off her shoulders.

She'd always been so desperate to make the Garlands proud of her. She'd worked so hard to make something of herself over those last couple of years, and she'd been thriving at school. She'd been daunted by the school when she first saw it, huge and white like the American campuses she saw on TV. There was no uniform either, pupils could wear what they wanted. Even teachers could be referred to by their first names. It fit in perfectly with Autumn and Max's relaxed vibe, but for a new girl, young and fearful of how people would regard her, it was terrifying. But after the initial difficult weeks, teachers like Mr and Mrs Tate brought her out of her shell. Estelle began to flourish, feeling her wings spreading, her grades improving. The parents' evenings Autumn and Max religiously attended began to include heaps of praise. There would even be celebratory dinners after: Autumn hugging her and telling her what a 'bright little thing' she was; Max leaning across the table and grabbing her hand: 'This is the time, Stel, when you're so young. The world is your oyster, grab it and lap it up!' It was hard not to be infected by it. Nothing had been expected of her before, just getting her to attend school each day was ambition enough for her previous foster carers. But with the Garlands, the world opened up. She was encouraged and *expected* to thrive, each small achievement a cause for celebration. It was invigorating, enlivening, and it would spill over into her moments with Aiden and Alice in that pink cottage as they excitedly discussed their futures: Estelle would be a famous chef, Aiden a singer-songwriter and Alice would be a world-renowned scientist, something Estelle didn't doubt, she was so clever. Autumn and Max had seemed so proud of their 'three children', as they referred to them.

So when Estelle learnt she was pregnant, she was terrified of losing all that: their home, their pride, their love. If they could celebrate achievements with such exuberance, what would happen when Estelle did something wrong? The worst possible kind of wrong for a teenage girl. Would they banish her?

But Autumn's reaction had shown her maybe love *could* be unconditional; that maybe her foster mother loved her in the good times and the bad, like good parents should. There were still moments of denial and anger as Estelle got used to the prospect of a baby. But it was easier with Autumn on her side. Over the next few months, Autumn helped Estelle to hide the pregnancy, buying her contoured clothes to conceal the bump and then, in the final weeks, telling people she was ill with glandular fever, and hiding her away in this room.

Estelle looked out at the glimmering sea now, the lights from the houses below reflected in its surface.

Where was Poppy right now, the baby who had grown within her?

She picked up her phone, quickly checking the news for updates. Then she froze when she noticed a headline. *Breaking news: Chris O'Farrell says daughter may have been groomed by predator.*

Estelle quickly clicked into the story.

TV presenter Chris O'Farrell believes his daughter, fifteen-year-old schoolgirl Poppy, may have been groomed before running away. He claims to have found an untraceable email on her computer from an older man giving only his first name, and lashed out at police, claiming they're not taking his daughter's disappearance seriously enough. More on this story as it develops.

Estelle put her hand to her mouth, feeling nauseous. Could Chris O'Farrell be right, could she have been groomed? Estelle flicked to the photo of the Polaroid she'd received, staring into Poppy's brown eyes. If so, that might mean whoever groomed her into running away sent this Polaroid to Estelle.

But who would do that?

Estelle went to the window, peering out over

Lillysands, heart thumping loud in her ears. 'Where are you, Poppy?'

As she asked the question, she caught a glimpse of a shadow in the garden. Her heartbeat trebled. She frowned, peering closer.

But the shadow had disappeared.

11

When Estelle awoke, it was early the next day, the sky bright and blue. Looking at her phone, she saw she had a voicemail. Could it be from Seb? She quickly accessed the voicemail and put her phone to her ear. But it was a message from Detective Jones instead, asking her to call him.

She dialled his number straightaway but the detective wasn't available so she left her own message.

It had been three days since Poppy had disappeared and with news of her possibly being groomed coming out, the detective must be as worried as Estelle now. Maybe he wanted to ask her some more questions? Or maybe he had new information?

She couldn't sit here and stew over it though. It would send her crazy. She needed to get out and clear her mind. So she pulled on her running gear then jogged downstairs. When she got to the kitchen, Autumn was laying out a large breakfast, a cigarette dangling out of her red lips. 'Honey, I do *not* remember you getting up this early when you lived here!' she said with a laugh.

'And I don't remember you getting up this early!'

'Then we've both changed.'

Estelle went over to her and kissed her cheek.

'Happy birthday, Autumn.'

'Thank you, sweetheart.'

'Isn't Max supposed to be making *you* breakfast in bed?' Estelle asked.

'I love doing this, you know that. Where do you think you got your love of food from? How do you want your eggs?'

'Oh, I'm fine, really. I prefer running on an empty stomach.'

Autumn raised an eyebrow as she looked her up and down. 'Have you lost your mind? Come here and get some breakfast inside you.'

She looked at the fry up. It brought back so many memories of having breakfast cooked for her each morning here by Autumn. It was tempting to say yes — she remembered the delicious breakfasts Autumn used to make. But now more than ever she needed to stick to her healthy eating habits. 'No really, it's fine, but thank you. I'll see you later.'

She walked down the hallway and opened the front door. Then, breathing in the crisp morning air, she set off down the pavement. But as she passed the tree in front of the house, something caught her eye. Propped up against the base of the trunk was an envelope with her name on. Estelle frowned, looking around her. Had the figure she'd seen skulking in the darkness the night before put it there? She reached down for it with trembling hands, then tore it open.

Something dropped out onto the dewy grass.

A Polaroid.

116

12

I see you found the photo.

I feel a stab of excitement. It's thrilling really, seeing the look on your face, knowing my handiwork is causing that.

Next time, I want to do something to really scare you. Something to make you realise this is serious.

But this will do for now.

I know why it feels so good today: I saw you with him yesterday.

The way it made me feel. The jealousy curling in the pit of my stomach. I hate it, hate how weak it makes me.

That's not why I'm doing this though. Not the main reason anyway.

But it helps. Doing something helps ease the pain of seeing you two so close.

Part of me wants to step out from the shadows now. Talk to you.

You would never guess it was me who left the photo there.

But I am so so angry with you. What if I lose control?

So, for now, I'll just watch.

What's going through your mind? Your eyes show nothing.

I suppose we're not so different. I keep everything pent up inside too. But it takes all of my energy. Leaves me exhausted by the end of the day.

I bet it doesn't tire you though. You're a real mistress of it. Face like glass.

I wonder what will happen when the glass shatters?

13

Estelle reached for the photo, barely breathing.

Then she let out a gasp.

It wasn't a picture of Poppy this time. It was a photo of Alice, in the distance. She was in the garden at the Garlands, peering out to sea from the edge of the cliff there, face pensive. It would have been taken from the path leading down to the beach, shared by all the houses along the road.

Taken without her knowledge?

Estelle ran her fingers over the photo. Someone must have taken very good care of it. It was in perfect condition, despite having been shot years ago. Polaroid photos faded. There'd been an old one hanging in Mr Tate's classroom, a picture of a house that had fallen into the sea. It was bleached white with time, the house barely discernible.

Estelle shivered. How long had someone been planning to send this to her?

How long had someone been watching her?

Her eyes moved to the bottom of the frame. Scrawled in messy handwriting was the message: *Watch your back or you might go over the edge.*

Fear trembled through Estelle. This confirmed it. Whoever was leaving her these Polaroid photos was right here in Lillysands. She looked around her then caught sight of Aiden driving up the road in a four by four. She jogged towards him, holding up the photo. She wanted to show him, have him involved. She couldn't deal with this alone.

He pulled to a stop beside her and powered down his window. He looked into her eyes a few moments, a mixture of emotions in his: the hurt she'd seen last night, some anger still, but some affection too. His eyes dropped to the photo. 'What's that?' he asked.

'Someone left it in an envelope by the tree. It's a Polaroid photo, just like the one of Poppy.'

He got out of his car and took it from her, examining it. 'Is that *Alice*?' he asked.

Estelle nodded.

'But what's that got to do with Alice?'

Estelle clutched onto the Polaroid, taking deep breaths. 'I don't know.'

Aiden went to speak to her again but before he had the chance, Estelle's phone rang. She looked down at it to see it was a London number. She put the phone to her ear. 'Hello?'

'Hello, Miss Forster.' It was DC Jones.

'Has there been any update?' she asked as Aiden watched her.

'Nothing so far. I'll be honest, we're grasping at straws. It's been three days now and as you can imagine, Poppy's parents are very concerned.'

'Yes, I can imagine. What about the grooming story?'

He sighed. 'It's just an avenue we're exploring. I just wanted to ring to see if you'd had any contact from Poppy?'

'No, not from Poppy.'

'What do you mean?'

She looked at the photo. 'I received another Polaroid photo this morning.'

'Of Poppy?'

Estelle swallowed. She peered at Aiden. 'Of my foster sister, Alice Shepherd. She died the day Poppy was born.'

Estelle thought back to the last time she'd talked to a police officer about Alice's death. The day she'd been interviewed about it a few days after, in her new care home. They'd got in touch with her social worker who'd told them where she was. The officers had been keen to discover Alice's state of mind before she'd died. Estelle had barely been able to string a sentence together, the shock at her friend's death still so severe.

DC Jones paused a few moments. 'Yes, I'm aware of your foster sister's death, I read the police notes. There was some concern around her death, wasn't there?'

Estelle's heart thumped against her chest. 'Concern? What do you mean?'

'Oh nothing,' the detective said, clearly backtracking. 'Can you email me a photo of the Polaroid photo? You have my business card?'

'Yes,' Estelle said sharply, annoyed with his evasiveness. He was obviously holding back information about Alice; what if he was holding back information about Poppy too? Not that he seemed to know very much about her whereabouts, he hadn't even got around to talking to Aiden yet. Maybe Poppy's father was right, maybe the Police weren't taking it all seriously enough? 'Have you sent officers to Lillysands?'

Estelle asked. 'I'm here and I haven't heard of anyone being questioned.'

'You're in Lillysands?'

'Yes.'

'Why?'

Estelle looked at Aiden again. 'I wanted to tell Poppy's birth father, face to face.'

'I see.' He sounded annoyed.

'Look, I really think you need to send some officers here. Whoever's sending me these photos is here.'

'I'll chat to the team.'

'Great, if — '

'I really must go now, Estelle. Take care.'

He put the phone down and Estelle let out a sigh of frustration.

'What's wrong?' Aiden asked. He looked worried, the anger from the day before gone for now.

She told Aiden about the conversation. 'I just don't think they're taking Poppy's disappearance and these photos seriously enough. And the stuff he implied about Alice . . . what if Alice really didn't commit suicide? What if — what if she was pushed?'

Aiden sighed. 'Not this again, Stel. She left a suicide note.'

'But think about it for a moment. Consider the possibility Alice was killed. What if whoever pushed her is the person sending me these photos? They're trying to send me a message, that I'll go over the cliff like Alice too.' She looked at the photo of Alice, fear trembling down her spine.

Aiden shook his head. 'You're overthinking things.'

'Really? Clearly there was doubt over her death — the detective basically told me as much.' Estelle traced her finger down Alice's red hair in the photo. 'This was taken a week or so before she died. She got her hair cut, I remember because she looked so much older and more sophisticated while I felt fat and — '

'Pregnant,' Aiden finished for her, voice brittle.

Estelle turned away. 'Whoever took the photo had been around just a few days before Alice died, perhaps even when she had died. So what are they trying to say to me? How is this connected to Poppy?'

Estelle thought about it. If Alice was pushed, then who would have wanted to kill Alice?

Alice's father?

Estelle thought back to what she knew of Alice's birth father, a drunken violent man not unlike her own birth father. He'd even served time for various acts. He'd not liked the fact Max and Autumn had taken Alice in. Aiden had told her how he had sat outside the house sometimes in those early months. There had been talk from social services of Alice being removed, taken to another town far away. But then her father had abruptly stopped. Aiden was sure it was because Max had had words with him, maybe even paid the man off.

But, the month before Alice died, she had told Estelle about how her birth father had rolled up in his car while she had been walking on the road, and shouted abuse at her. Alice had turned to Estelle, eyes wide. 'He's angry because I told my social worker I don't want visits with him anymore.'

'Her father was pretty angry with her just before she died,' Estelle said to Aiden now. 'Maybe he tricked her into meeting with him so he could confront her about the visits, then he pushed her in a moment of anger? Or maybe it was just an accident as they argued, I don't know.'

'But how is this connected to the Polaroids you've been receiving?'

'I — I don't know.' She frowned as she looked at the photo. Then something occurred to her. 'Alice told me he went to prison for blackmailing and threatening one of his customers, a local bank manager, after he found drugs in the manager's car.'

'Yeah, I remember that.'

'If he had form for blackmailing — '

' — then he could be blackmailing you?' Aiden finished for her. She nodded. 'I don't know, Stel. Seems a bit far-fetched.'

'Why not? Maybe he read an article about me doing well so thought he'd try to get some money by putting the wind up me.'

'But how on earth did he get a photo of Poppy?'

She dug her phone out of her pocket and found the article she'd read the evening before about Poppy possibly being groomed. 'Maybe he orchestrated meeting up with her?'

Aiden frowned as he read it. 'Just speculation,' he said, handing the phone back to her. But he looked worried.

124

'What does Alice's dad do now? Is he still a mechanic at that garage?' Estelle asked, shading her eyes from the morning sun as she peered towards where the garage was in the centre of town.

'Not after that blackmailing incident. He still lives close to it though, seen him coming in and out sometimes when I have work done on my car there. He lives in a house on the same street.'

'I need to talk to him,' she said, going to walk towards town. 'Even if it's just to rule him out.'

Aiden grabbed her arm. 'Woah, wait! This is getting out of hand. Poppy ran away. She hasn't been kidnapped, for God's sake. And Alice wasn't murdered.'

Estelle picked up the Polaroid, holding it up in front of his face. 'Then why all this?'

Aiden sighed, raking his fingers through his hair. 'I don't know.'

'She's our daughter, Aiden. We have to make sure she's safe.'

'Like you've been making sure over the past fifteen years?'

That comment stung Estelle. But she tried to hide her pain. 'Yes, actually. Why do you think I put her up for adoption?'

They both stared at each other, the friction in the air fizzing between them.

Then there was the noise of a door opening. They turned to see Autumn looking at them from the front door, her arms crossed.

Estelle quickly tucked the Polaroid in her pocket.

'What are you two doing out there?' Autumn

125

asked. 'I thought you were going for a run, Stel?'

'I decided against it.'

'You might as well come in for a fry-up then.' She turned to her son, putting her hands on her hips. 'And did you forget what day it is, young man?'

Aiden sighed, walking up the path. 'Of course not. That's why I'm here. Happy birthday, Mum.' He gave her a peck on the cheek then handed over her card with a small gift. Estelle reluctantly followed them back inside, the Polaroid seeming to burn a hole in her pocket. She wanted to go talk to Alice's dad right now. What if he knew where Poppy was, they couldn't waste any time. But she needed to figure out what she was going to say first.

Max was already in the kitchen, tucking into a cooked breakfast.

'So, the whole works?' Autumn asked Estelle and Aiden as she gestured to a huge frying pan full of sizzling bacon, sausages and eggs.

'Nothing for me,' Estelle said, but she was unable to stop her stomach rumbling in response. She used to love a good fry-up, especially the ones Autumn made. They were still strong in her memory, interlaced with that feeling of belonging she always felt here, especially on a Sunday morning when fry-ups were a regular occurrence.

But no, she couldn't indulge. She *had* to stay in control.

Max paused. 'Are you crazy?'

'I'm never hungry in the mornings.' Estelle liked to fast in the mornings, something she'd

126

trained her body to do. She'd then have a smoothie at eleven on the dot. She wasn't about to change her habits now.

'But what about the whole breakfast like a king philosophy?' he asked.

'That's a myth,' Estelle said. 'Our ancestors ate most of their food in the afternoons after they had a chance to hunt. Fasting for several hours overnight and into the late morning or afternoon is often beneficial for some people,' she added, repeating a line from her book.

Aiden raised an eyebrow as her tummy rumbled. 'I think your tummy says the opposite.'

'It's all BS,' Autumn said, dishing the breakfast up onto two large plates and placing them in front of Estelle and Aiden. 'Once you start eating, you'll be fine.'

'Autumn, you're being so sweet,' Estelle said. 'But I really don't feel hungry. I can cook you guys up a feast this afternoon though?'

Autumn opened her mouth to protest but Aiden put his hand up. 'Come on, Mum, she said she wasn't hungry.'

Autumn shoved the frying pan onto the hob, some oily mushrooms falling onto the floor. 'I suppose my food's not good enough for the Queen of Clean Eating,' she said, crossing her arms and sulking.

Max rolled his eyes and Estelle remembered how Autumn would get like this sometimes, go into sulks if she didn't get her way.

'I'm sorry, Autumn,' Estelle said, going over and giving her a hug. 'I really appreciate you cooking breakfast though.'

'Not sure I agree with all this clean eating stuff,' Autumn said, still slightly sulky.

'I hate that phrase, 'clean eating',' Estelle said. 'I think it makes food sound dirty. I'm not one of those clean eating advocates; I'm all about healthy nourishing fresh food.'

Max and Autumn both raised eyebrows. 'Well, she's passionate about her subject, that's for sure,' Max said.

Estelle felt her cheeks flush. 'Sorry, I do get a bit carried away sometimes.'

'Passion is good, sweetheart,' Autumn said, patting her arm. 'That's why you need a good breakfast inside you, it can be exhausting being so intense.'

Estelle rolled her eyes. 'You really don't give up, do you?' she said with a smile. She turned to Aiden, looking at him meaningfully. 'Anyway, Aiden promised me a tour of Lillysands' new sights.'

She hadn't quite figured out what to say to Alice's father but with each moment that went by, she felt she was losing time. It might not lead to something, but she needed to find out how Alice was connected.

Aiden paused as he lifted a forkful of scrambled eggs to his mouth. 'Did I?'

'Wouldn't Darren be better for a tour like that?' Max asked. 'He's helped develop some of the new buildings after all. I'm sure he wouldn't mind, considering he was chatting you up yesterday.'

Aiden narrowed his eyes. 'Don't try to push that idiot on Stel, Dad.'

Max's eyes sparked with anger. 'That idiot will be a millionaire by the time he's thirty-five!'

Aiden placed his toast on the side. 'Oh and I won't be, is that what you're saying? Money's not the be all and end all, you know.'

'Isn't it?' Max countered. 'Weren't you moaning the other day about the heating packing up in your house? The cellar still being damp from the flooding? Money would mean you wouldn't have to worry about all that.'

Estelle looked between them both. It was just like going back in time, watching them argue.

'At least I'm making an honest living,' Aiden said, crossing his arms.

'And Darren Kemp isn't?'

Aiden laughed bitterly. 'Really, Dad? You're asking me that?'

'Oh stop the bickering!' Autumn said. 'It's my birthday, remember?'

The two men went quiet.

'Sorry, Mum,' Aiden mumbled.

Max's face relaxed. 'Yes, sorry Autumn, darling.'

Estelle smiled to herself. Autumn always had a knack at diffusing a situation. Autumn leaned against the side with a small smile and opened the card Aiden got her. On the front was a painting of Lillysands at sunset, the town's buildings beautifully shadowed against an orange sky. 'Lovely card, sweetie,' she said, looking affectionately at her son. Then she opened the gift he'd got her to reveal a beautiful hand-crafted bracelet with silver shells around it. She walked up to Aiden and kissed him. 'I love it, darling. Did you make it?'

Aiden nodded.

Estelle looked at Aiden. 'You made it?'

He shrugged. 'Just something I like to do.'

'See, Max, money isn't everything,' Autumn said with a wink. She put the bracelet on and admired it in the sun streaming through the windows. 'My talented boy. Now, are you going to finish that breakfast?'

Aiden shook his head, laughing. 'Okay, Mum, if you insist.'

As Estelle watched them eat, sipping on a smoothie she'd managed to make from the fruit Autumn had, she smiled to herself. It really did feel like the old days.

Except her daughter was missing now, possibly kidnapped.

'Ready for that tour?' Estelle asked Aiden as he ate his last sausage, desperate once more for some answers.

Aiden wiped his mouth, holding her gaze. Then he sighed. 'Fine, if that's what you want. I can even pretend to be an arrogant fuckwit like Darren if it helps?' he added, eyes sliding towards his father.

Max rolled his eyes as Autumn smiled.

'No,' Estelle said, 'a rugged cliff-face climber will do just fine.'

Aiden smiled and she smiled back, noticing the way his eyes crinkled at the corners now he was older. She couldn't help but think of their first kiss. It was her second summer in Lillysands. She'd once dreaded the summer ending, the onset of darker colder nights

130

meaning she'd be made to stay indoors by various foster parents, a child chained. But in Lillysands, she felt free. Autumn and Max trusted her. And in the year and a half since she'd first arrived, she was beginning to feel like she belonged. And what a life! Darkness wasn't the enemy any more, it was embraced with fires on the beach, melting marshmallows and hot chocolate laced with whisky. As her and Aiden spent more time together, she felt the chemistry grow between them. He was only six months older than Estelle but he seemed so much older, more sophisticated with his ambitions and dreams. She'd been used to boys with crew cuts and bruised faces, forcing their tongues down her throat and trying to grope her while in care. Or the rich kids at the school in Lillysands, like Darren, the same really but dressed up in more expensive clothes.

But Aiden was different. He was her *friend*. He listened to her, respected her.

One night when it rained, they'd found shelter in the cave she'd found him in that first day and they'd talked into the night. As morning began to break, she'd impulsively pressed her lips against his. It had set off a whirlwind of feeling inside her and as he'd wrapped his arms around her, pulling her even closer, she felt she'd found something special.

The smile disappeared off her face as the memory came to her. She wasn't here to reminisce.

They both got up and walked outside. 'I guess you're appropriately dressed if Alice's dad decides to chase us out of his house,' he said, taking in Estelle's jogging gear. 'That's where I presume we're heading anyway?'

'He's that bad?'

'I don't know,' Aided admitted. 'Haven't heard much from him lately. How are we going to do this exactly?'

Estelle sighed. 'I have no idea.'

He went to his car, peering up at black clouds that were hovering on the horizon. 'I'll drive, looks like it might rain. When we get there, let me go in first,' he said when they both got into the car. 'Then I'll call you in if I need you.'

'No,' Estelle said, shaking her head. 'We do this together.'

Aiden smiled. 'I forgot what a firecracker you are.' She smiled back at him. Despite the negativity she often felt when thinking of the 'old Stel', there was no denying she'd had fire in her belly then.

He started the car and drove them down the cliff. Estelle didn't look out of the window, too focused on the thoughts swirling around her mind.

'I really am sorry I didn't tell you about Poppy, Aiden,' Estelle said.

His face clouded over. 'Her parents put Poppy in boarding school, you know.'

'Really?' she said, surprised she hadn't read this in any articles.

'Yeah, I read it in an article this morning. They barely saw her.'

'But the other articles, the photos I've seen suggest the opposite.'

'From the few times they probably spent together. I would never have done that,' he said. 'I've always said I'd keep my kids close.'

Estelle tried to ignore the pinch of guilt. 'I presume you haven't had any?'

'Apart from Poppy?' he said gravely, eyes sliding over to her.

Estelle sighed. 'Apart from Poppy.'

'No,' Aiden said, gripping the steering wheel. 'Did try for a while though.'

'Really?'

'Yeah, when I was married.'

She looked at him in surprise. 'You were married?'

He laughed. 'Don't look so shocked. It was a whirlwind thing with a girl I met in the States a couple of years ago. I went there with a friend to do some travelling. We got hitched out there. She came back here, we got a house together, made a go of it for a year.'

'What happened?'

He shrugged. 'We grew apart. She was so vibrant when I met her, so full of happiness. But coming here, she started getting miserable, moping around. I guess it was predictable considering we got married after a month together.'

'A *month*?'

He shrugged. 'You know me, wear my heart on my sleeve.' He gave her a meaningful look and her own heart responded, thumping wildly in her ears. She forced her eyes away from his.

'What did your parents think?' she asked.

'They weren't impressed. Mum hated her actually. But then Mum didn't see her best side.

133

It's tough coming here, trying to integrate yourself into the Lillysands community. You know how it is.' He looked out to sea, eyes narrowing. 'Even I feel like an outsider sometimes and I've been here most of my life.'

She looked out of the window. They were in the centre of town now; happy tourists were wandering in and out of shops on the cobbled streets. In the distance, the sails of the various boats docked up on Lillysands' marina fluttered in the breeze.

'You said you *tried* to have kids?' Estelle asked.

Aiden nodded. 'Clarissa — that's her name — she had some fertility issues. I'm sure we would've got there in the end. But we just didn't give it enough of a chance.'

'Do you miss Clarissa?' Estelle asked.

'A little. She's back in the States now.'

'I'm sorry.'

His face tensed. 'Don't be. It wasn't meant to be. I kind of suck at relationships.'

'Me too.' She thought of Seb. He still hadn't contacted her . . . and she hadn't contacted him. Did that mean it was over between them as easily as that?

He quickly looked at her and away again. 'So Darren Kemp was chatting you up last night, was he?' he asked.

'You know what he's like.' She thought again of the drunken fumble she'd shared with Darren. It had been just after the first kiss with Aiden. There had been a party on the beach and her tummy had tingled with anticipation, the way it does when you're just thirteen and you're naïve

134

enough to think one kiss can be something bigger and better. But Aiden had ignored her all night. She'd grown angry. When Darren had sidled up to her, offering her some wine from a bottle, she'd taken it. Two hours later, she was lying in the sand with him, his fingers crawling up her thigh. She'd pushed his hand away — she'd only meant to make Aiden jealous. Darren had been grumpy with her after, unused to rejection.

'Darren really is an idiot, you know,' Aiden said now. 'He's had it all handed to him by his dad.'

'That doesn't make him an idiot.' Estelle looked out of the window. They were in the busier part of town now. Children sat on the walls by the marina, licking ice creams and kicking legs with light tans against the bricks. Estelle unwittingly imagined being there with Aiden and Poppy and felt her eyes brim with tears.

They eventually entered a maze of small streets, leaving the pretty scenes behind. This was the rougher part of Lillysands, packed in with terraced houses, small shops and garages. They arrived outside a small building sitting next to a grotty-looking garage. It probably offered sea views from the back, but that was its only redeeming feature; the paint on its red door peeling, its bricks overgrown with moss. Outside was a wheelless Peugeot.

Not every part of Lillysands was pristine.

Aiden parked his car outside and they both sat quietly, looking up at the house.

'Right,' she said eventually. 'Let's do this then.'

They both got out, but Estelle hesitated before she walked down the broken path. What was she going to say? She let out a breath. She'd just wing it. That was what she was doing by impulsively coming here, after all. Why break a new habit?

She walked up to the door and knocked.

14

Look at you, being so brave. Taking charge.
Trying to get answers.

I don't quite know what you're trying to
achieve. But I can tell from the look on your
face, you're determined.

Then again, you always have been.

Me too in my way. Though it's only now
I've really started to feel some true passion and
ambition for something.

The past two days, I've woken with a thrill
of excitement and expectation.

What will today bring?

How can I ram the message home this time?

I like watching you. I like tracking the slowly
creeping fear and confusion.

The unravelling. That's what I want, to make
you unravel so you can't harm us.

I still have some reservations. Sometimes, the
excitement is overtaken by worry.

Am I doing things right?

Am I right to be doing this?

To you. Someone I once loved.

But there's no room for guilt.

So I swallow it down and plan my next
move.

15

They heard a man shout from inside. 'Connor! Door!'

Footsteps thundered down some stairs then the door opened, revealing a short red-haired man a couple of years younger than Estelle, arms bulging with muscles and filled with tattoos, spilling from a dirty white vest top.

Alice's brother. Estelle remembered him being a spotty, skinny little kid who had the bad luck of staying with his father. He'd sometimes turn up at their beach parties, watching from the distance. Estelle had wound him up once, flirting with him as he blushed furiously. Alice had jokily reprimanded her, telling her how sensitive her brother was.

She felt sadness swell up inside as she thought about the fact Alice never got the chance to watch her brother grow up.

'Yeah?' Connor said, looking them up and down. He didn't seem to recognise Estelle with her short blonde hair.

'Is your dad in?' Aiden asked.

'Who's asking?' a voice shouted from inside.

'Aiden Garland,' Connor sneered. 'He's got some bird with him too.'

There was silence then a sigh. 'Let 'em in.'

The man opened the door wide and Estelle and Aiden walked inside, getting a strong smell of body odour as they did. Estelle wrinkled her nose, pulling her hoodie around her as she entered the dingy living room. The curtains were drawn, the table dominating its centre full of rubbish and discarded food. It reminded her of her parents' house.

In one of the darker corners sat a sunken-looking man, and Estelle was surprised to see an oxygen tank next to him.

Was this man really capable of hotfooting it up to London, luring a teenage girl from her home and planting Polaroid photos for Estelle?

She looked at Connor. Maybe with the help of a strapping young man, he could.

'What are you doing here?' the old man said, squinting his eyes as he peered at Aiden.

'Just want to ask some questions about Alice,' Estelle said.

Alice's father glared at her. 'Who are you?'

'I lived with the Garlands,' Estelle said. 'I was fostered by them at the same time as Alice.'

Alice's father scrunched up his face in anger. 'Those fuckers,' he said, looking directly at Aiden. Then he turned to Estelle. 'And so are you if you lived with them, so both of you fuck the fuck off. The Garlands aren't welcome here.'

Estelle stood her ground, as did Aiden.

'You want me to get rid, Dad?' Connor asked, squaring up to Aiden. Aiden looked at him, curling his fists.

'Please, we loved Alice as much as you,' Estelle said. 'Give us a few moments.'

Connor frowned at her, clearly trying to remember who she was.

His dad started coughing. Connor came over

and patted his back, glaring at Aiden.

'Spit it out then,' Alice's father asked between coughs.

'Did you see Alice much before she died?' Estelle asked.

He shrugged. 'A bit, here and there.'

'You had visitation sessions with her, right?' Aiden asked.

He nodded. 'Until *they* poisoned her mind against me. Bloody accused me of sending her those threatening notes.'

Estelle froze.

'What notes?' Aiden asked.

'She got threatening notes slipped in her bag a few times,' Connor said.

'But that copper didn't give a damn about them,' his father added. 'And to think he's in charge now, Inspector Colin Campbell. *Inspector!*' he said, laughing as he shook his head. 'Bloody hoiked up the ranks for doing eff-all.'

'What do you mean by 'threatening'?' Aiden asked. 'Can you remember what the notes said?'

'Stuff about her not being as perfect as people thought,' Connor replied, brow creased. 'Threats to 'expose her' for who she really was — it was all ridiculous.'

Estelle and Aiden exchanged a look. They sounded just like the notes Estelle had been receiving.

She peered at Alice's father. He seemed genuinely upset about the threats, about Alice's death. She just couldn't see him being behind them.

But what about the notes to Estelle? What if he was looking to blackmail her? She looked around the small house, on the table beside her was a

140

pile of unopened bills marked urgent, a sight she remembered from when she lived with her parents. Alice's father clearly needed the money.

'Do you recognise me?' she asked, turning back to him.

He narrowed his eyes at her. 'No, should I?'

'I'm Stel.'

He frowned slightly as Connor examined her face.

'Oh yeah, I thought I recognised you,' Connor said. 'You look different.'

'Do you know what I do now?' she asked.

The two men looked confused. They clearly didn't.

'No, why?' the old man asked.

'It doesn't matter,' Estelle said with a sigh. So they didn't know. Sure, they could be lying, but something in their reaction told her they weren't. So that put the blackmail theory to bed.

'Why are you here really?' Connor asked her.

'Estelle hasn't been back to Lillysands for a while,' Aiden explained. 'It brought back memories of Alice.'

'So you thought you'd come over and give us the third degree?' the old man asked. 'Sticking your nose in like all the other people who walk around this town like they own it. The Garlands. The Kemps.' The man looked into Estelle's eyes, his chest rattling as he breathed in and out. 'It's not me you need to grill. It's them that are destroying this town bit by bit. My Alice was only the beginning. They're rotten to the core, all of 'em, and every little thing they touch turns to shit.' He glared at Aiden, who was clearly

141

included in his rant.

Aiden's face hardened, eyes sparking with anger. Estelle put her hand on his arm to calm him.

'What's that look for?' Connor asked. He marched up to them, getting right in their faces. He reeked of booze and stale sweat, just like Estelle's father had, and suddenly she saw her father standing over her, not Connor: eyes filled with rage, the reek of alcohol on his breath.

She started shaking, felt the room spin.

Aiden put his hand on her back. 'Estelle?'

'I'm fine,' she said, taking a deep breath to will the memories away. She peered at the two men. 'Did you ever have any suspicions about who was sending those notes to Alice?' she asked. 'Did Alice?'

'No idea,' the old man said. 'The girl was just fourteen, for Christ's sake. Who'd want to scare her like that?'

Estelle and Aiden exchanged a look. They both knew how mean Alice's father had been to her. But what was the point of bringing it up now.

'And her death,' Estelle said softly. 'I presume you were surprised she committed suicide.'

She avoided Aiden's annoyed look.

'Too right I was,' Alice's father said. 'She was driven to it! Everyone thinks the Garlands are perfect,' he said, sneering at Aiden, 'but those posh families always have secrets to hide.'

'Did Alice ever say anything to you about Autumn and Max mistreating her in any way?' Estelle asked.

Aiden opened his mouth to say something, but

she gave him a look.

'No,' Alice's father said. 'But the girl was fine with me.'

'Those bruises I saw her with the first day she arrived didn't look fine,' Aiden said, glaring at Alice's father.

Estelle noticed Connor didn't do anything this time. He just watched his father.

'Bruises? Bullshit,' Alice's father said. 'Something the social worker made up to take her off me.'

Aiden shook his head in disgust. Connor eyeballed him, and the atmosphere in the room sparked.

'Okay,' Estelle said, steering Aiden towards the front door. 'I think that's everything. Thanks for your time.'

'Nice of you to visit!' Alice's brother called out in a fake sing-song voice as they left.

They stepped outside, the door slamming shut behind them. Estelle closed her eyes, breathing in the fresh clean air.

'So Alice was receiving threatening notes too?' Aiden said. 'What's this all about?'

Estelle sighed. 'I don't know.'

'Funny place for you two to be hanging out,' a voice boomed from beside them.

They both looked up to see Darren Kemp crawling along in a sleek black Jaguar, the window down, his elbow hanging out of it.

'Funny place for you to be too,' Aiden said, narrowing his eyes at him.

Darren turned to Estelle, ignoring Aiden. 'You coming to the event I mentioned for local

143

investors, Estelle? It starts in a couple of hours.'

'I don't think so,' Estelle answered, mind still on her previous conversation. 'Thanks for inviting me though.'

'Oh come on,' Darren pleaded, flashing her a smile. 'You can go with Autumn and Max. I need our bright star there. Someone needs to make me look good alongside all those Chief Inspectors and MPs.'

Estelle frowned. 'Chief inspectors? Do you mean Chief Inspector Campbell?' she asked, thinking of what Alice's dad had said about the new Chief Inspector.

'You remember him?' Darren asked. 'Done well for himself, hasn't he? Yep, he'll be there.'

Estelle felt her heartbeat quicken. If Colin Campbell had been in charge of Alice's case, then maybe he knew something that could explain the link between her and Poppy?

'It'll be at the LS Hotel and Restaurant,' Darren added. 'The huge new building across from the marina? I own it.'

'Your *dad* owns it,' Aiden said.

Darren looked him up and down. 'I own a share, actually.' He turned to Estelle. 'So I'll see you there?'

'I'll be there,' she said, ignoring Aiden's incensed looks.

As Darren drove off smirking, Aiden turned to Estelle. 'What the hell are you doing?'

'You heard him. The police officer in charge of Alice's case will be there! Come along too, we can both speak to him.'

Aiden looked up at the sky in frustration.

'Seriously, Stel, I think you're reading too much into all this. Sure, someone's clearly trying to mess with your mind. But I think — I *hope* — Poppy has just run away. And I hope Alice just committed suicide because the alternative — ' He shook his head. 'It's too crazy to consider.'

Estelle stepped away from him. 'If you can't see something's wrong with all this, then *you're* the crazy one.'

Aiden sighed. 'I wasn't saying you're crazy! Look, I understand why you might be suspicious. But it's all a bit far-fetched, don't you think? Murder? Kidnap? I just — I don't want you to go storming in and questioning Chief Inspectors about things you can't be sure about.'

Estelle crossed her arms. 'I'm a grown-up now, Aiden. I think you can trust me to handle things carefully.' She looked towards the hotel where the luncheon was being held. 'And I'm going to that lunch, with or without you.'

'I was never able to stop you when we were kids, clearly I can't now either.' He smiled slightly then peered at his watch. 'I have a climb soon so I can't go anyway. Why not come see what I do for five minutes? Then you can go home and change for Darren's wankfest.'

She smiled at the boyishness she remembered. 'Sure.'

As they got back into his car, she couldn't help but continue smiling. This was the way it used to be between her and Aiden: arguments that were forgotten as quickly as they blew up. Despite the circumstances, she couldn't help but acknowledge it was good to be back in his company again.

They headed towards the sea. People were taking advantage of the sunshine, stretched out in jeans and T-shirts, reading papers and smiling. Some were eating fish and chips. Estelle and Aiden used to do that, cuddled together under a blanket, watching as the sun set. The smell of vinegar and salt always took her right back to those times, even now.

'There's a storm coming,' Aiden said, pointing at the gathering black clouds that were drawing closer. 'It'll come quicker than we think. The rain's been terrible here the past month. Not great for rock climbing: the cliff-face will struggle.'

'You sound like Mr Tate.'

'Ah, good old Mr Tate,' he said with a nostalgic smile.

'I saw him earlier actually.'

Aiden frowned. 'You heard about Mrs Tate?'

Estelle nodded.

'Why does bad stuff always seem to happen to good people?' He looked up towards where Alice had jumped. 'Have you thought about Alice much since you left?'

She looked at him in surprise. 'Of course.'

'Me too. I go over scenarios in my mind in which I was here to save her.' He clutched the steering wheel, his knuckles whitening. 'If only I was fucking here.'

'You wouldn't have been able to do anything if she was pushed.'

He looked at her, frowning. 'You really believe that, don't you?'

'I don't know.'

He took his eyes from the road briefly to look at her meaningfully. She turned away, sighing.

Aiden pulled up by the marina and they both got out, heading towards Lady Lillysands. In front of them was a small wooden hut with a hatch that was closed, and a laminated poster declaring a variety of different rock climbing opportunities beneath a banner saying 'Climb Lady Lillysands with a local expert'. On it was a photo of Aiden climbing the rock, looking over his shoulder and smiling into the camera, his blond hair lifting in the wind, his cheeks and forehead scorched brown by the sun. His green eyes were alarming against his tanned skin, his arms muscled. Anyone walking past would do a double take, just as she'd done the first time she saw him in that cave.

'Expert, hey?' she joked. 'Does that include the time you nearly broke a leg trying to climb Lady Lillysands?'

'I'll have you know I have all the required rock climbing qualifications,' he replied with a smile.

Estelle smiled back then she peered up at the curved rock above. It felt vast and endless, the blue skies accentuating the whiteness of the cliff. 'I thought I'd never see this up close again.'

Aiden walked to the cliff face, placing his palm on it. 'It's amazing. Sometimes, it feels like it's breathing.' Estelle frowned and he laughed. 'Seriously, come feel.'

She walked over and he took her hand, pressing it against the cliff. She tried to focus on the feel of the rock, not Aiden's skin against hers.

147

She was surprised at how warm the cliff was, and Aiden was right, it really felt like it was moving beneath her palm.

Estelle snatched her hand away. 'You're right; it's strange.'

Aiden pulled some keys from his pocket and walked to the hut.

'So do you get much business then?' she asked as she followed him.

'Summer's always good. Autumn not bad if the weather holds. It's the online group bookings that do it. I tend to squirrel away the money I get over summer and eke it out the rest of the months.'

Estelle peered out to sea, breathing in the salty air. 'It's so nice to be here. I love London but this place is, I admit, a nice contrast: the sea and salty air.'

'You miss it?' he asked. The look in his eyes suggested he was asking if *she* missed *him*.

'Yes,' she replied. *I do miss you*, she wanted to add, but didn't.

To break the spell, she got her phone out and took a photo of the scenery. She uploaded it to Instagram as Aiden looked over her shoulder.

Taking some time out for some reflection in the sun, she typed, aware Seb might see it. *Keep an eye out for some healthy fish and chip alternatives when my book comes out. #Pure-Eating*

'You like all this social media stuff, do you?' he asked.

'It's part of what I do really. I've been a bit slack the past few days; my publisher will be on

148

my back if I don't do something.'

'Don't you find it all a bit fake?'

She tried not to be insulted by that. It was what she'd built her business on. 'Well this certainly isn't fake, is it?' Estelle said, gesturing to the cliff. 'I think you've done great, you know, Aiden.'

He raised an eyebrow. 'My bank account disagrees.'

'You don't care about all that, do you? You never did when I knew you. You always said being a musician wouldn't pay the bills, you were doing it for the love.'

'Yeah, well, I was a naïve kid back then.' He frowned, his mood darkening.

'Do you still have your guitar?'

He shrugged. 'Somewhere.'

'Please tell me you still play it?'

He shook his head.

'That's a shame.'

'You sound like my mum,' he said. 'She keeps going on at me to get my guitar back out.'

'Then why don't you?'

His eyes flickered with sadness. 'Too many memories.'

'Alice used to love you playing. She'd be so sad if she knew you didn't play anymore.'

Aiden frowned as he opened the door to his hut. Estelle peered inside. It was messy but clean, a small fridge in the corner, a plastic chair inside. A pile of books and magazines sat on a wooden table, the two shelves above lined with various food items: sugary cereals and chocolate bars.

149

Aiden pulled a fizzy drink from the fridge, flicking it open. Estelle gave him a disapproving look.

'What?' he said. 'No calories, see?' He pointed out the label.

'It's not about the calories. You wouldn't believe what that does to your body.'

'I think it's a bit late for me to worry about that, considering the junk I've put inside me over the years.' He looked her up and down. 'Surely you allow yourself to indulge every now and again?'

'I have cheat days.'

'*Cheat* days?' he said, a look of confusion on his face.

'That's what I call them in my book. Except by cheating, I mean not cooking from scratch. So I'll have a pasta dish or something when I go out. Or I'll eat a Nakd bar.'

'Naked?'

'It's spelt N-A-K-D. Whole raw food in a packet.'

'Sounds delicious,' Aiden said sarcastically.

Estelle laughed. 'You haven't even tried one.'

'You can treat me to one later. How'd you get into all this healthy eating stuff anyway? Doesn't tally with the Stel I knew.'

Estelle kicked at the sand. 'I guess it was a way of controlling something, you know? Of doing something right?' She was surprised when that came out.

Aiden looked surprised too. 'You haven't done things right?'

'Not always — look at Poppy,' she said softly,

thinking that this was just one terrible mistake in a long line of mistakes.

'I thought you said it was the right thing to give her up?'

'It was but — ' She sighed. 'That doesn't stop me feeling guilty sometimes, wondering what if. Of course, I know it was the right thing. But doubts are bound to creep in.'

Aiden frowned. 'So advocating this healthy *clean* lifestyle is your way of making amends?'

Estelle laughed nervously. 'Wow, this is like a therapy session. I don't know, I think I'm reading too much into it,' she said, making her tone light. She forced a smile. 'I guess I just like healthy nutritious food!'

Aiden watched her, frown deepening. She looked away. Aiden sighed and pulled a deckchair out, setting it up on the sand. Then he opened the hatch of the hut and pulled a laptop from the bag he was holding, sweeping away some Lady Lillysands Festival leaflets from the hatch and setting it up there.

'The festival's in a couple of days, isn't it?' she asked.

Aiden nodded. 'Veronica ropes me into helping every year. This year, I'm in charge of setting up marquees and making sure they don't blow away into the sea like they did two years ago.'

Estelle smiled. 'Sounds fun.'

'Yeah, clearly the idiot who didn't realise the marquees needed weighing down thought it was fun too.' He leaned in close to her, lowering his voice. 'Oh, that idiot was Darren Kemp by the way.'

Estelle smiled to herself. He really didn't like Darren.

'Take a seat,' he said, gesturing to the deckchair. 'The group will be here in five minutes.'

Estelle perched on the wooden end of the deckchair but it nearly tipped over, the contents of her bag spilling out.

Aiden smiled as he leaned down to grab her bag. 'Lean back into it!'

She did as he asked, relaxing into it. It had been a long time since she'd sat in a deckchair and she felt out of control as her back bounced against the synthetic fabric, her legs lifting up.

Aiden laughed. 'You *have* changed.'

'I haven't been in a deckchair for ages, that's all.'

'That's the beauty of them, they make you *relaaaaaax* . . . something you clearly need to do more of.'

Estelle rolled her eyes. 'I do relax! You're making me out to be some uptight city girl.'

'Aren't you?'

'Not at all! My boyfriend says I'm too relaxed sometimes . . . ' Her voice trailed off as she remembered what had happened. She'd still not heard from Seb but that didn't surprise her, Seb was an expert at freezing people out. 'Or perhaps I should say, ex-boyfriend,' she added with a sigh.

'Ex?'

'We had a big fight. We argued about Poppy.'

Aiden raised an eyebrow. 'Why?'

'He thought it would ruin things for me if the

news got out that I was a teenage mum.'

'He's an idiot.'

'Why do you think I left him?' she said. She didn't add she'd actually left him to come to Lillysands to find Aiden.

They held each other's gaze then Aiden sighed. 'Looks like neither of us can keep hold of a relationship.'

'So you're not in one right now?'

He shook his head. 'Na.' Estelle found herself feeling relieved. So many years had passed. But somehow, as she sat there with him, she felt like that teenager in love again. The idea of him being in love with someone else would hurt, no matter how much she wouldn't have wanted it to. 'I flit around, fall in love a few times, you know what it's like.'

Estelle nodded. 'I do. Before Seb, I did the same.'

He picked up her book, which had fallen out from her bag. 'So this is it, is it? Your book.'

Estelle smiled as she looked at it. It was easy to forget about her book in the midst of all that had happened in the past two days. But there it was reminding her of how far she'd come since she'd been last sitting on this beach with Aiden.

'Yep, that's it,' she said.

'Wow, Stel. Just . . . wow,' he said as he looked at it. 'You did it, you really did it.'

She felt herself blush. 'Thank you.'

'Where can I buy a copy when it comes out?'

'The usual places,' she said. 'You can have that one if you want though; I have plenty spare at home.'

'You sure? You've left stickie notes in it,' he said, fingering the places where she'd marked parts to use in her speech.

'Sure I'm sure. The markers are for my book launch, but I noted the page numbers down on my phone. Just remember not to tell Autumn you have a copy before she does.'

'I promise.' He reached over and grabbed a pen. 'Sign it?'

She smiled. 'My first signing.'

She opened it and wrote inside: *To Aiden, climbing to new heights. Luv Stel. X*

She passed it back to him and he read it, a bright smile appearing on his face. It lit up his green eyes, made Estelle's tummy tilt. He peered up at her, holding her gaze.

Then a group of school kids approached.

'Here they are,' Aiden said, walking out of his hut. 'Fancy joining them on a climb?'

'No, I'll just watch,' Estelle said, distracted.

She watched Aiden walk over to the group, greeting them charismatically. The teenage girls in the group looked him over, giggling and whispering to each other. He led them to the hut, getting them all set up in their climbing gear and talking them through the rules. Then it was time to climb. As the group scaled the cliff with Aiden's help, Estelle couldn't help but think that things *had* worked out for him after all. Not much money, sure. But he was outdoors, among the elements, *free*.

Estelle felt a sudden urge to go up there too, feel the wind against the back of her bare neck. Lately, she'd been feeling constrained. First the writing deadlines then the looming launch party. Sure, it was all wonderful. When she'd first received the email from a literary agent asking to meet for lunch with a view to discussing a book, she'd been so excited. And then a few months later, a five-way auction with the country's leading publishing houses for the rights to a book based on an outline and a few photos. When her agent told her the sums they were offering, her mind had been blown. She'd been so proud when she'd seen the first instalment of her advance paid into her bank account. All the attention, the articles, the praise and admiring emails.

But lately, it felt suffocating. Maybe it was imposter syndrome? Or maybe it was all too much? Would she have been happier if she'd decided to keep Poppy, not been so obsessed with avoiding a life like her birth parents and having a life like the Garlands had? Deep down, she knew part of the reason she gave Poppy up was she knew she could never hope to have a life like theirs with a baby at fifteen. But she could have given Poppy a good life, she was starting to see that now.

How selfish she'd been.

Well, she was going to make it right. She was going to find Poppy. She pulled herself up from the deckchair. 'I'm heading off now!' she shouted to Aiden.

He was at the bottom of the cliff, chatting to the teacher. He quickly jogged over.

'You're going to the lunch?' he asked. She nodded. 'Be careful. People here don't like

155

outsiders sticking their noses in.'

'But I'm not an outsider.'

He looked into her eyes. 'Aren't you?'

★ ★ ★

Estelle looked out of the car window as Max drove her and Autumn through Lillysands later past the pretty houses, the stretch of silver sea, the smart shop fronts. Sat in the car with them now, it felt like she was twelve again on her way to a visitation session with her parents. While they had lasted anyway. They'd stopped the spring after she'd moved in with the Garlands. Alice had been with her too, that last time. They'd grown really close. Estelle had never had siblings, and not mixed with children much at an early age. Her parents had been young themselves when they'd had her, conceived when her mum was fifteen, her dad nineteen, probably on a filthy mattress while they were both strung out somewhere. Estelle's only other contact with children had been through the care system. But she hadn't grown close to other kids, hadn't *allowed* herself to. Truth was, she'd always yearned to have a little brother or sister, someone to share the burden of her parents with. And she was starting to find that with Alice. It felt good to have someone look up to her like Alice did. Autumn would call them 'two red bees in a pod' because of Estelle's dark hair, Alice's red, both heads bent over some book or another, their hair merging and mixing like the fur on a bee's back.

So when Alice had offered to join them on the car ride to the social services building where Estelle was to meet with her parents, Estelle had agreed. They'd sat in the back of the car, playing a game, taking Estelle's mind off the fact her parents probably wouldn't be there. Sometimes, they'd roll up, holding bags of dirty second-hand toys, eyes filled with tears. There would be promises to get her back, declarations of love. But soon they would both get tetchy, Estelle's mum clawing at her skinny arms, her dad fidgeting.

By the time Estelle was with the Garlands, she actually preferred it when they didn't turn up. But that day in spring was different. If her parents didn't turn up for that particular session, then that was it, no more. They'd missed too many sessions and her social worker felt it was only holding Estelle back. Estelle wasn't sure how she felt about that. They were her parents, weren't they? Her mother had pushed her out of her skinny pale body; her father had fed her and changed her nappies in that initial exhilarating promise-filled first few weeks of Estelle's life — at least, according to her social worker. But it had all turned sour when Estelle did what babies do: cried in the night, demanded milk, soiled her nappies. The few photos taken of Estelle as a baby showed a sullen little thing with a filthy face and a mess of dark hair, surrounded by cheap toys, a dented wall or two, and tins of lager in the background. Her mother would invariably be smoking a cigarette in any photos, her father wearing a scowl. The nicest photo Estelle found

157

was of her mother holding her on a small beach, skies bright and blue above her, her smiling eyes watching Estelle, a newborn in her arms. Estelle kept that photo for many years after. There weren't so many photos after that first year of Estelle's life, as if they got bored, the novelty worn off.

It was the same with the visitation sessions, initial enthusiasm tapering off into regular no-shows. When they didn't turn up on time for that session in spring, Estelle had been surprised at her disappointment. Autumn had hugged her after, whispering that she and Max would take the girls out for an amazing lunch to make up for it, go shopping for clothes, even go to the cinema. As Estelle had got back into the back of the car with Alice, she'd forced herself to feel hopeful, on the cusp of a true new start.

But then bony fists had started banging on the car window and her mother's pockmarked face was against the glass, right next to Estelle.

'Stelly, babe,' she called through the glass. 'We're here. We're just a bit late, that's all!' Behind her, her father lounged against another car, cigarette dangling from his mouth as he stared at her with empty eyes. Alice had leaned across to Estelle and squeezed her hand, giving her a look that told Estelle she wasn't alone.

Estelle had looked at her parents, then she'd looked at Autumn and Max who were regarding her with such love and sadness too.

'Just drive,' she'd said to Max, deeply embarrassed. 'I don't want to see them.'

But as Max drove away, her mother had run to

158

keep up. Max stopped the car and Estelle had wound down the window. 'Please, Mum, just let me go. I'm *happy* now.'

Her mother had frozen, first sadness on her face then anger. 'Fine,' she'd shouted back. 'The only reason we didn't get rid of you before you were born was 'cos we found out we could get ourselves a nice little flat with a baby. You were just a roof over our head for us, Estelle, that's all.' Then her parents had stormed off, jumping into their banged up old car. Estelle had watched them, her whole body trembling.

Autumn had gripped the headrest, turning to stare into Estelle's eyes. 'Look at me. Look at me, Stel! She's nothing, you hear me? Nothing. And you're everything. Don't you listen to her, don't you listen to a word.'

'Penny for your thoughts,' Autumn said now as they drove to Darren's event.

Estelle peered at Autumn. 'Oh, I was just thinking how much the seafront has changed,' she lied.

'Still lots more to change,' Max said. 'Peter and Darren are trying to get the marina developed; that's what this event is for. Speaking of which, here it is.'

Max drew up outside the restaurant, a two-storey glass-fronted modern building with an anchor etched into the glass. Two letters adorned its front: LS. The restaurant had been around when Estelle had lived there but it had been refurbished from the faded beach-front hotel it once was with its crumbling facade and murky windows. Instead, it was now smart and glossy.

Estelle got out, smoothing down the silk of the white dress she'd changed into before walking towards the hotel. People nodded hellos at Autumn and Max, looking Estelle up and down and smiling faintly. Estelle thought about what Aiden had said about her being an outsider. She shouldn't feel like one right then, wedged between her old foster parents, pillars of the community, but somehow she did.

When they got inside, Peter and Veronica came up to greet them. Darren wasn't far behind, looking at Estelle with approval. Several other people were already there. The usual Lillysands faces, of course. Some new faces too: mainly middle-aged, middle-class men in suits. The fact that Peter and Darren led Estelle, Max and Autumn over to them suggested it was these men they wanted to impress.

'Here we have a bona fide Lillysands success story,' Darren said, introducing Estelle to two large men whose faces were already red from the wine they'd drunk. 'You'll be seeing her food book all over the shelves next month. Am I right, Estelle?' he added, hand smooth on her back. His touch unsettled her, firmer than Aiden's, more controlling.

Estelle forced a smile. 'Well, I don't know about 'all over',' she said, shaking the men's hands as she looked around the room for the person she really wanted to speak to, the Chief Inspector that had been in charge of Alice's case. She hoped he was in uniform, otherwise how else would she recognise him?

Darren continued to introduce her to more

businessmen, implying Autumn and Max were her parents, that she'd spent her life in Lillysands. Estelle didn't correct him. It didn't matter. All that mattered was getting information on Alice and therefore Poppy too. She'd checked her phone again for developments before coming out but nothing had changed. What if she was out there, being held against her will, and everyone was brushing her off as a runaway?

'As you can see,' Darren said to one particularly large businessman, gesturing to the marina outside, 'the potential of this town is astounding. We already have a thriving tourism industry. If we could enhance the marina, then who knows where it could lead?' He raised an eyebrow, rubbing his thumb and fingers together. Estelle thought of what Aiden had said about Darren, unable to stop herself from smiling. 'And there you'll see preparations are being made for our famous annual festival,' Darren added, gesturing towards a group of men battling the strong coastal breeze to set a marquee up on the beach. 'The festival draws thousands of tourists in each year, and this year we have even grander plans for it.'

'Does the weather ever affect it?' one businessman asked.

'Weather?' Darren said with a laugh, indicating the tan line on his neck. 'We were bathing in beautiful sunshine this time last week.'

'Yes, but the flooding has been rather bad in previous years,' the businessman replied.

Max and Peter exchanged a look. 'That's a rare occurrence,' Max said. 'So, tell me, how's business your end?'

As they talked, Estelle noticed a grey-haired man walk in wearing a police uniform. He was with another officer, a woman, who disappeared to the corner of the room, phone close to her ear.

'Excuse me a moment, will you?' Estelle said to the men she'd been talking to. 'I've just seen someone I know.'

She quickly headed towards the Chief Inspector, fixing a smile onto her face. 'Oh my gosh, is it really you?' He frowned and she bit her lip. 'You gave me a telling-off when I was a kid. I was smoking on the beach?' He looked puzzled and she wasn't surprised. She'd never had any dealings with him. 'Estelle Forster.' She put her hand out, smiling at him. 'I promise, I don't smoke any more. In fact, the talking-to that you gave me possibly started me on my road to healthy living.'

Recognition flooded his face. 'Ah, the famous author!'

'You've heard already?'

'Who hasn't around here, with Max and Autumn as your biggest fans? Book's out soon, isn't it?'

She nodded.

A waiter with tiny canapés came over. The Chief Inspector took one, raising an eyebrow. 'Were these made by dwarves?'

She laughed. 'Not impressed?'

'I'm missing my wife's pie and mash lunch for this. But then I suppose you don't do roast dinners with all this healthy eating stuff, do you?'

'On the contrary. I do an amazing one-pot roast that's all about the flavour. I get rave reviews for it, honestly.'

He smiled. 'Maybe I'll get the wife to buy your book then.'

'I'll do one better and send you a copy to give to her.'

His smile deepened. 'That's very kind of you. Now, I better go talk to some of these investors about our impeccable crime record.' He raised an eyebrow, leaning down to her. 'I'll leave out the bit about the chain-smoking teenagers we have here. It was good to see you, Estelle. So wonderful to see you doing so well.'

He went to walk away but Estelle touched his arm lightly. 'Wait. I just wanted to ask you something.'

He paused. 'Sure, go ahead.'

'I know you dealt with Alice Shepherd's death.'

He frowned. 'Yes, I was involved with that along with Sergeant Beckett over there,' he said, gesturing to the policewoman who was talking on the phone.

'Before Alice died, did you ever have any dealings with her?'

Something flickered in his eyes.

'So you did?' Estelle said.

The Chief Inspector peered over at his colleague then away again. 'I really shouldn't be discussing this with you. I hope your book launch is successful.' He nodded and walked away.

Estelle clenched her fists in frustration. She

looked over at Sergeant Beckett. Clearly she also knew something judging from the way the Chief Inspector had looked at her. The policewoman put her phone down and Estelle went to walk towards her but then Max appeared.

'What was that all about?' he asked, watching as the Chief Inspector strode away.

Estelle forced a smile onto her face. 'I was just telling him off for all the crap he eats, he wasn't impressed,' she said quickly, watching as Sergeant Beckett headed over to the Chief Inspector, whispered in his ear before walking out of the building.

Max laughed, eyes still on the Chief Inspector. 'Sounds like you want to give us all a healthy-eating makeover.'

Estelle faked a laugh. 'I can but try. Right, I'm popping to the loo.'

'I'll save you a glass of champers,' he said. 'Only joking!'

Estelle smiled then walked towards the toilets, looking over her shoulder at Max. When she saw he wasn't watching, she slipped out the front. It was strangely dark outside, black clouds coating the sky. In the distance, she saw the policewoman opening the door of a car.

'Wait!' she shouted out.

Sergeant Beckett looked up, frowning.

'Hi, sorry,' Estelle said, jogging over to her and smiling. 'I was just talking to the Chief Inspector, he suggested I talk to you.'

'How can I help?'

'Did you work on Alice Shepherd's case?'

The Sergeant looked at her in surprise. 'That

was years ago! Why are you asking about that now?'

'I'm Estelle Forster. I was one of the kids Autumn and Max fostered. I lived with Alice.' Estelle looked towards the cliff edge. 'The Chief Inspector suggested there was more to her case. I had a feeling something was going on with Alice before she died.'

The Sergeant looked cynical.

Estelle looked into her eyes. 'She was like a sister to me. I suppose coming back here again has brought back all those memories and a bunch of questions too, especially as the anniversary of her death was just a few days ago.'

'Yes, I know.' The Sergeant sighed. 'Look, I can't remember the exact details, but yes, Alice came to us before she died.'

Estelle felt her heart start to thump. 'Why?'

'She was hurt and scared. Nothing serious but — ' Sergeant Beckett shook her head. 'No, I've already said too much. I really must go, I'm sorry.'

She went to step into her car but Estelle put her hand on the officer's arm. 'If Alice was being threatened, had been *hurt*, why did you so easily accept that she committed suicide? Surely her death would be deemed suspicious?'

'That's enough, Miss Forster,' the Sergeant said sternly, shrugging Estelle's arm off and getting into the car. As the Sergeant drove away, rain started hammering down on top of Estelle. But she stayed where she was, peering into the distance as she wrapped her arms around herself.

Alice had been *hurt* before she died, so hurt the police had got involved. More and more evidence was mounting up to suggest she may have been killed. But none that was definitive.

Estelle sighed and went to run back inside. But then she paused. In the distance was a blurry figure, long red hair trailing in the rain.

'Alice?' Estelle whispered.

16

You saw me. I'm getting sloppy.

But I don't think you recognised me.

Deep breaths. Calm down. It'll be fine.

I need to be smarter about this.

But am I really up to it?

Yes, of course I am! You're unravelling. I can see it.

Fake smile. Pristine hair. Perfect clothes.

But the eyes. They're starting to give everyone a glimpse of the real you inside.

Fear. Doubt.

Good.

For a moment, you were getting comfortable. You were starting to really think you could be part of Lillysands.

But you aren't and never will be.

I'll make sure of that.

17

'Did you just say 'Alice'?'

Estelle turned to see Autumn shivering behind her.

She thought of the figure, blurred by the rain. 'I — I thought I saw her, but of course that's not possible.'

Autumn put her arms around Estelle's shoulders. 'Come on, you're getting drenched.' Estelle let Autumn steer her into the building but twisted around to look over her shoulder towards where she'd seen the figure. It was raining so heavily, her eyesight was blurred. She was so sure it was a girl and her first thought, inexplicably, had been Alice.

Was she losing her mind? Maybe she really was — the stress of the past few weeks getting to her. No wonder she was jumping to conclusions about Alice's death, Poppy's disappearance.

She looked at Autumn. 'Do you think Alice really killed herself?' She needed someone else to back up her theory. Someone whose opinion she trusted, like Autumn.

Autumn looked at her in shock. 'Where on earth is this coming from?'

'I — I don't know. I just wonder if she was really capable of committing suicide, you know? The Alice we all knew, killing herself, actively choosing to jump from that cliff.'

Autumn raised an eyebrow. 'Darling, have you been drinking?'

'No, I just — ' Estelle sighed, raking her fingers through her soaking hair. 'Ignore me. I'm just over-tired, that's all.'

They walked inside.

'I better go dry off,' Estelle said, peering towards the toilets.

'Let me help you, I'm an expert at drying wine stains off clothes using a hand dryer, I'm sure my skills can extend to a bit of rain.'

'No!' It came out harder than Estelle intended, but she needed to be alone. 'I'll be fine, really,' she added more softly.

She strode towards the toilets. When she got into a cubicle, she sat on the toilet seat, her head in her hands. It was making her head throb: Alice, Poppy, the photos.

How was it all connected? Why could no one else see that something was wrong?

She quickly got her phone out, checking for more updates on Poppy. But nothing. It wasn't even headline news any more.

She had to get to the bottom of this all before it was too late. After what the Sergeant told her about Alice going to them hurt and scared before she died, she was beginning to see this might be about more than just threats. Someone had *hurt* Alice. If the same person was threatening Estelle and was with Poppy, then they could hurt her too.

She had to stop them before that happened.

But who *were* they? She hadn't got any closer to finding out.

She took some quick deep breaths then stood back up, moving out of the cubicle and looking in the mirror above the sinks. Her mascara was streaked, her hair a mess. 'Pull yourself together,' she whispered to herself. She dug around in her bag with shaky fingers and combed her hair, reapplying her lipstick. 'There. Back to normal.'

Then she walked back into the room. As she did so, she noticed Autumn being comforted by Max. *Oh god, she'd upset her and on her birthday too!* She quickly strode over. 'Autumn, I'm so sorry, I'm just — '

'Oh I'm not upset about that, sweetie,' Autumn said, sniffing.

'Our caterers have fallen through for the party tonight,' Max explained, blue eyes flashing with anger. 'I booked them months ago.'

'It's fine,' Autumn said, smiling through her tears. 'I'm being silly, crying! It's only a party. We can grab some platters from M&S. I'm sure people will understand.'

Estelle couldn't stand seeing her foster mother so upset. 'Let me cook,' she said quickly.

Autumn frowned. 'Really?'

'Really. I have plenty of experience. How many people will be there?'

Autumn and Max looked at each other. 'Forty, fifty?' Max said.

'That's fine. I have a whole load of canapé recipes on my YouTube channel. And I promise you, they'll taste divine *and* be healthy.'

'Are you sure, darling?' Autumn asked.

'Absolutely,' Estelle replied, feeling a surge of adrenalin. She could be of use, do something to make Autumn happy rather than going on a wild goose chase. 'It'll be all hands on deck, I'll need help. But yeah, I can do it.'

'This means you'll come to my party then?' August asked.

Estelle thought about it. She hadn't been sure that morning. But now she knew more was going on than she first thought, she realised the only way she had a chance of finding out was by staying in Lillysands, the place Poppy was born . . . the place where Alice had died.

'Yes,' she said.

Autumn's face lit up and she grabbed Estelle, kissing her on the cheek. 'You're an angel!'

★　★　★

After they left the restaurant, Autumn and Estelle made a mad dash around the local food market and supermarket. Though Autumn still threw in some party classics Estelle would rather avoid — dips and sausage rolls; trifles and crisps — Estelle was able to convince her to add some of her own favourites too. In fact, as they walked around, picking up vegetables and fruit, feeling their textures, sniffing them, it reminded Estelle of the time she used to spend with Autumn talking about and tasting food. Like the time Autumn had managed to get a booking at one of London's top restaurants for a seven-course meal to celebrate a glowing school report for Estelle. They'd travelled across the country in blazing sunshine in Autumn's silver convertible, staying in the plush apartment rented out by

Autumn's old school friend Becca for client meetings. Estelle had felt so grown-up, sitting in the beautiful blue dress Autumn had bought her, sampling some of the most delicious tastes she'd ever experienced, looking around with wide eyes at the ornate surroundings and beautiful people. After, Autumn had taken her behind the scenes and Estelle had got her first look at the kitchens of a world-renowned restaurant. The chef had been a woman, tall and elegant, not batting an eyelid during the mad rush of lunch. She was an old friend of Autumn's and let Estelle taste different dishes, even helped her cook up a delicious soup filled with spices and exotic vegetables. On the train journey back, weighed down with bags of food, she and Autumn had talked excitedly about Estelle becoming a chef herself. From then on, her evenings and week-ends were spent preparing meals with Autumn, helping her taste all the food she was sent by clients. 'Your palette is second to none,' Autumn would exclaim in excitement.

But then those dreams were shattered when Estelle found out she was pregnant. Even with Autumn's reassurances nothing would have to change once she gave the child up for adoption, Estelle felt tainted. How could she be like that elegant chef with a history like hers? How could she possibly rise above her grimy childhood if she was doing exactly what her mother had done at that age?

But she *had* risen above it. She had to keep reminding herself that. And having Autumn and Max so proud of her made her believe it too.

Seeing that figure in the road earlier had just been a glitch. She had to gain control, rein her emotions in, be the person she'd worked so hard to be. And she'd prove that by making all the food for the party.

When they got back to the house, they found Max and Aiden waiting for them dressed in aprons.

'Oh good, the help's arrived,' Autumn said with a wink.

Estelle couldn't help her tummy tilting as she took Aiden in, windswept from his time on the beach. Even in a frilly white apron, he still managed to have that effect on her.

'Right,' Estelle said, forcing the thoughts away. 'Chopping duty,' she declared, pointing at Aiden. 'And stirring duties,' she added, pointing at Max. 'We have two hours to produce enough food for fifty guests.'

Max and Aiden raised an eyebrow at each other.

'Yes, sir!' Autumn exclaimed, putting her hand to her head like a Sergeant Major.

Estelle smiled. 'Don't look so worried! We can still have fun while doing it. Music?'

Max's face broke into a grin. 'Fabulous.' He went to his iPod and switched it on, the rock music he and Autumn so loved soon pouring out of the speakers.

As Autumn unloaded all the food, Estelle set out the utensils, including the spiraliser she'd convinced Autumn to buy for the salad. For the next hour, they all worked at prepping the dishes, dancing to the music as they did so and giggling as Max and Aiden juggled the vegetables. In the background, heavy rain battered down, turning the skies dark. But it somehow added to the atmosphere, making the kitchen feel like the only bright spot on the planet. Estelle's heart swelled. It was just like the old days when Estelle, Alice and Aiden would help Autumn prepare and serve the food for the various dinner parties they'd throw for Max and Peter's business associates.

'How the hell do I work this?' Aiden asked, trying to get to grips with the spiraliser.

'Here,' Estelle said, placing a carrot into it and twirling the handle around.

As orange spirals curled out of the end, Aiden's eyes widened in wonder. 'Wow. I need me one of these.'

'They're amazing, the vegetables are a great substitute for pasta and spaghetti.'

He raised an eyebrow. 'I very much doubt that.'

They both smiled. She realised he seemed more relaxed now. Had he got over his initial anger at what she'd told him about their daughter? She hoped so.

'You'll see!' she said. 'Here, have a go.' She let Aiden take over, the smile on his face widening as he produced spiralised carrots and courgettes.

Estelle scooped the carrot up and placed it in a bowl, then reached for some rice wine vinegar, splashing it in with some soy sauce and grated ginger. She then sprinkled in some sesame seeds and chopped cucumbers before lifting the bowl and shaking it about. As she placed the bowl down, she realised the room had gone quiet. She looked up to see Autumn, Max and Aiden watching her with wide smiles on their faces.

'You're a natural, sweetheart,' Autumn said, with a look of pride.

Estelle felt her cheeks flush. She'd heard it so many times — from Seb, from her publisher, from visitors to her YouTube channel and social media followers — but somehow, to hear it from Autumn felt extra special.

'You won't be so impressed if we don't get this done in time,' Estelle said with a wink, turning away so they couldn't see the happy tears in her eyes. 'Chop chop,' she added, clapping her hands.

'I'm sorry my darlings,' Autumn said, pulling her apron off as she looked at the clock. 'But I have a hair appointment so will have to leave you to it.'

'And I have some work to do,' Max said.

'Slackers!' Aiden declared.

His parents smiled. 'I'm sure we can trust the chef and her assistant to produce the finest party food,' Autumn said. Then they left the kitchen.

As they got back to work, Aiden continued watching her. 'You really are talented,' he said.

'Oh, come on, it's just salad,' she replied, taking a quick photo of it for Instagram.

'Exactly, just salad,' he said, picking a forkful up and putting it in his mouth. 'But it tastes amazing.' He looked into her eyes. 'You've really found your niche.'

'So have you,' she said. 'I saw the way you were with the group earlier; they were hanging on your every word.'

His brow creased. 'Na, it's not the same.'

'Isn't it?'

'I don't love it, Stel. Not like you clearly love this.'

'You loved singing, writing songs,' Estelle said gently.

'Yeah, well, those days are over.'

'Why do they have to be? Why can't you dig your guitar out?'

'I'm not a kid any more. I have to pay the mortgage.'

'It doesn't have to be your job, Aiden. It can be something you do in the evenings for fun. You have to try again, you can't just give it up. You were so talented.'

'*Were* talented, you've got that right. Not any more though.'

'Nonsense, I bet you still are. How do you know you haven't still got it if you don't give it a go?' She tilted her head, examining his face. 'There's only one way to find out and I'd *love* to hear you play.'

His face hardened. 'No. That's the past.'

Then he pulled off his apron and walked away.

★ ★ ★

Estelle tried not to think about the sadness she'd seen in Aiden's eyes as she walked around the party later, a huge tray of canapés in her hands. Around her, people laughed and drank, Autumn's favourite rock music booming out of the speakers. The doors between the kitchen and dining room had been opened wide and all of

Lillysands' great and good were there, drinking wine, laughing uproariously. Amongst them, Autumn floated around in a long, sheer emerald dress, her blonde hair piled on top of her head. Estelle felt a burn of pride inside. It felt good to know she'd helped Autumn have a great party. For so many years, she'd felt guilty about the way she'd just walked out. Maybe, in some way, she was making up for it now. She'd never dreamed she'd be sharing another birthday with Autumn again and yet here she was. Not just that, she was playing a pivotal role in it, cooking all the food.

All she needed now was to know Poppy was safe and sound, and she could live her life with a little less regret and guilt.

Estelle placed the tray on a nearby table and headed to a quiet corner, quickly checking her phone for any updates on Poppy.

But still, nothing.

She felt disappointment and frustration thread through her. She was completely helpless.

'My wife is such a beauty, isn't she?' a voice said. She looked up to see Max watching Autumn hugging one of the guests.

'She is,' Estelle replied.

'Remember how people used to think you were her birth daughter?' Max said. 'Same curly hair. Same wicked smile and colourful clothes. She liked that, the idea of having a daughter.' He looked into her eyes. 'Still does. The way you just stepped in with the food earlier.' He smiled. 'You're a good girl, Stel.'

Estelle felt herself blush at his emotion.

177

'Anyone would have done the same.'

'Cooked for fifty people? I don't think so.' He gestured to the bottles of champagne on the table. 'Sure I can't tempt you with some champagne? We brought it back from our trip to France last year and I can promise you it's the best of the best.'

'It certainly is,' Autumn said, appearing by his side. 'Come on, darlin', we won't tell anyone.' She held up a bottle of champagne and a glass.

Estelle laughed. 'You two will never give up, will you?'

She'd been surprised when Max had served her with wine during that first dinner in the house all those years ago. 'The kids drink all the time in France,' he'd said, leaning back and putting his feet on the wall surrounding the terrace. 'Does them no harm, they're better behaved than British kids.'

'Yes, drink up, little one,' Aiden had said, blond hair flopping in his eyes as he put his feet on the terrace as well as if he was so much more grown-up than her instead of the mere six months that separated them. 'Then you'll end up just like Alice and I, *bons petits enfants*.' Alice caught his eye and they shared a smile.

If there was one thing her birth parents did, it was not let her drink and go near their drugs. 'Don't want you ending up like us, Estelle,' her mother would say in more sober moments. So it was a surprise to be offered alcohol at just twelve by the Garlands. Before she'd even had a chance to say no, they had poured some wine into her glass. Alice had given her a look that said 'I

178

know, weird, right?' Estelle had raised the glass to her mouth, not wanting to disappoint them. When she'd taken a sip, Max and Autumn had clapped, like it was something to be proud of. 'That mouthful was worth ten pounds,' Max had said as Autumn laughed. She found out later she'd been drinking wine from a five hundred pound bottle, brought out especially to celebrate her arrival. It had thrilled her, that thought. Made her feel important.

But now things were different. She was a woman, she knew her own mind. 'The one glass I had earlier is enough, thank you,' she said.

'But you're a clean eater, aren't bubbles good at cleaning?' Autumn said as she poured some champagne into a glass. Estelle resisted the urge to tell Autumn, again, that it wasn't about being 'clean'. Instead, she watched the champagne fizz and pop, the gold bubbles reflecting the lights above.

'Imagine these bubbles tickling your throat, the happy feel of it spreading to your head, making it swim, *cleaning* you good and proper inside.' Autumn squeezed her hand and smiled.

Estelle laughed again, shaking her head. 'Nice try, Autumn, but water will do just fine.' She clinked her glass of water against Autumn's champagne glass and winked at her.

'Right,' Max said. 'Time for a speech. Come on,' he said, taking Autumn's hand and leading her up to the front of the room.

'Oh god,' Autumn groaned. 'A speech!'

Max had always enjoyed making speeches at parties.

'Okay everyone,' Max said, going to the front of the room and clinking his glass as the music was turned down. 'Believe it or not, I'm not going to bore you over the next hour with a speech.'

'That'll make a change!' Peter shouted. Everyone laughed.

'All that really needs to be said is can you believe that stunning woman over there is *sixty*?' He gestured towards Autumn and she struck a pose. 'From the moment I met you, all those years ago, after you crashed into my new Mercedes with your friend Becca, I knew you would cost me a fortune.' Autumn narrowed her eyes at him. 'But,' Max continued, face going serious, 'you're worth every penny. The love of my life, my light in the darkness, everything I ever wished for.' He lifted his glass up. 'To my beautiful Autumn.'

Everyone else raised their glasses too. 'To Autumn!' they declared.

As they did, Estelle got a flashback to a party her parents had held in a local village hall for her mother's twentieth. The sight of her father with his hand around her mother's neck, pressing her up against the wall, glass shattered around them, the man he'd accused her of kissing sprawled on the floor with blood pouring from his nose. And in the distance, the sound of sirens.

'Daddy, please don't,' Estelle had begged, pulling at his other arm.

He'd looked down at her with hatred in his eyes. 'Get off,' he'd said, shoving her away. She'd stumbled into someone behind her, their lager spilling all over the pretty pink dress that her mother had found at the local Oxfam and she'd been so excited about wearing. Her father had laughed. 'Look at you, all filthy, like your filthy whore of a mother.'

'I'd also like to say a huge thank you to our Stel,' Max said. Estelle blinked, the memory dissolving at the sound of Max mentioning her name. Everyone turned to look at her. 'What would we have done without you, Stel? This beautiful talented girl saved the day today by cooking up a storm with these delicious canapés. She even had Aiden and I in frilly aprons to help out.' Everyone laughed, then Max's face grew contemplative again. 'In all seriousness though, and I say this with complete sincerity, having Stel back here has been the best birthday present Autumn could ask for. Am I right, darling?'

Max turned to Autumn and she nodded, her eyes filling with tears. 'Absolutely.'

Estelle felt her cheeks grow hot. She smiled, trying not to cry herself. The people in the room parted so Autumn could walk to Estelle, put her arms around her and kiss her on the cheek. 'It means everything that you're here, darling,' she whispered. 'Thank you.'

'Speaking of birthday presents . . . ' Max said. 'Autumn is currently wearing one of mine right now.'

Autumn fingered the diamond necklace around her neck, mouthing a *thank you* to Max.

'But there's just one more,' Max said. 'And this one is from Aiden, so I'll pass you over, son.'

Aiden walked into the room then . . . with his

guitar in his hands. Estelle was shocked. He'd seemed so against playing again earlier.

He looked so handsome in skinny grey jeans and a white shirt, his tanned face stubbled, his blond hair combed back.

Autumn put her hand to her mouth. 'He has his guitar,' she whispered.

Aiden peered at his mum. 'This is for you, Mum. Happy birthday.'

He looked down at his guitar, and a strand of hair fell in front of his eyes. Then he started strumming the strings, singing a song Estelle recognised from a time before everything went wrong in Lillysands. Nobody but Estelle knew he'd written the song for Alice, about a lost girl who was found.

Estelle lost herself in his voice, just as she used to all those years before. It was deep and mesmerising, his face intense. It felt like the words were wrapping themselves around everyone in the room. And it took her right back to the cottage, to Alice, to the feel of Alice's soft cheek on her shoulder as they listened to Aiden.

By the time Aiden got to the last verse, Autumn was crying and Estelle had to take large gulps of her water to chase her own tears away. As the song came to a close, she looked up to see Aiden's eyes were on her, a solitary tear gliding down his cheek.

Then he walked from the room. Everyone applauded, raising surprised eyebrows at each other.

Estelle instinctively went to follow him. But Autumn put her hand on her arm. 'Leave him be. He needs time; that took a lot, getting his guitar out again. Go have fun, sweetie. Lots of people want to catch up with you! You've been carrying food around like a waitress all evening when I've been telling you not to. So, go,' Autumn said, shooing Estelle away. 'Have some fun.'

So that was what Estelle tried to do over the next hour. But as much as she tried, she couldn't allow herself to 'enjoy' this party, as Autumn had insisted she should. Not when she knew Poppy was still out there somewhere missing. There was nothing she could do about it for now, but she would keep her ears peeled for any gossip and her eyes open for anyone who seemed uncomfortable, even unhappy around her.

But as she talked to people, all she felt was herself being enveloped in Lillysands' warmth. They all seemed so proud of her.

'Look how well our Stel's done,' a woman who owned a clothes boutique in town declared. 'You must come in and have a look at our new stock; you could wear a dress to your launch party! Autumn said you'd be having a launch party? We'd give you one for free, of course!'

'That's very kind of you,' Estelle said.

'It's so glamorous,' Veronica said. 'Lillysands' very own food writer. I remember when you first arrived, darling, such a pretty lost-looking thing.'

'Oh yes!' another woman declared, and Estelle remembered she owned the local gym with her husband. 'I remember when my daughter and her friends said they would take you under their wing.'

Estelle smiled, remembering the woman's friendly daughter with her long strawberry-blonde hair. She'd come up to Estelle on her first day of school and tucked her arm into hers, telling her any friend of the Garlands was a friend of hers.

'Maybe you can do a talk at the library if you have time?' a short man with kind eyes that Estelle vaguely recognised said.

'Oh, I'm not sure how long I'm staying,' Estelle replied, blushing at all the attention. 'But I can donate a signed copy of my book? God,' she said, laughing at herself, 'that sounds weird, saying that out loud. *My book*.'

They all laughed.

'And so modest too,' Veronica said.

'You've done us proud,' the storeowner added, squeezing Estelle's arm. 'Really proud.'

'You're all being so sweet, thank you,' she said with a happy smile. 'I'll catch up later, must top up my orange juice.'

She took the chance to walk away, still beaming from all the compliments. They made her blush, sure, but it felt good, to have people be proud of her. She remembered as a child coming home with a picture she'd drawn, a sketch of a local church that her teacher said was fantastic. But instead of praise, her parents had laughed at it, saying it looked like an elephant. The next day, she'd found it scrunched up in the bin.

So to have people express pride over something she'd done — a whole community! — felt special.

She walked to the kitchen then paused, hearing her name being whispered. It was Lorraine, Autumn and Max's neighbour who ran her own PR company.

' . . . can't change the fact she had a junkie mother. Makes out she's all good and clean, but we know she isn't, don't we?' Estelle stepped into the shadows, heart thumping as she listened. 'You remember what she was like when she arrived?' Lorraine continued.

'Oh, a complete mess,' the woman with her said. Estelle recognised her voice, it was the woman who owned the gym. 'Max was horrified. Autumn had to convince him to let her stay, he was nearly on the phone to social services to have her taken back.'

Estelle's stomach plummeted, all the pride she'd felt a few moments before dissipating in an instant. She looked towards Max who was topping up someone's glass as he laughed with them. Had that really happened? Had he really been ready to get rid of her that easily?

'They tried to scrub that past of hers away,' Lorraine continued. 'But you can't teach a dirty dog new tricks. You can even see it in her now. No matter how hard she tries with all that pure eating of hers, she'll never stop us all seeing her for what we know she is: a junkie's daughter. Rotten to the core.'

Estelle stumbled away. She ran out to the veranda, gulping in huge breaths of fresh air.

How could she have been so naïve to think she could be accepted by Lillysands so easily? Had they been judging her all this time, thinking of her as 'dirty' and 'rotten' as Lorraine had said? She hadn't even realised they knew so much of her childhood. And Max. Had he really tried to have her taken away?

She heard movement in the darkness and turned to see Aiden standing in the shadows, looking at his phone. She walked over to him. She needed to know if it was true about Max. 'Aiden, I — '

'You seen this article?' He held the phone up for her, his jaw set. 'It's pretty buried, the media seem to be growing bored of Poppy's story now.'

She frowned. 'What article?'

He handed his phone to her and she looked down at it. It was a short article from a national tabloid.

Poppy O'Farrell's Heartache

Poppy's former nanny has exclusively revealed that the runaway teenager would often ask about her 'real mummy and daddy', something TV presenter Chris O'Farrell struggled with. The teenager, who has now been missing for nearly four days, attended ongoing therapy sessions to deal with issues stemming from her adoption.

'What the hell did you do to our daughter, Stel?' Aiden said, his green eyes filling with tears. The pride she'd seen in his eyes as they'd cooked in the kitchen earlier was now replaced by disappointment.

'It was the right thing to do!' she replied, protesting weakly.

'Stop telling yourself that! It won't change anything if you keep saying it like a useless mantra. The fact is, she's a fucking mess and it's your fault for giving her away.'

He shoved away from the wall and stormed off the veranda going down to the beach.

Estelle squeezed her eyes shut. She thought of the moment she handed Poppy over to Autumn, her little face scrunched up, the sound of her crying.

The guilt came in waves, punching at the core of her. Aiden was right, she told herself it was the right thing to do, over and over, hoping she might convince herself. Hell, she *did* convince herself for so many years. But the evidence was right in front of her now. The girl had run away, she was in therapy, her heart was broken. Poppy had been neglected by Estelle just like Estelle's parents had neglected her. And look what it had done to her.

It was like Lorraine said, no matter how much she tried to tell herself otherwise, she was just like her parents. Dirty, filthy, soiling every relationship she had.

She looked inside and caught sight of the champagne bottle Autumn had been trying to tempt her with.

Imagine these bubbles tickling your throat, the happy feel of it spreading to your head, making it swim, cleaning you good and proper inside.

Nothing she did could cleanse her. None of the food she deprived herself of, none of the vitamins she pumped into her body. What was the point? She just wanted her head to swim. She *needed* it to.

Before she knew what she was doing, she was heading towards the bottle. She grabbed it while nobody was looking, and then walked to the table full of pre-packed party food Autumn had insisted on buying, piling a plate high with cheesy nachos, mini hamburgers, cocktail sausages and sticky cheese dip; cream-filled cakes and After Eights. She thought of the times she'd done the same at her home in London, raiding the local newsagents with one of Seb's baseball caps pulled low over her eyes like some criminal, grabbing chocolate bars and packets of crisps, shoving them in her mouth as she walked up the street, thinking he had no idea as she added items to her secret stash. She was dirty, just as Lorraine had said. No matter how hard she tried, she couldn't outrun her past; couldn't get beyond her rotten core. No wonder Max had wanted to get rid of her.

She ran outside, the plate and bottle clutched close to her chest. She took the narrow steps down to the beach, the moon beaming on her from above as tears flowed down her cheeks. The skies had cleared now, the setting sun casting an orange glow across the clear sea as it began to dip under the horizon. Estelle sunk down onto the smooth pebbles and stared out to sea, the distant stars smudged through her tear-filled eyes.

'I'm sorry, Poppy,' she whispered.

She breathed in the clogging chocolate of the

188

cakes and the powdery cheese of the nachos, her tummy rumbling in anticipation.

Then she looked at the half-filled bottle of champagne.

She ought to be strong, like her therapist had taught her. Just throw it all away. She had the chance to do that right now, there was a bin just a few strides away.

But then she heard Aiden's words again: *She's a fucking mess and it's your fault.*

She quickly brought the neck of the champagne bottle to her nose, breathing in the tart sweet smell. She licked her lips, then brought the bottle to her face, felt the foil on her mouth, smelt the intoxicating scent of the champagne again. The liquid fizzed against her tongue as she tipped the bottle slightly, teasing her taste buds. Then she tipped the whole bottle up. As the golden liquid slid down her throat, Estelle groaned, the taste bringing back heady memories of her birthdays here in Lillysands, the popping of bottles, the giggles as she shared a cup with Alice.

She closed her eyes, saw Alice standing at the edge of the cliff, fear in her eyes as she looked over her shoulder. Then Poppy, her daughter, eyes filled with sadness as she looked into the camera.

What was the connection?

Whoever had sent the Polaroids clearly hated her. And who could blame them?

She took another sip of champagne, surprised to realise she was sobbing against the opening. The champagne flooded her mouth, almost choking her. As the effects of the alcohol spread inside her, her head seemed to blossom, the light of the bubbles flooding the dark corners inside.

She put the bottle down, wiping her mouth, then eyed the plate of food. She reached for one of the nachos, trying not to think of the chemicals slathered on that one solitary chip. She brought it to her nose and sniffed it, memories flooding her mind: three sets of tanned hands dipping into a plastic bowl, Alice laughing as Estelle shoved them into Aiden's mouth.

She licked it, tongue lighting up at the memory of its taste. She paused a moment then bit into it, taste buds sparking at the crunch. She grabbed more, shovelling them into her mouth like she used to when she spent time in care homes. Before she knew it, the plate was empty, the bottle nearly empty too.

She leaned back, her heady fuzzy from the champagne, the pebbles digging into her palms as she stared out towards the darkening sea, the sky above her now black, stars sparkling savagely. She and Alice would come to the beach often in the summer, bring a blanket and food, curl up together as they talked.

Could she have saved her, if she hadn't been so selfish, so focused on *her* troubles? Just like she might have been able to save Poppy if she hadn't given her up for adoption?

What a mess she'd weaved.

Suddenly her phone started buzzing in her pocket. She pulled it from her pocket.

It was Detective Jones.

18

She took a moment to compose herself — she couldn't have the detective knowing she'd been drinking. Then she put the phone to her ear. 'Is there any news on Poppy?' she asked, hoping against hope he was calling to tell her Poppy was home safe and sound.

'I'm afraid not.'

Disappointment rushed through her. 'Oh. Then why are you calling, Detective Jones?'

'Just checking in after you got that last photo. Any more since then?'

'Nothing.'

'How's it going in Lillysands?'

She looked down at the food in her lap. 'Not bad. Look, what are you guys doing to find Poppy? I noticed her story's no longer top of the media's priorities.' She didn't mention the article Aiden had shown her.

'What the press print is out of our control, Miss Forster.'

'Is it really?' she asked, the alcohol making her brash. 'You have a media department. Get them to keep the pressure up. If someone recognises her, they'll call. But that won't happen if Poppy isn't in the news.'

'I don't need someone to tell me my job,' the DC said, clearly put out.

'But I'm not just someone, I'm Poppy's mother!'

'Poppy has a mother: Mrs O'Farrell.'

She flinched at his words then slammed the phone down, tears squeezing out of the corner of her eyes as she tipped more champagne into her mouth.

She meant nothing to the police. Even with the notes she'd been receiving, she was just the woman who gave the baby up. She'd seen it in their eyes when they'd visited, the disdain. How could a mother hand over their newborn like that?

Estelle pinched her eyes shut, more tears falling down her cheeks.

Maybe they were right to hate her. Didn't she hate herself?

She heard the crunch of pebbles behind her and turned to see Darren standing above her. He was wearing a suit; he always seemed to be wearing one. His dark hair was neatly swept to the side, his face cleanly shaven.

She quickly wiped her tears away. He looked at the bottle and the plate and raised an eyebrow.

'Naughty girl,' he said suggestively, sitting beside her, not seeming to notice her tears.

Or not caring.

'I'm having a cheat day,' she said, barely registering that her words were slurred. 'Want some?'

'If there's any left?' he replied playfully.

'A few mouthfuls.'

'That'll do.' He picked the bottle up and downed what remained as Estelle watched in surprise.

'What?' he said, laughing. 'Is a property mogul

drinking champagne any more controversial than a healthy-eating writer gobbling up cheesy nachos and cocktail sausages?'

She moaned. 'I'm so going to regret this tomorrow.'

'Why? Like you said, it's a cheat day. Just as well I'm having one too.' She noticed the way he was watching her, his eyes slowly taking her in.

'You have cheat days?' she said.

'Sure I do.' He patted his svelte stomach. 'You think I look like this eating nachos every day of the week?'

She looked at his handsome face. He was so like Seb. Undeniably handsome — square jaw, sparkling eyes, tanned skin. But there was no depth there.

She thought of Aiden's angry eyes as they'd looked into hers earlier, full of emotion. Maybe she didn't deserve that; maybe she deserved someone shallow, someone like Darren. Aiden was better than her. Always had been. She was bad. He was good. She'd never deserved him.

'I know Autumn and Max would love to see you doing this,' Darren said. 'I just had to tell them off for saying you need to loosen up.'

So Lorraine and her friend weren't the only people talking about her at the party.

'Maybe I do need to loosen up,' she said.

'No,' Darren said, looking into her eyes. 'I like you the way you are. You're in control. I like to see that in a woman. The three Cs: clean, controlled, cute.'

'I wouldn't agree with that statement right now,' she said, gesturing towards the bottle of champagne and food.

'You're allowed a night off every now and again.'

She held his gaze. Was it so wrong, him being like Seb? Isn't that what she deserved: shallow, suave and selfish?

'And I like the fact you use the name Estelle,' he added. 'Sounds classier than Stel. So, shall I let Autumn and Max know you're indulging?' he teased.

'No. That's half the fun,' Estelle teased back, peering up at the lilac house, which loomed above her in the darkness, music and laughter tinkling out of it. 'Drinking and eating crap without them even knowing.'

'Ah, a secret feast.' Darren took her empty plate. 'Want me to get more?'

She smiled despite everything inside her crying 'no'. 'Absolutely.'

Over the next hour, they drank more champagne and ate all the foods Estelle advised against. In the back of her mind, she knew it was wrong. But something inside her — the old Stel — rebelled against her conscience.

One night, just one night, she told herself. Then after this, no more binging.

But guilt still hit her like a cricket bat as she thought of all she'd just eaten.

'Excuse me,' she said, standing up and swaying. 'Just popping to the loo.'

She walked across the beach, grasping onto the metal pole as she walked up the steps. When she got into the house, she slipped past the revellers to the bathroom, slamming the door shut behind her and kneeling in front of the toilet. She stared down at a sight achingly familiar to her, tears sliding down her cheeks. Then she stuck her fingers down her throat, retching into the toilet and bringing up all the food she'd just consumed. With each retch, she felt the slate inside her getting cleaner and cleaner.

When she was finished, she looked at herself in the mirror. She tidied her hair, wiped her mouth and ignored the disappointment in her eyes. It had been a while since she'd done this. She thought she'd gained control of it.

It was just the one time, she told herself.

She took a deep breath then walked out of the door, banging straight into someone.

'Oh hello, Stel!' She looked up to see Mr Tate smiling down at her. But then his smile disappeared, his brow furrowing. 'Are you okay?' he asked quietly.

'Of course I am!' she said, a little too brightly.

He peered behind her into the bathroom then back at her again. 'You're still seeing someone, aren't you?'

She frowned. 'Seeing someone?'

'A therapist? You look very thin, Estelle, I'm worried — '

She crossed her arms, heart pounding. Mr Tate had always been one step ahead of her. At school, he'd referred her to a therapist before she'd even realised she had a problem. 'I'm fine.'

'You don't seem it. Maybe it's not a good idea you being back in Lillysands, you know what this place is like. Are you returning to London soon? I think you should consider it, you know how

195

this town can chew you up and spit you out.'

'If it's so bad then why are *you* still here?' She felt a stab of guilt as she said it. The drink was making her cold, it always did.

'My wife, Estelle. You know how she loves this place. But *you* don't have to stay.' He put his hand on her arm, his eyes pleading with hers. 'And when you do go back, get help, quickly. We both know how this can spiral out of control for you.'

She pulled away from him. 'I'm not a little girl any more, *Geoffrey*,' she said, using his first name, feeling rebellious like she did at school when she addressed teachers like that.

Then she stormed off. She couldn't be doing with Mr Tate's sad brown eyes and concerned looks. It had nothing to do with him! She was an adult now, she could do what she wanted.

She jogged back down to the beach, relieved to see Darren there. Darren was always good for forgetting things, for burying things away.

'I forgot how gorgeous it is out here,' Estelle said, sitting down next to him. He handed her the bottle of champagne. She hesitated. She'd just purged all that. But what harm would more do, she needed to drive away the memory of Mr Tate's expression anyway and she could always get sick again. So she took it, taking a sip. She peered towards the white marquees that had been set up on the beach in the distance. 'I always liked it when the festival took place. The atmosphere, the buzz.'

'You wouldn't like it living with my mum; she goes a bit mental in the lead-up.'

'Well, she is the brains behind it.'

He examined her face. 'Do you miss the sea?'

'I do,' she said wistfully.

'Strange place to move then, London.'

'I needed a change.'

'Why did you leave so abruptly?'

She looked into his eyes. For one drunken moment, she considered telling him everything. But then she stopped herself.

'I was being a dramatic teenager. I bet you live right by the sea,' she asked, wanting to change the subject.

'Of course! You'd be a fool not to.' He pointed towards one of the tall white buildings overlooking the marina. 'I live in a penthouse there and rent out a couple of the other flats. I think Max had his eyes on it as an investment. But, you snooze, you lose.'

'What a life, fighting over penthouses!' she teased.

'Oh, it wasn't a fair fight really. Max wouldn't have been able to afford it.'

She looked at him in surprise. 'Really? I hear his business is thriving.'

Darren laughed. 'You're kidding! The man's as skint as his son.'

Estelle spluttered on her champagne. 'What?'

'All these houses?' Darren said, peering along the stretch of gleaming houses that lined the cliff above them. Max and Darren's father had decided to keep two each to rent out as long-term lets and they'd both made a lot of money from them . . . or so she'd thought. 'Thanks to some recent landslides,' Darren continued, 'including one big one a couple of years ago, people are reluctant to spend as much money on renting out these places so the ones Dad and Max have sit empty. Luckily, Dad has lots of other healthy income streams. Max on the other hand.' He sighed and shook his head.

'Jesus. Alice used to talk about the landslide threat here, she was so obsessed with that kind of stuff, but I had no idea it was a genuine issue.'

'Really? Surely you've seen how half the gardens have disappeared up there? Same with the other houses down Seaview Terrace. And as for the cottage gardens at the front of the street, they're in real trouble.'

Estelle thought of Mr Tate and his ill wife, guilt whirring inside. 'Do you think the houses will go into the sea?'

'One day, yes. Dad's made quite a loss from it all, but luckily he's been sensible with his other investments. Max on the other hand — ' Darren shook his head. 'Never known a couple to spend so much money they don't have. But then Autumn probably doesn't have a clue about the debt, bless her.'

'But where does Max *get* the money from?'

'Loans.'

Estelle looked up at their house, so full of light and laughter. She just couldn't believe it.

'It's not the first time either,' Darren said. 'Dad told me Max is always getting in trouble with money. But somehow manages to claw himself back to the surface again without Autumn noticing anything is wrong.'

'Poor Autumn.' This new information about

Max just reiterated what Lorraine had said about him earlier. He wasn't the person she thought he was. But then was anyone?

'You mustn't mention any of this,' Darren said, suddenly looking panicked. 'Dad would go mental. I'm serious, Estelle, you can't tell anyone.'

'I won't.'

'Good,' he said, his face relaxing. 'I know I can count on you. You're — '

'Clean, controlled and cute,' she said robotically.

'Very cute,' he said, eyes running over her face.

'Caught in the act!' a voice said from behind them. They turned around to see Autumn and Max weaving down the beach in the dark towards them, Darren's parents Veronica and Peter not far behind, more bottles of champagne in their hands.

Estelle looked at Max, still trying to process what she'd learnt about him that evening.

'Remember, not a word,' Darren whispered into her ear, his lips tickling her skin.

'I promise.'

'Well well well, Stel,' Max said with a raised eyebrow. 'Do I detect leftover cheesecake on your lap, young lady?'

'And a half-empty glass of champagne in your hands?' Autumn added, sinking down beside her and giving her a hug. Estelle looked into her eyes. How could Max have kept his money troubles from her? Or maybe she knew but just didn't want to accept it. 'I knew you wouldn't be able to resist,' Autumn continued. 'And look how much more relaxed you are. See, a little naughtiness every now and again does nothing but good.'

Darren raised an eyebrow at Estelle and she waited for her tummy to tingle in response. But there was nothing.

'Speaking of which . . . ' Veronica said, joining them and reaching into the pocket of her red dress. 'The icing on the cake.'

She pulled out a spliff. Darren's eyes widened as he looked at it. 'Jesus, Mum.'

'Oh come on, don't pretend you didn't know,' she said.

Darren rolled his eyes, embarrassed.

'Want some?' Veronica asked Estelle.

Estelle watched the orange sparks on the spliff, breathing in the familiar musky scent. She used to sit in the cave she'd once found Aiden in, smoking the weed they'd stolen from Autumn's stash — a stash so large her and Aiden knew she'd never notice. She'd told them she took it for medical purposes, to ease the muscle pain she sometimes felt after a gym session. It had seemed a weak excuse to Estelle, but she was so desperate to regard Autumn differently from her drug-taking parents, she'd accepted it. And the truth was, her stash rarely went down. Estelle recalled the delicious loosening of her brain cells when she smoked it, the way it made her relax.

'Not Estelle, Veronica,' Max said in a low voice.

Estelle narrowed her eyes at Max. He couldn't mould her into a perfect little girl like he clearly wanted all those years ago.

'Well, it is a cheat day,' she said defiantly.

She reached for the spliff, desperate to feel its papery texture between her fingers again. Everyone watched her, eyes bright.

'Just one little drag,' Autumn said.

Estelle looked out to sea, still tasting the acid from her retching earlier. She imagined Alice in there, reaching up to the surface, eyes wide with fear. Then Poppy, dark hair swimming around her pale face.

She quickly put the joint to her mouth, sucking the smoke in, letting the images shimmer from her mind.

★ ★ ★

'What about the time you and Alice scaled the statue in town?' Darren said, shaking his head at the memory a couple of hours later.

'Oh god, yes! We draped pink frilly knickers around the statue's head,' Estelle remembered, snorting with laughter as she took a puff of the next joint. They were sitting around a fire on the beach, ten or twelve stragglers from the party, familiar faces that dotted memories of Estelle's teenage years there. Aiden was nowhere to be seen and Estelle presumed he had gone home. Maybe that was a good thing, she didn't want him seeing her like this. He'd already looked so disappointed in her.

Autumn squeezed her close, her arm around her shoulders, both of them huddled under one of her thick wool blankets. Estelle leaned her head against her foster mother's shoulder and peered up at her. She'd forgotten how much she'd loved Autumn, how comforted and welcome she made her feel. And now she knew how hard she'd fought her own husband to keep Estelle in Lillysands, it meant even more. That was real love.

She gazed out to sea, head fuzzy from champagne and marijuana, the familiar lilac blot of the mansion on the cliffs above, the soft lapping waves ahead. Her heart soared with an intense happiness and love. Screw Max. Screw Seb. Screw Aiden. As long as Autumn loved her, that was all that mattered.

She took a quick photo with her phone, uploading it to Instagram with the caption: *Cheat day with the family. #LoveLillysands*

She jumped up, flinging off the blanket. 'I want to swim,' she declared.

Darren laughed. 'This brings back memories. Remember when we all used to skinny dip as kids?' Estelle smiled at the memory. When there were summer parties on the beach, they all used to run out into the waves at midnight, shedding their clothes and diving into the warm waves.

Autumn stood up. 'I think it's time we old folk leave the young kids to have some fun,' she said with a wink. 'Who fancies some bacon butties?'

Everyone stood with her, walking inside and leaving Estelle and Darren alone.

'We going into the sea then?' Darren asked, eyes crawling all over Estelle.

Estelle swayed slightly, taking another puff from her joint. 'Why not? But I'm keeping my underwear on this time.'

Darren pouted. 'You sure?'

Estelle rolled her eyes. 'Yes, I'm sure.'

He smiled and stood up, unbuttoning his shirt to reveal a well-muscled chest. Estelle pulled her dress off, aware of Darren's eyes on her. He was probably used to frills and lace, not organic white cotton underwear.

Five minutes later, they were both in the sea, splashing each other and laughing under the moonlight like they used to as teenagers. But then Darren's face grew serious. He swam up to Estelle, taking her hand as his eyes travelled over her. 'It's been good having you back,' he said in a husky voice.

He went to move towards her to kiss her. For a moment, she thought about letting him. But then she thought of Aiden. She stepped away, water splashing between them. 'No, Darren.'

His eyes flared with anger. 'But you've been giving me the come on all night!'

She rolled her eyes. 'No, I haven't. Just because a girl talks to you, doesn't mean they want to kiss you, Darren.'

He looked at her, his jaw flexing and unflexing. Then he turned away. 'I'm heading back,' he shouted over his shoulder.

Good, she wanted to be alone. When he was gone, she lay back, floating like a starfish as she looked up at the stars.

'Can you see the stars where you are, Poppy?' she whispered.

She thought of Aiden, of how they would swim beneath the moonlight together. After that first kiss, and the party where Aiden had ignored her and driven her into Darren's arms, she thought the kiss had meant nothing to him. But one particularly hot night, after Alice had gone to bed, Aiden had suggested they go swimming. So they'd both tiptoed into the sea in their underwear and she'd felt his eyes on her as she'd laid back just as she was doing now.

'We shouldn't have kissed,' he'd said.

She'd stayed where she was, closing her eyes so he couldn't see her disappointment. Then she'd felt his lips against hers and she knew in that moment, he didn't really mean what he'd said.

Each night that summer, they would come out and swim. And each swimming session got more heated, until eventually . . . Estelle took in a deep shaky breath at the memory. That was where they had conceived Poppy, one of those late summer evenings, beneath the waves, her legs wrapped around Aiden's waist, the feel of him inside her making her gasp. To lose her virginity with Aiden had been special, and then all the times after where they'd made love, it just got more and more intense.

Then she'd fallen pregnant. They'd been stupid, thought the water would mean she couldn't get pregnant.

Estelle turned onto her belly and swam farther out, desperate for the silence she and Aiden used to share on their midnight swims together, moonlight tracking her then just as it was now, the salt of the sea lapping her lips. Her arms ached, her head was fuzzy, and the heaviness of all the processed food she'd consumed that night was weighing her down.

She went to lie on her back again but paused, seeing a figure watching her from the garden of the pink cottage above. She waded her hand in water, making herself upright so she could look properly. She wondered for a moment if it was Mr Tate, but the figure had long hair.

Her heart started pumping, the irrational thought of it being Alice buzzing through her mind again. She headed closer to look, but the figure was now gone. As she trod water, something felt different, her legs heavier, the water thicker. She looked down and was shocked to see the sea had turned a deep red.

Was she bleeding?

She swivelled around, saw the redness was all around her under the bright moonlight, too much for one body to produce.

She started panicking, her breath coming in gasps. What was happening? She thought of the figure again. Was she hallucinating, losing her mind?

She went to tread back to shore. She no longer felt safe in the water. But suddenly she was pulled by something, a swirling pressure beneath her, her whole body buoyed out into the dark deep sea.

A riptide.

She'd grown used to them living in Lillysands, the intense and unpredictable flow of water that could sweep you right out to sea in the blink of an eye. She'd learnt how to deal with them the first time she'd been gripped by one thanks to Alice.

'Swim parallel to the shore,' Alice had shouted out to her as she got caught up in the current, accidentally swallowing mouthfuls of water as she was bounced up and down. 'It won't pull you under, Stel, swim parallel.' The calmness of her voice had kept Estelle calm too and within seconds, she was out of it and safe, both of them laughing.

But there was no Alice here tonight and Estelle was filled to the brim with alcohol and drugs.

Panic flooded her chest.

She worked her arms and legs harder, gasping as she tried to twist around to face shore, the blood red sea splashing in her face.

No, she mustn't face shore. Parallel, Alice had said parallel.

She swirled round again, taking in a huge gulp of red water. She coughed, spluttered, arms flailing, making her sink under, a strand of bloody red hair covering her face.

'No,' she screamed. 'No.'

The world seemed immeasurably red, the sea a thunder in her ears. Her breath was shallow, her arms and legs growing weak.

She tried to find shore but the moon disappeared beneath a cloud and made the world pitch black.

Was she under already? She looked up, saw stars, then a wave of water gushed over her.

Was this it? Was she going to die?

And just when she thought that, she saw a swirl of red hair in the distance.

'Alice.' She reached her hand out . . .

Then strong arms were gripping her.

She looked up into bright green eyes.

'Aiden?' she whispered.

It was Aiden, blond hair plastered against his head, chest bare. 'It's okay,' he said. 'You'll be okay, just stay still for a sec.'

'Aiden,' she moaned. 'There's blood. It's everywhere.'

'That's not blood, Estelle. It's clay falling from the cliffs. Be still. Let me bring you in.'

She did as he asked, felt his fingers on her waist, his body against hers as he swam her closer to shore. After a while, he stopped.

'We're in shallow water now, you can stand.' He helped her upright, her bare feet sinking into the sand. 'You okay?' he asked, steadying her by putting his hands on her waist.

He was swathed in red clay, eyelashes thick with it. She looked down at her hands, bright red too.

'I — I think so,' she said.

He paused, looking into her eyes. 'I came down here earlier to look for you and saw you with Darren.'

'I don't care about Darren,' she whispered. 'I was remembering what we used to do here. Do you remember?' she added, head light from the drink and drugs.

His brow creased. He didn't say anything.

'I miss us,' she said. 'We never had a chance, did we?'

'You're drunk.'

'I'm right though, aren't I? We had no chance at all. I got pregnant, you went off to boarding school, then Alice died. It's such a bloody waste, all of it such a waste.'

His eyes swam with emotion.

'There's not been anyone like you, Aiden. Not even close.' She stroked his glistening cheekbones with her fingers. 'The way you made me feel back then. The way you *still* make me feel.'

She stood on tiptoes, impulsively pressing her lips against his, tangling her fingers in his soaking hair. For a moment, she thought he might respond. But then he pushed her away.

'What are you *doing*, Estelle?' he asked.

She stared at him, not sure what to say, the rejection burning her.

'You're drunk,' he said again, shaking his head. 'Come on, let's get you back.'

★ ★ ★

Estelle hugged her knees to her chest, looking out to sea as she sat outside the pink cottage. The moonlight cast an eerie glow over the red sea below, making it even more vibrant. Aiden had said it was from rock and sand sliding into the water from the cliffs. She thought of what Darren had told her about the gardens disappearing into the sea. Was it really that bad? She'd wanted to ask Aiden more, but she hadn't got a chance to find out, he'd left immediately after returning her to the party. And now here she was, sitting outside the pink cottage on the very bench her and Alice used to sit on, the trees branches swaying above, the cliff edge so close.

The cliff edge from which Alice jumped . . . or was pushed.

Estelle took another slug of the gin she was holding and wiped her lips. She'd got even more drunk with everyone after Aiden disappeared, trying to erase the look in his eyes after she'd tried to kiss him. Even *he* thought she was too soiled to kiss. She'd found it hard to join in with the revelries, brooding on it all. After a while, she'd snuck out, taking a bottle of Max's gin with her as she headed to the pink cottage.

She leaned against the bench, looking up at the black sky, her head swimming.

She and Alice used to squirrel stuff away in the burrow of this tree, she realised with a dizzy start. She got up from the bench and knelt on the grass, using the light from her phone to illuminate the burrow. She reached her hand in, her drunken mind not registering there might be insects in there, smiling when she felt something at the back. She couldn't believe she'd actually found something, could it really be something she and Alice had stowed away all those years ago.

She pulled out a small tin box with a delicately petalled lid. She opened it, finding a photo of a mother with a baby inside. On the back was a date: *1988*. The year Alice was born. It must be a box that had belonged to Alice.

She swallowed, tears pricking at her eyelashes as she glided her finger over Alice's young face. Beneath the photo was a folded sheet of paper. She opened it, laying it out flat on her thighs and lighting it up with her phone. It looked like a pen drawing of a cliff with houses on top. Scrawled over it were arrows and notes relating to

209

'frequencies' and 'slopes' with phone numbers of various authorities such as the local council and the environment agency written down the side. A name was written along the bottom: Alice Shepherd.

It must be Alice's handwriting. Estelle got a rush of feeling then, memories of her old friend tumbling through her mind. She looked out to the sea that had taken Alice and shook her head. 'Oh Alice,' she whispered. Then she turned her attention back to the box.

There was just one more item in the box, a postcard. It was illustrated like a typical seaside postcard — typical except for the fact the woman on the front was naked, tall and buxom, legs spread on the beach. A man stood above her, a fishing rod in his hands, visibly excited, judging from what was protruding from his pants. The caption beneath it read: *Always something saucy to catch in Lillysands.*

Estelle turned it over. There was a message scrawled on the back. Estelle hovered the light of her phone over it.

To Alice. Forgive me for last night. I didn't mean for it to go that far. Are we still friends, my gorgeous redhead? x

Estelle frowned. Who would send a postcard like this to Alice? As far as she knew, Alice didn't have any boyfriends. But then, Alice had grown into quite a beauty. After her fourteenth birthday, a few months before Estelle fell pregnant, she seemed to bloom, her body filling out, her hair a crimson cascade down her back. The first time she'd really registered other boys taking notice of Alice had been at Aiden's fifteenth birthday party. It was held on the beach, a local band playing, lots of drink flowing. When Estelle walked towards the crowds with Alice, for once all eyes hadn't just been on Estelle. They were on Alice too. So why should Estelle be so surprised Alice might have been seeing someone?

And yet they told each other everything. Surely Alice wouldn't have kept such a thing from Estelle.

As she thought that, she heard a sound from nearby. She looked into the darkness, heart thumping as she saw something move amongst the shadows.

Or *someone*.

'Hello?' she asked, her voice echoing around the cliff top. But there was no answer.

A ribbon of fear ran through her as she thought of the Polaroid photos. She tucked Alice's box under her arm then stood up, swaying a little, before hurrying up the road in the darkness, searching the shadows for any movement. When she got back, she was relieved to see Max and Autumn were still awake along with a few others.

'More drink?' Max asked her, holding up a bottle.

'Why not?' she said, looking back out into the darkness, heart thumping.

19

The sound of hammering rain woke Estelle the next morning. She flinched, quickly covering her ears with her hands as she turned away from the sound, which seemed to be exploding in her head, yelping when something dug into her hip. She pulled whatever it was out from under her to see it was a glass bottle, the remnants of the liquid within splashing over her chest. She looked around. She was in the Garlands' living room, on the sofa, more bottles scattered everywhere, Autumn and Max snoring on a nearby floor cushion, Peter and Veronica tangled on the other sofa. They all looked older in the harsh reality of day after a night of excess.

Nausea built inside Estelle.

She slowly got up, the room swaying, then ran to the bathroom, retching into the toilet.

'Jesus,' she groaned, wiping her lips with some toilet tissue. She stood on wobbly legs, and looked into the mirror, horrified at what greeted her: bloodshot eyes, short blonde hair standing on end, a grey pallor to her skin. Her stomach turned again as memories of the remainder of the night before accosted her: hamburgers shoved into her mouth. Champagne poured down her neck. Dancing with Darren to nineties music, his hips grinding into hers. Laughing as

212

Autumn stumbled into her cake, sending it crashing to the floor.

And before all that, the figure she'd seen on the cliff, the blood-red sea, Alice's box . . . and the kiss she'd forced on Aiden.

What the hell had she been thinking?

She went upstairs and took a hot shower, cringing each time she thought about her antics the night before. How could have undone all her hard work? Sure, she had some binging episodes before this, but never anything as bad. It made her feel dirty, ashamed. And if anyone found out about her excesses . . . she shook her head. What a mess.

She walked back to her old room. She was reaching into her bag for some clean clothes, when she noticed something tucked into its pocket.

Another Polaroid photo.

And this time the girl in the picture was her.

20

I got too angry when I watched you sleep.
Even circled my hands around your neck.

   Imagined squeezing, squeezing, squeezing.
Skin turning blue. Eyes bulging. Tongue purple
as you grappled for breath.

   But then I stopped myself.

   That isn't the plan. Stupid, stupid, stupid.

   I need to be more controlled. But it's so
hard. You make it so hard for me. I saw you in
the sea with him.

   Teasing him. Tempting him.

   Since when did you turn into such a seduc-
tress?

   But I won't let your behaviour with him rule
my actions.

   And yet it plays on my mind, makes me lose
focus. As you unravel, so do I.

   But I won't allow myself to.

   I have to keep calm. Very calm.

   There is work to do.

21

Estelle reached for the photo with shaking fingers. In it she was slumped on the sofa, mascara over her cheeks, mouth open as she slept. Curled in her arm was a half-drunk bottle of champagne, a smouldering joint next to her. Laid on her lap was a whiteboard with a message scrawled on it.

Imagine if this photo gets into the wrong hands?

Estelle dropped the photo like it was on fire and backed away. Whoever this person was had been there at the end of the party. Or had it been someone who had left earlier then come back once she was asleep? Either way, they'd approached as she was sleeping and put the whiteboard in her hands. In her mind, she ran through everyone she'd seen last night, but she couldn't settle on any of them.

Could she trust *anyone* in Lillysands?

'Idiot, idiot, idiot,' she hissed to herself as she looked out of the window towards the sea. For so long, she'd thought she was in control. But a couple of days in Lillysands and she was back to being that easily influenced *stupid* young girl again. She had to leave. As she thought that, an uneasy feeling filled her. The last time she'd left, she'd had to endure several months of hell. She'd been put into a care home at first, a residential home with a warden and her own room and small kitchen. It had been horrific, all the memories from her last days in Lillysands and the pain of not being able to talk to Aiden crowding into that small room. There had been times when she wanted to run back, especially when she learnt of the money Max had transferred into her account. But shame kept her away. The look in Autumn and Max's eyes as she'd handed the baby over. The horror of Alice's death. She couldn't go back. So she'd kept her head down, buried herself in books. That wasn't enough though. The other kids didn't like it. They noticed the expensive clothes she wore, clothes that had been bought by Autumn, and started calling her 'Snobby Stel', the tension mounting until one day she was set upon by two thirteen-year-olds, room trashed, clothes ripped, shoved against the wall and hit. She was quickly removed four months after leaving the Garlands and placed in a foster home with a young couple new to fostering. 'You're a foster carer's dream now, Stel,' her latest social worker had said. 'Just keep on the road you started with the Garlands.' And she'd tried, really tried. But then six months in, a family friend had come to stay and tried to coerce her into kissing him one night. No one believed Estelle — she'd stupidly cried wolf once before. So she ran away to London, seeking out the chef she'd met with Autumn during their visit to London, sitting outside the restaurant in the rain until she came out. She just wanted a job, she told the chef. She'd wash up, clean the floors, do *anything*. The chef had looked like she might take her up on that offer to begin with. But then she said she'd call Autumn and that was that, Estelle was gone. Finally, she was placed with the Halls who she stayed with until she was eighteen.

Estelle sighed at the memories as she looked around her. She couldn't stay there any longer. She shoved her clothes in her bag along with the photo and Alice's box. Then she shrugged it over her shoulder, jogging down the stairs and heading outside, pulling her hood over her head to protect herself from the downpour. As she walked down the road, she noticed someone in the distance: Mr Tate in his dressing gown, standing outside his cottage in the rain, his phone to his ear, an umbrella in his other hand. He looked panicked, pacing up and down.

Estelle walked up to him. 'What's wrong?'

He looked at her, eyes filled with worry. 'There's been a landslide, our garden's completely disappeared. I'm trying to call emergency services, but reception here is bloody useless and our landline's gone down too.'

Estelle peered towards his garden, shocked to see he was right: it had disappeared . . . and the tree outside the pink cottage had completely vanished, presumably right over the edge. If she hadn't found Alice's box in it the night before, it would have been gone forever.

In the distance, the upcoming festival's white marquees quivered in the breeze. How would visitors take to the news a whole section of the cliff had fallen to the beach just a few hundred metres away from where they would be having fun very soon?

'Jesus, I was sitting out there last night,' Estelle said.

'It happened just now. I heard the racket.' Mr Tate gestured for her to join him under his umbrella as his eyes filled with tears. 'I'm terrified the house will go over the edge too.'

Estelle peered around her. Were they safe? 'We need to get help.' She pulled her phone out to see she had no reception either.

Mr Tate raked his fingers through his thinning hair. '*I knew* this would happen after the landslide last year! It was only small but it took some of our garden, some of the others gardens along this street too. I've been warning Max and Peter for years! Even last night, I went to the party to talk to them about it after seeing the weather forecast for the next few days. But, *Oh no, it would all be fine*, they said.' He threw his hands up, exasperated. Estelle had never seen him like this. He was usually so calm.

She put her hand on his back. 'I'm so sorry, Mr Tate.'

'We've lived here for nearly thirty years,' he said, peering up at the pretty cottage. 'We were here way before those posh new houses were built by Max and Peter. We moved in the day after we married.'

Estelle squeezed his shoulder, her heart aching for him. She suddenly got a memory of the way she'd spoken to him the night before. 'I — I wanted to say sorry, for last night . . . '

He shook his head. 'It's fine. Don't worry about it.'

'Well, I don't think it's safe for you to stay here

218

anymore,' she said, looking up at the black skies. 'If this rain gets any heavier . . . ' She let her voice trail off.

Mr Tate nodded, a resigned look on his face. 'Mary's still in bed, she's very weak.'

Estelle peered in the direction of the train station where she'd been heading. But there was no way she could leave now, however much she wanted to. She couldn't just turn her back on this man and leave him to watch as his house crumbled into the sea.

'Okay,' she said, taking a deep breath. 'Let me go back to the house, see if the landline works there. I'll make some calls and gather some people to help.'

She went to walk back to the house but Mr Tate grabbed her arm. 'I don't want the Garlands and the Kemps in my house,' he said, face angry. 'Only you and Aiden.'

Estelle frowned. 'Is this because they ignored your warnings?' He nodded. 'Okay. But I must call 999.'

She jogged back to the Garlands', letting herself in. Autumn was awake now, making tea in the kitchen, a dressing gown wrapped around her.

'I need to make some calls,' Estelle said.

'What's wrong, darling?' Autumn asked.

'There was a landslide last night. The gardens behind the cottages have disappeared.'

Autumn's eyes widened. 'Holy shit.'

'What's going on?' Max asked as he walked in, yawning.

'The gardens behind the cottages have

219

disappeared,' Autumn repeated, peering out of the window with worried eyes.

'We need to get help,' Estelle said. 'Mr and Mrs Tate's cottage is right at the edge of the cliff, it could go any minute.'

Max shook his head. 'It won't go,' he said firmly. 'It'll be fine.'

Estelle looked at him in disbelief. 'Are you kidding? Their back door opens over the edge of the bloody cliff now, Max. And unless you haven't noticed, the weather isn't going to help.'

He looked at her in surprise. She took in a deep breath then walked to the phone but it too wasn't working. 'Even the landlines aren't working,' she said, shaking the phone about.

Max and Autumn stood in the middle of the kitchen, looking at each other. Estelle thought about what Darren had said the night before. Was Max just thinking about the money he would lose if Mr Tate's cottage did in fact fall into the sea? It would confirm how weak the cliff was ... and therefore, how at risk the other houses he'd ploughed his and Peter's money into were.

'Right, I'm going to gather some neighbours to help get the Tates' possessions out,' Estelle said. 'You both stay here and keep trying to get the emergency services, okay?'

'Of course,' Autumn said, grabbing her mobile phone.

Estelle ran outside, knocking on people's doors and gathering them to help the Tates. As she jogged down the road, she saw Aiden climb out of his car, face wet and hair dishevelled.

'I saw the landslide from my hut,' he said. 'I drove straight up.'

'The cottage gardens have disappeared,' Estelle said, trying not to think about what she'd done the night before. 'The Tates can't stay there any more, it's too risky.'

Mr Tate ran over then, grabbing Estelle's hand. 'Will you go to Mary and help her change? Just put some stuff over her nightie. Everyone else,' he said, shouting at the five or so neighbours with Estelle, 'it would be wonderful if you could help me grab some items from the house?'

They all nodded and entered the house with Mr Tate.

'Just up there,' Mr Tate said, gesturing to the stairs. Estelle walked upstairs to find a painfully thin Mrs Tate in bed. Estelle was shocked. She used to be a PE teacher, strong and vibrant with glossy auburn hair. She looked so different now.

A smile appeared on Mrs Tate's face when she saw Estelle. 'Oh look at you, all grown up!'

She put her hand out to Estelle and Estelle took it. 'Hello, Mrs Tate.'

'Call me Mary!' Her brow creased. 'Does it look bad out there?'

'It's not great,' Estelle admitted as she gathered some clothes from the Tates' wardrobe. 'I'm so sorry this is happening to you.'

Mary's eyes filled with tears. 'We saw the sea turn red last night so knew clay was falling. Geoffrey was going to call someone in the morning but it all happened so quickly. He *knew* this would happen eventually. But no one listened. Only Alice ever seemed to understand.'

Estelle paused. 'Alice?'

'She was doing a project on coastal erosion and landslides for Geoffrey's class, remember? She came here to take samples of the rock. We thought Max might listen to her considering he'd commissioned the building of the houses. Plus he was renting some out to unsuspecting people. But no such luck.'

Estelle frowned. Alice was always so smart and interested in how the world worked. She knew Alice was fascinated by landslides. But to have uncovered all this then go to Max who had dismissed her fears, Mr and Mrs Tate's fears too . . .

'Here,' Estelle said, helping Mrs Tate pull a jumper over her nightie.

'Thank you, sweetheart.' She looked into Estelle's eyes. 'How are you doing now?'

'Good, really good.'

'Oh good. I remember Geoffrey always used to worry about you.'

Estelle avoided her gaze. 'Let's get these on, shall we?' she said, helping Mrs Tate get on a pair of trousers under her nightie.

As she tried to manoeuvre Mrs Tate out of her bed, she heard footsteps up the stairs and Aiden appeared. Estelle tried to compose herself as she looked at him, remembering how it had felt to press her lips against his. But then she remembered the humiliation too at being pushed away from him.

He caught her gaze then looked away, obviously thinking about it too. 'Need some

222

help?' he asked Mrs Tate.

Mrs Tate put her arms out to him. 'You can carry me downstairs. You're a strong lad.'

'Of course.' Aiden walked over and picked Mrs Tate up. 'Long time since I carried a beautiful woman in my arms, Mary,' he said, smiling down at her.

'Oh you're such a charmer, Aiden,' she replied, face lighting up. 'But remember I'm the one who made you do thirty press-ups after I caught you smoking behind the school?'

He laughed. 'Nothing's changed. Let's get you downstairs.'

They all walked downstairs, the sound of sirens ringing out in the distance. Below, neighbours were carrying boxes of possessions: piles of books with battered spines, the kind Estelle remembered from her classes with Mr Tate, and framed photos of the couple on various holidays. They'd never had children, but Mr Tate always said their pupils were enough.

Aiden gently put Mrs Tate down, helping her to stand up, and her husband went to her. They both held each other, eyes brimming with tears as they looked out at their vanished garden.

'This is it, isn't it, Geoffrey?' Mary whispered.

'I'm afraid so, darling,' he replied, his voice breaking.

Estelle felt tears spring to her own eyes. Aiden gently took her hand, his brow creased as he looked out to sea.

★   ★   ★

Autumn threw some bacon onto a pan as Max handed cups of tea out an hour later. They were all sat in the kitchen, still shocked from what had happened.

'Mr Tate told me you knew this might happen,' Estelle said to Max and Peter. 'Mrs Tate mentioned that *Alice* knew as well.'

The atmosphere in the room tensed at the mention of Alice's name.

'Really?' Max responded, looking surprised. 'Nobody said anything to me.'

He was lying. She could see it in his eyes. Lying right to her face. How could she not have seen this side of him before?

Aiden paced the room, shoulders tense. 'We need to do something,' he said. 'The whole town's going to fall apart if we have more landslides.'

'Don't be dramatic,' Max said. 'The town will be fine. Those cottages aren't fit for purpose anyway, everyone knows that.'

Aiden stopped pacing, flinging his hand towards the back garden. 'Is this house not fit for purpose either then? What about the other houses on Seaview Terrace? This isn't just about the cottages. How do you explain losing fifty foot of your garden over the past few years? You need to stop living in denial, Dad.'

Max's face hardened as Peter and Veronica exchanged raised eyebrows. But Estelle was used to seeing the two men argue. Like that first dinner.

'Feet off the table!' Max had exclaimed as they'd eaten pudding.

224

Aiden had shot his father a wide-eyed look. 'But you have your feet up.'

'I'm allowed.'

'Fuck's sake,' Aiden had muttered under her breath.

Max had leaned over the table and grabbed Aiden's arm, glaring at him. 'Don't ruin Stel's first dinner here with your vulgar language.'

Alice had sunk into her fur coat, eyes blinking as she looked between the two of them.

So even rich people are a mess, Estelle remembered thinking to herself. She'd caught Alice's eyes and something had passed between them, a mutual understanding.

Autumn served up the food now and brought plates piled high with greasy sausages, bacon and eggs to everyone, placing one before Estelle.

'No thanks,' Estelle said, pushing it away.

'Come on sweetheart,' Autumn coaxed. 'Please eat something. You must be starving!'

Estelle peered towards the fridge. 'I think I have some smoothies in the fridge.'

Laughter came from the door as Darren walked in, rubbing at his wet hair with a towel, another towel draped around his waist. She hadn't even realised he'd stayed. 'You really don't remember much from last night, do you, Stel?' he said. 'We made cocktails out of your smoothies.'

Aiden's face darkened as he looked between Darren and Estelle.

'What a night,' Autumn said, shaking her head. 'The best in a long time. Honestly, Stel darling, you're the life and soul.'

'*The* life and soul,' Darren said, looking into her eyes.

A panicked thought occurred to Estelle. They hadn't done anything, had they? Her memory was fried after all that drink.

Beside her, Aiden tensed.

'Great, a Garland fry-up,' Darren said, walking past Aiden and slapping his back as he took the stool next to Estelle. 'None for you, Estelle?'

She shook her head.

'Do you remember when Stel decided to become a vegan after doing that farming project at school?' Darren said to Aiden. 'The whole point was it was supposed to make students appreciate the good farming does.'

'You do realise the cottage's gardens just disappeared into the sea, don't you?' Aiden hissed.

Darren frowned. 'What? When did this happen?'

'Just now, darling,' Veronica said.

'Shit. I was sleeping.'

'Jesus,' Aiden said under his breath. 'Stupid is as stupid does.'

Darren glared at him. 'What was that?'

Aiden didn't reply, just glared at him.

Autumn handed Darren a plate of food, her brow creased. Darren bit into some bacon, the oil oozing down his chin. 'All I know is investors won't take too kindly to that if they find out,' he said, grey eyes sliding over to Max.

Estelle looked at the two cottages on the horizon, a whole thirty years of memories soon to disappear into the sea for the Tates. And yet all Max, Peter and Darren seemed to care about was what it would do to the town's reputation

. . . and their wallets too. How could they be so shallow?

'I need some fresh air,' she said, standing up.

Aiden looked into her eyes. 'I'll join you.' They both walked out, Darren's eyes on their backs.

'Jesus, can you believe them?' Aiden said when they got outside.

'I know. They really don't seem to care about the people in the cottages; it's all about the town investments.'

'That's Lillysands for you.'

She looked at him, thinking of the way she'd kissed him the night before. 'What I did last night . . . ' she said.

'Forget about it. You were drunk.'

Yes, she was drunk. But did that mean she hadn't *wanted* to kiss him? 'I know but — '

'I said forget about it,' Aiden said softly. 'You said Alice knew about the coastal erosion issues here?' he asked, clearly wanting to change the subject.

Estelle nodded, recounting what Mrs Tate had told her. Then something occurred to her. She opened her overnight bag and found Alice's box, pulling out the drawing. 'I found this in the burrow of the oak tree, remember we used to store stuff in there? It's Alice's.'

Aiden took it, anger flaring in his eyes as he stared at it.

'I'd thought it was just a sketch at first, but now,' she paused. 'Now I think it has something to do with what's happening here, the erosion of the cliffs.'

Aiden nodded. 'She figured out there was a

227

major landslide risk on the plot where Dad and Peter's development is,' he said with certainty, then put his finger to a number she'd written in one corner. 'Looks like she called local authorities too to get more information. And look,' he added, pointing to a small bit of writing which had been scribbled out.

Estelle peered closer and saw it said: *Cover-up? People paid off by M & P?*

'Jesus,' she whispered.

Aiden's green eyes flickered with anger as he looked over his shoulder into the house. 'Alice thought Dad and Peter covered the landslide risk up so they could continue their development, that they even *paid* the authorities off!'

'Mrs Tate said she confronted Max about it. Do you think your dad knew about this all along?'

'I guess there's only one way to find out.'

He went to walk back inside but Estelle held him back. 'Maybe it's best not to go steaming in there.'

'Why? He's my dad. I need to know.'

'Calm down a bit first. It'll do no use storming in.'

He smiled. 'Have we reversed roles? I used to be the one calming you down when we were kids.'

'I guess we have.'

'You know how I feel then.' He shook her hand off and marched into the kitchen.

Estelle followed.

'Can we talk, Dad?' Aiden asked immediately, folding his arms as he stood in front of his father.

Max looked up from his breakfast as Darren raised an eyebrow.

'You sound very serious, son,' Max said.

'Did you cover up the landslide risk so you could build your development here?' Aiden asked outright.

Darren's brow creased as Max's face grew serious. 'Where's this coming from?'

'Just answer the question, Dad,' Aiden said warily.

Max shot his son a quizzical look. 'That building work took place years ago.'

'Doesn't matter when it happened. Did you and Peter cover up the landslide risk?'

Peter looked at Aiden in shock. 'I had no idea about the landslide risk!'

'Neither did I,' Max replied airily. As he said that, Darren regarded him with hooded eyes. Max peered at Estelle then back to Aiden again.

'You're lying,' Aiden said. 'I can always tell when you're lying.'

Max's face hardened.

'That's quite an accusation, Aiden,' Peter said.

'An unfounded accusation,' Darren added.

Aiden pointed at him. 'This has nothing to do with you.' He turned back to his father. 'So? Why don't you tell the truth for once?'

Darren narrowed his eyes at him.

Max stood up so he was nearly nose-to-nose with his son. 'Don't you talk to me like that,' he hissed.

Estelle felt her heartbeat accelerate.

'Stop it, you two!' Autumn, who had been uncharacteristically silent up to now, said, trying to pull at Max's arm.

But he swept her away. 'Our son is making groundless accusations. I have a right to be angry.'

Estelle walked up to him with Alice's sketch. 'Groundless? Really? Alice knew, didn't she?'

Max looked at the sketch then at Estelle, his eyes glistening with anger. 'Where'd you get that?'

'It doesn't matter,' Estelle said.

'This has nothing to do with you either,' he spat, looking Estelle up and down. 'You come marching back into our lives, not a word from you in years. Think you can be a Garland again — that you ever *were*? Think again. Just because you're a stuck-up bitch now doesn't mean people forget the scum you came from.'

Estelle stepped back, shocked. She stared into her foster father's furious eyes, saw the spittle on his chin, the way his fists were curled. It reminded her of her birth father and made her feel sick.

'Leave her alone,' Aiden said in a low warning voice.

Max laughed bitterly. 'Well, you would stick up for your little girlfriend, wouldn't you?'

Estelle went very still as Aiden blinked.

'What?' Darren said.

'You think we didn't know about you two?' Max hissed, looking between Estelle and Aiden. 'Why do you think we convinced you to get rid of the kid, Stel?'

Autumn marched over to Max, slapping her husband around the face. 'How dare you?' she

230

screamed at him. 'How fucking dare you?'

Peter stood up. 'Okay, I think this is our cue to leave,' he said, and Veronica, who had sat back and watched the scene unfold, stood with him.

But Darren remained seated, looking between Estelle and Aiden. 'You were *fucking*?' he said.

'Come on!' Peter said, grabbing his son's arm and pulling him towards the hallway.

'I'm not dressed!' Estelle heard Darren exclaim.

'You can change in the car,' Peter retorted.

After the door slammed, Estelle turned to Autumn. 'You knew?'

'Of course we knew, darling,' she said quietly.

'Why didn't you say anything?'

'I wanted to, so desperately.' Her face darkened as she looked at her husband. 'But Max insisted.'

'Fucking disgusting,' Max said. 'Not like you've stopped either, I saw you in the sea last night.'

Estelle felt her face flush.

'*We're* disgusting?' Aiden said in a trembling voice. 'You're the ones who were happy to get rid of your own granddaughter, for fuck's sake.'

Max's face exploded with anger and he shoved Aiden up against the wall. Estelle and Autumn darted towards them, grabbing at Max's arms. But Max caught Autumn's cheek with his hand. She stumbled back and Estelle helped her upright, shocked.

'Don't you fucking talk to me like that,' Max hissed into Aiden's face.

Autumn got up, redness blossoming on her

231

cheek. 'Leave him alone, Max,' she said in a calm voice. 'Leave my son alone right *now* then get the hell out.'

Max looked at his wife. Autumn was tiny but she seemed to dwarf his large form as she stood before him. His eyes dropped to her bruise and all the anger seemed to drain out of him.

'You heard what Mum said,' Aiden said calmly. 'Get out.'

Max turned to Estelle. 'I hope you're happy pulling this family apart again,' he said before sweeping out of the house.

★ ★ ★

Estelle sat on the window seat of her old room, looking out at the stormy sea as Max's words ran through her mind. She'd thought Max was a good man, he'd saved her when she was a teenager. But had that all been a sham? Had he *always* thought she was 'scum'? Even when he'd held her after she'd fallen off her bike and broken her wrist? Or when he'd wiped the tears from her eyes when yet another birthday went by with no card from her own father?

She wrapped her arms around herself. All her memories of the time she'd spent here felt fake now.

Her phone buzzed. She quickly glanced at it. Just an email from a friend. She was hoping there might be an update on Poppy from DC Jones. She quickly checked the news but there was nothing about her at all. They'd already forgotten.

232

She was just a runaway girl and the novelty had worn off.

But she was still missing.

'Mind if I come in?' She looked up to see Aiden at the door.

'Sure.' She rubbed her eyes and sat up as he took the chair across from her.

'Mum's pretty upset downstairs,' he said. 'She's worried you took Dad's words to heart.'

'I'm worried about her! He *hit* her, Aiden.'

'To be fair, I think that was an accident.'

'But he didn't blink an eye about it.'

'Mum and Dad are always arguing, don't you remember? She gives as good as she gets. It's the drink, Stel, you know what they're like.'

Estelle thought back to when she lived there. Aiden was right. There *had* been arguments, shattering the silence at night. One particularly bad one had Estelle and Alice running onto the landing, eyes wide with fear as they heard Autumn and Max screaming at each other accompanied by the sound of shattering glass.

'What are you fucking looking at?' Max had shouted up at Estelle and Alice when he'd seen them watching. So they'd both scurried into Estelle's room, covers up to their chins as they endured the rest of the screaming match.

Funny how her memory could be so selective about her time in Lillysands.

'Look,' Aiden said with a sigh. 'You know my dad didn't mean all that, he's clearly still feeling the effects of the alcohol from last night and he says stupid things when he's drunk. Plus you know what he's like about Peter and the

Lillysands set, desperate to impress, desperate to do Peter's bidding.'

'Seemed to me like he meant it.'

Aiden looked pained. 'He loves you, Estelle; like a daughter.'

'I don't know. I'm starting to doubt a lot of things lately.' She shook her head as she recalled the argument from an hour ago. 'Like how could they have kept the fact they knew about us a secret for so long?'

'This is Lillysands, Stel. Lies and secrets.'

'I don't remember it being this bad.'

He raised an eyebrow. 'You've clearly been away too long.'

Estelle turned to look out of the window again. Police were at the front of the cottages, men in rain jackets too, cameras out as they investigated the back of the houses.

Estelle looked up at Aiden. 'Do you think your dad covered up the landslide risk?'

'I hope not. But nothing surprises me anymore.'

Estelle thought back to the way Max had shoved Aiden against the wall. 'If Alice confronted him, he would have been angry with her,' she said. She'd been thinking this ever since she'd seen Max explode with temper earlier. She'd seen what that temper had done to Autumn, she could only imagine what it could have done to Alice.

Aiden frowned. 'What are you saying?'

She held his gaze then shook her head. 'Nothing.' How could she say to Aiden, *Hey, I think your dad might have hurt Alice?* She stood up, grabbing her bag. 'I think it's time I got out of this place. The main reason I came in the first place was to tell you about Poppy.'

'And to try to figure out who'd sent the photo of Poppy,' Aiden said.

Estelle went still as she thought of the last photo she'd got. She didn't want to tell Aiden about it. He'd only ask to see it. She was too embarrassed.

'I'm not a detective,' she said. 'I've tried but I just can't penetrate Lillysands. It's like a bloody clam. I know it's all connected somehow, and I have a feeling Alice is all part of it but — ' She let out an exasperated breath. 'No, it's time to go.'

'Train?'

'Yep. The journey will give me time to think.'

'About what?'

'Me.' She thought of what Mr Tate had said to her the evening before. He was right. She thought she was handling things, had believed it for years. But any hint of stress and she was back to her old ways again, binging, getting sick, pretending everything was okay. She needed to clean herself up and she clearly couldn't do that in Lillysands. It had all started here after all. The first summer when the sun came out, the girls at school all obsessed with being skinny even at just twelve. One girl — another rich kid like Darren — had whispered to Estelle in class that she'd seen her mother get sick after a big meal.

'That's why she's so skinny,' the girl had explained. 'So I started doing it. Honestly, it's the best. You feel all empty and clean after.'

So each lunchtime in the school bathrooms

she'd flushed away all the filth. She'd stopped for a while with Mr Tate's help after he twigged what she was up to. She'd even seen the school counsellor. But then, thanks to Autumn and Max's business dinner parties, she felt more pressure to fit in, to be clean.

When she was placed with her next long-term foster parents, Carol and Justin, things abated for a while. They were the calmest years of her life, a complete contrast to the Garlands: quiet, studious, affection not shown through hugs and kisses but smiles and awkward taps of encouragement on the back. Estelle welcomed it. She needed a cave to hide in and that small house in Ealing with its piles of books and musical instruments was just what she needed. Just the three of them, living together, eating together, quiet, peace.

Each day was carefully planned by the couple, breakfast at the same time, lunch and dinner too. Fish on a Monday, a lean roast dinner on Sundays. Justin had come from a family rife with obesity and heart attacks. Estelle remembered being shocked when she'd met his brother, a man so big he could hardly fit through the door. So all the food in their house was low fat, no sugars, a restriction on carbs, a complete contrast to the Garlands.

Things got so good, Estelle even felt she could work at the patisserie next door in the evenings and at weekends. It was a chance to test her discipline, a test she passed most of the time. But sometimes she would slip into her old ways. There was one time when particularly bad snowfall meant a surplus of leftover cake. She'd had a bad day, some other schoolkids coming into the shop and taking the mick out of her. As she sat there, waiting to close up, the shiny chocolate wafers and succulent cream calling to her, she suddenly rushed at it, gorging herself. The guilt that came after, the nausea and the filth all over her hands and face, was overwhelming. So she'd run to the toilet to throw it all up. But the guilt that followed that was *worse*. So she forced the desire to binge away.

Of course, it wasn't as easy as that. When she failed to get clients as a nutritionist after leaving university, the setback made her struggle at home too, ignoring her carefully planned meal schedule and binging on food before throwing it up. And ever since, it would crop up now and again, the 'friend' she could turn to when things got tough.

But she was getting somewhere with her life now. She was determined to put an end to it once and for all. And being in Lillysands wasn't going to help with that.

She explored Aiden's face, so familiar to her despite the years that had passed. 'It's been good seeing you, Aiden. We'll keep in touch; we have each other's numbers. We'll keep an eye on the news about Poppy too, and if I get to the bottom of the Polaroid photos, I'll call you.'

'And vice versa.'

She tried to explore his face to see if he was disappointed. But he gave nothing away.

'I hope the rock climbing stuff works out for you,' she said.

'And the nutrition stuff for you.'

She raised an eyebrow. 'I'm not so sure after

237

last night,' she said.

'That was just a lapse — you're human. It'll make you more determined.'

'Maybe.'

They stood looking at each other for a few moments. Part of Estelle wanted to hug him but she was worried it would ignite something inside her again and she already knew Aiden no longer felt the same. So she headed for the door, Aiden following. She felt him close behind her as they walked down the stairs, his breath on her neck. She couldn't help her thoughts straying to the night before, the feel of her lips on his . . .

They walked through to the kitchen to find Autumn on a stool, head in her hands, a smouldering cigarette on the side.

Estelle walked over to her, putting her hand on her back as Aiden watched from the doorway. 'Autumn?'

Autumn peered up. Her eyelashes were wet, her cheeks mascara-streaked. It made Estelle think of other times she'd seen Autumn like this after a fight with Max all those years ago.

'You okay?' Estelle asked, taking the stool next to her. She could smell brandy, Autumn's choice of booze, coming off her. She looked at the glass by her side, half-drunk already.

'Oh, just my husband being a complete arsehole, that's all,' Autumn said, taking a drag of her cigarette and blowing it out of the side of her mouth, the smoke swirling around Estelle's head. Autumn looked into Estelle's eyes, her own looking pained. 'He shouldn't have talked to you like that.'

'Does he often get angry like that?' Estelle asked gently.

'More so lately. He's been under a lot of stress.'

'What sort of stress?'

Autumn peered out towards the sea. 'Money doesn't come as easy as it used to.'

'I had a feeling that might be an issue,' Estelle said with a sigh.

Autumn forced a smile onto her face. 'But that isn't something you need to worry your pretty little head about. Look what I found,' she said, gesturing to a box on the side. Inside were photos, the top one of Estelle's first Christmas with the Garlands. She was sitting under a huge tree with Aiden and Alice, a slightly over-whelmed look on her face. It had only been a couple of weeks since she'd arrived in Lillysands, after all. A lot for a kid used to bad memories at Christmas to take in. The festive season just brought excuses for more alcohol and drugs for her birth parents, more time cooped up indoors, more fists clashing and words flashing, her mum's panda eyes bubbling with tears, a smear of red lipstick across her face, the Christmas tree toppled against the TV. Estelle had learnt at a young age to retreat to her room as soon as she could after Christmas dinner and allow the carnage to unfold without her. Sometimes it spilled into her room, the alcohol-fuelled anger directed at her.

'Look at you,' her mum would hiss. 'Dirty little girl, hair a mess, filthy clothes. You ought to take more care of yourself.'

She'd just been a kid. That tangled hair, the

239

filthy clothes — how could she have possibly done anything about it? She'd tried her best, even figuring out how to turn on the taps of the bath to try to clean herself when her parents lay on the sofa in drunken stupors. But the bath had been filthy, the ceramic black from dirt. It was always impossible to feel clean in that house.

As Estelle looked at that first Christmas photo with the Garlands, she remembered feeling truly *clean* for the first time in a long time that day, dressed in the new clothes they'd bought her, cleaned raw by the hot power shower they owned. If only that feeling had lasted . . . now she felt filthy again.

The sooner she got away from Lillysands, the better. She needed a detox when she got home, a proper forty-eight-hour detox to strip all the ugliness from inside her. Her mind started whirring over the ingredients she'd use, each one going through her mind like a calming mantra: Grapefruit. Beetroot and dandelions. Mint . . .

'Look you two,' Autumn said with a sigh as she glanced over at Aiden. 'Regarding what Max said about the two of you . . .'

'We don't need to go over it,' Estelle said, shrugging her bag over her shoulder and backing away. 'I'm going home now.'

Autumn gave her a wounded look. 'No!'

'I have to.'

'Oh darling,' Autumn said, flinging her arms around Estelle's shoulders. 'I'll miss you. You will keep in touch, won't you?'

'Of course.' But as Estelle said that, she knew she wouldn't. It just felt too suffocating, the past and the memories she wanted to forget were too close.

'Let me give you a lift to the station,' Aiden said, grabbing his keys.

'That'd be good, thanks.'

'One more hug?' Autumn said, beckoning Estelle over again.

Estelle smiled and hugged her again. She felt a sense of uneasiness as she hugged Autumn this time, the arguments earlier still tingling.

'Look after yourself, darling,' Autumn whispered into her ear, her voice catching. As Estelle looked into her eyes, she could see Autumn knew this might be the last time she saw Estelle. Her heart clenched. She'd miss Autumn, just as she had all those years ago; leaving her behind had been as big a wrench as leaving Aiden behind.

She extracted herself from Autumn's arms and walked out with Aiden. She took a backwards glance at the house, remembering the last time she'd left. Would she ever come back again? Probably not, she thought.

No, *definitely* not.

As she thought that, she realised it was the same thought process she'd gone through when she'd left after giving birth to Poppy. Hesitation followed by determination.

Aiden drove in silence to the train station, his eyes darting over to her every now and again. When they pulled up outside the station, they said nothing for a few moments.

'I — '

'We'll — '

'You go first,' Estelle said, smiling.

241

'We'll keep in touch,' Aiden said.

Estelle nodded. 'Yes, we will. Thanks for the lift.' She quickly leaned over, giving him a kiss on the cheek. 'Take care,' she said, looking into his eyes.

His face flooded with emotion and he nodded. 'You take care too, Stel.'

It was hard, saying goodbye to him. At least last time, she hadn't had to see the pain on his face.

She let herself out of the car, feeling his eyes on her as she walked away, trying to contain the tears in her eyes.

As she walked into the station, she noticed people milling about. Then she realised why: all trains were delayed by at least two hours because of the weather.

'Great,' she hissed to herself. She walked to a café and found a seat, buying a bottle of water.

'Hello you.'

She looked up to see Darren peering down at her.

'The Jag in for a service?' she asked.

He took the seat across from her. 'Have a client due in, said I'd meet them, but looks like they won't be getting in any time soon.'

Estelle sighed. 'No.'

'So, you and Aiden.'

Estelle didn't say anything; she didn't have the energy.

'Hey, it's cool,' Darren said, shrugging. 'Rather kinky too, if you ask me.'

'Oh please.'

Darren's face darkened. 'And you had a kid

too, hey? What happened to it?'

Estelle tensed. 'Adopted.'

'Thought that might be the case.' He leaned back, stretching his arms behind his head. 'Max lost it a bit back there, didn't he? Said some nasty things?'

Estelle's eyes lifted to meet Darren's. 'It wasn't pleasant.'

'No. But then Max isn't exactly the most pleasant of men. Poor Alice got the brunt of it before, didn't she?'

Estelle's heart started thumping. 'What do you mean?'

'I saw them arguing once, on the beach. Was just a week before she died actually.'

A week before . . . about the time Estelle thought that Polaroid had been taken of Alice.

'What — what were they arguing about?' she asked.

'I don't know the details; all I know is Max was very angry.'

Estelle thought of the diagram she'd found. Was that when Alice had confronted Max about her findings? Had she made him angry . . . angry enough to retaliate?

Angry enough to hurt her?

The thought made Estelle feel weak. 'What do you mean?' she asked Darren.

'He shoved her.' Darren frowned. 'I wanted to tell him to leave it out but I was a kid, not as strong as I am now. She looked pretty scared of him.'

'Jesus,' Estelle said under her breath, remembering what the policewoman had said to her about Alice being hurt before she died.

Darren stood up. 'See, I'm not stupid like Aiden says. I notice things,' he added, tapping his temple. 'And I've noticed for a while Max isn't as chilled as he likes to make out.' He looked her in the eye. 'Good luck, yeah? It's good you're getting out of Lillysands. Just wish I could do the same.'

Estelle raised an eyebrow. 'I thought you loved it here.'

'Why would you think that?'

'You've make a life for yourself here. You had a good childhood.'

'Did I? Just because my parents are well off doesn't mean I didn't have a tough childhood like you.' His brow knitted. 'It's hard being pushed every minute of every day to succeed, you know.'

Then he walked away.

Estelle watched him, not quite sure what to think. Part of her thought it was laughable he was comparing his childhood to hers. But then maybe he was right? Just because she'd come from a deprived background didn't mean her childhood was any worse than those kids who came from a privileged home. With parents like Peter and Veronica, the pressure on Darren must have been intense.

Still, it wasn't quite in the same league really.

Estelle spent the next couple of hours staring out at the increasing rain, thoughts of Poppy and Alice whirring around her mind. Could Max have hurt Alice? Could he have *pushed* her from the cliff? He had a motive. Alice had learnt about the corners he'd cut building the clifftop houses, what a risk it all posed to the town. Imagine if that had got out?

But if Max had killed Alice, could that mean he'd sent Estelle the Polaroids too? And if so, that meant he'd seen or had contact with Poppy at some point after she ran away.

Estelle sat up straighter in her chair. What if Poppy had somehow found out where she was born and ran right here, to Lillysands? She thought of the girl she'd seen in the road, on the cliff. The one she thought was Alice. Could it have been Poppy? Her heart started thumping. Could Poppy have been in Lillysands all this time?

As she thought that, a loudspeaker declared all trains were now cancelled. It felt like fate.

She headed towards the B&B that she remembered. But the sign outside said No Vacancies. She tried the plush new hotel, but that was full too, the frosty receptionist telling her the flooding meant roads were closed and trains weren't running so people couldn't get into the town for the festival.

She looked down at her phone and found herself dialling the number of the one person she wanted to see more than anyone. The one person left in Lillysands who she felt she could trust.

Aiden.

★ ★ ★

Estelle jumped into the passenger seat of Aiden's car, flinging her bag in the back.

'Thanks, I really appreciate this,' she said, watching his reaction. He'd been surprised when she called to tell him all the trains were cancelled and all the hotels were booked up. She hadn't wanted to invite herself to his, especially after the kiss she'd imposed on him the night before. Luckily, he offered, but it had been hard to tell how he really felt from his voice.

Now, as she watched him, he seemed fine. Even smiled.

'No problem,' he replied. 'Don't want you sleeping on the streets. Or worse, at my parents' again.'

She laughed awkwardly.

He looked at his watch. 'How about I cook you a nice lunch?'

Estelle raised an eyebrow.

'Ye of little faith,' he said with a laugh. 'I actually went shopping earlier and have a whole fridge full of fresh fruit and vegetables.'

'If you insist.'

He started the engine and they headed away from the sea towards a set of bohemian-looking terraced houses gathered around a small square. She and Alice would walk past them on the way to school and often talked about renting a flat there together when they were older.

She thought then of what Darren had told her earlier about Max and Alice arguing. But she didn't want to spring it on Aiden. He already found her theories outlandish. She'd see how he was later.

Five minutes later, he pulled up in front of a house and they both got out of the car. 'Don't judge me,' Aiden said as he gestured to the overgrown lawn and chipped blue door. 'It's been pretty manic at work and all the rain makes the grass grow wild.'

'I'm not judging,' Estelle replied. 'I always liked these houses.'

They walked down the path. 'I bet your front lawn is immaculate,' Aiden said.

'I don't have one. Front lawns are at a premium in London. I have a roof garden though.' Or, *did* have one, she thought. Maybe she wouldn't if things were really over with Seb. She still hadn't heard from him. And if she did, would she really want to still be with him? Something inside told her no, she wouldn't.

She looked at Aiden. Maybe seeing him again had played a part in that.

Aiden raised an eyebrow. 'Oh, a roof garden, how divine.'

She laughed. He really did seem in a better mood.

They stepped inside, Aiden kicking a pile of newspapers to the side as he led her down the hall. The floor was tiled in black and white, and slightly dusty. Along the white walls of the narrow hallway were drawings of Lillysands' famous cliff and pretty marina.

'Right,' he said, clapping his hands. 'Welcome to my humble abode.'

'How long have you lived here?'

'Since I got married. I bought my ex out. Had to live on baked beans and cereal dinners for a few months. I'd like more time to look after it,' he said. 'But the job doesn't allow for that at this time of year. Tea? I haven't got any green tea before you ask.'

'That's okay. I have some teabags with me.'

He laughed. 'I'll pop the kettle on.'

She followed him into a long galley kitchen with a small round table at the back looking out over a narrow garden that seemed to go on forever. She took a moment to take it all in. It felt strange to be here, in Aiden's 'grown-up' home. All she knew was him in his parent's house.

'Was meant to be the perfect family home,' he said, gesturing for her to sit at the table.

She looked at the table and imagined sitting around it with Aiden and Poppy. She sighed. 'I'm sorry that didn't work out for you.'

He shot her a brave smile now. 'It's fine. It's what's meant to be, right?' He poured some boiling water into a chipped mug for her and brought it over. She got her green teabag out, dipping it in.

'Right,' Aiden said, turning his back to her to hunt in the fridge. 'I better get on with your lunch.'

'Are you sure you don't want me to cook?'

'I think you've done enough cooking. And don't look so worried! I promise you the sea bass will be the best you've ever tasted. Fred the Fisherman told me it's top notch.'

'Fred the Fisherman?' Estelle asked with a raised eyebrow.

'You're doing me a favour anyway,' he said. 'I need to cook more. I tend to survive on microwave meals lately.'

Estelle couldn't help but wrinkle her nose.

'I know you're wrinkling your nose,' Aiden said without turning. 'I can *sense* it.'

She laughed. 'Microwave meals are the devil's work.'

'They're angels when I've been climbing cliffs for twelve hours.' He pulled some items from the fridge.

'I can show you some easy thirty-minute recipes,' Estelle offered.

'Oh come on. You know those recipes take an hour really, they never include the chopping and preparing.'

'Mine really *do* take less than an hour, usually half an hour from start to finish.'

He looked at her. 'You're going to be a saint to cliff climbers all over the country.'

'That is exactly why I became a nutritionist.'

He pulled out a frying pan, splashing some olive oil into it. 'I think your reasons were far more noble. You had a friend with diabetes, right?'

'You know about that?'

'I've been reading your book, Stel. It's really good.'

She felt her cheeks flush. She hadn't realised he'd start reading it so quickly. 'Thank you.'

Estelle stood up and went to get a knife to chop some onions but Aiden brushed her hand away.

'Go sit back down. And you know what? Forget about the tea, have some wine. It's *organic* wine,' he added.

'No,' Estelle said firmly. 'Not after last night's mess.'

'Best cure. Hair of the dog and all that.'

'You sound like your parents.'

He shook his head. 'I'm talking a couple of glasses, Stel. My parents' hair of a dog is a bottle of Bucks Fizz.'

They both laughed.

'No, really, it's fine. But you have one,' Estelle said.

'Must be good to know you help so many people with their health?' Aiden asked, pouring himself a glass.

'I guess,' Estelle said. 'I get lots of emails from people and messages on social media saying so.'

He was quiet for a few moments, just watching her.

'What's up?' she asked.

'Nothing. I just . . .' He sighed, looking down into his drink. Then he peered up at her, his face serious. 'You've turned things around. You've done really well for yourself.'

'So have you.'

'I'm not on Inster and Twitgram though, am I?'

Estelle burst out laughing. 'It's Instagram and Twitter. Where's your phone? Let's set you up. I think a hot rock climber is just what the social media world needs.'

'Hot?' Aiden said, raising his eyebrow. 'I don't think I've been described as that since I was fourteen.'

Estelle's face flushed.

'So, what do I do then?' he said, digging his phone out.

Over the next half an hour, as the sea bass

cooked in the oven, Estelle helped set Aiden up on Instagram.

When the food was ready, Estelle organised it on a plate for him. 'Needs to look pretty.' And they took a photo, uploading it to their respective accounts.

'This is delicious,' she said as she had her first taste. 'I was genuinely worried when you said you were going to cook; I remember the raw egg milkshakes you'd make me back in the day.'

Aiden smiled to himself. 'I never had a chance to learn! You know what my mum's like — I'm not allowed to lift a finger. I couldn't even make pasta when I moved out. My ex couldn't believe it when we got a place together. If only Mum had given me a little more independence.' He shrugged.

'You're blaming your mum for your divorce?'

He smiled wryly. 'You know what I mean.'

'I do.' She thought of her own childhood, picking at the leftovers of a stale takeaway as her parents slept off another party.

'Estelle will get fat if all she has is takeaways,' she remembered her social worker warning her mother during visits. Maybe Aiden was right, parents — and social workers with comments like that — were the root of everything.

'Sorry,' Aiden said now. 'I shouldn't moan.'

'Yeah, you were lucky.'

'It must have been tough with your parents?'

'They loved me, in their way.' Did she really believe this, though? It was the line trotted out by her social workers; a line to make her feel better. But the way her parents treated her, how

251

could that be described as love?

'Not noticing a three-year-old leave the house in the dark with no shoes on is love?' he asked, remembering one of the stories she'd once told him.

'They didn't express love the way we do,' Estelle said. 'Love means different things to different people.'

'Do you love them?'

'When Mum died — '

Aiden's eyes widened. 'She'd dead?'

Estelle nodded. 'Two years ago.'

He put his hand on hers. 'I'm sorry.'

She kept her eyes on the table, taking comfort from the warmth of his hand over hers.

'She was found behind a pub, slumped against some rubbish bins. Had been there for hours. Overdose.' She peered up at Aiden, eyes brimming with tears. 'When they called me to tell me, I felt sad. But it wasn't the same way I felt when I learned Alice had died, that was worse.'

She thought of the ashen look on her social worker's face when she'd told Estelle Alice was dead. Two girls ripped from Estelle in two days. Estelle had gone out that night from the care home she'd ended up in, body still aching from giving birth, and walked into the sea. It wasn't an attempt to take her own life. It was to deal with the horrible raging storm of grief inside that needed placating, not just for losing Poppy but losing Alice too.

'I didn't know it hit you that hard,' Aiden said.

'Of course it did! I loved Alice like a sister.

252

And — and I felt so guilty.'

'Guilty?' Aiden said. 'You don't have anything to feel guilty about, do you?'

'I — I should've realised what was going on in her mind. I should have stopped her.'

They looked into each other's eyes, both of them filling with tears.

Then Estelle saw movement out in the garden behind him — a figure darting away.

'Poppy?' she said, standing up and running to the back door, yanking it open and staring out into the rain. 'Poppy!' she shouted again. But the figure had disappeared.

Aiden stood with her, staring out in the garden. 'Why are you calling for Poppy?' he asked.

'I — I thought I saw someone out there,' Estelle said. 'A girl, like the girl I saw on the road yesterday and on the cliff last night. I thought it was Alice but — '

'Alice? What are you talking about, Stel?' He was looking at her like she was mad.

'What if Poppy is right here in Lillysands? If your dad was the one who took the Polaroid photos of her — '

'My *dad*?'

Estelle sighed. 'I discovered your dad and Alice had an argument before she died, possibly about what she'd learnt about the development.'

Aiden frowned. 'Jesus. Who told you this?'

'Darren.'

He shot her a cynical look. 'And you believed him?'

'Why not? What does he have to gain by telling me that?'

253

'*You.*'

Estelle laughed. 'Don't be silly.'

'It's true! If he can be seen to be helping you, maybe he can get into your good books. No coincidence he tells you that after overhearing our big family argument.' His jaw clenched. 'Do *not* trust anything Darren says.'

'I never got a chance to tell you this, but I spoke to the policewoman who dealt with Alice's case. She backed up what Darren said. She told me Alice was hurt before she died.'

'What do you mean 'hurt'?'

'She wouldn't say. Just that Alice came to the police, that she was scared.'

'And you think my dad did it?'

'I saw how violent he got with you! Maybe — maybe he even pushed Alice off the cliff?'

Aiden turned away, raking his hands through his hair.

'I know this sounds mad!' Estelle exclaimed. 'But think about it for a moment. And — and what about the Polaroids I've been sent?' she added, voicing thoughts that she'd been contending with over the past few hours.

Aiden turned towards her. 'What are you saying?'

'What if Max sent them? He has motive. You heard what your mum said about them not having any money. Poppy's parents are rich. That article in *The Times* mentioned the size of my advance. If Max tracked down where Poppy was living, then he could have coerced her into coming here, taken those photos to blackmail me, her parents. For all I know they received photos too!'

254

Aiden put his hands up. 'Woah, wait a minute! Have you received a ransom demand?'

'Not yet,' she said.

Aiden sighed. 'My dad might be a wanker, Stel, but he did not kill Alice, he does *not* have Poppy holed up somewhere.'

Estelle went to the window and looked out. 'Call me mad, but something in my gut tells me Poppy is in danger. It might have started off with her simply running away. But it's developed into something else now. Whoever has her — Max, *anyone* — they could be moments away from us right now, enjoying their little game and — ' She stopped talking, slowly looking down at her feet. Hadn't Max said Aiden had a cellar which was damp after being flooded?

A cellar where Aiden could keep a young girl safe and quiet.

His young girl.

22

This morning I wondered, for the first time, if I'd gone too far.

And all because I was beginning to be pulled back in by you.

I started feeling guilty. Started thinking my suspicions about you were wrong, and you were right.

But I am right. You are asking too many questions, trying to destroy the town and the people I love.

It has to end. And for it to end, I have to stop letting my emotions cloud my judgement.

I've been right at the bottom, so have you.

Maybe in different ways, different circumstances. But I have been there, you know, looking up, desperate for someone, anyone, to save me.

And I was saved, as you were too. We both dragged ourselves up, didn't we?

But you seem to want to fall again, destroy all that has been given to you.

What if you want to take me with you?

No. I won't let you drag me back down there again.

So that's it, no more guilt, no more allowing myself to be deceived by you.

This is serious now. Time to dig deep.

23

Estelle slowly looked up at Aiden. 'Did you know about Poppy before I told you?'

'What?'

'Just answer the question, Aiden.'

He went to take her hand. 'Estelle, what's this about?'

She shoved his hand away, backing away and nearly stumbling over the chair behind her. 'You were angry I'd kept her a secret,' she said. 'If you found out *before* I told you, then you'd be furious.'

Aiden's face paled as it dawned on him what Estelle was saying. 'So furious I'd kidnap my own *daughter?*'

'Maybe.' Her voice faltered. Was she really accusing Aiden of this?

But wouldn't it make sense? If anyone had a reason to hate her, it was Aiden.

She looked towards the door next to the cooker. Did it go down to the cellar? Only one way to find out. She marched towards it.

'What are you doing?' Aiden asked.

'Checking,' she said, pulling the handle down and opening it.

Aiden stayed where he was, arms crossed as he watched her. She didn't want to believe it. But what if the truth had been staring her in the face all along?

She found the light switch, flipping it on. Light

flooded the cellar. She jogged down the stairs. 'Hello?' she asked, heart thumping as she explored the large space. There were lots of cardboard boxes down there, an old pedal bike, tools and paint.

But there was no one there. No Poppy.

She stood in the darkness, taking deep breaths. What had she been thinking?

'So?' Aiden called down to her.

She walked back up to the kitchen and slumped down on a chair. 'Nothing,' she mumbled. She peered up at him. How desperate must she be to think *Aiden* would do something like that? 'I'm so sorry, I don't know what I was thinking.'

'I can't believe you really thought I'd kidnap my own daughter,' Aiden said. 'Don't you trust me?'

'I — I don't know what's got into me,' she said. 'I shouldn't have accused you, I'm sorry.'

His face flickered with anger then he sighed, the anger suddenly gone. 'I know you find it hard to trust people,' Aiden said softly. 'But I'm not your parents, Stel. What they did to you, especially on that day — ' He crouched down in front of her, taking her hand. 'It wasn't the norm, you know that, don't you?'

She dropped her head, more tears falling down her cheeks. 'I'm exhausted with it all. I just want Poppy to be safe . . . and — and I want Alice to be alive. I've made a mess of everything. I want to go back in time and keep them both wrapped up in my arms.'

Aiden tilted her chin up, looking into her eyes.

258

'Me too,' he whispered. Then he gently pressed his lips against hers. She froze for a moment, shocked. But then her body melted into him and she wrapped her arms around his neck, returning his kiss with an urgency she thought was long forgotten. He lifted her off the chair so she was on his lap, her legs tangling around his hips, feeling how much he wanted her as their kisses grew more urgent.

She moaned against his lips, moving her hands down to his neck, then his back, feeling the muscles beneath her fingertips. Aiden's lips travelled down her neck, across her collarbone. She looked down at him, her fingers in his blond hair, mind and body stirring with the thought it was Aiden, *her* Aiden.

He paused, peering up at her and she realised his eyes were full of tears. 'Estelle, I — '

Then the doorbell went.

Estelle climbed off his lap and Aiden sat up straight, both of them taking deep calming breaths as they looked at each other.

'I better get that,' he said, standing up and raking his fingers through his hair.

Estelle watched him as he walked down the hallway, mind buzzing with what had just happened between them. She peered at her reflection in the patio doors. Her cheeks were flushed, her lips still held the taste of his, brown eyes sparkling. She looked towards Aiden's front door then to see someone on the doorstop.

It was Veronica. She looked on edge, tired.

'I thought I'd pop by to check everything's in hand,' she said to Aiden. 'What with this weather, I'm worried no one will want to come to the festival tomorrow.'

'Well, they won't if they can't get *into* Lillysands,' Aiden replied. 'You do realise trains have been cancelled, roads closed?'

Veronica frowned. 'I've been assured the rain will subside overnight, so the trains should be up and running by morning, the roads will open too. The forecast suggests it might be dry throughout the morning as well, maybe even some sunshine.' She smiled but Estelle could see the despair in her eyes. 'But what I *am* concerned about is cover in case it *does* rain. If we can make it clear we have marquees, marquees that *won't* go flying into the sea, maybe people will be convinced to come.'

'It's sorted, I promise,' Aiden said. 'They're up and secure already.'

'I know but — '

'Trust me, Veronica!'

Veronica looked relieved. 'I do.'

Estelle's phone started ringing. DC Jones. She quickly silenced it, not wanting to take a call about Poppy with Veronica there. But it was too late, Veronica was peering down the hallway.

'Oh! I thought you went home, Stel,' she said.

Estelle gave Aiden a panicked look and he shrugged. She forced a smile onto her face, standing and smoothing her skirt down. 'No trains.'

'I offered to let her stay here,' Aiden said, holding Estelle's gaze and making her tummy tingle.

'So how's the festival shaping up?' Estelle

260

asked Veronica as they walked down the hallway.

Veronica sighed. 'I'm worried, to be frank. The weather's worse than it's ever been and then with the Tates' cottage looking so precarious . . . I mean, it's truly terrible for Geoffrey and Mary, of course it is!' she quickly added. 'But the fact remains, it doesn't bode well for visitors to the festival if they find out a cottage is hovering on the precipice.'

'Maybe you should cancel the festival?' Aiden said.

Veronica shook her head. 'I've worked too hard to give up on it.' She looked at her watch. 'We have our final meeting soon in the café. You'd be welcome to join us to reassure everyone else about the marquees?'

'I'm sure you'd do a better job than me at reassuring them,' Aiden said, folding his arms to indicate the subject was over.

'Right.' Veronica smiled weakly at Estelle. 'Maybe you'd like to come, Estelle? Offer your publicity expertise.'

Estelle couldn't think of anything worse than leaving Aiden in that moment. She just wanted to kiss him again, feel his arms around her. 'Maybe,' she lied.

'I better go. Lots to do!' Veronica gave a little wave then grimaced at the pouring rain before striding off under her umbrella.

'Veronica is *freaking* out,' Aiden said as he closed the door and walked back into the kitchen with Estelle.

'It's important to her, bless her.' Estelle looked down at her phone. She had a missed call from

DC Jones. 'The officer on Poppy's case just called. I better call him back.'

Aiden's brow knitted.

She tried the detective's number but it was engaged so she left a message. When she put her phone down, she sensed Aiden watching her.

'Look, Stel,' he said. 'Maybe we should slow things down.'

Estelle frowned. 'I wasn't aware we were going so fast.'

'The kiss,' he said, peering at the chair where they'd been tangled up in each other a few moments before. 'It was the heat of the moment and — '

'I get it,' Estelle said, feeling wounded. 'It's fine.'

Aiden's eyes look pained. 'It's not that I don't want to . . .'

'You don't have to explain!' Estelle said, standing up, her face flushing. 'In fact, maybe it's best I don't stay.'

Aiden's brow creased. 'Of *course* you can stay.'

'Do you really think that's a good idea?' she asked, looking into his eyes. Part of her wanted him to say 'It's a very good idea, Stel. Stay!' and she could see the hesitation in him.

But then he nodded. 'Maybe you're right,' he said.

She tried to hide her disappointment.

'Look, I know someone who works at the B&B,' Aiden said. 'They have rooms put aside for staff on late shifts. Let me put a call in, maybe they can squeeze you in.'

'Thanks.'

He made the call and his contact at the B&B managed to find a small single room for Estelle. She pulled her overnight bag over her shoulder. 'Well, I guess this is another goodbye.'

'No way you're walking in that rain.'

'I'll be fine.'

'I'll drive you, I insist.'

A few minutes later, he was driving her through town, his windscreen wipers angrily mopping the heavy rain away. The roads were heavy with rain, people scurrying down the streets under umbrellas, the sea in turmoil in the distance. The atmosphere in the car matched the world outside.

'We're getting flooded every year now,' Aiden said, voice strained. 'It's like Lillysands is sinking. This morning's landslide won't be the last.'

They pulled up outside the small B&B. 'I'll help you with your bag,' Aiden said.

'I'm fine, thank you though.' She put her hand on the door handle then looked at him. 'I feel like we keep saying goodbye.'

He frowned, looking down at his hands. 'At least we're getting the chance this time. We didn't say a proper goodbye all those years ago.'

Guilt whirred inside. 'I know.' She wanted to reach out and touch him but stopped herself. He'd already made his feelings clear and she couldn't face being rejected a third time. 'Well, I might find myself at the festival tomorrow if the trains are still cancelled.'

'If the festival goes ahead.'

'Veronica seemed quite determined,' she said.

'Yeah, maybe.' He examined her face then turned away. 'Hope the journey goes okay,' he said. 'Goodbye, Estelle.'

'Bye, Aiden.'

Estelle sighed then let herself out, pulling her hood over her head as she ran to the B&B. She paused at the entrance, watching Aiden drive away and wondering if she'd see or talk to him again. The fact was, Poppy was still missing so they probably would need to stay in touch. They were in this together, even if he didn't believe her yet.

She walked to reception and checked in. Afterwards she tried DC Jones again but still got his voicemail. As she was about to head upstairs, she noticed Mr Tate sitting in the small bar, head down as he nursed a cup of tea.

She walked over. 'Mr Tate?'

He peered up. 'What are you doing here?'

'Trains all cancelled.'

'Not staying at the Garlands' then?'

'I couldn't face being there another night,' she said.

He raised an eyebrow. 'Come join me, have a cuppa.'

She took the chair across from him, leaning back and closing her eyes.

'Been quite a day, hasn't it?' he said.

'Not compared to the day you must be having. Is Mary upstairs?'

Mr Tate nodded.

'What are you going to do?' Estelle asked.

'We'll find somewhere new.'

'I'm really sorry.'

He shrugged. 'I knew it was coming.'

'Aiden and I confronted Max about it all.'

He smiled. 'Good for you. What did he have to say for himself?'

'Not much. Well, that's if you count shoving Aiden up against a wall and having a go at *me* not much.'

Mr Tate sighed. 'Yes, Max has always had an issue with his temper.'

'What do you mean?' Estelle asked, thinking of what Darren had told her.

'We were in the same year at school,' he said. 'He was always quick to get angry, got himself into fights. I knew to steer clear of him.'

'That isn't the Max I remember,' Estelle said with a sigh.

'Maybe you just choose to remember him a certain way.'

'You might have something there.' She peered out towards the cottages. 'I think he might have hurt Alice before she died.'

Mr Tate frowned. 'Really?'

Estelle nodded. 'When she confronted him about the cliff erosion.'

He looked mortified. 'I suppose I hoped that cliff erosion project I set would lead to more scrutiny of Max and Peter's cover-ups. But I didn't want anyone hurt.'

Estelle remembered that project. She'd thought it was odd at the time, because he'd set it to both Estelle and Alice's class, despite being in different years. After giving them a lesson about cliff weaknesses and landslide dangers, he'd instructed them all to go out locally to find evidence of it.

265

Looking back, it was a clear flag from him that Lillysands was under threat. If his peers wouldn't listen to him, then maybe they'd listen to their clever children — *especially* Alice who was always so convincing.

'So that was the reason you were so passionate about that assignment,' Estelle said now.

He nodded sadly. 'Only Alice really ran with it. Such a bright girl! I'm not suggesting you aren't,' he quickly added.

'No, no, it's fine! I know Alice was particularly clever, we all saw it.'

Mr Tate went quiet for a bit. 'Do you think that's why she took her life? Because of something Max did?'

Estelle leaned forward, looking in her old teacher's eyes. '*If* she took her own life.'

'What do you mean by that?'

'What if she was pushed?'

His eyes widened. 'Are you suggesting Max . . . ?'

Estelle thought about it. It sounded so dramatic out loud. But why not? There was proof he'd been violent. That he was self-centred and highly motivated. And proof that Alice had uncovered something. 'Maybe,' she admitted.

Mr Tate shook his head. 'I can't see that, I really can't. Sure he has a temper, but murder? What possible motivation could he have had?'

'To keep Alice's mouth shut about the cliff erosion?'

Mr Tate looked down at his tea, brow puckered. 'I can't believe Max could be capable of that.'

'I can't believe it either. But Lillysands is a

good place to cover things up.'

Mr Tate's eyes lifted to hers. 'Like a pregnancy.'

Estelle's froze. 'You know? Who else . . . '

'Just a handful of us. I thought you were aware of that?'

Estelle went very still.

He closed his eyes. 'Oh dear. I've put my foot in it, haven't I?'

'How long have you known?'

'Autumn let it slip to Lorraine many years ago, probably during a particularly drunken night. Lorraine told a couple of her friends, then my wife Mary found out. She then told me.'

Estelle shook her head, unable to believe it. 'All this time, you all knew but didn't say anything the past few days?'

'I'm sorry, Stel, I didn't think it was my place to mention it until you did. And with Darren being a big shot in town, I didn't think he'd want it getting out either.'

'Darren?'

'Oh. I presumed he was the father, I know you had a thing.'

Estelle shook her head. 'He's not the father. It — it's Aiden.'

Mr Tate's eyes widened. 'Aiden?' he asked, disbelief in his voice.

Estelle nodded, tears brimming. 'You must think I'm disgusting,' she said, repeating Max's words to her. 'He's my foster brother.'

'Disgusting? Don't be silly, Estelle. You aren't related, are you? You need to stop looking at yourself like this.'

'Like what?'

'Like you're soiled in some way.'

Estelle flinched. It reminded her of what one of her primary school teachers would say to her in front of the whole class when she used to wet herself . . . or worse. 'Estelle has *soiled* herself again.' Her mum would get a phone call and she'd drag Estelle home, shouting at her for being a dirty little girl.

'I thought I was saved when I came to Lillysands,' Estelle whispered. 'But it's all fake. At least when I lived with my parents, it was all laid out on the table. But here the filth lies beneath a glossy surface. All the lies and the fake smiles.' She shook her head. 'I've been sat talking to these people the past two days. No one said anything. Even Veronica and Peter pretended not to know when it was brought up earlier. They're all so good at hiding the truth.' She looked out into the darkness. 'Maybe they've been doing the same with regard to Poppy's whereabouts too?'

'Poppy?'

Estelle looked at her old teacher. 'The daughter of the TV presenter who ran away? She's my birth daughter.'

Mr Tate blinked. 'My God. That's why you're back?'

Estelle nodded. 'And I keep seeing her around Lillysands. I think she might have been kidnapped. That she's being kept here by someone.' She frowned. 'But then I also thought I was seeing Alice.'

He raised an eyebrow. 'Alice?'

'I know. Maybe I'm losing my mind.'

'Your mind's making associations — it's a stressful time.'

'Yes, there's been a lot of stuff going on.'

'You know you can talk to me, Estelle.'

He was right, she could. Mr Tate was always the teacher pupils went to with any problems. And why should that change now? So she explained about the photos.

'And you think someone from Lillysands is sending them?' he asked.

'Yes, I think so. Maybe even Max.'

Mr Tate raised an eyebrow. 'He is rather manipulative. I told him about the landslide risk years ago but he continued to rent those houses out to unsuspecting people. I even think he may have known before he started building the properties, but just ignored it, putting his monetary gain first.'

'That's what I suspect too.'

But did she really believe Max could be behind the Polaroids and Poppy's disappearance? Something just didn't ring true about it. She put her hands to her head.

'You okay?' Mr Tate asked her.

'All this speculating and worrying is giving me a headache.'

He put his hand on her shoulder. 'Then you should rest.' He sighed, peering above him. 'And so must I. I better head back up. You take care okay?'

Estelle nodded. He was right — she needed rest. But as Mr Tate left the room, a shadow fell over her. Estelle looked up to see Alice's brother, Connor, standing above her, his arms crossed, an angry look on his face.

She tried to focus on the boy she used to know, swallowing her fear down. 'Hi Connor.'

'Saw you as I walked past.' He gestured to the seat across from her. 'Okay if I sit down?'

'Sure.' She tried to hide her discomfort. She had no idea why he was there but it still worried her.

He sat down, his bulky frame filling the chair. As she looked at him, she couldn't help but think of Alice. He had the same colour hair as hers, that deep silky red. And his eyes were the same shape, oval and large and staring right into hers.

He raked his hand through his hair. 'Been thinking a lot since you came to visit yesterday,' he said. 'Seemed like you were trying to figure out what happened to Alice before she died.'

Estelle leaned towards him. 'I was. I *am*.'

He peered around him then leaned towards her too, lowering his voice. 'She found some stuff out about Max Garland.'

'About the landslides?' Estelle asked.

'Yeah, she tell you about it too then?'

Estelle shook her head. 'I only found out recently.'

'So you know Max covered the landslide threat up so he could build those poncey houses of his?'

'That's right.'

'Alice tried to confront him about it, even spoke to some other people around the town, councillors and the like. But no one would listen. So she went to a local journalist she found in the paper.'

270

Estelle raised an eyebrow, then smiled. 'Wow, she always was like a dog with a bone when she got something in her head.'

Connor grinned slightly. It made his look less fierce, less angry. 'Yeah, that was Alice for you. After she moved in with the Garlands and got all serious about school and stuff, I saw a change in her. She really started believing in making something of herself.' The smile disappeared off his face. 'She would've gone far if she hadn't died, can tell you that for certain.'

Estelle felt sadness sweep over her. He was right. She didn't really see it back then, Alice's potential. She knew she was clever, inquisitive. But that determination to succeed was very clear now.

'Anyway,' Connor said. 'The journalist liked her story and started asking questions, digging around, according to what Alice told me.' He frowned. 'But then it all stopped.'

'Stopped? Why?'

Connor peered around him again, checking nobody was listening. 'The journalist was fired. Alice thought it was mega weird as he'd got awards and stuff for his writing.'

'So she thought Max had got him fired?'

'Yeah, maybe.'

'Do you remember the journalist's name?'

'Eddie Lazell. He drives taxis around here now.'

'Maybe I should talk to him.'

Connor nodded, face animated. 'Yeah, do it! The taxi place is just down the road, on the left. He might be there, not like he'll be busy tonight with the flooding and stuff.' He clenched his fists. 'It always played on my mind, that Max

271

Garland and his rich buddy Peter Kemp could roll around here in their posh cars, all the time keeping the landslide stuff hidden. I thought about saying something myself, but who'd take a loser like me seriously?'

'You're not a loser, Connor. You clearly have some integrity, which is a lot more than most people here in Lillysands, as I'm beginning to discover.'

His nostrils flared as he looked down at his large hands. 'Yeah, well integrity gets you nowhere here, does it? I know what I am. It's like my dad says, lazy good for nothing.'

Estelle's heart went out to him. Her dad would say the same about her sometimes. If she'd stayed with her parents, maybe she too would still be living at home with them, not fulfilling her potential. She leaned over, grabbing Connor's hand. 'Connor, look at me.' He peered up at her. 'What you're doing now, coming to me with this information, that's not *nothing*. Alice would be proud of you.'

'Not written a book though, have I?' he said, quirking an eyebrow. 'You done all right for yourself. I think Alice would be proud of *you*.'

Estelle moved her hand away, frowning. 'I'm not so sure.'

'You kidding? She loved you, Stel. Always went on about you.' His brow knitted. 'Made me jealous sometimes, how you got to see her all the time when I couldn't. But then, back then, I could see she had a chance at a good life with the Garlands . . . that was until I knew the truth about Max anyway. Dad always treated her like

272

shit.' His jaw clenched. 'I know why, too; Alice reminded him of Mum too much and Dad don't like being reminded of her. So when Alice went to live in that big house, I was happy.' His face darkened. 'At first anyway. Then she goes and tops herself. Why would she do that?'

Estelle followed his gaze towards where Alice had fallen from the cliff edge. 'I don't know,' she whispered.

'She was special, wasn't she, Stel?'

Estelle's eyes filled with tears. 'She was.'

'Too special for this place,' he said, watching people running through the rain. 'A place that chews people up and spits them out if they don't conform. Well,' he said, standing up. 'Better go or my girlfriend'll think I've stood her up. Let me know what you find out, yeah?'

'I will.'

He gave her a quick nod then walked out of the hotel, head down as he stepped into the rain.

Estelle thought about what he had said. If Max had somehow got the journalist fired, that suggested a worryingly sinister side to him, one she'd seen hints of over the past day or two. Was it a side that could be capable of playing games with Estelle? Of sending her unsettling notes?

She needed to find out once and for all.

After placing her bag in the room, she headed out into the rain, pulling her hood over her head. In the distance, the whites of the festival marquees stirred in the downpour. Her heart went out to Veronica. She just couldn't see the festival going ahead if the weather continued like this.

She headed towards the tiny taxi office Connor had mentioned, just a few doors down from the B&B. A bell rang out when she let herself in. It was quiet, empty. 'Hello?' she called out.

She heard movement from out the back. A man appeared with greying dark hair — the same taxi driver who'd given her a lift into town from the train station when she'd arrived. He had a pair of glasses perched on his nose, a crime novel in his hands.

'How can I help, luv?' he asked her.

'Is Eddie Lazell around?'

'Yep, that's me.'

She examined his face, thinking of what Connor had told her. Once an award-winning journalist, now a taxi driver. Not that there was anything wrong with being a taxi driver, but it was quite a contrast. Had Max really snatched his career away from him?

'You gave me a lift the other day?' she said to him. 'My name's Estelle.'

'Yes, I remember.' He peered out behind her. 'Afraid there'll be no driving today, Estelle. I was going to wait it out but the rain's just getting worse so might lock up and head home.'

'Before you do,' Estelle quickly said, 'I was wondering if we could have a chat?'

His brow puckered. 'A chat? About what?'

'Max Garland.'

His face clouded over.

'I hear you used to be a journalist,' Estelle said.

'*Used* to be,' he said bitterly.

'What happened?'

274

He sighed. 'That's a question I've been asking myself a long time. Why are you so interested?'

'I was fostered by the Garlands and was very close to Alice Shepherd.'

His eyes narrowed in curiosity. 'So you lived with Max Garland?'

'Yes, as a child. But — ' She paused. 'How can I put this? Certain things are coming to light lately that are making me see a different side to him.'

Eddie examined her face then walked around the counter, gesturing to the two small chairs on the side. 'Sounds like we need to sit down for this.' They both took a seat, then Eddie turned to her. 'Has Max done something?'

'I'm not sure yet. I can't go into detail. But if you told me what happened to you, it might help.'

He took in a deep breath, taking off his glasses and rubbing them on his blue jumper. 'I was working on a story, a bloody good story.'

'About Max covering up the landslide risk?'

The journalist paused, raising an eyebrow. 'You know about that?'

Estelle nodded. 'I know Alice found out and came to you about it.'

'That's right,' he said, face softening. 'One clever girl, that. She'd even done a little diagram for me. Very determined to make sure the information got out. And I was too. So I started digging, uncovered a few things in the process.'

'Like what?'

'Like Max had been seen having lunch with an official from the environment agency, an official

275

known for enjoying under-the-table bribes.'

'So Max was paying people off to make the landslide risk seem less severe?'

'Yep. It was turning into quite a story.' He stopped, eyes darkening. 'But then it all went to pot.'

'You got fired.'

'Came out of nowhere. The editor seemed reluctant. I knew he'd had his hand forced. Maybe he was blackmailed, I don't know — he did have a penchant for visiting ladies of the night, if you see what I mean.' Eddie sighed. 'But it didn't stop there.'

Estelle frowned. 'What do you mean?'

'I decided to continue the investigation anyway, maybe send it off to a national. But people must have noticed I was still digging. First thing that happened was my membership was revoked from the local gym. Had been going there for years,' he said, peering towards the glass-fronted gym across the road. 'When I asked why, I was told I'd broken membership rules. Bullshit, of course. Then the apartment my wife and I were about to buy in the new complex owned by the Kemps falls through. *Quelle surprise*. I learn later Veronica Kemp had vetoed my application.'

'*Veronica*?'

'Oh yeah. This wasn't a bulldozer operated by one person, Estelle. There were several on board this one. The worst thing was my boy being turned down for a place at the local comprehensive.' He shook his head, eyes flashing with anger. 'No way that was right. We lived around the corner and he was a good kid! I did some

276

digging and guess what? The head teacher ran in the same circles as the Garlands and the Kemps. See, this wasn't just about Max, Estelle, it was about the whole community turning against me.'

Estelle wrapped her arms around herself, peering out into the darkness. If he was right, that the community worked together to destroy people, what did that mean for Estelle?

What if they were *all* behind the threatening notes?

'Life went downhill after that,' Eddie said. 'My kid got into all sorts of trouble when he had to go to the school on the other side of town — a rougher school. Targeting me, I could handle,' he said. 'But my family? Na, game over. I gave up, let the story go. And they left me alone.'

'That's awful.'

'That's Lillysands for you.'

'Why are you still here?'

He looked towards a photo that was hanging on the wall of a pretty blond woman. 'My wife loves this place. Has family here. I tried to get her to leave. But she'd never leave her parents behind, her sister. I couldn't ruin her life. So I stayed, behaved. And here I am,' he said sarcastically, looking around him. 'Running my own taxi empire.'

'I'm sorry this happened to you.'

He looked her in the eye. 'I don't know what's going on, but don't let this happen to you, okay? Watch your step with this place.'

Estelle opened her mouth but he put his hand up.

'I don't want to hear anything about your

277

story. Not willing to take the risk of pissing them all off again.' He stood up, the look on his face making it clear the conversation was over. 'You look after yourself, all right?'

Then he disappeared into the back office.

Estelle sat still, blinking.

The whole community, not just Max.

As she made her way back to the B&B, Estelle caught sight of the marquees in the distance and a memory suddenly came to her of the last time she went to the festival, the May before she fell pregnant. Pupils from the school always contributed to it and, that year, Estelle had baked some cakes, the first time she'd tested her cooking on someone other than the Garlands. They'd gone down a storm, Autumn's friend Becca who was visiting even asked her to bake some more for a party she was throwing back in London. Estelle had never felt more proud. It made her wonder if she really did have some talent. She'd been so happy at that festival knowing people were loving her cooking, skipping along with Alice.

'Why are you smiling so much?' Alice had asked her.

'It's the first time I've felt part of something.'

Alice had frowned. 'Be careful, you never know how long that'll last here.'

As the memory dissipated, Estelle wrapped her arms around herself. Alice knew. She knew how Lillysands could be, saw it for what it was and yet Estelle had been blind.

And now she was the target? But why, what had she done wrong?

Then something occurred to her. The article that had appeared in *The Times*, the one which Autumn was so proud of, mentioned that Seb's brother Dean was the presenter of the *Outing Rogues* radio show. Maybe Max and the others were worried Estelle knew about the landslides and might let it slip to Seb's brother? It seemed a bit extreme, but then it was clear this community was paranoid about keeping the town's reputation intact.

In the distance, Estelle saw Veronica hurrying to the café with three other women, including the owner of the gym. *Of course,* she thought. Veronica had mentioned there would be a meeting about the festival. Estelle found herself walking out into the rain after them, pulling her hood over her head. She needed to see these people — the stalwarts of the community that had punished Eddie Lazell and were possibly punishing her. She needed to look them in the eyes and see if she could find the truth there.

She approached the café, remembering when it was once a run-down place owned by a pot-smoking hippie. She and Alice would go there and pretend to be all grown-up, sipping coffee and gossiping. It had had a makeover since. The new owner was clever enough to see its potential given that it overlooked the marina. Now its walls were painted pale grey, distressed white wooden tables and benches dotted here and there.

Estelle smoothed her skirt down and planted a smile on her face as she walked in. There was a table of people in there, heads bent over a flyer.

They all looked similar: perfectly highlighted hair, nice tans, colourful but tasteful clothes, and that included the men too.

They all looked up when Estelle walked in, going silent.

Estelle looked at them all, trying to see the secrets in her eyes.

Then Veronica smiled. 'How wonderful, you came! Budge up,' she said to Lorraine who reluctantly shuffled up the bench to let Estelle sit down.

Everyone's eyes drilled into Estelle's, making her feel uncomfortable.

'So tell everyone how you can help, Stel, darling?' Veronica asked, pouring Estelle some tea from a delicate teapot as everyone else around the table exchanged looks with one another.

Estelle cleared her throat. 'My friend Christina runs a lifestyle blog,' she said, thinking on her feet as she watched all the faces around her. 'It's really popular. Part of what she does is recommend places to take kids. How about I put a word in, see if she can rustle up a piece about the festival this evening? She'd share it on her social networking platforms; she has a bunch of followers.'

Veronica looked at her, face full of hope. 'You'd do that?'

Estelle looked into her eyes, unable to wrap her head around the thought she'd been involved in trying to destroy Eddie Lazell's life here . . . and possibly, Estelle's.

'Of course,' Estelle said, forcing a smile. 'I love this place as much as you do. I *want* to help.'

280

Veronica's eyes sparkled. 'That would be wonderful. Are you sure she can do it at such short notice?'

'She owes me.'

Veronica put her arm around Estelle's shoulder and squeezed her. 'It's so good having you back, darling Stel. Here, have some cake. Don't worry, it's made from honey, not processed sugars.'

Estelle went to take some cake then froze. Lying on the table among various festival flyers and documents was a photo of Poppy.

24

Well, I've never seen you look more frazzled.

Dark circles under your eyes. Hair a mess. And your cardigan, inside out!

The others have noticed too. Some of them look uncomfortable about it.

They shouldn't! I'm doing them a favour. They'd want this as much as I do if they knew what you were really like.

You're talking too much, digging too much.

I even saw you talking to that journalist just now. That proves it, you're trying to ruin Lillysands!

It's time for this to stop.

Lillysands needs to come first. I love this place and I'll fight for it.

If that means shutting you up, then so be it.

And I know plenty of ways to make you shut up.

25

'Why's this photo here?' Estelle asked, heart thumping as she picked it up.

Veronica frowned, following her gaze. 'Oh, it's Poppy O'Farrell, the TV presenter's daughter who ran away.'

Panic flooded Estelle. Was this some kind of trap — were they all in on it?

'I know who she is. Why the hell have you got a photo of her?'

The people around the table looked at each other, frowns creasing their perfect foreheads.

'Each year we choose three charities to give proceeds from the day to, remember?' Veronica said. 'Poppy's parents have set up a fund to help runaway teenagers.'

Estelle looked around her at the familiar faces, not believing her words. 'You chose *that* charity, out of *all* the charities you could've chosen?'

'I can't remember who recommended it,' Veronica said hesitantly. 'I think it was a suggestion made via the website? Anyway, what's the problem? It makes sense to highlight something that's in the news right now, helps people connect with it. And, well, I know this will sound cynical, but it might help raise the festival's profile considering her father's a celebrity.'

Estelle jumped up, making the table shudder and spilling drinks. The people around it tutted, mopping up the mess as they raised their eyebrows.

'I don't believe you,' Estelle shouted, the café going silent. 'You chose her charity on purpose to get to me because you know! I'm *sick* of everyone pretending. You *know* where Poppy is. You all know and you're using it as leverage to shut me up about the landslides!'

They all exchanged confused glances. But Estelle knew it was a charade.

'I think that's enough,' Veronica said sternly. She stood with Estelle and took her arm. 'Let's get you back to Max and Autumn, they — '

'No,' Estelle said, pulling her arm away from her. 'I'm not a child any more. I see you all for what you are. It's all just lies and lies and even more lies in Lillysands. Jesus Christ,' she said, waving the photo about. 'Do you think I'm stupid? Admit it, you all know Poppy O'Farrell's the daughter I gave up for adoption and you were discussing your next move in this stupid game of yours. *That's* why you have her photo. That's why you chose her charity. You're taunting me.'

Veronica gasped, putting her hand to her mouth as everyone else's mouths dropped open. They were pretending to be surprised about Poppy being her daughter. But then the people in Lillysands were good actors.

Estelle backed away from the table. 'This isn't a game,' she said, tears falling down her cheeks. 'A girl is missing and you know who's taken her, I can see it on your faces. I *will* find her.'

She stumbled from the café, feeling their eyes on her back.

Then she heard footsteps running after her. She quickly turned, ready to tell whoever it was to stop following her.

But it was Autumn.

'Honey, what happened in there?' Autumn asked. 'I was running late for the meeting and saw you storm out!'

Estelle looked at her foster mother. 'Do you know about my connection to Poppy O'Farrell?'

Her eyes flickered with something.

'You *do* know,' Estelle whispered, unable to believe it. 'You know she's my daughter.'

'Only recently,' Autumn said quickly. 'I saw you on the beach when you left during the party last night and was about to join you when I realised you were on the phone to someone. You — you said you were Poppy's mother, and you mentioned Detective Jones's name. I did some digging, put two and two together.'

'Why not say something to me?'

'I was going to! But I wanted to wait until *you* told me first. I didn't want to force it out of you.'

'Well, it's too late now, most of Lillysands seems to know I had a baby anyway,' Estelle said pointedly. 'I know you let slip to Lorraine a couple of years ago. Then she told a bunch more people!'

Autumn sighed. 'Oh darling. I'm so sorry. I've been kicking myself ever since.'

'Why didn't you tell me people knew?'

'I didn't know what to say. You didn't bring the baby up, so I didn't either.'

'*Didn't know what to say.* Jesus, why can't people be open around here? It's like you and Max knowing Aiden was the father all along.' Estelle said. 'What *is* it with this place and

285

covering up the truth?'

'I'm sorry. It wasn't a vindictive move on my part. I didn't want your homecoming tainted with — '

'Homecoming.' Estelle laughed bitterly. 'Lillysands isn't home, Autumn. It's very far from home. London is my home now.'

Autumn's eyes filled with tears. 'It was home for a while though, a very special home. That's what I hoped for anyway, Stel. I worked so hard to makes sure you felt secure, safe.' She stepped forward, taking Estelle's hand. 'I can see you're hurting, darling. Come back to the house; I'll make you tea.'

Estelle stepped back. 'No, I'm not going back there.'

'Okay.' Autumn put her umbrella up to cover Estelle's head. 'But I'm not leaving you. What's going on, Estelle? You say we're not being open, but what about you? I've sensed it from the moment you got here.'

Estelle looked into Autumn's eyes. Despite her worries and doubts about the community, she just couldn't bring herself to believe Autumn would deceive her. Maybe Max, yes. But not Autumn.

So Estelle told her about the photos.

Autumn put her hand to her mouth. 'Who would *do* that to you?'

'So many people here seem to know I had a baby, it could be any one of them. Hell, maybe it's all of them.'

Autumn examined Estelle's face. 'What are you saying?'

'They all want to protect their interests,' Estelle said. 'Maybe this is a joint venture.'

'Estelle, listen to yourself!'

'You don't understand.'

'Are you well, darling?' Autumn asked, clasping Estelle's hand.

Estelle snatched her hand away. 'I'm fine.'

'No. No you're not. I could see it in your eyes when you turned up the other day, the same look you had when you first arrived here all those years ago. Lost, scared.'

'I'm not lost,' Estelle retorted with frustration.

'Aren't you? It must be overwhelming with the book coming out. And then learning about Poppy. It must have all come rushing back, those old feelings of inadequacy.'

Estelle frowned. 'Inadequacy?'

'Oh darling,' Autumn said. 'Don't you remember what a mess you were with the binge eating? It's never truly gone, has it? Never can really, always just a case of *managing* it. We tried to rebuild the foundations for you — make you strong. But it's an impossible task with a childhood like yours, with what your parents *did* to you.'

Estelle felt herself stiffen. 'You're making out I'm a mess.'

'You're not, you're so *far* from it! But cracks appear in moments of difficulty, they're bound to.'

'Then I'm just like Lillysands,' Estelle spat. 'Built on rocky grounds, ready to fall apart at any sign of stress.'

Autumn sighed. 'Look, you're exhausted,

worried, scared for your daughter. Come back to the house, get some food in you, *sleep*. Everything will feel better in the morning.'

'I told you, I'm not — ' Estelle paused. In the distance, a figure appeared in the darkness, their shadow bouncing off the wet tarmac, long hair lifting in the breeze, hood pulled over their face.

'Poppy?' Estelle called out.

Autumn peered in the direction Estelle was looking. 'What? Estelle, what is it?'

'I keep seeing someone,' Estelle said, striding to the spot where she'd seen the girl. 'At first I thought it was Alice but then — '

'Alice?' Autumn looked at Estelle, concern in her eyes. 'Alice is dead.'

Estelle looked around her. 'I know. I just — ' She took a deep breath, putting her fingers to her temple. 'It's difficult to explain. It's just a feeling. I was so sure it was Alice the first time but now I think it must be Poppy. She's here, maybe being hidden by someone.'

She realised she was rambling, Autumn watching her with a creased brow. She clearly thought Estelle was unhinged, just like everyone else.

'Are you sick again, Estelle? I know it used to make you weak, disorientated . . . '

Estelle backed away, shaking her head. 'I'm not imagining things.'

Autumn put her hand out. 'Please come back to the house.'

'Stop saying that!' Estelle shouted, rain blurring her vision. 'I need to be alone. I don't need you. I'm sorry, Autumn, but — but I don't need you.'

Then Estelle ran away into the darkness.

★ ★ ★

The ringing of her mobile phone sounded like it was coming from underwater. Estelle opened her eyes into darkness. She groaned, pulling herself up and looking at her phone. Another missed call from Autumn. Estelle threw the phone to the side and got off the bed, walking to the window and looking out into the night. The road looked like a river of rainfall glistening under the moonlight as relentless rain pummelled on top of the town.

She'd come straight to the B&B after seeing Autumn. When she'd got to her room, she'd just lay in darkness, staring up at the ceiling, trying to figure out her next move.

If the people of this town knew about Poppy and *were* hiding her, she had to find a way to save her. But right now, she just couldn't figure out how.

Her tummy rumbled. She looked at the small fridge in the room.

'Why not?' she said to herself.

She yanked the fridge door open. Inside was an assortment of fizzy drinks and alcohol. On top of it was a rack of snacks: salty peanuts, crisps, chocolate bars. She gathered several of them up and plucked out a small vodka and a Diet Coke.

Then she went and sat on the bed, staring at the pile on her lap. She needed energy, didn't she?

She quickly opened the packet of peanuts, popping one in her mouth, luxuriating in its salty taste. When she'd finished those, she tucked into a Mars bar, the synthetic chocolate taste bursting in her mouth.

It was only when there was knocking at her hotel door that she stopped. She peered up, chewing on some salt and vinegar crisps, the taste of them suddenly making her nauseous. What had she been thinking?

'You in there, Estelle?'

It was Aiden. She hesitated a moment, aware of the empty crisp and chocolate wrappers around her. She quickly gathered them up and threw them in the bin, before wiping her mouth. Then she took a deep breath and opened the door to him.

'Come in,' she said.

He walked in. 'I heard about what happened at the café.'

Estelle rolled her eyes. 'God, word really does spread around here.'

'Why did you even go there, Stel?'

'Did you know your mum told Lorraine I'd had a baby when she was drunk a couple of years ago? People have known all along, Aiden.'

'Nobody said anything to me,' Aiden frowned. 'But then, I don't have many friends here.'

'They probably knew Poppy was mine all along too. Do you know what it means if they do? It could be *anyone* sending me those photos.' Estelle looked towards the pink cottage. 'Whether Alice jumped or was pushed, Lillysands killed her.'

'Lillysands?'

She looked into Aiden's eyes. 'Yes, and I was

part of that. I wish I'd been here for her then. I could have done more. I *should* have. She was my friend.'

Aiden examined her face then he pulled her into his arms. 'You loved her as much as I did.'

'Yes,' she whispered.

They stayed like that a few moments then she peered up at him.

'I sometimes think . . . ' Estelle's voice trailed off. She should probably keep her mouth shut.

'What?'

She turned away from him. 'Nothing.'

He gently took her chin, making her turn back. 'What, Estelle?'

'I think if I hadn't made such a mess of things back then, maybe we'd still be together. We'd have brought Poppy up together, she'd be safe, we'd be out of this godforsaken town.'

He frowned, his face pained.

'I feel I need to make up for what a mess I made back then,' Estelle said.

His brow puckered. 'How?'

'By doing what I've been trying to do the past few days, I guess. Doing all I can to find my daughter. *Our* daughter. I need to be more honest with myself. I've been pretending I'm something I'm not, I see that now. The healthy eating, even the bloody hair colour,' she said, flicking a strand of her blonde hair up. 'I don't think I've been honest with myself for a long time. I'm going to get back to London and I'm going to start being more honest with myself.'

'That's good, Estelle,' Aiden said softly. 'You can't keep living a lie.'

'Neither of us can,' she said, looking into his eyes. 'What is going on with us, Aiden? What happened yesterday, then at your house earlier . . .'

He swallowed, eyes travelling all over her face. 'It's just always been the way with us, hasn't it? Right from the first time I saw you . . .'

' . . . When you were crying in the cave.'

His face flinched.

'Why were you crying?' she asked softly. 'I never asked.'

'I'd had an argument with my dad,' he said. 'He told me I'd amount to nothing. Any time he said anything to me, it'd be a criticism. Looking back, I could see it was his way of pushing me to succeed. But it was difficult hearing that as a kid, especially as I felt so ignored at it was.'

'You did?'

'I guess Mum and Dad were so wrapped up in the houses, and having Alice to care for as well, then you coming along, I didn't get a look-in.'

'Oh Aiden, I'm sorry.'

He sighed. 'I shouldn't moan. If they didn't do what they did, I wouldn't have met you and Alice.' He smiled. 'I remember that first time I saw you, Stel, marching along the beach all brave and stubborn with that messy brown hair of yours, those crazy tartan trousers. You got me right here,' he said, punching his stomach. 'Honestly, you took my breath away. I'd never seen anyone like you, never spoken to anyone like you.' His face grew serious. 'There's been no one like it since. I've not admitted that to myself before. But I see that now, as clear as day.'

Lightness seemed to spread throughout her to hear him say those words. Could he really mean it? Yes, he did, she could see it in his eyes. The happiness she felt at that was off the scale.

'And . . . ?' she said, daring to hope he might want to kiss her again.

'And this.' He hesitated a moment, eyes exploring her face. Then he pressed his lips against hers. She wrapped her arms around him, tangling her fingers in his hair, feeling the familiar texture of each strand, breathing in his musky scent. They both stumbled to the bed and fell onto it; Aiden kicking his shoes off and pressing his lips along Estelle's neck, her collarbone. His face looked distressed, like he was angry at himself. But his hands and lips were telling another story. Estelle understood; she thought she'd left those old feelings behind, dismissed them as childish. But they were so much more than that; she realised that now.

He ducked his head, nudging the neckline of her top down with his lips. She looked at him, breath coming fast. Was it really Aiden? Or was she dreaming?

He peered up at her, cheeks red. 'You okay?'

'Yes,' she said, smiling. 'Very okay.'

'Good,' he murmured, lips moving against her nipple as she moaned. He gently pulled her skirt up, his eyes on hers as his head dipped down even further, his tongue slipping beneath the lace of her knickers.

As Estelle lay her head back against the pillow, she felt like a teenager again, all her feelings and emotions buzzing at the surface.

26

Sunday, 7 May

Estelle watched Aiden the next morning, her fingers playing with his hair and dancing down his arm. Sunlight streamed through the gaps in the curtains, the rain now gone.

'It's like we've gone back fifteen years,' Estelle said. She felt happy as she looked at him, more content then she'd been for a while. It was like she'd come home. Not here, to Lillysands. It held too many dark memories. No, *Aiden* felt like home. Safe, secure, right.

'No,' Aiden replied, shaking his head. 'We're different people now. This is new.'

'*New*. I like that.' She explored his face and saw Poppy in his long eyelashes, the curve of his cheeks.

She sighed.

'What's wrong?' Aiden asked.

'It feels wrong, being here with you while our daughter is out there, somewhere.'

'Maybe she just ran away, Stel. Have you considered that this theory about her being kidnapped may stem from your guilt at giving her up?'

She moved away from him, looking him in the eye. 'No, it's not about that! I know I said I feel some guilt, but those are just fleeting moments. On the whole, I know I did the right thing, I

294

couldn't have her living the life I lived with my parents.'

'Jesus, Stel!' Aiden said, raking his fingers through his hair in frustration. 'We would have been nothing like your parents.'

'Really? My mum was fifteen when she got pregnant with me. She was in care too. Can't you see the similarities?'

'Yes, but that's where is stops! You're nothing like your parents. And you're nothing like the kid you thought they saw when they looked at you.'

He went to grasp her hand but she pulled away from him.

'This isn't about my parents,' she said, feeling frustrated. After all they'd shared, she'd hoped Aiden would be a hundred per cent on her side now. Why was he still being so stubborn about all this? 'This isn't about *me*. This is about a fifteen-year-old girl who's scared and alone out there somewhere.'

Aiden looked up at the ceiling, grimacing in frustration. '*Nobody* has kidnapped Poppy.'

Estelle swung her legs out from the bed and grabbed her jeans, yanking them on. 'You're in denial, Aiden. You want to believe she's safe so you don't have to admit to yourself the town you grew up in — the *father* you grew up with — might have something to do with your daughter's disappearance. Fine, if you're not willing to help me find her, I can do it on my own.'

Aiden got up too and started putting his clothes on. With them both dressed, the magic seemed to have dissipated. She turned her gaze back towards the gloomy old B&B room now, bed sheets dishevelled. She noticed the holes in Aiden's blue jumper, the circles under his eyes and she caught sight of herself in the mirror, the hair under her arms, too busy and preoccupied the past two days to shave. Her roots were beginning to show too, her skin dehydrated.

This was the reality of her and Aiden, not the fantasy she'd dreamed up of the past. She'd spent so long running away from her past but now it was here, in this room, the true reality of it, the good and the bad . . . did she want it?

Maybe.

She grabbed some deodorant, sliding it on before pulling her top over her head. Then she checked her face in the mirror, smoothing her hair down and rubbing some moisturiser into her skin.

'Where are you going?' Aiden asked.

'I'm going to look for Poppy. I'm going to *physically* walk around and look.'

Aiden shook his head. 'Jesus, Stel.'

She grabbed her phone and purse then went to the door. 'Come find me if you fancy helping to find your *daughter*.'

'Wait, let me come,' Aiden said, fumbling for his jacket.

They both walked out in silence. They wandered the streets of Lillysands for the next twenty minutes, looking for Poppy in Lillysands' alleyways and backstreets. Estelle knew Aiden was only doing it to appease her and that annoyed her even more. Part of her *knew* it was ridiculous. But the other part — her *gut* — knew Poppy was there somewhere.

Soon they gravitated towards what remained of the edge of the cliff where Alice had jumped. They sat down.

Estelle looked out at the sea. 'Alice said something once, about how being part of something wasn't always so great.'

Aiden examined her face. 'That was the thing with Alice. She got under the skin of things. She knew this community for what it really was.'

'And what's that?'

'Rotten.' There was a hardness to his face when he said it that surprised Estelle.

Estelle followed his gaze to the drying flowers at the edge of the cliff. She leaned her head against his shoulder. It was a habit, something she would do when they watched the sun set from this very spot, sat on the dusty windowsill of the abandoned cottage. Now, here they were again but several years older and their daughter missing.

Their daughter . . .

If only things had been different.

'One movement and we'd both go over the edge,' Aiden said.

She frowned. 'That's a scary thought.'

His face hardened. 'Imagine how Alice must've felt to be forced over the edge.'

'I thought you believed she committed suicide?' Estelle said.

'Yeah, sure, physically. But who gave the emotional push? Who drove her to it?'

Estelle looked down into the sea and wondered who would be the one to drive her over the edge.

27

Four steps and I'll be right behind you.

All it would take is one shove and boom! Over the edge you'd go.

Aiden would be devastated though. He doesn't see through your charade like I do.

Like the rest of us do.

Some caught on sooner than others.

I admit, it took me a while. I was beguiled by you.

But not now. Not after I learnt of all the damage you're trying to wreak.

I can't let that happen.

I must hold onto the life I've built up for myself here, the bright future ahead.

It's all at stake because of you.

I need your games to be finished once and for all.

28

Aiden moved away from Estelle, looking at his watch. 'I promised Veronica I'd double-check the marquees.'

Estelle peered up at the skies. The sun was really out now, but dark clouds hovered nearby. 'You think the festival will go ahead?'

'You know Veronica. She'll make sure it does.'

'Just like she made sure Eddie Lazell's life was ruined.'

'Eddie Lazell?' Aiden asked.

Estelle explained what she'd learnt about the journalist and how the community had come together to push him down.

Aiden shook his head. 'I can't believe this place.'

'I know. It just gets worse, doesn't it? Well, I'm not going to the festival, I can't face them all. I might sit here for a bit,' Estelle said. 'I have a good vantage point here in case Poppy turns up.'

'Then after?'

She peered towards the train station. If she didn't see Poppy, would it be time to go home? What exactly could she do if she stayed? What would be the point if there was no sign of Poppy? Nobody was going to open up to an outsider. And that was what she was, wasn't it? An outsider. Maybe that was what she'd always been.

But what about Aiden?

She knew part of her had hoped something

would come of the night before. But as she sat here in the cold light of day, she knew she was being unrealistic. They both had new lives. They couldn't turn back the clock. And being with Aiden would only mean her past would press even closer, a reminder every single day.

No, she needed to go home and get her head in gear, really think about things. Maybe go to DC Jones with all she'd learnt. Sure, he might not take her seriously, but at least she'd know she'd tried.

'I'll go home,' she said to Aiden. 'If the trains are running anyway.'

'So this is another goodbye,' he said, and she thought she could hear disappointment in his voice.

'I suppose it is.'

She wanted him to tell her to stay, or to say that he'd go with her. But he just looked at her, emotions rushing between them. Maybe he also felt that there was just too much baggage. She'd given up his daughter, after all.

As though in answer, he stood up, and walked away without saying anything. But she under-stood. It was too much, all of these goodbyes.

Everything was too much.

She stayed where she was for a while, watching as the final details were added to the festival: stall owners turning up with their wares, a man with a clipboard ordering people about, balloons being tied to some chairs. She looked at the sea, which was a hazy red in areas. She tried to find Poppy amongst the people gathering below, but there was no sign of her.

Estelle took a deep breath then stood up, peering over the edge of the cliff and imagining Alice falling from it all those years before. She shuddered then walked to the road, surprised to find a car parked up.

Darren's car.

He had his window down and was peering out at her through a pair of expensive sunglasses.

'Looks like the sun's coming out for my mother's festival,' he said.

'Maybe not for long,' Estelle said, eying the black clouds on the horizon.

'Yep, and the beach will be sodden after that rainfall last night. Mum won't be happy, she was hoping it would subside. At least the roads have reopened.'

'You seem to turn up a lot in your car when I'm around,' Estelle said, looking at him suspiciously. Did he know everything about her, like the rest of the town seemed to?

'It's a small town.' He paused. 'I heard about what happened last night at the café. Fancy a coffee? Maybe you need a friend to talk to.'

She scrutinised his face. 'Are you a friend?'

'You know I am, Stel. I know I can be a bit of a dick sometimes, but I know when someone's in need of a strong cup of organic coffee and a chat. And I had no idea about you and Aiden having a kid together by the way, my mum told me last night.'

Maybe he was a friend then. Estelle raised an eyebrow. 'Organic coffee in Lillysands?'

'No, but I have some at my place,' he said. 'Come on. I won't bite.'

She looked into his eyes. He seemed genuine.

And maybe he could tell her more than his parents and anyone else seemed to be willing to. This was her last shot then that was it, she was returning to London.

She opened the passenger door of his car and jumped in.

'That cloud really doesn't look too good,' Darren said, arching his neck to peer at it through the windscreen.

'There's bound to be more rain.'

'Mum's convinced the marquees will save the day.'

'Didn't they blow away last year?'

'Yep.' A smile lit up his handsome face. 'It was hilarious.'

She couldn't help but smile back. 'You're cruel.'

'Don't tell my mum I said that,' he said, and raised an eyebrow.

She noticed a slight bruise above his eye. 'Been in a scrap?' she asked him, pointing to it.

He smoothed his fringe over it. 'Boxing. I like to indulge every now and again.'

'Tough guy.'

'That's what I like to tell myself.'

As they passed the beach, Estelle looked out at the calm sea, the sails of ships below fluttering in the warm breeze.

After a few minutes they drew up outside a huge block of apartments overlooking the marina with sparkling windows and a glossy white exterior. They both looked up at it . . . all ten floors of it.

Darren clicked a button on his keys and the double gates opened, welcoming them into an underground car park.

'Very nice,' Estelle commented.

'It'll do,' Darren said, peering at her sideways. He parked up and they both got out, walking to a lift. When they got in, Estelle felt self-conscious, aware she hadn't showered nor applied makeup. But Darren didn't seem to care as he pressed his finger onto a fingerprint reader. 'Security is better this way. No one gets in or out without permission,' he said with a wink.

'Sounds like Lillysands.'

He smiled. 'True.'

The lift pinged when it got to the top floor and opened onto a large penthouse apartment with gleaming white walls and floor-to-ceiling windows.

'Wow,' Estelle said, looking around her.

Darren smiled. 'Still needs some more bits and pieces to make it feel like home, but it's getting there.' He threw his keys into a black glass bowl and led her to an open-plan kitchen. 'So, organic coffee?'

'Decaf?'

'Of course.'

'Yes please.' She needed to at least *try* to return to normal eating today.

She sat on one of the stools and peered out of the windows towards the grey sea.

'You look tired,' Darren commented.

She put her hand to her hair, conscious again of how she must look. 'It's been a tough night.' As she said that, a memory of Aiden's lips on her skin, the feel of him inside her, shivered through her mind. She blushed, looking down at the table.

'So Poppy O'Farrell is your daughter?' Darren asked, pushing the plunger of his coffee maker down. 'Yeah, Mum told me that bit too. She was really shocked.'

Estelle raised an eyebrow. 'Oh come on, they all knew already.'

Darren frowned. 'Mum insists they had no idea. I mean, they knew about the pregnancy, sure. But that was it.'

'It's hard to believe what people say here, Darren. You must understand why it's so difficult for me to trust people in Lillysands?'

'Of course.' The smell of coffee filled the air and he poured Estelle a cup, taking it over to her. She held it in her hands, breathing in its scent.

'I know I seem like I love it here,' Darren said to her. 'But the place does my head in too, Estelle. I'm tied here.'

'But you have money,' Estelle said, peering around her. 'You can leave it you want.'

'My money is all tangled up in my dad's business here. My dad relies on me. If I just upped and left, it wouldn't be fair.'

'But you said your childhood wasn't great. Why the obligation to stay for them?'

His face darkened slightly as he looked down into his cup. 'Despite the pressure they've put on me, they've been there when I've needed them most.'

'Needed them most?'

He looked up, face now unreadable. 'Oh, you know, the usual teenage stuff.'

'You're lucky they were there for you.'

Darren examined Estelle's face. 'But your parents weren't, were they? Obviously, I know you had to go into care as a kid. But I never knew the details of why.'

'It's how you'd imagine really. Two alcoholic parents. Neglect. The usual stuff.' She didn't want to go into the horrible details of the incident that led to her finally being put into care.

'Then you had Autumn and Max. I wouldn't call them teetotallers exactly. But you could never accuse them of being neglectful.'

'True. Though I've seen a different side to Max lately,' Estelle said.

Anger flared in Darren's eyes. 'Yes, me too. I think he really did cover up the landslide risk, you know.'

'You really had no idea he did that?'

'Not at all. It's very serious.' The anger in his eyes showed he wasn't happy at all. It seemed Max had angered a lot of people, just not the core Lillysands set who supported him. Darren forced a smile onto his face. 'But let's stop with the depressing talk. Tell me about your book launch, are you excited?'

The book launch. Right now, that part of her life seemed a million miles away.

'Excited, yes,' she replied. 'Nervous, even more so.'

'Oh come on! You have nothing to be nervous about, your book will be a hit.'

'You can't guarantee that.'

'But that's the excitement, isn't it?' he said, grey eyes sparkling. 'The not knowing. That's what stops so many people from achieving their full potential. Fear. Sure, people like you and I can be scared sometimes, nervous too.' He laughed. 'I was a nervous wreck before the event I threw for those businessmen.'

'You didn't show it!'

'Precisely! We both know how to project the right image. And we do *not* allow our fear to stop us. That's why I have confidence in you, Estelle. And yeah, myself too.'

Estelle couldn't help but smile. He was self-assured, that was for sure. But it was contagious. He was right, wasn't he? She'd battled her way through everything, beaten the fear down, to get where she was. She had to try to keep hold of that; be proud of it; not let herself fall apart like she felt she was in that moment.

That was why she needed to go home, get back on track.

She peered around her. 'Well, you've certainly done well for yourself.'

'Lots of hard work,' he said.

She took in the open-plan living room, a large space with a huge black leather corner sofa and glass coffee table. As she peered closer, she noticed a pile of article printouts lying on top of the coffee table. She realised, with a start, that they were articles about her.

Darren followed her gaze, the tops of his cheeks flushing. He rushed over and tidied them

306

away. 'Just doing some research so I could show you off at that event the other day.'

'Right,' Estelle said, not quite convinced. She took quick sips of coffee, welcoming its strong taste but suddenly keen to get away. 'This is delicious, thank you.'

'Made from one of your recipes.'

'Oh?'

'The coffee bean and cocoa one?' he said.

She frowned. 'Wow, you really have been doing your research,' she said, feeling uncomfortable. 'I thought I could detect some cocoa.'

He smiled, looking proud of himself.

'So, do you really think Poppy might be here in Lillysands?' Darren asked.

Estelle frowned. Why the sudden change in subject? 'My gut tells me she is,' she said.

'And you have a good gut, from what I recall,' he replied, eyes travelling down to her stomach.

She pulled the bottom of her top down, her skin crawling slightly.

'God, sorry, that was crude,' Darren said. 'It's just that I remember thinking that all those years ago when Max held that dinner party for his business associates. Remember that top he made you wear?'

Estelle frowned, confused. 'What top?'

'Don't you remember? Max was desperate to seal the deal. He knew the men were into young girls so got you and Alice to dress provocatively. Alice had the shortest dress on ever. You had a crop top and tight trousers on. Mum was scandalised, but I thought you both looked pretty hot.'

Estelle thought back to the dinner. She *did* remember now. How could she have forgotten? It was a few weeks before she got pregnant. She'd felt slightly uneasy about it. But Max had pitched it as innocent, only clothes, nothing else. Afterwards, she'd been desperate for a bath to scrub away the looks the men had given her. Alice must have felt worse, she'd barely been fourteen.

She peered down the hallway. 'Look, I feel a bit gross. I didn't shower today.'

Darren wrinkled his nose then smiled. 'Use my shower! You'll love it.'

'No, it's fine. I just wouldn't mind splashing my face with some water. Can I use your bathroom?'

'Of course. It's the second door on the right.'

She got up and walked down the hallway then froze.

On the walls were seaside postcards, each one featuring a crude but distinct illustration, mostly buxom women in compromising positions as men gawped at them.

Just like the one she'd found in Alice's silver box.

29

I notice the way you're holding yourself. Arms wrapped around your waist, head bowed — like you're dirty.

You look vulnerable. Scared too. It's endearing really.

You'll be wanting to be leave Lillysands soon. I can see it in your eyes.

I ought to be happy about that. But the truth is, I can't decide how I feel. Something inside me wants you to stay.

And yet you need to leave. You must.

But what to do now? It was so simple at first: a Polaroid photo here, a threatening message there.

Or some kind words, a hug. Make you feel you belong despite all you've learnt.

A few manipulations and untruths. Make you think you're imagining it all.

I know, I know, I was toying with you.

I have to admit, it's satisfying, watching the effect this is all having on you.

How easily you unravel.

This is the true power I've been told about. The ability to pull someone's sanity apart.

But photos and words aren't enough now. I need to do more.

30

Estelle peered over her shoulder at Darren and he flashed her a smile. She returned it weakly then quickly went into the bathroom, closing the door behind her and leaning against it, heart thumping.

Why did Darren have those postcards? Could he be the person who sent Alice hers? That would mean they'd been dating. It wasn't so unbelievable. All the girls used to fancy him, why should Alice be any exception? And she *had* grown to be so beautiful in her last few months.

The only way to find out was to ask him. She quickly splashed her face with water, drying it on his pristine white towel, then opened the door again and marched through to the kitchen.

'That was quick!' Darren exclaimed.

'Was there something going on between you and Alice?'

The smile disappeared off his face. 'Strange question.'

'Not really. It's quite a straightforward one. So?'

Darren seemed to think about it for a while. Then he put his hands up. 'Okay, I admit it. We fooled around a bit. But then I fooled around with a lot of girls back then, didn't I?' he said, a knowing smile spreading over his face.

'What exactly happened between you and Alice?' Estelle asked, trying to get back on track. 'Was it serious?'

His face darkened. 'Hardly. Just a few innocent kisses.' He shrugged.

'But why didn't Alice tell me?'

'She told me you two weren't as close as you used to be.'

Pain stabbed at Estelle's heart.

'Thanks for the drink,' she said, grabbing her coat. 'I think I better go.'

'Why?' Darren said, jumping up and following her. 'You only just arrived.'

'Because I'm sick of people lying to me.' She thought of Aiden, the only person other than Autumn to have told her the truth.

She walked to the lift, jabbing at the button but nothing happened. Of course — she needed his fingerprint.

'Don't go, Estelle,' Darren said, striding after her and grabbing her arm hard.

She turned and looked at his fingers pinching into her skin. 'Get off me.'

He let her go, his face going hard. 'Fine, go. It's not like anything could have happened between us anyway, no chance I'd date a girl like you.'

'A girl like me?'

He looked her up and down, curling his lips. 'Damaged goods.'

He leaned over, pressing his finger into the pad. The doors of the lift pinged open but Estelle stayed where she was, blinking at him.

'Go on,' he said, gently pushing her into the lift. 'Go have a shower, *Stel*.'

The doors closed, her last view of him glaring at her, his hands on his hips. She turned to look

311

at her reflection in the mirror as the lift sank to the ground floor, at her dishevelled hair and creased top. When she got out, she suddenly felt an urgent need to see Aiden. She wanted to feel safe and Aiden made her feel safe. And she was regretting the way they'd left things. She tried to call him but he didn't answer.

In the distance, she heard people laughing.

The festival. He'd be at the festival.

She headed to the beach to see people crowding the front of the cliffs, the two large marquees buffeting in the wind. Balloons featuring the Lady Lillysands' distinctive curves bounced up and down as they were carried along by children. A small food market lined the marina, people walking amongst the stalls, buying fish and chips, and mussels and whelks; the smell of the salty chips drifted over to Estelle.

Whenever this time of year came around in the years after she left Lillysands, Estelle would always think of the festival. The whole town got so excited about it, its flagship event, especially the kids, eager to see what new faces it would bring. Estelle had been nervous at that first festival, the year after she arrived. It wasn't the sort of event her parents would attend, but that didn't stop her worrying they might show up, eyes scouring the crowds as Alice bounced in excitement beside her and Aiden strolled along with his hands in his pockets.

When Estelle watched the crowds now, she tried to see Poppy's face amongst them. Was she here? She hadn't heard from DC Jones that

Poppy had returned home. It had been too long now, surely. The detective seemed worried the last time he called her. What was he worried about? That she might be hurt?

Estelle shuddered at the thought. She wanted to leave. But being at Darren's, realising that even he had weaved a web of lies, made her see she had to get to the bottom of Poppy's disappearance. She needed to know who had been sending the notes and how it was all connected. But she felt like she was banging her head against a brick wall, a brick wall lined by the residents of Lillysands. After everything she'd learnt from Eddie Lazell, it just made it all seem more real. The community was closing in, punishing her. But for what?

When she reached the central tent, she spun round to look at each of the faces. People she had known since she was a girl. Tourists too. And then Veronica standing nearby, looking anxiously up at the skies; Lorraine, ordering people about in the distance; Peter patting a suited man on the back. Shop owners. The vicar. The couple who owned the gym.

What were they hiding?

She noticed Aiden in the distance, hammering something into the ground, face grim.

She walked towards him. Her heart went out to him — he looked so miserable.

'Hey,' she said when she got close to him.

He looked up, surprised.

'I thought you said you were leaving,' he said, examining her face. 'You okay?'

'I was just at Darren's.'

Aiden's hands curled into fists. 'What?'

'Him and Alice had a thing.'

'A thing?' he said.

'They dated.'

Aiden's face grew even angrier. 'What the — '

Estelle noticed movement out of the corner of her eye and turned to see Mr Tate jogging towards them.

'Been trying to find you,' Mr Tate said to Aiden, leaning down to catch his breath. 'Your dad's in hospital. I was just there picking Mary up from an appointment and bumped into your mother. She pleaded with me to come tell you on the way back, she's been trying to call you.'

Estelle's breath caught in her mouth.

'Jesus. What happened?' Aiden asked.

'He was found on the beach last night,' Mr Tate responded. 'Hit his head pretty bad on some rock. Few bruises too. Said he got into a fight with some local kids and slipped over.'

Aiden and Estelle exchanged a look.

'He'll be all right,' Mr Tate said. 'Your mum will be back from hospital soon. She said she'll be at the house. I better go, Mary's waiting in the car.' He turned to Estelle, taking in her dishevelled appearance with concerned eyes. 'You okay, Estelle?'

'I don't know, to be honest,' she replied truthfully.

'The trains are back up and running,' Mr Tate said, putting his hand on her arm. 'I really think it's time you went home, got back into your normal routine.'

He was right, but how could she now?

314

Mr Tate sighed. 'Well, take care, okay?' Then he jogged back off down the beach towards his car.

'I better call Mum,' Aiden said. He got his phone out and dialled her number.

'Mum, is Dad okay?' Estelle overheard him say when he got through to Autumn. 'Yeah, he just told me. What the hell happened?' He listened to his mother then shook his head. 'That's ridiculous. What was he doing on the beach at that time of night anyway? What?' His green eyes flared with anger. 'Darren fucking Kemp. I'm going to kill him.'

He snapped the phone shut then looked around, eyes scouring the beach.

'What's this about Darren?' Estelle asked.

'Mum said Dad was having dinner with Darren last night to discuss some business matters. Can't be a coincidence, can it?'

Fear tingled down Estelle's spine. 'Darren had a bruise above his eye.'

'If he beat my dad up . . . ' He shook his head. 'So help me God.'

'But what motivation would he have?'

'Dad convinced Darren to invest in the rental properties a few years back, told him he was renovating them, making them more attractive to people.'

'Darren didn't tell me that,' Estelle said.

'Why would he? It's embarrassing, he's lost a lot of money,' Aiden said, and Estelle thought back to the conversation she'd had with Darren on the beach at Autumn's party. He'd talked about the rental properties but not once mentioned his involvement. 'Dad covered up about the landslides, didn't he?' Aiden continues. 'Darren must be angry at him as it's all falling apart around their ears now with them being empty so long.'

Estelle thought of the fury of Darren's face when he talked about Max. 'I just can't see Darren being handy with his fists though,' she said.

'I couldn't see Darren and Alice together, but apparently they were!'

As he said that, Darren appeared in the crowd with his parents. Estelle and Aiden instinctively walked towards them. Veronica arched an eyebrow when she saw Estelle approaching. She was wearing a long summery dress that looked strange under the darkening skies, the pinpricks on her arms showing how cold she was in the morning breeze.

'What a pleasure,' Darren said sarcastically.

'Were you with my dad last night?' Aiden asked him, forgoing any platitudes.

Veronica frowned.

'Of course not,' Darren said.

Aiden crossed his arms, looking Darren up and down. 'Where were you then?'

Darren laughed. 'Okay, PC Garland! I cancelled dinner with your dad because I had a better invitation from a particularly gorgeous *clean* brunette,' he said, narrowing his eyes at Estelle. Estelle wrapped her arms around herself. Then realised she didn't want to be made to feel like crap by someone like Darren, so she looked back at him defiantly.

'Why are you asking where Darren was?' Peter asked.

'Dad's in hospital,' Aiden replied, his eyes still on Darren. 'He was pretty badly beaten up last night.'

Peter and Veronica exchanged a look.

'You don't look surprised,' Estelle said. Then something occurred to her, turning her blood to ice. She looked up towards where Alice had jumped to her death — or was pushed. 'Have you got a propensity for violence, Darren?' she asked him. 'Did you hurt Alice?'

'This is ridiculous!' Darren said, shaking his head.

'Just answer the question,' Aiden said.

'Of course I bloody didn't! This is fucking ridiculous. I'm not putting up with this.'

He went to walk away but Aiden grabbed his wrist.

'Did you fucking hurt Alice?' he hissed into Darren's face. 'And did you hurt my dad?'

Darren shoved Aiden away. 'Of course I didn't. You two have officially lost it!'

Veronica's brow creased slightly and Estelle saw something in her face that suggested she knew all about it.

Veronica and Peter marched after their son. 'Were you with Max last night, Darren?' Estelle heard Veronica hiss at Darren.

His cheeks flushed pink. 'What? Of course not, Mum!'

'Don't lie to me!' she whispered.

The tension between them was palpable. What did Veronica know?

Then it occurred to Estelle exactly what Veronica knew.

Estelle chased after them. 'You *knew* Darren hurt Alice, didn't you?' Estelle said to Veronica.

Veronica's face paled.

'It was just the one time,' she said, peering around her to check no one was looking.

Peter closed his eyes, shaking his head.

'Mum!' Darren's eyes filled with alarm as he looked at Aiden.

'I'm sick of it, Darren!' Veronica said. 'You're not a kid any more. You need to take responsibility.'

'So you *did* hurt Alice?' Aiden said, eyes flaring with anger as he walked towards him.

'It was just a slap,' Darren said, backing away. 'I was drunk. She was kicking off about something to do with landslides, she was obsessed, telling me to talk to my dad about it as Max wouldn't listen. I lost my rag. Big fucking deal.'

'He's had anger management therapy,' Peter explained. 'It's under control.'

'Where did it stop exactly?' Estelle asked Darren, looking him in the eye. 'Were you with Alice when she died?'

Veronica and Peter's eyes widened.

'What are you suggesting?' Peter asked.

'You *know* what I'm suggesting,' Estelle said to him.

'Are you implying Alice didn't take her own life?' Veronica asked. Estelle took a deep breath. 'Maybe.'

'I'm sorry, Estelle, but you are completely off track with this,' Veronica said in a shaky voice.

'That girl committed suicide. I can assure you of that.'

'How do you know for sure?' Aiden asked her.

'She tried once before — before she lived with Autumn and Max,' Veronica replied. 'She was just eleven, took some pills. Autumn told me.'

'Like mother like daughter,' Peter added.

Aiden and Estelle exchanged a look. Could that really be true? Why hadn't Alice told them?

'But the fact remains,' Estelle said, trying to process the information, 'Darren did *hit* Alice. And that means he's capable of other violent acts — like kidnapping.'

'Oh God, not this again!' Veronica said, shaking her head.

'Do you own a Polaroid camera, Darren?' Estelle asked, ignoring Veronica.

Aiden tried to put his hand on her arm. 'Stel . . .'

She shrugged him off and glared at Darren. 'Do you?'

Darren laughed. 'You are officially losing it. You think I kidnapped your illegitimate kid?'

'Why not?' Estelle countered. 'I saw all those articles you had about me. Maybe you did it to get my attention? Maybe you're angry I didn't reply to your emails? Maybe you're jealous I rejected you and chose Aiden? Maybe you're in financial trouble too and are planning to blackmail me. I don't know, there are *countless* reasons.'

People around them had gone quiet, looking over with raised eyebrows.

'And you,' Estelle said, turning to Veronica

319

and Peter. 'This explains why you've kept so many things covered up, why other people in Lillysands have. You've been protecting your son. You've convinced others to as well.'

'Do you realise how you sound?' Peter asked her. 'You sound hysterical, Stel. Quite mad. And I'm not the only one who thinks it.' He gestured to the crowds, familiar faces from Lillysands loosing out at her, whispering, some even laughing in disbelief.

Estelle felt tears prick at her eyelashes. She was sick of this, of being suspicious of everyone, of having no idea who was guilty, who wasn't. She was sick of people thinking her mad and paranoid.

She just wanted her daughter safe.

'Come on, let's get out of here, Stel,' Aiden said.

But she didn't move. A mother walked past with her child, a little girl of about five. They stood at the cliff, peering up at the curves of Lady Lillysands. Then the little girl placed a teddy at the foot of the cliff, adding to the growing collection there. It was a tradition each year to leave gifts at the feet of Lady Lillysands, all the items were then donated to a local charity. Estelle imagined doing the same with Poppy if things had been different. She let out a sob.

'What a mess I've made,' she said quietly.

'Come on, Stel,' Aiden said softly. Without looking back, she let him lead her up the hill towards Autumn and Max's house.

When they got inside, she slumped on the sofa.

'Mum said she'll be home with Dad soon,'

Aiden said. 'We can grill him about Darren then.'

As Estelle looked at Aiden, she noticed something behind his head, a crack that extended from the top of the wall to the bottom. 'That wasn't there yesterday,' she said.

Aiden followed her gaze and sighed. 'Yeah, it appeared overnight. Mum texted me about it; I was going to pop over after the festival to look.' He walked over to it, placing his fingers on it. 'Doesn't look good.'

'Could it have something to do with the landslide down the road?'

'Yep, quite possibly. Jesus, this whole town really is falling apart.'

'Just like I am,' Estelle whispered. 'Everyone was looking at me like I was mad. *Am* I going mad? It feels so believable to me, the idea that Poppy is here, somewhere; that there are secrets here. But to everyone else, it seems preposterous . . . even you.'

'You're not going mad,' Aiden said, sitting beside her and taking her hand. 'Maybe you're just looking in the wrong direction? Maybe you need to look at yourself, at why someone might want to do this to you.'

She went silent. He was right, she hadn't really thought about it properly. Maybe she hadn't *wanted* to.

The front door clicked open and they both looked up to see Autumn walking in, Max behind her. His cheek was bruised, his eye swollen. He was clutching his arm close to his side.

'Jesus, Dad,' Aiden said, going up to his father. 'Who did this to you?'

321

'Kids,' Max mumbled.

'Bullshit. Was it Darren?'

Max stared at his son then shook his head. 'I need to rest.'

'Was it?' Aiden asked, following him to the stairs.

'I told you, it was just some kids.' Then Max walked up the stairs.

Autumn shook her head as she watched him. Then she noticed Estelle sitting in the living room. 'Estelle, what's wrong darling?'

Estelle realised she was crying. Autumn hurried into the living room and sat beside her, pulling Estelle into her arms. Estelle breathed in her familiar scent, letting Autumn comfort her the way she used to. She'd never felt more safe than she did when she was with Autumn. Right at that moment, she just wanted to curl up with her and make all the bad stuff, all the confusion, go away.

Autumn put her hands on Estelle's face, forcing her to look at her. 'Look at the state of you.' She peered up at Aiden, who was watching with hooded eyes from the doorway. 'Give us a few moments, Aiden.'

He nodded and walked out onto the veranda.

'Now, dry those tears,' Autumn said to Estelle, using her thumb to wipe Estelle's tears away. 'Veronica called me. She said you and Aiden had argued with Darren. What was all that nonsense about?'

Estelle explained it all: Darren's relationship with Alice, her concerns he may have taken Poppy. 'You're a mother, you understand,' she said when she'd finished. 'I just feel in my gut that Poppy running away wasn't straightforward.' She peered out of the window. 'I *know* she's here, I can feel it.'

'A mother's instinct can't be beaten,' Autumn admitted, squeezing Estelle's hand.

Estelle felt relief. At least someone didn't think she was mad.

'I just want Poppy safe,' Estelle said.

'We all do. She's our family too, a Garland.'

Estelle caught sight of the large crack which stretched across the wall. Here she was, moaning. And yet Autumn's house might be falling apart.

Autumn followed her gaze. 'Looks pretty bad, doesn't it?' she said.

'Are you worried?'

'Not yet.' Autumn put on a brave smile. 'And don't you worry either, sweetheart. It'll give me an excuse to get this whole place redecorated again, won't it?'

'By Becca?' Estelle said.

'You remember her?' Autumn asked, looking surprised.

'Of course. I remember she had really long black hair she'd tie up in a bun, I was so fascinated with it.' She wasn't sure why the memory of Becca was so vivid, she'd only seen her a couple of times, and not for over fifteen years. And yet it seemed like Estelle could remember her perfectly, as if she'd seen her only last week . . .

'Oh, I don't use her any more,' Autumn said quickly. 'I have this fabulous new designer, a gay guy called Diamond. I mean, it's clearly not his real name but . . .'

As Autumn jabbered on about her new designer, a mounting unease filled Estelle.

'I just need to pop to the loo,' she said, standing up.

'Everything okay, darling?' Autumn asked, looking up at her through her heavily mascaraed lashes.

'Everything's fine,' Estelle lied.

She walked quickly to the downstairs bathroom, feeling Autumn's eyes on her back. When she got in, she locked the door and leaned against it a few moments, the sound of her breath filling her ears, her thumping heart seeming to bounce off the walls. Then she got her phone out, her fingers trembling as she googled 'Chris O'Farrell wife'.

As she waited for the results to appear, she held her breath.

Then there she was. Poppy's adoptive mother, Rebecca O'Farrell. Piercing blue eyes. A smiling face. Glossy black hair in a bun.

Estelle put her hand to her mouth. It was her, Autumn's rich London friend, *Becca*. Becca who had lent them her apartment. Becca who had liked Estelle's cooking.

Estelle strode out of the bathroom, heart thumping. 'Poppy's adoptive mother is Becca!' she said, thrusting the phone at Autumn.

Autumn stared at it, green eyes blinking.

'Why didn't you tell me?' Estelle asked, the betrayal stinging. She'd trusted Autumn and yet she'd withheld this huge fact from her?

324

'What's going on?' Aiden asked, appearing in the doorway.

'Your mum's friend Becca is Poppy's adoptive mother,' Estelle said. 'She's the interior designer, remember? The rich one who came on trips from London. The one who went to school with your mum.' Estelle showed him her phone while Autumn remained uncharacteristically silent.

'It is her,' Aiden said. He looked up at his mother. 'Why didn't you say, Mum?'

'Gosh, look at you both, so serious!' Autumn said in an unsteady voice.

Estelle searched Autumn's face. She was smiling, but Estelle could see the panic in her eyes as she twisted her necklace with her fingers against her flushed chest.

'Poppy's adoption was done properly, wasn't it?' Estelle asked Autumn. 'It was all done through the council's adoption services, right?'

'Of course,' Autumn said.

'You're lying,' Aiden said.

Autumn sighed. 'Fine. We arranged it ourselves — what can I say?'

Estelle's heart plummeted. 'What do you mean 'arranged it'?'

Autumn shrugged, examining her nails. 'Becca is infertile; she was desperate for a baby. You didn't *want* your baby, Estelle! She lives hours away so you'd never bump into her. It made sense.'

'Jesus, Mum,' Aiden said.

Estelle sank to the sofa, putting her head in her trembling hands. The feeling of betrayal was overwhelming. Autumn had provided a safe

325

haven for her, had enveloped her in love and trust. But that was all torn apart now. Her whole world felt fragile.

'How much?' Estelle asked, looking up at Autumn. 'How much did you get for Poppy, Autumn?'

'You're overreacting!' Autumn said, trying to put her hand on Estelle's shoulder. But Estelle batted it away.

'No,' Aiden whispered. 'No, Mum, please don't tell me you sold our daughter.'

'Thirty grand,' a voice said from the hallway. They all turned to see Max standing there, clutching his ribs. 'They paid thirty grand. Oh, don't look at me like that, Stel. You benefitted from it too.'

'Benefitted?'

'The five grand I transferred into your account after you left?'

Estelle suddenly felt sick. The room began to spin. Tears sprang to her eyes. She thought that money had been their gift to her, something to help her after she'd left, but now she realised it was guilt money.

'Look at me, Stel,' Aiden said, crouching down in front of her. 'Look at me.'

'My — my child was sold,' she whispered, looking into his eyes. 'I made money from it.'

As the truth surrounded Estelle, she felt herself slipping back to the hours, all those years ago, just before social services finally took her from her parents for good. Her mum shaking with cold in the back seat of the old car Estelle's dad had borrowed. Estelle perched on her lap, a pink blanket wrapped around her thin shoulders. Her mum kept kissing her cheek over and over, smiling a desperate smile with tears in her eyes. Her dad sat rigid in the front, knuckles white on the steering wheel.

'Maybe they won't come,' Estelle's mum had said.

'They will,' Estelle's dad had spat back, looking over his shoulder at them. Then his eye had caught Estelle's and she saw a glimmer of the dad he might have been if he hadn't been ravaged by alcohol and drugs. But then the hardness came back.

'What's happening, Mummy?' Estelle remembered asking.

'Just — just some nice people,' her mum had said, wiping tears from her grimy face. 'Some really nice people are going to take you away for a while.'

'Take me away?'

Her mum had shot Estelle's dad a nervous look, then she'd given Estelle a shaky smile. 'Just some people who want to look after you, baby.'

Those people didn't turn up. Instead, an undercover police officer did. It turned out Estelle's parents had tried to sell her. Five hundred pounds. Just five hundred pounds.

And Estelle had gone and done the same thing to her own daughter.

She started crying, the sobs making her shoulders shake. Aiden tried to pull her into his arms, whispering to her, 'You are not your parents, Stel,' but she shoved him away and jumped up, running outside.

It was raining again, hard; the black clouds that had been hovering out to sea were now directly above the town. In the distance, the festival was being packed up, the revellers finally giving up; even the staunch Lillysands community couldn't stop a storm.

Estelle jogged to the pink cottage and what remained of the garden, and came to stand right at the edge of the cliff, as Alice had once done, rivulets of water falling down her cheeks, soaking her top. She understood now how Alice must have felt.

She *had* jumped, Estelle knew that now.

If she'd tried to commit suicide when she was eleven, as Veronica had said, it seemed more likely it was suicide rather than someone pushing her. She remembered what Alice had said at the festival that time, about Lillysands' goodwill not lasting long. She was so right. Alice was the only one who really saw Lillysands for what it was in the end; saw Autumn and Max for what they were. Why hadn't Estelle helped Alice? Why had she trusted Max and Autumn so much? Alice hadn't been so stupid, she saw the rotten core of the town, of its people, and couldn't take it.

'Estelle?' She looked up to see Aiden jogging towards her.

'Go away,' she shouted.

'She's safe. Poppy's safe!'

'What?'

'Look,' he said, showing her his phone when he reached her, large drops of rain landing on its screen. Beneath them, Estelle discerned a headline: *Breaking news: Poppy O'Farrell*

328

returns home to TV presenter father safe and sound.

'How can we be sure that's true?' Estelle asked, not daring to believe it. 'After everything we've learned? And the Polaroids that were sent to me?'

'Why would they lie?' Aiden said. 'This isn't the only article about it.'

'But — '

'She's safe, Stel!' Aiden said, grabbing her arms. 'Our daughter is safe!'

Estelle tried to match his happiness, but she was overcome with conflicting emotions. Could she have been wrong this whole time? She peered out over Lillysands. No, she wasn't crazy. She could not believe the people here weren't in some way involved.

But the fact was, if the reports were true, Poppy was home; she was safe, and that's all that really mattered. Estelle allowed herself to feel some relief.

'She's safe,' she whispered. 'Thank God.'

Then the ground shifted beneath their feet.

They both froze, looking into each other's fearful eyes.

A loud creaking sound filled the air, followed by the splashing of rocks tumbling into the sea below.

'Another landslide,' Aiden yelled in panic.

They both scrambled backwards as the ground seemed to disappear from beneath their feet. Estelle watched in horror as what remained of the grass broke away and fell into the sea.

'We need to get away from the edge,' Aiden

said, taking her hand.

They ran around the side of the cottage, its pink walls trembling as a deafening popping sound filling the air. Estelle turned as she ran down the path away from the cottage, looking over her shoulder just in time to see the windows of the pink cottage shattering, the walls now shaking violently.

'It's going over,' she whispered.

They stopped on the road, and stared as the walls of both cottages slid inwards, the roof crashing down into the middle. And then all seemed to go still, silent, before first the blue cottage then the pink one slid into the sea before their eyes; the crunching and creaking sending seagulls squawking away, their white wings panicked triangles against the darkening skies.

Estelle thought of all the time she'd spent in that cottage with Alice and Aiden, the memories drifting into the sea with the bricks and mortar.

Estelle looked up the street, watching in shock as the land started falling away from Seaview Terrace too. On the beach below, people screamed and ran through the rain to get away from the falling debris, abandoned balloons drifting up into rain sodden skies.

Estelle kept her eyes on the crumbling rock, tracing it up to one house: Autumn and Max's house.

'Your parents' house,' she said to Aiden.

People were coming out of their homes, flooding the road as they ran to safety. Estelle pushed her way through them as Aiden followed, finally coming to the house she'd once loved, cracks zigzagging up its lilac façade, jagged and cruel.

A window cracked and a hush fell over the people running past. Estelle could see something in their eyes, a sudden realisation that their beautiful town wasn't as perfect as they thought.

A creaking sound pierced the air. The crowds rolled back farther, screams echoing around them. Autumn and Max ran out of the house, faces desperate, terrified as they reached Estelle and Aiden. Estelle couldn't help but feel sorry for them, despite everything she'd learnt. Everyone stood very still. Even the sea beyond seemed to freeze: once wild now calm. Estelle felt Aiden's hand on her back and she moved closer to him.

'It's going over, isn't it?' Autumn whispered.

'I think so, Mum,' Aiden replied as Max pulled her close.

The blue lights of a police van swirled around them; two police officers jumping out.

'Everyone back!' one of them shouted out. 'This house is about to go. It's dangerous.'

Autumn's face went pale. 'I thought I'd live here until I died,' she whispered.

Estelle put her hand on her shoulder. Despite all the lies, she could still sympathise with Autumn. She wanted to say it was only bricks and mortar. But she knew more than anyone how a place could tangle itself into you. Like Lillysands — how she so hated it yet loved it too, pretty ivy needling itself into the core of her.

Autumn leaned her head on Estelle's shoulder. 'I'm sorry,' she whispered. 'We betrayed you.'

As she said it, the walls of the house toppled in on themselves.

Autumn collapsed into Max, sobbing into his chest as tears flooded Aiden's eyes. Then a terrible roar filled the air and the Garland's grand lilac house crumbled into the sea.

31

One month later

'Over there. No, there, by the champagne glasses.' Estelle pointed towards the round wooden table to the right of her.

Her publicist Kim smiled and moved the origami apple. 'Here?' she asked.

'Left a little,' Estelle instructed. Kim moved the apple a few centimetres to the left and looked at Estelle for confirmation.

'Just a tiny bit more', Estelle said.

Kim inched the apple across. 'Now okay?'

Estelle smiled. 'Perfect. Thank you!' Everything was just as it should be.

'Oh, and here's the book you're doing your speech from,' Kim said, handing Estelle her copy with its stickie notes jutting up from inside.

Estelle took it and surveyed the room. It was on the second floor of a vegan restaurant she often dined at, overlooking Borough Market. Dotted here and there were distressed wooden tables adorned with canapes and drinks. Lining the shelves of the four white columns in the room were copies of her book.

Her book.

Finally, the day had come: her launch party.

The scent coming from the food rose into the air, making her tummy rumble.

Her editor Silvia strode in, pulling Estelle into

a hug. 'You look amazing.'

'Thank you, so do you! What about the room, does everything look okay?' Estelle asked, peering around her.

'It's perfect.'

'Five minutes until everyone arrives,' Kim called out.

'Right,' Estelle said, smiling nervously as she smoothed down her white dress, simple and pure, sweeping her blonde fringe from her eyes. She'd had it newly highlighted and the return to her old diet had made her skin clean and clear again. Everything was back on track, and nobody knew any different.

'Do you want a moment alone to take it all in?' Silvia asked her.

'Yes, that would be good actually.'

Silvia and Kim both nodded, leaving the room. Estelle took a deep breath, looking at the food she'd created, the books, and the champagne. This was the sum of her; of what she'd worked so hard to become. She walked around the room, gliding her fingers just above the mini sweet potato burgers and small glass jars filled with rainbow salads; courgette roll-ups and salmon oatcakes.

She passed a mirror and paused, looking at herself. Her hair was shorter, neat and bright, her face looking healthy from her short holiday with her friend Christina. But there were dark circles that hadn't been there two months before; something new in her eyes too, a sadness. She thought of Poppy. How sad she'd appeared when she was dragged in front of the cameras a week

334

after she returned home. Estelle hadn't liked the way her father had gripped her arm to make her change position, the hard look in her mother's eyes. It made Estelle sick to think how unhappy Poppy must be. She still couldn't wrap her head around the fact Poppy's mother was Becca.

DC Jones had told her Poppy was just a typical troubled teenage girl, wanting a little freedom. As for the Polaroids, though Poppy hadn't admitted to it yet, the detective's theory was she'd run away with an older boy. Perhaps that boy had somehow learnt Estelle was Poppy's birth mother — easier to uncover, considering she'd been privately adopted — and had been planning on blackmailing Estelle.

But it rang false for Estelle. Why wouldn't she have received a ransom note of some kind? And why that photo of Alice?

Of course, when Estelle had questioned DC Jones about it further, he'd told her she needed to move on. Poppy was safe. Wasn't that all that mattered? It wasn't like Estelle could do anything about it after all. He'd also made it very clear there was to be no contact between her and Poppy unless Poppy asked for it.

And clearly Poppy hadn't asked for it.

So Estelle had done just as he'd advised, throwing herself into planning for the launch party, taking in the news items about Poppy's return but not dwelling on them too much.

Thoughts of her time in Lillysands still lingered. Autumn had tried to call her, even sent a few emails, but Estelle had ignored them. She'd not heard anything from Aiden. After the

335

house collapsed into the sea, he'd had to be there for his parents. But a look had passed between them as they said goodbye, a look that told her that evening in the hotel was a one-off. It was time to leave the past behind, proper closure, finally. So Estelle had taken the chance to slip away and return to London. She'd sent him an invite to tonight but he hadn't RSVPd, so she was sure he wouldn't be there.

That was a good thing. The Garlands were firmly in her past now, Lillysands too. Even if the people of Lillysands were behind the Polaroids, the fact was, she hadn't received any others and Poppy was safe. Clearly miserable, but safe.

She had to concentrate on throwing herself back into her clean, pure lifestyle, focusing on the book launch and finding a new place. She and Seb had agreed to part ways during a fraught lunch. Estelle had called him on her return and arranged to meet up. Seeing him, she'd felt nothing, such a contrast to the way she felt around Aiden. So she'd suggested they break up. He'd agreed. She couldn't tell if it was what he really wanted, like her he was a master of hiding his true feelings. So now she was renting a place a few miles from where she'd lived with Seb as she searched for a permanent home.

And now here she was. Her big day.

She took a deep breath, smiling at herself in the mirror. 'You've done it,' she said. 'You've really done it.'

Kim peered through the door. 'Ready? People are here.'

Estelle took a final calming breath. 'Ready.'

336

The door opened and guests started pouring into the room: journalists and bloggers, friends and associates. Over the next hour, she moved around the room, speaking to old and new acquaintances, thanking people for coming, and signing books. Every now and again, thoughts of Poppy and those few days she'd spent back in Lillysands crept in. But she buried them deep, along with thoughts of the Garlands.

As Estelle was talking to a journalist, Kim walked over to her and whispered in her ear, 'We're ready for you.' She gestured towards the small stage area with a lectern set up, a pile of Estelle's books on a table nearby.

Estelle took in a deep shaky breath. She might be able to talk to a camera for hundreds of thousands of people in her videos, but public speaking was all together another thing.

She looked towards the corner of the room where all her friends were. Christina gave her a thumbs up. Estelle smiled at her, drawing strength from her presence, then she walked up to the lectern, the book she was going to read from in her hand.

A hush fell over the room.

'Thank you so much for coming tonight,' Estelle said, looking around the room. 'It means more than you know that you're all here to join my journey into the world of pure living.' She paused, raising an eyebrow. 'However, the writing of this book was anything *but* pure. You should see the green tea stains on my laptop from the endless nights I spent agonising over the words to write.'

The room laughed and she felt herself relax.

'It's been quite a journey.' She looked out of the window over the city spires, imagining the sea's whisper a long way away. 'From difficult beginnings,' she said, looking at Louis, the journalist who'd visited her and subsequently published his article, misinterpreting her abrupt ending of the interview for shame about her birth parents. 'Something I'm *not* ashamed to talk about because it's what made me who I am. And now this,' she said, sweeping her hands around the room. 'Look how far I've come. Little old me, shivering in the corner of my room as my parents argued all those years ago. I'd never have dreamed this would be my destination.'

People in the room whooped, others applauding. She'd been nervous about bringing up her childhood, but Kim had convinced her it was the right thing to do after the newspaper interview came out.

She thought of Lillysands' windswept shores and of her daughter. Of course, there were *some* secrets best kept hidden away.

'But here I am, even if I can't believe it. And here *this* is,' she said, holding her book up and giving it a kiss as people laughed. 'A dream come true.'

Everyone clapped and she tried to bask in the glory of it. But an emptiness consumed her. She clenched her fists, willing it away.

Enjoy this moment, she told herself.

'I'd like to read a passage or two if you don't mind, and as I do, these wonderful people will be encouraging you to taste some of the very recipes

I talk about,' she said, gesturing to the serving staff now filing into the room with wooden trays of food. 'That's if you haven't eaten enough of the canapés already,' she added with another raised eyebrow.

The room laughed.

She opened her book to the page she'd marked with a Post-It note.

'So this passage is from my section on pure party food, which seemed appropriate for this evening,' she said, peering up at the crowds. 'You'll have noticed I open each section with a personal anecdote. And this one is particularly . . . '

She paused as she looked down at the page, brow furrowing.

It didn't make sense.

The words she'd expected to be there were gone. Instead, there were the same lines printed over and over, so achingly familiar:

They say you're as pure as the driven snow. But I know you're not.

I'm watching you. I know <u>everything</u> about you.

Watch your back or you might go over the edge.

Imagine if this photo gets into the wrong hands?

Estelle flicked through the book with trembling hands, her breath coming quick and loud, muffling the microphone. The other pages were fine. It was just this one, the page she was going to read from.

Then something slipped from the book. A creased piece of paper, yellowed with time.

Her breath caught in her mouth as she recognised the writing.

Alice's writing.

To anybody who still cares, it began. *The next time you'll see me, I'll be in the sea . . .*

Estelle smothered a gasp then quickly shoved it in her pocket, aware of everyone's eyes on her. Then she looked up at the room, laughing nervously. 'Well, typically, I bring the wrong book with me.'

She looked at the columns filled with her books. Were the same lines printed in those? *People had been reading them.* Surely someone would have said? She peered towards the table of books beside her and grabbed one, quickly opening it to the page she'd been reading, relief flooding through her when she saw the words were as they should be.

Then she flicked back through the doctored copy in her other hand, and something caught her eye. A scribble inside. She opened it to its title page and peered closer.

To Aiden, climbing to new heights. Luv Stel. X

This was the book she'd given to Aiden. His copy was the one she'd marked up for the speech on the train journey to Lillysands. When she'd returned from Lillysands, she'd marked up a second book with Post-its in the same places for the speech . . . the book she thought she had in her hands now.

So why was she holding Aiden's book instead?

As she looked up, she saw Aiden at the back of the room, walking towards the exit.

Ignoring the confused whispers of the crowd, she jogged down the steps towards him.

Her editor stepped towards her and softly grasped her arm. 'Everything okay, Estelle?' she whispered.

'Can you take the stage for a moment,' Estelle said, eyes pleading with her editor. 'I just need to speak to someone. Thank you.'

'Sure. But — '

Before Silvia had finished, Estelle was out the door, and Aiden was waiting for her.

'*You* did this?' she whispered when she reached him. 'How?' she added, looking at the book in her hands.

'You gave me an early copy of your book, remember?' he replied, as people looked over at them. 'Easy enough to have a new page glued in then come here and swap your book for mine, especially when you leave your bag lying about.'

She looked at him in shock. What was going on? Was she losing her mind. 'But — but why?' she asked.

'They're your words, aren't they?' he said.

What did he mean? Estelle examined his face, he looked different somehow from the Aiden from her childhood; from the Aiden she'd spent the night with a month before. The warmth was gone.

'These arc the words you sent to Alice,' he said bitterly.

Estelle's breath slowed, a strange buzzing in her head. She looked into Aiden's eyes.

He knew.

341

32

My stomach is huge now. It seems to swallow me all up.

I feel like I've been trapped in my bedroom for months. Watching Alice and Aiden have fun together made me sick with jealousy, but he's gone now and I feel more alone than ever. And if that isn't bad enough, Alice is making the most of my absence from all the events we usually attend — birthday parties, beach BBQs, the annual funfair — to suck up all the attention I used to get. Trying to usurp me and cement herself into Lillysands.

Well, that's all going to change, isn't it?

From my window, I see a movement on the cliff outside.

Is it you, Alice? I think so.

Then I see your long red hair, and I know it is.

Maybe today is the day you will finally leave Lillysands. Maybe you're taking it all in one last time before you go. I thought the photos and notes weren't enough, that I'd have to plan something else.

But maybe they've worked.

I peer closer. You're standing right at the edge of the cliff.

I feel that guilt again. Once a trickle — now something more.

Maybe it's the hormones making me weak. Sentimental.

I know I have to stay strong. I have to make sure you don't ruin our family and the town I've grown to love.

I know you want to destroy it. I overheard Max and Peter talking about the fact you want to ruin everything. That Max might even have to sell the house, stop fostering too if they didn't have enough rooms.

And that would mean I'd have to leave them.

No.

I don't know what you've done, but I just can't let that happen! I've worked so hard to finally be accepted by a family; to feel part of a community.

And now you want to ruin it all.

Autumn and Max have saved me, so now I'll save them. And it's working, I really think it is! I can tell you're going to leave town, very soon. You were so quiet at dinner last night.

Yes, I've done a good job. I saw the look on your face when you found that last photo I'd taken of you, the way you'd looked shocked and scared as you'd read my little notes. Just some little digs about us all knowing you for what you really are, a pretender.

I know how embarrassed you are about your life before you came to the Garlands, just as I am. How keen you are to appear like a clever perfect little thing. Protecting that would come above anything, even your attempts to destroy the very people who took you in.

And it's working, isn't it? You're unravelling just as I'd known you would.

I ought to be happy. So why do I feel so sad?

But this is what you do. Make me feel like you're a good person when really you're not.

And you're not, are you, Alice? You're not good. I saw the way you flirted with Aiden any time you could. I know you want to take him off me. What have I done to you? What have Autumn and Max done? Why are you punishing us?

And yet it's so hard to believe sometimes, that you really want to destroy us all like Max told Peter. You're so convincing. The way you smile at me. The love in your eyes. Like a sister . . .

You're still at the cliff. Even closer to the edge now.

You turn. See me watching you.

Something's wrong. There's a look in your eyes . . .

I reach for the handle on the window. I don't mean to. It feels like an automatic reaction.

But then the pain. Scorching, debilitating pain ripping through my stomach.

Oh God. The baby's coming.

I lose sight of you just as another contraction rips through me.

33

Estelle tried to organise the jumbled thoughts inside her head.

She'd run from away from Aiden, into the darkness of an empty Borough Market. The stalls stood still and quiet, a crow pecking at a discarded piece of meat on the ground.

She reached into her pocket with trembling hands, opening Alice's letter, knowing what it was — her suicide letter. Estelle had never seen it before. She had left so soon afterwards, consumed by guilt not only for the daughter she'd given away but for the foster sister she had baited to protect her family, not knowing that Alice would take a more drastic step than simply leaving Lillysands like Estelle had planned. It had not been what she had intended, *never* what she intended, but she was only a child, and she had been so consumed by jealousy and worry for Max and Autumn, and the home she thought Alice was trying to take from her.

As Estelle had spotted Alice that day on the cliff edge, she had realised she'd taken it too far and was going to call out to Alice, to stop her . . . but never got the chance.

Estelle wiped a tear from her eye and looked at the letter.

To anybody who still cares,

The next time you'll see me, I'll be in the sea.

God, that sounds so dramatic, doesn't it? But it's the truth. As I sit here writing this note, looking out to the water. It seems like the most simple option.

I'm tired.

I'm so tired of being let down by the people I love the most. Who I really thought loved me the most.

Just when I feel I'm safe and in the arms of people who might finally accept me for who I am — make me feel I belong — trust is snatched away again.

What's the point? If at every single turn I'm rejected?

Maybe I could have carried on if I knew there was someone left, anyone, who I could say for sure loved me. I once thought there was.

But I was wrong.

At least none of you will need to try so hard to get rid of me now. At least I've saved you that last bit of trouble.

Goodbye and I'm sorry, for whatever it is I did.

Alice x

Estelle closed her eyes, the image of Alice standing at the edge of the cliff that day coming to her. If only she'd stopped her, begged her forgiveness.

She heard movement. She looked up to see Aiden walking towards her. Above him, the

346

moon was a wicked crescent smile, the leaves on the trees stirring slowly.

'How did you find out about the notes I left Alice?' she asked.

'Alice's diary,' Aiden said. 'I found it in the silver box in the tree burrow.'

'But — but I found that box. There was no diary in there.'

'Because I took it. I put the box back just as it was — minus the diary.' He looked Estelle in the eye, his own green eyes hard. 'She guessed you wrote those threatening notes to her the day she died, Stel. That's why she jumped. She wrote all about it, every single sickening detail and kept each and every note.'

Estelle backed away from him, shaking her head.

Alice had known?

The thought was unbearable. She looked at the restaurant, and thought of all her guests. What if they found out?

'You killed her. You killed our sister,' Aiden said. 'I just need you to admit it.'

'I didn't! She jumped.'

'But why? Why did she jump, Stel?'

Estelle couldn't bear to answer that. She leaned against a wall, trying to wrap her head around the fact Alice had known it was Estelle who had sent her the threatening photos. The thought Alice *hadn't* known was the one small comfort Estelle had taken after she learnt Alice had committed suicide.

But Alice *had* known. And now Estelle had to live with that.

'I — I was just fifteen,' she said quickly. 'My head was a mess with pregnancy hormones and I'd overheard Max telling Peter Alice might destroy them with some kind of information she found. He said they might lose the house, move somewhere else. That Alice and I wouldn't be able to go with them. I now know that was about the landslide. If I'd known . . . '

'Don't make excuses,' he said. 'You wrote those notes. You took the photos.'

A car swooshed by, its headlights in Estelle's eyes. She put her hand over her face, turning away. He was right, it was just an excuse.

Applause sounded from inside. Estelle thought of her editor on stage talking to the crowds.

What if Aiden told them all?

She turned back to Aiden. 'Please don't say anything.'

He laughed bitterly, shaking his head. 'You never learn, do you? It's all about protecting yourself.'

'And what about you? What's this all about for you, Aiden?' Her voice was shaking, her teeth chattering. 'I presume it's been you all along, sending me those photos, those flowers?' He nodded and she wrapped her arms around herself, unable to comprehend it. Then something else dawned on her. 'Did you suggest Poppy's charity be used at the festival too?'

'Yes, anonymously via the website.'

'To play mind games with me.'

'To remind you what you gave up.'

'We slept together, that night at the B&B,' she whispered.

His jaw hardened. 'It was a mistake.'

'But there was real feeling there. I *know* there was, Aiden.'

'You loved Alice, didn't you? But you were still able to hurt her,' he said.

He held her gaze but she looked away.

'What about Poppy?' Estelle asked. 'Did — did you take the photos of her?'

'Yes.'

Estelle frowned. 'So you found out about her before I told you?'

He nodded. 'I read about it in Alice's diary when I found it last year.' His jaw clenched. 'I was so angry. I'd never *felt* such anger. For you to have given our daughter away without even giving me a chance.'

'I explained that. I was — '

He put his hand up. 'No more excuses.'

She swallowed her words away. 'How did you find Poppy?'

'A hunch. I knew how desperate my parents were for money at the time she would have been born and remembered one of Mum's old school friends — a school friend who happened to be married to a rich TV presenter — was struggling to have a baby. It all clicked into place.' His face softened slightly. 'The moment I saw Poppy's photo after tracking them down on Facebook, I knew she was mine.'

'So you contacted her through Facebook?'

He nodded. 'I didn't tell her I was her father at first. But after she told me what arseholes her parents are — sending her off to boarding school, barely paying attention to her — I had to tell her the truth. That's the difference between you and me, Stel.' He looked her up and down. 'I tell the truth.'

She couldn't help but laugh. 'But look at all the lies you've told me!'

His face hardened. 'Because I had to.'

'As did I,' Estelle said in resignation.

'No, you didn't.'

She looked up at him. 'I thought I was protecting the only family I ever really knew. I thought I was protecting myself.'

'All selfish.' Maybe he was right. But she had been a mixed-up teenager when she'd done all that. Aiden was an adult now.

Estelle peered up at the crescent moon, trying to gather her thoughts. 'Did you tell Poppy about me?'

'Not at first,' Aiden replied. 'Why would I want her to know you were her mother, the person who killed a fourteen-year-old?'

Estelle flinched. 'Stop saying that. I didn't *kill* Alice.' But deep down, that was the guilt she had carried, the knowledge that the photos she'd sent to Alice had driven her to suicide. Perhaps that was why she was so quick to let herself believe Alice might have been pushed.

'She committed suicide because of what you did,' Aiden said, voicing her fears. 'You might as well have pushed her. I bet she thought that as she stood on that cliff after finding out what you'd done. Almost like you were reaching out and shoving her yourself.'

Estelle felt nausea work its way up inside as she remembered seeing Alice from the window

350

of her bedroom. She'd been so close to opening the window and calling out to her. If she had, would things have been different?

'So Poppy came to Lillysands then?' Estelle said.

Aiden nodded.

'I knew it,' Estelle said. 'That's who I saw, wasn't it? The figure with the long red hair?'

Again, Aiden nodded. 'She turned up in Lillysands one day after finding out where I lived.'

'The day she ran away?'

'Yes.' He smiled. 'That was quite some day, seeing her walk down the beach. I knew it was her, instantly.'

'What's she like?' Estelle yearned to know. It blew her mind to know Aiden had *met* their daughter.

His eyes lit up. 'Beautiful. Clever. Intense, like you were back then.' Then his eyes filled with sadness. 'But mixed up too, angry. A beautiful disaster like you once were. Maybe still are.'

Estelle's heart sank. She closed her eyes. 'Oh Poppy,' she whispered.

Aiden sighed. 'When I found out she'd run away, I tried to convince her to return home but she refused. Stubborn as anything, that one. So she stayed at mine for a couple of days while I tried to figure things out.'

Estelle thought back to then. 'But I was at your house.'

'She wasn't staying there then. I actually thought she'd gone back home; she'd disappeared while I was at Mum's party; I'd gone

351

home to get my guitar and saw she was gone.'

'That's why you were so upset at the party?'

Aiden nodded. 'I was out of my mind with worry, especially when I didn't see any official news about her going home later that night. Turns out, she remained in Lillysands, just didn't want me to know. She wanted to track her real mother down. That's why you saw her in the garden the next day, watching us.'

Estelle's heart ached at the thought of Poppy desperately trying to find her birth mother, watching Aiden for any clue.

Estelle felt tears slide down her cheeks. 'Did Poppy ever find out I'm her mother?'

'Yes, she figured it out. She texted me, said she knew it was you, that she'd been following you and could see how much you both looked like each other.'

Estelle closed her eyes, the knowledge unbearable. 'How did you get the Polaroid photo to me in London?' Estelle asked.

'I bribed the butcher's son. I'd seen photos of him and his dad on their stall on your Instagram. In one of your captions you mentioned your weekly deliveries. It was easy enough to track him down, ask him to slip in the little note for fifty quid. He had no idea what was inside, of course.'

Estelle examined his face. 'Sounds like a lot of planning went into this little game of yours.'

'Not really, it was rather impulsive. Watching Poppy, seeing what a mess she was, it made me even more angry at you. Two girls' lives ruined by *you*. And yet there you were, in all those

articles with your smiley face and perfect life.'
He curled his hands into fists, shaking his head.
'I had to do something.'

'So you thought you'd take some sneaky
photos of your daughter while she was upset
then send it to me with those horrible words?'

'They were your words, Stel. Messages you
sent to Alice!'

Estelle paused. He was right. 'But to use our
daughter like that.'

'Not really, she had no idea. And I wasn't the
one who gave her away, was I?'

'Have you spoken to her since?'

He nodded. 'A few times, on the phone. She
knows everything now.'

Estelle went still. 'Everything? What — what
do you mean?'

'About Alice.'

Estelle's stomach dropped. 'But why?'

'The truth. She deserves it.'

'How did she react?'

Aiden's eyes filled with sadness. 'Not great.'

Estelle sunk down onto a nearby brick wall,
shaking her head as tears filled her eyes. 'She
hates me.'

Aiden frowned. 'No, Stel. She's just trying to
process everything.'

She looked up at him. '*You* hate me. Why not
her?'

'I don't hate you. I just need you to admit the
truth. Being pure isn't about all this,' he said,
gesturing around at the restaurant where the
party was still taking place. 'It's up here,' he said,
tapping his temple. 'The guilt. The shame. You

need to accept you're not perfect, that you never will be, that's when the slate will truly be clean. I did this for you, Stel. That's what it turned into by the end of our few days together in Lillysands last month. I ended up wanting to save you.' She saw a flicker of affection in his eyes.

'Estelle?' Estelle turned to see Kim standing awkwardly by the door. 'I think Silvia's running out of things to say now.'

Estelle stood up, smoothing her dress down. 'Give me a few more minutes.'

Kim sighed. 'Okay.'

When she left, Estelle turned back to Aiden. She felt winded, head spinning with it all. For so many years, she'd kept the guilt buried away. But now it was out, exposed. It made her feel like her nerves were exposed too, that her skin had been stripped away to reveal the very core of her.

And maybe that wasn't such a bad thing? The burden of guilt she'd shouldered all these years felt a little lighter. And the knowledge Aiden knew everything, Poppy too. Yes, at first that thought horrified her. But now? It felt right. The two most important people in her life knew her for what she truly was.

And that was what Aiden had wanted for her ultimately, despite the twisted way he went about it.

Aiden sighed slightly, as though he could sense her thoughts. 'It feels better, doesn't it? Being truthful. Having it all out in the open.'

'Yes,' she admitted.

He stepped towards her. 'I know you think I'm unbelievably cruel for doing this. But I know

354

you, Stel. I know you more than anyone. Reading all those articles about you, seeing those photos of you, sure it made me angry. But I could also see you've been desperate to start again. And yet how could you, with all those secrets and lies? Now they are out in the open, you can truly begin again, can't you?'

Estelle peered in at the stage. 'Not truly out in the open.'

Aiden frowned.

Kim walked out again. 'I am so sorry, but . . . '

'It's fine, I'm coming,' Estelle said.

'Thank you,' she whispered to Aiden. Yes, he had been cruel. But the way she was feeling now, open and raw and true, was better than she'd felt in a long time.

There was just one thing left to do.

She walked slowly to the stage, feeling as though her legs were made from rubber. People's smiles turning to frowns as they noticed the look on Estelle's face. Was it so obvious? She'd grown so adept at hiding how she felt, but now it was all on display and she couldn't rein it in.

Her editor mouthed a 'What's going on?' at her as they exchanged places at the lectern. But Estelle didn't reply. Instead, she clutched onto the lectern and looked out towards the crowds: her editor and agent, her friends.

And Aiden — who was no longer alone. Beside him stood a young woman.

Poppy.

Estelle's heart started thundering as she looked into her daughter's eyes. She was beautiful in the flesh, hair long like Estelle's had once been, back to its natural brown colour too. But her eyes were sad, dark circles beneath them.

Estelle felt a heady mixture of guilt and love explode within her. She wanted to run to her but knew she couldn't; that she didn't *deserve* to. First, she had to make amends. She had to really get everything out in the open.

She coughed then leaned down to the microphone. 'Sorry about that. Saw an old friend. Anyway, let's get on, shall we?' She paused, taking a quick sip of water. Then she picked up one of her books, eyes still on Poppy. '*Pure* is the title of my book.' she said. 'Which is interesting as they say cleanliness is next to godliness. And yet no matter how much I try to clean myself, I don't think I'm anywhere near that. You see,' Estelle said, finding her voice now. 'I have kept something trampled down inside me. A truth that — that is so very far from the *pure* façade I like to show you all.' She pursed her lips, tears flooding her eyes. 'Fifteen years ago, I did two things, two terrible things. I betrayed one girl and — ' She paused, taking in a deep shuddery breath as she watched Poppy struggle to contain her emotions. 'I gave another away. A beautiful special baby girl who is now a beautiful special teenage girl. Something I have regretted *all* my life.'

People around the room gasped, her editor and publicist exchanging panicked looks. But Estelle kept her eyes on her daughter whose brown eyes were now flooded with tears, her red lip caught in her teeth, something Estelle did too when she tried not to cry. God, they were so alike. But Estelle hoped against hope that was where their similarities ended.

'When I say betrayed,' Estelle continued, 'I mean I drove a girl to suicide. A beautiful girl called Alice. All for selfish reasons. For jealousy. Spite.'

Her editor walked up to her. 'Estelle, maybe you should stop now.'

'No,' Estelle said, shaking her head. 'I won't stop. I am so sick of hiding the truth with — with kale smoothies and spiralised courgettes. I am impure and I fucked up, big time. I'm sorry, Alice. I'm sorry, Aiden.' She looked at her daughter, holding her gaze. 'And I'm so sorry, Poppy.'

Poppy let out a sob and ran from the room.

'Wait!' Estelle called out. She scrambled down the steps and ran through the crowd after her daughter. But Aiden grabbed her arm at the door.

'Give her time,' he said.

'Did you know she was coming to the party?' she asked, watching as her daughter headed into the darkness, fighting the urge to run after her.

No, not her daughter. *Their* daughter. She looked at Aiden. She ought to be angry in some way, considering how underhand he'd been with all this. But how could she be?

She understood. She deserved it after all.

'She threatened to come,' Aiden said. 'I tried to convince her not to, to wait to set up a proper face-to-face.' He quirked an eyebrow. 'I guess she's like her mother, stubborn.'

'Will she be okay?'

'She'll be fine. She's a survivor,' he said, softly, 'like you. And you will survive now, Stel, I can see it in your eyes.'

'I think I will thanks to you.'

And what of us two? she wondered. Aiden was the love of her life, she saw that more clearly than ever now, despite all he'd done, all *she'd* done.

But because of all that too, she knew nothing could ever come of it. Maybe as parents to Poppy, they could forge some kind of long-term connection. Any more than that was out of the question, she could see it in his eyes despite what had passed between them in Lillysands.

She looked back towards where Poppy had disappeared. 'I need to see her,' she said. 'I need to *explain.*'

'I think she gets it now. She'll come to you when she's ready.'

Estelle looked at the space where her daughter had just been, and her mind went back to that moment fifteen years ago as she held her baby in her arms. The reality of what she'd done to Alice had come rushing at her. Maybe it was seeing a newborn in her arms, realising the vulnerability and innocence of people.

Of Alice.

When Autumn had asked Estelle if she was sure she wanted her newborn daughter adopted, there had been a moment of hesitation. But then she'd thought of the look in Alice's eyes standing on the cliff a few hours before.

'Take her,' Estelle had said to Autumn, turning her face away from the tiny baby in her arms and handing her over to Autumn. 'I don't deserve her.'

'Maybe I don't deserve to know my daughter,' Estelle said now.

'You're getting there,' Aiden replied. 'First step is telling the truth. Next step is forgiving yourself.'

She looked into Aiden's eyes. 'You didn't forgive me.'

'I guess that's one of *my* steps.'

They both turned to look out into the market, where Poppy was walking away. As Estelle looked at her daughter, she promised herself she would do everything she could to deserve her, to bring her back into her arms. She would begin again, if she had to, as long as she had Poppy.

Though she would never get a chance to make things right with Alice, it was not too late for her and Poppy. She would do everything she could to do things right this time, for Poppy, for herself . . . and for Alice.

A new life. A new truth.

Poppy paused, peering over her shoulder at Estelle. Estelle held her breath. Then Poppy smiled at her, a huge life affirming smile, before walking into the darkness.

Estelle let go of her breath and it felt like her first.

Acknowledgements

This is the first novel I've written while being a full-time author, something I dreamed about since being a child. But I'm not saying that's made it loads easier: you find with the luxury of time, there's more time to doubt, to worry, to second-guess yourself.

Luckily, I have the most amazing support network, from my friends who allow me to let off steam with fun dinners and mad Halloween adventures. A particular shout out to Emma Cash for reading a first draft of this and giving me invaluable advice; Elizabeth Richards as ever for her constant support; and Jenny Ashcroft, always there for a quick chat over coffee in busy London or breezy Brighton.

And of course, my amazing family. The endless support of my mum and stepdad, and my dad and stepmum who take the strain off what is often a manically busy life as a mother and author.

My husband is a constant support, putting up with my 'creative' mood swings and tantrums. I love you, Rob, and I promise I'll buy you that Santa Cruz V10 CC mountain bike one day! And my daughter Scarlett and my new puppy Bronte for . . . erm . . . keeping me on my toes (I mean, seriously, who thought getting a new puppy in the midst of book edits was a good idea?!). But in truth, all my writing and hard work is for my darling Scarlett, even when she's keeping me on my toes! There's no better motivation than making your child proud.

I write this in memory of my dog Archie too, who padded off to Rainbow Bridge last winter. His constant companionship in the early days of writing this novel was invaluable. I miss you, boy.

I'd also like to thank my wonderful agency, Hardman & Swainson: to Jo for being there when Caroline was on maternity leave and Caroline for being there in spirit.

And then there's the Avon team. Wow, what a super team, especially my new editor Rachel Faulkner-Willcocks who, honestly, has blown me away with her brilliant editorial support and comments (and yes, her pedantic ways which I LOVE as someone has to be pedantic while I live in my messed up crazy writer's head). My copy editor, Jade Craddock, is a superstar for finely tuning this manuscript and those eagle-eyed proofreaders too.

A final huge thanks goes to YOU, my readers. Your support has been amazing, and the regular emails and messages I receive from you keep me afloat. Thank you, thank you, thank you! I hope you enjoy my latest novel, do let me know!

Sign up for my newsletter for exclusive updates and competitions. http://www.tracybuchanan.co.uk/sign-up

We do hope that you have enjoyed reading
this large print book.

Did you know that all of our titles
are available for purchase?

We publish a wide range of high quality
large print books including:
Romances, Mysteries, Classics
General Fiction
Non Fiction and Westerns

Special interest titles available in
large print are:
The Little Oxford Dictionary
Music Book
Song Book
Hymn Book
Service Book

Also available from us courtesy of
Oxford University Press:
Young Readers' Dictionary
(large print edition)
Young Readers' Thesaurus
(large print edition)

For further information or a free
brochure, please contact us at:
Ulverscroft Large Print Books Ltd.,
The Green, Bradgate Road, Anstey,
Leicester, LE7 7FU, England.
Tel: (00 44) 0116 236 4325
Fax: (00 44) 0116 234 0205

NO TURNING BACK

Tracy Buchanan

When radio presenter Anna Graves and her daughter are attacked on the beach by a crazed teenager, Anna reacts instinctively to protect her baby. But her life falls apart when the schoolboy dies from his injuries. The police believe Anna's story, until the autopsy reveals something more sinister. The evidence seems to connect Anna to a decades-old serial murder case. Is she really as innocent as she claims? And is killing ever justified, if it saves a child's life?

WHAT ALICE KNEW

T. A. Cotterell

Alice has a perfect life. A cool job, great kids, a wonderful husband. Until he goes missing one night. The phone rings and then goes dead. Unexpected gifts appear. Something isn't right.

Alice needs to know what's going on.

But when she uncovers the truth, she faces a brutal choice. And how can she be sure it is the truth?

Sometimes it's better not to know . . .

THE ORPHANS

Annemarie Neary

Eight-year-old Jess and her little brother were playing at the water's edge when their parents vanished. For hours, the children held hands and waited for them to return. But nobody ever came back. Years later, Jess has become a locker of doors. Now a lawyer and a mother, she is determined to protect the life she has built around her. But her brother Ro has grown unpredictable, elusive and obsessive. When new evidence suggests that their mother might be alive, Ro reappears, convinced that his sister knows more than she claims. And then bad things start to happen . . .

THE MARSH KING'S DAUGHTER

Karen Dionne

When the notorious child abductor known as the Marsh King escapes from a maximum security prison, Helena immediately suspects that she and her two young daughters are in danger. No one, not even her husband, knows the truth about Helena's past: they don't know that she was born into captivity, that she had no contact with the outside world before the age of twelve — or that her father raised her to be a killer. And they don't know that the Marsh King can survive and hunt in the wilderness better than anyone . . . except, perhaps, his own daughter.

IF YOU KNEW HER

Emily Elgar

When Cassie Jensen arrives on the intensive care ward in St Catherine's hospital, Alice Marlowe, the chief nurse, is fascinated by this young, beautiful woman who strikes her as familiar, and yet she doesn't know why. But then Alice is astonished to discover something about Cassie that she has been keeping secret from everyone, including her devoted husband and family — a secret that changes everything . . . Frank is a patient on the same ward who has locked in syndrome, so can hear and see everything around him but cannot communicate. Soon he comes to understand that Cassie's life is still in danger; and as the police continue to investigate what really happened to her, only Frank holds the truth, which no one can know and he cannot tell . . .

GOOD AS GONE

Amy Gentry

Eight years ago, thirteen-year-old Julie Whitaker was kidnapped from her bedroom in the middle of the night. In the years since, her family have papered over the cracks of their grief — while hoping against hope that Julie is still alive. And then, one night, the doorbell rings. A young woman calling herself Julie claims to have come home. But certain things don't add up. Julie's story doesn't quite ring true. And before long, the family are in danger of being torn apart all over again . . .